The Ring
Is Closed

The Ring Is Closed

KNUT HAMSUN

Translated by Robert Ferguson

Souvenir Press

First published in Norway in 1936 by Gyldendal Norsk Forlag
Under the original title: RINGEN SLUTTET

This translation first published 2010 by Souvenir Press,
43 Great Russell Street, London WC1B 3PD

Published with a translation grant from NORLA

ISBN 9780285638686

Typeset by M Rules

Printed in the UK by CPI Bookmarque, Croydon, CR0 4TD

I

I

WHEN PEOPLE GATHER ON THE COASTAL BOAT DOCK THEY
don't gain much by it, but then it doesn't cost them much either, so it
works out even, with maybe a little minus for the wear and tear on the
shoes. So if it doesn't exactly do any harm, it's not often anyone prof-
its by it. An unforgettable experience, a sight fit for the gods, some sort
of benediction or other? No no no. A few people and boxes ashore, a
few people and boxes on board. No-one says anything, neither the mate
at the ship's rail nor the agent on the dock needs to say a word, they
look at the papers, they nod.

That's about it.

People have a pretty good idea what they're going to find there
each day, still they go.

Is there really never anything else?

Well, now and then there's the blind hurdy-gurdy man who gets
led down the gangway and causes a stir among the young, or some

3

dandified sportsman who disembarks with his skis and his rucksack, even though it's now the month of May and Easter is long gone.

But then that's about it.

Quite a crowd here by now. As well as children of all ages there are the town's older residents and elders, buyers and fishermen, a couple of Customs men just passing the time, Smith the photographer with his wife and daughter, and a great many others. Now and then Captain Brodersen would show up, the man who used to command the barque *Lina* but then retired to become the lighthouse-keeper. For a while the captain stands in conversation with Robertsen the Customs man, whom he addresses as Mate, then he steps down into his boat and rows back out to the lighthouse.

No lack of young girls here either: Lovise Rolandsen, the well-built and nubile daughter of an artisan family, a bit dry and boney but blue-eyed and really not too bad at all. Usually she was with Lolla, no great beauty either but with a fine body and good breasts, she looked as if she could whinny. When that handsome sportsman came ashore she shifted her feet twice and stared at him. The chemist, who was a bit of a wag, once described her as overqualified.

But it was the children, dressed in every conceivable hue of blue and red and yellow and black and grey, who dominated. There were perhaps twenty of them, pretty children, little girls mostly, some of them big and already in love, walking out with the big boys. One of the chemist's daughters was a definite centre of attraction, she sat on a crate and held court. Her name was Olga and the others followed her lead. The lighthousekeeper's son was squeezed in among them, but he wasn't considered of much acount. A cheeky little lad, freckled, not yet been to Confirmation, his voice was breaking too, Olga said he spoiled the mood. She couldn't stand him. Why didn't he go home with his father? Look, there he's goes, he's rowing!

Abel said nothing.

But he wasn't always so quiet. From a time when they were much younger than they were now he and Olga had been in the habit of quarreling about everything. Once she boasted that her father could throw a stone at a magpie and hit it. But my father can do card-tricks, said Abel.

4

They had shared a lot of things through their childhood years. They were as mischievous as each other when they stole carrots from Fredriksen's country mansion and didn't go to him afterwards and own up. Once they drowned a cat together, a big tomcat that had clawed open the chest of Olga's cat, another tom. Naturally a murder like that had to be accompanied by an oath of silence and carried out in the dead of night, for this was a well-known cat, he lived at the customs shed. They made a thorough job of it: a heavy stone in a sack, the cat into the sack, string tied around the neck and the whole bundle tossed overboard into deep water. Each of them took an oar as they rowed back to the quay, each one in it as deep as each other, but it was Abel who had blood on his hands.

He might have won Olga's eternal gratitude for this service but instead squandered it all just a couple of days later. She'd climbed up on the roof of one of the shacks down by the vacant lots and Abel was standing stood down below laughing and looking up her skirt instead of helping her down. It made her so mad she hopped right down on him without a moment's thought and tumbled both of them into the nettles and the piled rubble so that they both bled.

For a long time after that they weren't friends.

But time passes and everything shapes itself to time, they grew up, they matured. They went to the cinema and saw the pirates and the horse-racing and the dancing dogs, along with the others they played on the merry-go-round down on the vacant lots. The chemist's daughter had started wearing finer clothes than the other little girls, finer even than Lovise Rolandsen and Lolla, who were both grown up. But Abel didn't change a lot. He wasn't much to look at, but his friends stuck with him because he was helpful and was always able to find a way out of a tight spot. During the summer egg-gathering once him and another boy got into mortal danger, but it was after he had learnt to swim, so he was able to save both himself and his friend. He had strangely small fists, strong enough and work-lined, but quick as those of a thief.

He wasn't rated as highly as Helmer, who was already apprenticed to a blacksmith, and nowhere near as high as Rieber Carlsen, who was enrolled at secondary school by this time and was destined to be a someone. But then both these gentlemen were older. Yes, but he wasn't even respected as much as Tengvald and Alex, who were the same age as him, what could the reason for that be? They had been taught better manners at home, they had uncles and aunts who slipped them a few extra shillings, their shoes were in a better state of repair, and sometimes the sandwiches they took to school with them for their dinner had slices of expensive banana in them. No, Abel had none of these worldly refinements, he was from the lighthouse, where his father sat and watched over the lamp at night and slept during the day and lived his modest little life. That's the way it was.

And yet Brodersen the lighthouse keeper could have lived in a little more style if he'd wanted to. But he didn't want to. He was so frugal.

Brodersen got married again fourteen years ago. His first marriage was childless, Abel was the son of his second marriage. For many years he'd commanded the barque *Lina* and made a profit, and people thought he must be very comfortably off. And maybe he was too, but if so he didn't flash it around and he kept his son Abel on a shoestring.

But Abel didn't know any other way and he thought it was all quite alright. He thought the lighthouse on Holmen was just as good as any house in town, and anyway he had treasures out there that were beyond the dreams of town-dwellers. What did they have compared to him? He boasted of the place to his friends, said it was the only place he'd ever known and that he'd never swap with them, they could just keep their houses, even the chemist's house, big, with a balcony and an extension, you could keep that too.

You're just lying about your lighthouse, said Olga.

Come and see, said Abel.

And he went on about it for so long that one day Olga and a group of little girls came out to the lighthouse with him. She took Tengvald along too, him being an especially looked-up-to older person.

The visit didn't work out too badly, the landscape on Holmen was scaled-down and strange, with secret hideaways between the rocks. It was fun to see the hedgehogs and the rabbits, and pretty too, with all the flowering bushes planted out along the friendly patches of earth. Here was the wreck of a cutter that was used as a barn, and these sea-gulls here came back to breed year after year, and here too was the endless soughing of the sea, all of these things unknown and strange to the children.

Well, said Olga and the little girls, it's certainly different out here.

But it didn't overwhelm them enough to strike them dumb: What's this hole for? Is this the well? Yes, but what about when gulls fly over the well and do their . . . you know what I mean.

Ha ha ha!

And not one single little road, just mountains and mountains . . . no, sorry, Abel, but really . . .

We haven't been inside yet, said Abel.

They went inside and raced up into the tower. It was a disappointment. The keeper explained to them about the lamp and about the rotating screen, but it was too early to turn it on, so they didn't get to see the powerful light beaming across the sea. So they probably thought, well, it's just a big light.

We haven't looked in the living-room yet, said Abel.

They went down to the living room. There was a large collection of curiosities the lighthouse keeper had picked up cheap in foreign countries, furniture from the Australian outback, a ship in a bottle, empty coconut shells. Abel described it all to them the way he'd heard his father do, but the children weren't interested.

We better get home before it gets dark, said Tengvald.

The little girls stuck their noses into the kitchen and into the cubbyholes, but one door was kept locked, Abel's mother wasn't always sober.

A place of contrasts, that lighthouse home on Holmen: a father who was teetotal and parsimonious to the point of meanness, and a mother who drank to cure her bronchitis and her loneliness. She was still only in her forties.

With the coming of the Christmas holidays things went bad again, the people who were usually away all returned home and Abel went back to being a nothing again. He put up with it fairly well, but he wasn't old enough and wise enough to keep out of the way, he imposed himself and he was rejected. And now that he'd finally got himself a new cap the others had bought hats, and Tengvald new shoes as well.

But the winter was alright, in its way. Around that time he quite often sought out Lili's company. She was a bit younger but tall and pretty for her age, she was kind enough to listen to what he said, and since she lived on the other side of the bay and had a long way to go to school he sometimes gave her a lift in the boat. That's so nice of you to do that, she said. That's just the way I am, he replied.

And things didn't work out too well for him in the spring holidays either, first at Easter and then Whitsun. He might have stayed at home at the lighthouse and not taken any chances, but he was still not smart enough to realise that and when the postboat arrived a trip to the dock was always a temptation. The girls turned against him: Here comes Abel, of course, they said when they saw him coming. All he ever talks about is his lighthouse, said Olga. And then when he sat down with them and prodded with a stick in the sand she said: Ugh, now you're getting us all dusty!

But Lili was different, she was a friendly girl, one he could get on with. Olga was a witch, and yet in all those years she was still the only one for him. He even went so far as to deny the lighthouse, and to speak slightingly of the lamp and the gulls and the rabbits. All he got was laughter: Yes wouldn't you just know it, he's on about his lighthouse again!

No matter which way he turned, he was facing a wall.

One evening he waylaid Olga with a present, a gold bracelet he had stolen from Jesus in the church. The old, unmarried daughter of a priest had hung this costly bracelet on Jesus in gratitude for something or other, and there it stayed, hanging on his wrist throughout the spring, and because it was a holy place and a beautiful gift and a pious gift, no-one had the heart to remove it.

But Olga wasn't brave enough to take the bracelet from Abel's hand and thank him for it. Of course she tried it on, with her eyes shining and her heart beating and all that, but then she gave it back and said: What on earth do you think you're doing?

Abel said nothing.

I don't want it, she said, so you'd better put it back.

Abel said nothing. He was pale, disappointed.

Let me just see it again. Oh goodness . . . and it fits me too . . . but you must understand . . . When did you take it?

Just now. Whitsun, he said.

I've never heard anything as wicked. Did you climb up and take it?

Reluctantly, haltingly, he confessed that he had let himself be locked inside the church on Whit Sunday, stolen the bracelet at night, and slipped out again at Mass on Whit Monday. Quite a lad, godless as you please.

In intense excitement she asked him: Did you spend the night in the church? Weren't you afraid?

For a moment his mouth trembled, but he made a gesture with his fist as though hitting something away.

Didn't you see anything?

Abel said nothing.

Olga with finality: Anyway, you're insane. How are you going to get it back on him again?

Dunno, he said, wretched. And for the second time he felt himself on the verge of tears.

We have to get hold of the key to the church, she said. Can you do that?

He said: Yes, I think so. The sexton has it.

Together they made up their minds that things had to be put right, the wrong had to be righted. When he stole the church key from its place on the wall he was as light-fingered as when he had had taken the bracelet from Jesus' wrist. Olga stayed outside by the church-windows and kept a lookout while he hung the bracelet back.

But his mad gesture didn't win him her lasting favour. On the contrary, she threatened him sometimes, hinting that she knew something about him, that she could get him sent to jail. She was a damned witch and he had to keep out of her way.

He rowed Lili home each day so as to have someone to be with. There were only two windows in her house, it had just one room, the smallest house in the whole village, her father worked at the sawmill so he didn't have a big house. Abel once went all the way inside with her carrying two loaves that she'd bought in town. It wasn't too comfortable inside, the place smelled of something, whatever it was, the clock had stopped, the bed was unmade. There were food and clothes on the little table by the window, and on the window-sill some boiled potatoes still in their jackets.

Lili looked embarrassed. Would you like to sit down? she asked hesitantly and wiped off a chair. Mother, this place is in a terrible mess today!

You can say that again! the mother rejoins. But I've just got in, so I've not had time to tidy up here. I'm washing clothes today.

Mother does the laundry for some of the casual labour at the sawmill, Lili explains.

Someone has to do it, Abel replies in his most grown-up way.

Yes, he took comfort in Lili's company in those bad times when he had no-one else. And it was quite okay that she was from a poor home and not one of the snobs. Lili was calm and good, even when he kissed her once later that summer she didn't give a start and jump back, she just put a hand over her eyes. He was ashamed of himself for what he'd done, so he gave her a quick shove and shouted out *last one home is a . . .* whatever it was, and set off running.

And time passes, the summers, and winters, and years. And Olga didn't deliberately break the peak of his cap, and when he saw what had happened he laughed feebly, but she did say: That serves you right! But then felt bad about it afterwards. Now the peak hung down with one broken half on each side and was a sorry sight.

He climbed down into his boat, baled it out boat and rowed home. Next day he was back at school again just his usual self. He had started wearing the cap back to front, but with the peak dangling down he didn't look good in it.

Olga took him to one side and said: You can hit me if you like.

When I hit something it leaves a hole! Abel answered, and swaggered away from her. It was something he'd heard someone say down on the dock.

Yeah! She called after him, the peak was nothing but cardboard.

Shut your mouth!

Just varnished cardboard.

Your father sells worming powder . . .

It was Lili who came up with an answer: You can buy a new peak for the hat from Gulliksen's. My father did that once.

10

How much did he pay?

I don't know that. But I'll put it in for you.

That's so kind of you.

He was Confirmed the same summer as Olga. The sexton gave them instruction in the schoolhouse, and Olga didn't know anything and was often left dumb and blushing furiously when she was asked something. Once he rescued her by tipping all the things off his desk so that the sexton lost his temper with him. She never found out that he'd done it for her sake. Of course, Olga was a witch, but it made him unhappy to see her in a fix for just for old Pontoppidan's sake, she knew a lot more than that old sexton about all sorts of things, now she was quite the young lady, she used perfume and had Visiting Cards that she handed out to people. After Olga was Confirmed she was going off travelling with her mother.

I'm off travelling too, said Abel.

You? Where are you off to?

To sea, he said.

He was going to sea, right enough. He had in a manner of speaking no alternative, since his father felt he couldn't aford to keep him at home anymore . It was what the son wanted for himself anyway.

So, you're off to sea, said his mother. Fourteen years old, she said and shook her head.

Nearly fifteen, said Abel.

Just the same age as I was, said his father. And you're sailing with the best people, not like I did.

As they took their leave of each other up in the lighthouse he was given a piece of good advice by his father: he mustn't shove his money down into his pocket like the seagoing lads did, he was to hide it away in this leather wallet. Here, take this with you! There's quite a bit of money passed through that in its time.

Abel went downstairs and opened the door to the kitchen. As he did so his father shouted down the stairs: Don't you touch that poison of hers!

No, replied Abel.

His mother was sitting with a pair of grey mittens in her lap and

11

she looked vague. Her face was a mottled red. Now and then she turned the waffle-iron on top of the stove, and a few waffles lay ready to eat on a plate.

There was no need for him to shout, she said. I wasn't going to offer you a drink.

No, said Abel.

It's nowhere near ready to drink yet anyway, she went on as she moved a pipe and lifted a lid and had a look.

Well goodbye than, said Abel and held out his hand.

Stay a while longer, don't you want some waffles?

No, why would I? Father's taking me straight to the boat, and I'll get food on board.

I only made them for you, she said sadly. Don't you want these mittens either?

Abel hesitated, then he said okay, okay.

I worked on them at night.

Yes but it's summer now.

I dropped a few stitches, but I picked them up again

Yes, thank you for the mittens, they'll probably come in useful.

His father came down from and hurried him along: We better get going.

That was all the goodbye he got. His mother didn't get up to watch him leave, just wished him a slurred goodbye and slumped back in her chair.

II

IT WASN'T AFTER THIS FIRST TRIP AWAY THAT HE CAME BACK SO changed in his appearance and his ways, but more after the next one, when he came back changed for life.

But he was different after this first time too, four years older, bigger, more experienced, steadier in his behaviour, yes, and even better looking, the freckles had gone. He had started smoking a pipe and swaggered with his shoulders when he walked, now and then he used a foreign word. Oh yes, he'd seen hurricanes and been shipwrecked, broken a rib and got into fights in distant ports, he'd completed the course. But he didn't boast too much about it, and the others of his age listened to his stories with interest.

He hadn't been at sea the whole four years he was away, he'd jumped ship in America and worked ashore, sometimes in factories, and picked up skills like woodworking and metal-turning. He'd take evening classes at college, sailed on the Great Lakes, gambled, learnt to

13

drive, how to box and a lot of other stuff. He'd also been in a spot of
bother with the police, like the time he 'borrowed' a jalopy and made
off in it with a girl. Quite a lad, and still young.

The style of his storytelling came from the everyday way
Americans talked, with a smattering of the tabloid press and the Police
Gazette. He was new on the quayside with his stories and easily gath-
ered a crowd of listeners.

Never heard the like of it! the lads could say – and what happened
next?

Well, after that he just paid up. A bullet into a mirror, that was
nothing for Lawrence.

The lads, disappointed: Didn't he get arrested?

Arrest Lawrence? The police were sick of him.

Really? He was that tough, was he?

He used to try to outdo me in all the breaking into shops and stuff
like that when we needed clothes. But Lawrence hadn't the knack of it
and he had to give it up. But when I ran into him again in the autumn,
sheer need had made an expert out of him and you wouldn't have recognised him. He was at it all the time, even stole clothes to sell on board
ships, didn't even draw the line at pickpocketing. But Lawrence had a
good heart, and when he was drunk enough he could take to weeping
and give away the stolen goods. A remarkable man, good-looking too.

Silence.

But how much did he have to hand over for the mirror, since it was
so big?

You mean did he try to make a deal? Not on your life. Just slapped
down as many notes as he thought it was worth, and one more for the
waiter. And then we moved on somewhere else.

The young girls wandered by, it was pretty much a question of which
ones, but when it was Olga Abel stood up politely from the bench and
doffed his cap. She was four years older now, but he recognised her at
once and got up. Not that it did him much good. She was the chemist's
daughter, the town beauty, engaged to marry Rieber Carlsen who'd
done nothing but read for the past four years and was now a trained
priest.

No, it didn't do him much good. The first time she reacted as though his politeness was his way of being rude. She stopped and said: Is that you, Abel?

None other.

So, you're back home.

Just a quick visit.

She nodded and wandered on. Her fiancé hadn't said a word.

The next time he stood up and greeted her didn't do him much good either, she didn't even look at him. Fair enough, he sat back down on the bench and said loudly, as if it didn't matter at all: Oh yes, that Lawrence was a real hellraiser!

Did you ever get in a *really* tight spot? asked the lads.

Sure. Once, in a dive. It's a bowling alley, Lawrence said, a nice place, they shot a man there last week. Let's go there.

I wanted to go straightaway, but I didn't want to lose my job at the workshop, so I pinned on a blue Temperance League ribbon I happened to have.

Three men were bowling and they asked us to join them. I sat down in a corner to think about it, but Lawrence started drinking with them, just to be sociable. They all got drunk, and Lawrence could be unbelievably stupid when he was drunk. Suddenly a shot rang out, and a man fell to the floor. What the hell, I thought, did they shoot him? And who did it? They turned him over, he was covered in blood and quite dead, and his two friends were making a huge commotion. Lawrence was out of it. Be quiet! he said a couple of times, and just sat there on the chair, drunk. The men came across to my corner and accused me of firing the shot. They flashed police badges showing they had the right to search me, and they found my gun in my back pocket. I protested my innocence and showed them my blue ribbon and shouted for Lawrence to come to my assistance. Leave him alone! Lawrence shouted back and went on sitting in his chair. Are you prepared to pay compensation? the men asked. No, I said, why should I pay? So they dragged me to my feet and they were about to leave with me. Supposing I was to pay, I asked, how much? Because I didn't want to get involved in something and lose my place at the workshop. Yes, how much? they started asking each other. I don't have anything, I said.

Yes, but the man can't just lie there, they said, we've got to get him out of here. It's none of my business, I said. What, you won't even pay five dollars towards the cost of the funeral? they said. I'd been thinking it through, of course, I'd be acquitted in any court, but it might take time.

But now listen up! In the meantime the attendant had run out the back way and gone for the police. The moment two bulls appeared on the scene up jumps the dead man and runs out the main door with his two friends. It was as if the wind blew them out, and no-one moving quicker than the dead guy.

That left just Lawrence and me to face the police.

Silence.

Yes? And then what happened? asked the lads.

Nothing happened. The police recognised him. So, you're back in business again, are you Lawrence? they said. But once we'd explained the story to them they just laughed and said it was an old trick these three had been trying on. They'd been done for it before but they didn't give up.

They took my gun, I said.

Well, greenhorns pay, said the police.

But Abel didn't spend his whole time sitting on the dock telling tall stories and recounting adventures, he could be serious too. With his own money he bought a motor-boat that he loaded up at the sawmill and used to transport the offcuts over to the lighthouse. It took him quite a few days, because the boat couldn't carry much at a time.

At the sawmill he met Lili again. She was sixteen years old now, slender and sweet, she'd taught herself to read and write, and now she had a little office job at the mill. They talked about everyday things, there was no question of them falling in love or anything like that, just a few things they recalled from their schooldays, while other things were too trivial to bring up again.

You've travelled a lot since you left home, she said.

Round the world, he said.

Oh just imagine, all round the world! I heard you were in America.

Yes.

16

All I do is sit in here at this desk, it's like, nothing.

You shouldn't talk like that. There's plenty of people who would envy you your job.

Do you think so? Well, if I'm good at it, I might get promoted.

You'll be good at it, Lili.

Do you think so?

As far as I can remember, you're always good.

So then Lili probably thinks she has to say something friendly in return and she says: I hear you load your boat to the gills here at the mill. But you shouldn't . . .

Oh?

No, because it's quite a long way, out to the lighthouse.

The boat turned out to be useful in all sorts of ways. In my day we used our arms and rowed, said his father, because he didn't much like the motor. And yet things were better now with a motorboat and the only expense was the petrol. He went fishing a long way out with it, took it to town to pick up things, and when his mother died in the autumn he used it to transport the body over to the cemetery. His father was annoyed with him and obstinately insisted on rowing his own boat and was a long way behind him.

They both joined in the psalm-singing at the grave, dressed in black, sombre and serious. And on the way back the engine packed up. It did what? That's right, it packed up. Abel set about tracing the trouble, and he knew enough to find the fault but he couldn't fix it out on the water. Since he didn't have a pair of oars on board he drifted helplessly. Finally his father showed up and then just rowed on by. Ho! shouted Abel. His father kept on rowing. Abel looked round to see if there was anyone else, but saw no-one. Surely the old skipper realized that something was wrong? He carried on rowing. Hey, father! Abel finally shouted, and waved. At first the old man just sat there and stared, but after another wave he rowed as slow and reluctant as you like over to the distressed boat.

Abel, somewhat feebly: Ha, you see, I forgot the oars . . .

Oars? His father said distantly.

Because the engine's packed up.

17

Oh really? I'm a little slow-witted today: what would you need oars for?

Abel said nothing.

What did you say about the engine?

That it's packed up, listen to me. But I can fix it as soon as we get ashore.

You're not telling me the engine's broke down out here in the middle of the sea?

Abel said nothing. He fastened the boat to his father's and he said: Let me row!

You sit down! said his father, and started hauling away.

Abel went forward and tried to take the oars.

Sit down! Captain Brodersen ordered sharply, and carried on hauling at the oars.

Neither one spoke again until they were ashore. Father was pretty worn-out, but his irritation had passed and, as though a little ashamed, he said: Well, Abel, now you see what a lot of rubbish these engines are!

Now that the old lighthousekeeper was a widower he couldn't manage without a little female help around the house. He advertised for a housekeeper and got Lolla. A great bit of luck! Lolla would be fine, she was quick around the house, used to chickens and pigs, unmarried, four years older now, in good health and quite pretty. Tengvald was after her, a trained blacksmith now and working as a journeyman, they could have got married any time and started a family. But Tengvald held back. Why? Probably because he lacked the courage. He was a quiet, rather shy blacksmith, nothing especially outstanding about him, but honest and steady. It wasn't easy for him to break up with Lolla, but she had those crazy nostrils that fluttered every time she looked at him. His excuse was that he had to take care of his mother. Okay then, said Lolla, who wasn't too brokenhearted about it. What was Tengvald the blacksmith to her? But when, a little while later, the very same Tengvald began courting Lovise Rolandsen, and even ended up marrying her, Lolla started started passing a lot of sly remarks: that, by God, those two were made for each other, because one thing was for sure, he

18

wouldn't be forcing his attentions on her too often, and she wouldn't be having to repair any children's clothes! And how could Lolla know something like that?

Not long afterwards she was halfway engaged again, this time to the chemist, the man who once called her *overqualified*. But now people said that this time it was Lolla who held back and wouldn't dare. The chemist had a bad limp, and in addition to this he helped himself too liberally to the alcohol used in his own shop, so that it was impossible to walk down the street with him, since he kept bumping into her. She had no physical disabilities herself.

That was when she boldly went into service at old Captain Brodersen's, out at the lighthouse.

She must have had her own reasons for this, and when Abel came to fetch her in his motorboat she didn't even cry when she said goodbye to her parents. I'm not that far away, she said, only over at the lighthouse.

She showed moderation in all her ways, she was frugal with the housekeeping to please the old lighthouse-keeper, and she was understanding and motherly towards Abel. It was remarkable how well she adapted. Surely she wasn't thinking she might be wife to a man forty years her senior? Wouldn't he soon have to retire from the lighthouse, and then probably live out the rest of his days in a little house down on the beach? Abel, the boy, was quite out of the question, and she seemed to be on her guard against the very idea. Of course they spoke together during the daily round of things, they could discuss things and mull over things in conversation, that was all he asked of her, and perhaps that was all she would have permitted him as well.

But it's not much of a life for you lads at sea! she said. Just men all the time. I can imagine what that's like. Okay during the day maybe, but at night . . .

Yes, said Abel.

I suppose you make up for it when you get ashore, but then that's just an emergency solution.

Yes, said Abel.

Lolla got up, put one foot on the chair and drew her stocking a long way up. She was that motherly she gave no heed to his quick glance. She did the same thing again the next evening, by lamplight, and Abel laid a hand on her leg.

What is it? she asked with a smile.

Nothing.

But the old man sitting up in the tower probably started worrying. There was something not quite right about the fact that he sat there high up in the air passing his time doing card-tricks for himself while down below the young ones quietly got on with God knows what. He would have to speak up.

You mustn't mess about with him, he said.

With who – the kid? she shouted back.

Yes, you mustn't mess about with him. He's off again soon.

Fine by me. He's only going to show me how to use the motor-boat.

Don't get me wrong, Lolla, I'm old enough to be your grandfather, don't mess about with him. You young people, you're so wild.

Lolla smiled: As for that, you're young enough yourself to be doing all the messing about that needs doing out here.

He looked her up and down, to see if she was giving him cheek: I was already a married man by the time you and your parents were born, he said expansively.

That seems so strange! Lolla said. But I remember when you came back home in that big barque of yours . . . what was the name of it again?

The *Lina*. Yes, she was a lovely little ship.

I was standing there and saw you when you came, and I rowed out to the ship. You probably don't remember, do you?

So many people came aboard. But yes, I think maybe, possibly . . .

I was just a little girl, but I thought you were such a handsome man.

Well I'm damned!

You know, we girls, we're not that old before we start to get the feel of it.

Yes, so I gather.

So in a kind of way, I'm your old sweeetheart.

Ha ha ha! the old skipper laughed along, tolerant with the youngster.

*

Some time after Abel had left, with everything back to normal again, old Brodersen seemed to be doing an unusual amount of thinking. It was nice having a young woman out at Holmen, he trimmed his grey beard and combed the long hairs across his moon. Often he invited the girl up into the tower and did card-tricks for her, he was in a good humour, they were spending so little on coffee and butter. Smart girl, that Lolla. Okay, since she'd learnt to handle the motorboat she was often in town, and that meant a fair amount of petrol, but on the other hand it suited him well to have her out of the way and not clanking about the place while he was trying to take his afternoon nap. All things considered it was a piece of good fortune to have got hold of her.

The courtship didn't come to much. No, he was too old. For a while he dandified himself up with a thick chain across his waistcoat and leather boots with glossy turnovers to make himself look a little bit more the sea-captain than the lighthouse keeper, but it didn't last long, he was irrevocably old. The snows disappeared, the sap rose in the bushes on Holmen, spring came to the people again, but for old Brodersen it all went the other way, he felt himself growing older and drier than ever. He was still carrying a touch of influenza from the winter and wasn't getting boiled fish as often as he did when Abel was home, and life really was't that much fun anymore. Nor did Lolla make any effort to make him feel alive and young again, after her fresh opening in the autumn. Now she'd heard his talk and seen all his card-tricks – *finito*. Lolla really was using far too much petol in that motorboat. He really would have to have a word with her.

You're in town such a lot, Lolla. I'm not saying you neglect your work, I'm not saying that, but you're using a lot of petrol.

Yes, said Lolla. But what else should I do? Sit here on Holmen with an old man and not move a muscle?

He couldn't flare up and send her packing, he had to put up with the truth. He would try to entertain her a bit, he really would. Come here into the living room, Lolla, there's all sorts of strange things here from faraway lands! He was touching in his enthusiasm as he started to show off his curios, explaining what part of the world they came from, the year in which he had acquired them, what they'd cost. It was worthless junk the lot of it, gathered during his earliest days at sea, bows and arrows, seashells, a little buddha made of lead, a box with a shell on it, a big painting of the *Lina*, done in Nepal. He gave her a silk scarf from China. He folded it up nicely and lingered over it before he held it out to her.

She said : What shall I do with this?

It's silk. You can have it, as a present.

Oh thank you. I can fold it into a little scarf to put round my neck.

Yes, that's right. It's from China. I don't remember what I paid for it, but you can have it.

But the collection in the living room was soon exhausted, and he was unable to entertain her any longer. It was obvious she didn't belong in his house, the young are so demanding these days. But there again he couldn't get rid of her after such a short time and be a person people didn't stay long with. He was Brodersen, the respectable captain and lighthouse keeper, a man with bank accounts, well respected by one and all.

A letter arrived from Abel, he'd been paid off in Sydney and was now studying at a Seaman's School, he wrote. A real hard-working lad, he wanted to get on in life and make something of himself. His father was proud of him and when he was in town told people that now Abel was studying at the Seaman's School. Sure, Abel's going far, people answered. He might end up the town's big hero, there's no one else anyway, they said.

But nothing much came of his efforts in Sydney. His next letter arrived from New Zealand, from Wellington, where he was studying to be an engineer. He could have made a lot worse choice and his father still had high hopes of him. A trick Abel was able to do was bend his fingers over backwards, they were that supple, and he used them to make a brass box with a double bottom that had no keyhole in it but sprang open as if by magic. There was a lead weight between the two bottoms, and moving it back and forth a certain number of times brought it to the exact right spot where it touched a spring . . . and up flew the lid! Fantastic invention. Old Brodersen had heard his son explain the mechanism, but beyond that hadn't bothered much with

22

the box. Now he took it out and showed it to Lolla, this last and most remarkable curio.

But apart from that he didn't want to make a fuss of Lolla any more, he only wanted to keep the atmosphere between them good until the end. She'd been over a year at the lighthouse and he couldn't put up with her anymore. It wasn't just that she wasted his savings on petrol for the engine, but she didn't always come back to the lighthouse at night. What she was up to might have been a matter of indifference to him, for any day now he would be retiring and finding himself a place to rent in town; but he would have preferred it if, out of respect for him, at least, she made some show of wanting a good reference from him. But staying away all night – what was the point of that? He heard the odd story about her in town: when she was home at her parents she said she was going out to the lighthouse at night, and at the lighthouse she said she'd spent the night at home.

He went down to the motorboat in the morning, baled it out and scraped around the inside of it with a nail and that kind of thing, but later in the day, when Lolla wanted to use it, the engine wouldn't start. The Captain was taking a nap so she couldn't turn to him for help, but she didn't let that stand in her way, she rowed off in the lighthouse rowing-boat and went to town anyway. One smart woman, that Lolla, but so easily led astray. It looked as if things were alright again between her and the chemist, people had seen her going in by the back door when the chemist was on duty. It was most unsuitable.

Maybe it was all one to Captain Brodersen, but still, it put him in a bad light. It was during the year she spent at his house, under his supervision, that she had become so flighty. And one day he had the painful experience of seeing the chemist in the street, limping along, drunk, with the Chinese silk scarf dangling from his breast-pocket. So that's where it ended up, the silk scarf he had bought with his savings back in 1887.

He had all the bother and stress of moving away from the lighthouse, but again, Lolla was efficient and helpful. They gathered everything together and packed it all up, a busy time, so there wasn't much talking. When she asked and was told that he had rented himself a little attic room she nodded and said it was in a good neighbourhood.

Have we got everything now? she asked. Yes, he thought so. He'd rented a shack for all the bits and bobs he didn't have room for in the attic, and he'd sold his animals. All that was left behind were the handful of decorative bushes Abel's mother had planted. It must have been around ten years ago, before she got sick, and now she was dead. Yes, and the bushes still there. Brodersen shook his head – what was the point of it all? There was no way the new lighthouse keeper was going to give him anything for those bushes.

So he and Lolla parted company. Thanks for your company, they said to each other.

III

LODGING IN TOWN WORKED OUT BETTER THAN HE HAD expected. He wrote and told Abel that he'd rented an attic room and furnished it with his own bed and table and a couple of chairs, it looked just like his old bedroom out at the lighthouse. He kept going on dried food and ate his main meals out at a restaurant. The main thing was to make sure his pension lasted, he wrote.

His daily life carried on, without much excitement but without significant difficulties either. In the morning a stroll down to the fish-dock when the mackerel boats came home. At the cemetery he had the graves of two dead wives to look after, to keep up appearances. Then a long nap after his main meal. Now and then he met some old friend in town, some worn-out old skipper out walking to kill time in the same way as he was. There were quite a few of these, Kjørboe was one, and Krum, Tengvald's father, and the father of Rieber Carlsen, the priest. Kjørboe was almost the best one to meet, he was so decrepit he more or less vegetated and didn't cause his head any bother.

They walked along together as far as the little park, chatting away. By the time they got there were tired and sat down. Good to sit for a while, next to a little chat there was by God nothing as good as a rest. They're so full of loneliness and age, so wizened, and already they've started to die. Kjørboe is seventy five.

They don't have much else to talk about than mutual acquaintances from seagoing days, old captains who have retired, among them one who'd been unfortunate enough to lose a dog he'd been so fond of, and another who had had to sell his last share in a ship in order to survive. That was Rieber Carlsen, the one who'd paid for his son to study for the priesthood. Everyone had something on their mind. And come to think of it, it was an idiotic affectation of Norem's to walk around town with that dog at his heels, he wasn't born with it, because Jakob Norem was really common and an ordinary humble man, like you and me.

What was wrong with the dog?

It got too old.

Then I supposed he'll get himself a new one?

I couldn't tell you. Last time I spoke to him he couldn't make up his mind.

A housewife has stretched a line between two trees in the park and hung out washing on it. You weren't supposed to do that, so they passed a comment on it. A pair of women's bloomers hanging there in broad daylight with their shameless opening, they both pretend they aren't looking at them. They wonder what kind of housewife it is who dares to let the whole park down like that. Mind you, the wash is clean and white, and they aren't looking at the bloomers but staring fixedly at a pillow case next to them, as if it was an interesing shape in its squareness.

It develops like this:

If only those bloomers weren't there, says Kjørboe.

I'm not looking at them, answers Brodersen.

Can I help it? Aren't they hanging there?

Well you know you've always been a great one for stuff like that.

At least I haven't worn two wives out like you, ha ha ha.

No. But would that be six or twelve kids you're father to, you old goat?

Nothing but good humour and friendship. They flatter each other, they make out they're still up to it.

From one thing to another, says Kjørboe, did you read about that storm in the Atlantic?

No.

No because you've gone all religious. I bet all you read is 'The Messenger'.

I don't even read that, I can't afford magazine subscriptions.

What are you saving up for then?

For my last resting place in the cemetry.

After his friend has thought about this for a while he says: Oh, you'll live a long time yet.

Silence.

A dog goes over to one of the trees, cocks his leg and lets fly. Fair enough, but there's a lovely bunch of dandelions directly below him and a bumble bee has to take off from the dandelions and get away. The dog's finished, he trots away, sniffs, finds himself another tree—

What are you talking about? says Kjørboe. What do you mean, can't afford it? The banks are all stuffed with your money.

Brodersen is offended: You're an ignorant so-and-so.

Then it dies away and neither of them has the wit nor the intelligence to keep it going. If it's a warm day they might doze off.

From one thing to another, says Kjørboe, to hide the fact that he's asleep: Have you got anything to drink up at your place if I pop up one of these days?

Me, something to drink? I'm lucky enough if I've got something to eat each day.

I was only asking.

I've just had half-soles put on my shoes, four bloody kroner it cost me.

The money just leaks away. I oiled my boat last week.

I don't have a boat any more, says Brodersen.

No, you got a lot of money for them.

Brodersen ignores this and says: I should have had my hair cut, but I'll have to leave it now. You know how much they charge!

And then it all dies away again, and again they fall asleep.

The evening is drawing on, a breeze passes through the trees and the leaves of the aspen rustle against each other with a silky sound. Loneliness everywhere. Here and there a small bird.

A few minutes later they wake up again, and of course, no-one has been sleeping. They're more lively now after the nap and ready for more chat. Kjørboe starts off:

I just can't understand what Norem wants with a dog.

No, says Brodersen, agreeing.

Remember that chap in Brevik who retired and bought himself a parrot to sit on his shoulder?

Brodersen shakes at his head at such folly. He says: If you ask me now the best thing is to be dragging as few things as possible around with you.

You sold your motorboat to Robertsen the Customs man, I heard?

Yes but it wasn't mine, so I'll be sending the money to Abel.

What does Robertsen want with that?

You tell me. He's already got two boats.

He was your Mate once.

I know that.

Then he started in the Customs.

You think I don't know that? I see him every day. But three boats—

And then Kjørboe fades away a bit, he shivers his shoulders, he's cold. Why are we still sitting here? he asks.

Yes, why, answers Brodersen and slowly starts to get to his feet.

Finally his friend gets up too and yawns. I wouldn't mind being back home again, he sighs. It's a long way.

Brodersen, who is five years younger: That little bit of a path is no bother to me.

Well, I wasn't asking you to carry me neither.

And they quarrel away the homeward path, helping each other along like that.

Kjørboe: Looks to me as if you're falling behind.

Well I can't keep up with a youngster like you!

Yes you can, but you don't want to be wearing out those new half-soles of yours.

They toddle along. Long way to go—

A while later Abel wrote that he'd arrived in Sydney. He'd left the engineering school in Wellington, the course was too long, the prospects uncertain, and anyway, for the three weeks he'd spent in Wellington the weather had been terrible. Here in Sydney he'd enrolled at the Seamen's School, but the teachers had ignored him, they said he wasn't capable of following the lessons. And it wasn't all that easy for him in a foreign language, and with not much money for his keep. So now he'd signed on for a trip to Quebec. He knew Canada from before and he was pretty sure he'd be alright there—

Bit of an oddball that Abel, roaming round all the time and not settling down anywhere. And what about that idea he had of making something of himself? As it happened he stayed on in Quebec for quite a while and even wrote the odd letter there. He was working as some kind of mechanic or blacksmith on a new fort that was being built. Two years had passed since he left home this time.

Old Brodersen wasn't quite so keen to talk about his son now, only when people asked him, then he might say thanks for asking, Abel was doing fine, he was a mechanic at a fort and earning good money. But when a letter arrived from that capricious lad to say that he'd left Quebec and was now working in a sawmill in the forests his father shook his head and began to doubt whether Abel would ever make anything of himself. One good thing about him: he looked after himself and never wrote home asking for help, he seemed actually to be content with his changing fate and didn't complain.

So the days passed, with old Brodersen sinking into decrepitude, still living out his lazy dog-days on the dried food in his attic at home, with his main meals out at the restaurant. Not a bad life, but not enough to keep an active man going. There weren't mackerel boats to watch at the fish-dock all year round, and by this time there wasn't a single street in the town he wasn't familiar with. Naturally he went along every evening to his vantage point and kept an eye on the lighthouse and made sure

29

the lamp was lit, if it was blinking, somebody had to check. But it wasn't enough for an active man.

For company he had the Robertsen family. The husband had been his Mate when Brodersen was a captain, but since he was no great shakes as a seaman and had no prospects of getting a ship of his own he'd gone into the customs service. He'd risen through the ranks there and managed fine with his steady wage. There were two almost-grown daughters in the house, and the parents were in their forties.

A pleasant home to visit, straightaway they brushed off a chair for old Brodersen and he could fill his pipe for nothing at the Robertsens, on top of which they always called him Captain, a habit from the days when Robertsen was his Mate.

Now you just sit yourself down, Captain, and have a spoonful of mushy peas with us, says the wife.

Fine by Brodersen, it means he saves his krone for his main meal. And the mushy peas were delicious—boiled with smoked pig's knuckle, with timian and onion and plenty of peas. And a pipe to follow.

As usual the family asked after Abel. The wife and daughters were always very interested, as if they had some kind of stake in it. Brodersen didn't answer, he talked about other things:

I hear there's been a dreadful storm in the Atlantic.

Ferocious, said Robertsen. Good job we weren't there, Captain!

Well, we would've managed alright.

I don't doubt it for a moment. I saw you in action enough times.

I don't understand it, says Brodersen, they make too much out of a storm these days. They start shouting and carrying on and telegraphing round the world. We had the odd storm in our day too, Mister Mate.

Robertsen nods his head. They remind each other of this time and that time.

The coffee arrives.

Yes please, but now I didn't exactly call in expecting a three-course meal, says Brodersen.

The wife asks about Abel. Isn't he coming home?

Ha, him! is all the father says and shakes his head. How are you getting on with the motorboat, Mate?

Not bad at all. Goes like a bomb. I've painted it now.

Ok, so you're getting the use of it?

Oh you bet! Robertsen is a 'boat-maniac', once he gets onto the subject of boats you can't stop him. Everyone has a hobby horse, it might be postage stamps or politics. Shrewd boy, that Abel, he says. The boat's eighteen foot long with a three horse-power engine—

And Robertsen could have kept going, but the wife interrupts: You didn't answer my question about Abel, Captain. Hasn't he written?

Yes, of course. A letter from every country on the map. But the Mate sits there, and I'm sitting here, and *we* knew where we were going, we stuck to the course.

Robertsen: Abel's a shrewd one alright. I was thinking two horse-power is not enough and four too much for the size of it – but Abel *knew*.

Be quiet, says the wife. Does he write from every country, Captain? So he's travelling around a lot?

Brodersen curtly: Yes.

Robertsen's been overpowered on this occasion and falls in: Well, he's having a look round, nothing wrong with that. Last thing he was at a fort. And you can bet it's only the chosen few who get a look in behind all the secrets there.

Last thing at a fort yes. But that was last year. Then at a sawmill—

That Abel! He wants to learn everything.

And now he's gone to the States.

The wife: Have you just had a letter?

Yes. Not long ago.

But he is doing fine, isn't he?

No, Brodersen snaps. He's got married.

Married! the wife and daughters gasp.

Well now that's strange, says Robertsen.

The family recovers, and there are more questions: Then she's probably got a lot of money? What does she look like? He has sent a photo, hasn't he?

Brodersen's replies are curt and angered, like round numbers: He sends nothing and no information. Just that he's tired of wandering round and now he's got himself married to a southern girl.

31

Silence descends upon the room. Robertsen has to rescue the situation and he says: You'll soon see, she's a rich heiress.

Old Brodersen dismisses this prospect entirely, because in that case he would have sent a cheque to his old dad. Would that have been asking too much? But even if she did have a million the lad should have made something of himself before running off and getting married. Look at young Rieber Carlsen – climbed right to the top and already preached in our church in his dog-collar and his gown. Abel settles to nothing out there, just change and change again. What's he going to do when he brings madam back home here? He's neither an engineer nor a seaman, he won't be able to get a ship—

Robertsen is bored already and yawns: He's still so young.

Brodersen thanks them and leaves.

A procession passes the window, a landau with two horses, a bridal procession. What's this? The women flock to the window and talk over each other: It's Olga, she's gone and got married! Will you just look, she's only ridden up another road and come down here so the whole town can see!

Brodersen from a long way off: Olga?

The chemist's Olga. She's so wild, she's had no-one to keep her in check since the mother died. Imagine, and before that she was engaged to Rieber Carlsen who became a priest, then she broke up with him last autumn when he was called away to preach up in Finnmark. Oh no, Olga wasn't going up there. So she got engaged to young Clemens, the magistrate's son, but he's no great prospect . . .

Old Brodersen toddles off homeward. Of course he's upset about Abel, but saving that krone for his main meal makes it easier to bear. He calls in at his local shop for food and toothpicks, but he's drowsy after the pea soup and looks forward to his nap at home.

There's a wedding in town, says the old shopkeeper.

Yeah yeah yeah yeah, flags flying and two horses on the wagon, same thing here as in the South in America. But what did you and I do, Westman? We waited until we'd made something of ourselves before we got married.

Yes, in a way . . . yes, I suppose we could say that . . .

But what do they do now? Run off and get married twenty-four

32

years old, with no trade to speak of, and no skill they can make a living out of.

Well, young Clemens is, after all, studying law with his father's firm.

And, of course, to a girl without a penny in her pocket.

I don't know who you're talking about, the shopkeeper says sharply. The chemist is a rich man.

Who's talking about the chemist? I'm talking about Abel, my boy. Gone off and got married. Is there no shame? Where's the rhyme and reason in it? You don't know Kentucky, she might even be black . . .

33

IV

AND AFTER THAT ABEL DIDN'T WRITE ANY MORE.

Old Brodersen lived up in the loft and it wasn't too bad, not bad at all, one day ran on into the next. The autumn was tough, mind, and he had to think back to his younger years when autumn and snow and darkness were all just good fun to him. Not like that now, but he'd avoided contact with doctors and medicine the whole time. People thought he looked after himself well. In his own opinion he was suffering with a minor heart problem. There was a description of it in his 'Doctor at Sea' book.

Lolla started to visit him. It was almost a bit odd, but Lolla came, and it didn't exactly displease him. She hadn't had a position since she was out at the lighthouse, she stayed at home with her parents, and you didn't hear any more scandalous talk of her. She had no husband and child, no, but then she didn't have the chemist anymore either. Over. Finished. But things at home had gone downhill, the house had been sold and the family moved down to a little house down by shore. Fate. And in the midst of it all something unpleasant emerged, involving her father and the serving girl. The whole thing was a disaster.

Well, one afternoon Lolla turned up in the attic. Brodersen had had his nap and was well-rested.

Oh my dear, is that you, Lolla? he greeted her.

I don't know who else it would be, she replied. She looked good, bright. She took a look round and said: Yes, I thought so, I should have come here a long time ago and done the cleaning and tidying up.

Brodersen said he'd had a woman who came in and did the cleaning for him now and then, but Lolla was scathing: A funny sort of cleaning that. Look at this! And this! And look at your ceiling!

Then she took off her coat, fetched some water from the tap, rooted about until she found the things she needed and started work. She had lost weight and was slimmer, it seemed to him, but as she worked away her skin turned pink and and she looked pretty and chatted away to him the whole time in a lively fashion. Remarkably capable girl, that Lolla, a lot nicer than she used to be, and her nostrils a lot less frivolous. She climbed up on a chair to wash under the gable, he sat there and watched, it didn't occur to him all that often to study her legs.

When she was done she said: So, now do I get some coffee and a bite to eat?

Yes, he said, but I don't have much. Look in the drawer!

She made the coffee herself and found the dried food. Oh yes, it was good, she ate as though she was hungry.

A couple of days later she was back again. It put a bit of a strain on the coffee and the dried food, but it was nice to have her around, he bought in extra for her, to keep her happy, and in the weeks that followed he often said to her: It's kind of you to look out for me, Lolla. So she kept on coming, at intervals, and was welcome.

She couldn't be forever washing the room or the curtains, but she could make the bed and now and then sew on a button and do the odd bit of mending, Lolla could do it all. She asked him to show her his card-tricks again, though his fingers had grown too stiff, and in return he got her to write letters to Abel for him, he couldn't handle a pen as well as he used to. Write that it's over two years since his father has heard from him. Tell him his father has written two letters and got no reply. Oh just write anything you want. Did you know he got married?

I heard that.

Yes, a fine business.

But time went by, and Abel didn't answer Lolla's letters either. The letters weren't returned to sender, so he couldn't have been dead.

Abel didn't write anymore.

Brodersen stayed at home most of the time and only met a few people. Kjørboe was okay, Krum and Norem too, but there wasn't much life to them, no, they were old and silly. He stopped calling in at Robertsen the Customs man's house, the Robertsen family didn't seem to care about their dear old Captain anymore – for whatever reason. And if he did meet the Customs man by himself on the quay, all he got was nothing but endless talk about boats.

After a while Lolla started coming less often. She'd got herself a position now, with newly-wed Olga and her husband, young Clemens. The couple really didn't need a housekeeper, it was just something you had to have. Clemens himself carried on at his father's office and opened a legal business of his own on the side in case any business came his way. It wasn't easy for someone just starting up, and besides he was probably too decent a person to be respected.

The Clemens' sometimes visited the wine-bar and enjoyed themselves in town. Olga was a gorgeous young wife, she smiled at the world and hung on her husband's arm.

It was inevitable that Captain Brodersen would find out about a document in the vaults of the Private Bank that bore his signature. It was bound to come out in the end, wasn't it?

But before it did, Lolla turned up at the attic late one rainy evening, Brodersen had gone to bed and was trying to sleep when she arrived. She was cold and wet, she asked if she could take off some of her clothes, but of course that didn't warm her up much. There was a puddle on the floor where she stood.

What in the world, said Brodersen, why are you so wet?

It's my evening off, said Lolla.

Have you been out walking?

Yes. Walking and thinking.

He took pity on her and told her to start a fire.

Yes, she said, right . . .

But then she came over to the bed and felt down inside, how warm it was.

Let me just snuggle in to you a little while, she said. Next to you.

Here? he managed to gasp. And he sat up as though to relinquish the bed to her.

Just here at the very edge. Until I get warm. And she took off more of her clothes, and by the time she got in she was wearing almost nothing.

They didn't speak until a few moments had passed.

Where did you get so cold?

Out. I was walking and thinking.

Thinking?

But I'll soon be warm. It's so good here.

Come on over here to me. The bed's wide enough.

Thanks, she said, and wriggled over to him and cautiously lay her arm across his stomach under the blanket.

He tucked the bedclothes in around her and made himself comfortable. Miracles and fairy tales. Hadn't happened to him for maybe a half a century. But all nice and modest, his marital bed from the lighthouse was wide enough for both of them.

Thinking? he repeated, not understanding.

Yes, thinking. I can't say anymore now.

They were silent for a while.

You're clothes are lying there and they're not getting any drier.

It doesn't matter. Once I've got warm I'll put them on and dry them on my body.

And he recognised sensible Lolla in this. She was never at a loss.

I'm already warm now, so if you think . . .

Lolla come over here properly and get warm. I won't eat you.

Presently their legs and breasts came together and they stayed there. They fumbled with each other under the blanket . . .

37

Afterwards they boasted of each other's passion:

I certainly never expected you to be such a stud.

It was because of you, Lolla. You're wild.

I just hope nothing goes wrong, she said.

Wrong? Not at all! Suddenly he became very honourable and responsible: And if anything does, I'll do the right thing. Remember that.

Yes.

I'm man enough.

Oh goodness me yes, you're man enough.

I have to laugh when I think about Kjørboe, he said. Do you know Kjørboe?

Yes.

Captain Kjørboe. He's so old, nothing but dust. He was trying to do a long-distance spit once, but with no teeth he couldn't get it out and it flopped down into his shoe.

Lolla laughed. Ha ha ha!

Yes, it must be terrible to be so far gone! But Krum isn't any better. You probably know Krum, and Norem too? Not a jot better. Now I'm going to get up and fire up the stove for your clothes, he said, and he got up, wanting to be younger than he'd ever been before.

Absolutely not! I'm getting up now and leaving.

But are you warm now?

Yes, she said with a sly smile. Yes, I'm warm now.

Alone again, Brodersen lay awhile. He felt unreal and strange. It didn't happen and it couldn't've been him. Then he collapsed into a deep sleep.

She didn't come again.

After four days he went out with the plan of waylaying her. No. He didn't dare ask after her at young Clemens' house, but hung around in the vicinity in case she came out and headed for the market. No. He walked to her home by the sea, but Lolla wasn't there. He was getting very worked up. After a week he knocked on the kitchen door at the Clemens'. He met the lady of the house. Old Brodersen stood there, drooling and lost.

Lolla? No she wasn't in at the moment. Was there any message for her?

Absolutely not. Not at all. It was nothing . . .

Alright then.

It probably sounds a bit odd, but . . .

No it doesn't sound odd, Captain, the young lady says in a friendly manner. After all, Lolla was out at the lighthouse with you.

Yes, right, out at the lighthouse with me. We know each other. But it was nothing really. But at the door he managed to say: It was just something about her mother. Nothing.

Where could Lolla be, what was going on? Brodersen was by now completely besotted by her, the very caricature of an old fool. Where could Lolla be? He got himself all dressed up again, with the watch chain and the knee-length boots, he splashed out on a haircut, he had disgraceful dreams at night. No letters from Abel, old Brodersen was alone in the world.

Robertsen the Customs man came to see him and pleaded with him to guarantee for a bank loan.

Me? said Brodersen. No.

A tiny little loan, sixteen hundred, he needed it to build an extension to his house.

No, no, I won't want hear another word.

Yes, because now his daughters were both as good as full grown, and they needed a bigger room now, maybe one each, young people wouldn't settle for less nowadays.

Brodersen just shook his head.

Robertsen: I'm a safe bet: steady job in the public sector, three boats, a house and garden . . .

It's no good, Mister Mate, I won't do it. Coming to me like this! That's something I've never done.

Oh no? asks Robertsen.

No never.

Well according to what I've heard, Captain, you have done it before.

Me? Done what?

Signed.

39

Never, Mister Mate. And there's an end to it.

And there was another annoyance to contend with. The new light-house keeper had informed him that he had no intention of paying for the ornamental shrubs that had been left behind on Holmen. Brodersen had been a real cheapskate and hoped to get some recompense for them, but no luck. He could take his bushes, here you are . . .

And no Lolla to talk to about it this time either. He was alone in the world.

V

THEN LOLLA CAME.

Lolla had to come, her father had disappeared, left home, left town, run out on everything, left her in a real jam with a debt of a thousand kroner and a forged bank draft in the Private Bank.

It was a nasty shock for Lolla when her mother told her the news, but she was strong, she was fearless, she went into service with the young Clemens'. Very little work to do, but not enough money either to pay off the bank, she had every reason to go out on that 'evening off' and 'think'. Lolla's idea was that she would get Brodersen himself to redeem the forged document. So she went to him and she was with him. That was the first time.

She also worked out that she shouldn't rush her next visit . . . let him wait for her . . . crave her. But then she met Robertsen the Customs man one day and realized she was in danger. Robertsen said: I went to see the old lighthouse keeper and tried to get him to guarantee for a loan

41

and he turned me down! Lolla answered: Yes, but did you ever hear tell of him guaranteeing for a loan for anyone? And Robertsen said yes, and he looked at her, yes, I did hear something to that effect . . . since you ask!

That meant Lolla was in danger, and she went to Brodersen for a second time.

It wasn't in the evening, but in the middle of the day, in broad daylight. So each of the two occasions were completely different.

She was insecure, glancing sideways at him, wondering if he already knew something. No. He was just burning up for her and he said: Bless you, where have you been all this time?

Me? she said, all at once sorrowing and desperately unhappy: she was in terrible trouble, her very life, she was in danger . . .

What on earth . . . ?

Everything had gone wrong for her.

How? Surely not. What nonsense.

That something like this should have happened to her! From now on she might as well be dead, the grave was her only home . . .

Calm down. Come over here and sit on my lap.

But, she said, I've no-one to blame but myself. It's just that I was so cold that night.

Brodersen is completely obsessed with his own desire, he wants her to take off her clothes and stay with him.

It's all my own fault, she said, shaking her head. Didn't you say, she asked, that you would help me?

Yes. Oh yes of course.

And support me? Because now is when I need it.

Don't say that, you're just afraid, you'll see.

Oh but . . . I'm afraid I'm the best judge of that.

Silence.

A little money is nothing to you, Captain. But for me . . . my life . . .

Alright, alright, let's just calm down and think this over.

She seized the opening: Yes, that's good of you, to want to help me.

But why didn't you come, Lolla? Do you know how long it is since you were here? You could've come.

42

I couldn't face it.

Well now you're here anyway – take your things off and make yourself comfortable.

I'm going to need a thousand kroner.

What! he gasped.

They couldn't agree about anything. He wanted to postpone things, they should wait and see if anything happened. Take off your things and make yourself comfortable! She asked how he could think of such a thing and refused to come near him. Never again!

But if she left without achieving her goal now she would be back where she started, so she had to keep at it, the danger was imminent.

And I don't have time either, she said. I'm going to the market.

Then come back this evening!

No, she said and shook her head

No?

Why should I? You won't help me, like you said you would.

But of course I will. But Lolla, a thousand kroner . . .

You don't know what's at stake.

How much does a dress cost? he asked.

I don't need it for a dress.

But how much does a dress cost? I've been thinking of buying you a pretty dress. Shall we say fifty kroner?

Abruptly Lolla sits herself in his lap and says: Now let's not joke about it anymore. A dress with a hat and shoes and gloves costs at least two hundred and fifty.

Does it? is all he says, so overwhelmed by the fact that she's sitting in his lap, so silly now that he'll say anything at all.

So if you want to give me enough for a silk dress—

I'm sure I'll manage that, he replies. Will you come back this evening?

Yes.

He wants to go with her to the bank and get the money, but she says no. He's to write her a note, a cheque, and give it to her.

Lolla was a fast learner.

*

43

And with that she was gone again. No, she didn't come to him in the evening, and she didn't buy a dress. She paid the precious cheque into the bank as a down-payment on the loan and earned a few months respite. Here you are, down-payment courtesy of the guarantor himself!

It was difficult for her to avoid him in the days that followed, a lot of thought and skill was required. She frequented a distant market place, she walked down the streets with her eyes wide open and a gaze that reached farther than others.

And yet . . . Lolla 'thought' again, and now she began to doubt her own strategy. Was it really so smart? She still owed a lot of money, and she had her mother to take care of in the house on the beach. And every hour of every day she ran the risk of the story of the forged document coming out. By the time, therefore, she had organized matters so that she and Brodersen would encounter one another in the street she had made her decision.

Just for a moment it looked as though he might turn away, avoid her like some wounded and hurt soul. But she waved, and held him.

She took a quick look round and spoke quietly: I've been worrying myself sick the whole time about you-know-what. I've been crying day and night, because you know it doesn't take much for it all to go wrong.

Yes.

Yes. But now it looks as if I'm in the clear, I hope.

There you see! he said enthusiastically. I knew it.

She looked around even more carefully: I can't say any more here, but I'll come to you this evening if you like.

He began muttering something about how she'd promised and lied to him once before, but soon stopped. And even though he was on his way to the cemetery to the graves of his two wives he turned back immediately and went home to get ready.

She came that evening.

Lolla was nice and pretty and bold. I'm not wearing the new dress, she said. I can't afford to.

It doesn't matter about the dress.

Listen: I think I'm alright now.

There you see! I knew it! And now he probably thought everything was alright again and he started to fumble with her buttons.

She didn't want that.

But I've waited so long for you, he protested. There was just the once, and then you were gone.

Yes, but . . . yes, you're right. Can't you forget that?

No, he couldn't forget that.

Was what we did so unforgettable for you?

All he could do was nod his head, yes, it was unforgettable for him.

I've been thinking, she said. And then paused for a long time. She let him undo a couple more buttons on her blouse. I've been thinking — how would you like it if I was here with you all the time?

How would I . . . ? No, no.

That I didn't . . . go away anymore?

He muttered something about not being able to afford her, his meagre pension, he didn't understand . . .

I mean, that we get married.

Brodersen gasped. A moment later he asked in disbelief: D'you think so?

They sat there, each with their own thoughts. He mutttered something about being too old, that she didn't mean it, that there were so many handsome young men around—

Yes, she said, and sat in his lap. Maybe so. But in a way, you know, I'm your old sweetheart.

Well, he had to smile at that.

From childhood, you know. And a thing like that you don't forget.

They got married as soon as possible, neither one of them wanted to spin it out, married in the parish church with choir and organ. Old Brodersen managed to stay on his feet, the priest called him Captain and spoke of this young girl who by your side stands. A lot of things could happen in the course of their marriage, but they must be sure not to let the sun set on their wrath. Five other skippers sat there, alternately listening and dropping off, listening and dropping off. So now Brodersen was married for a third time. Lolla wore a pretty dress with hat and gloves and shoes, she had achieved a goal.

They continued to live in the attic. Lolla was very sensible about it, they were two people alone together, the attic was big enough, so was

45

the bed. If they got themselves any bigger living quarters her mother would have to move in, but for a number of reasons it would be better if she carried on living in the house on the beach.

They wrote to Abel about 'the change' that had taken place, and the letter wasn't returned to sender this time either, but still no reply. Strange man, that Abel.

And a strange marriage too, as might have been expected. Lolla wanted nothing to do with her husband, and he made no great demands of her either, just a little in the beginning, an old man's passing ardour, a flicker only. The odd time when he thought he might want her she brushed it aside and said: Oh, come *on*!

Is that any way to talk to your husband? he asked.

But dear, you can't do anything.

Can't I ? That first time you said I could?

Yes, and you couldn't back then either.

Insults and silence.

Then he got angry and jealous: Then there must be someone who can with you, even if I can't.

She didn't answer.

Brodersen, angrier still: Not to mince my words, one day that silk scarf of mine from China, one day I saw it hanging out of a strange man's pocket.

Oh him, she replied with a disdainful pout.

Remember, I saw it.

Him! she pouted again. Well really!

It would have been much better if you'd given it back to me.

You'll get it back, she said.

Well, I don't want it now, he sulked. And when she didn't say anything he continued: How? By going to him and getting it back? Wonderful! Go to him at dusk, maybe, maybe at night, when he's on duty . . .

There there there, don't make such a fuss about it anymore, please. I'm your old sweetheart, you know that.

Be quiet, Lolla, I've got a right to talk about it.

Yes you have. But we're not to let the sun set on our wrath.

No, the sun was not to set on their wrath, every time Lolla was smart enough to smooth things out. But old Brodersen was badly stung and so upset afterwards that he went into a decline and started to fade away. He sought out his old companions again. They had been in the habit of showing him respect because he was a man with two bank accounts. But they weren't the same now, some were envious, others enjoyed his upset: How do you like being married, for once? they would ask. How do you get on at night? Isn't she a bit young for you? Kjørboe was the worst, even though he was oldest and so repulsively toothless. I've been thinking a bit about making a few 'changes' in my life too, said Kjørboe, but if I did I'd need 'help' from the postman. How about you?

Not yet, answers Brodersen and stands up.

No, sit down a while and have a chat.

No, I have to go.

So you're at it all the time now that you're married?

That's not why I'm going, says Brodersen uncomfortably. I can't be bothered to sit here anymore listening to your drivel.

He wandered down to the cemetry, to the two graves. He probably didn't give the dead women much thought, but he pulled up a few weeds and dead leaves. So that passed a bit of time, and he conducted himself in the appropriate fashion while he was about it. But it was no use, he was upset and he remained upset, and it ended with him joining the Salvation Army. And he could have done a lot worse things, he became religious, he found peace of mind and did good deeds, he burnt the old deck of cards that he'd used for his card-tricks, he said grace in secret at the table and abandoned as much as he could of this sinful world. But his decline was shocking over a very short period of time.

And Abel didn't write.

He said to Lolla: I should have sent Abel the money for his motorboat.

Yes, said Lolla.

Can you arrange it?

Yes, Lolla was good at that kind of stuff too: the bank will send the money as soon as you tell them, she said. How much is it? He gave her a little note, a cheque to take to the bank.

You must get a receipt, Lolla.

Of course I will.

So that was that. Good to get rid of money that it was sinful to hang onto. And perhaps he ought to reimburse the Robertsen family for all the thick pea soup and the rest of what he'd had there, and all the times he'd filled his pipe at the Mate's house? But when the Mate came to him with a request for his signature that was another matter entirely, as good as a robbery, he never signed.

In a way though it was also sort of an advantage to have a wife in the house. At heart it was best for him that she sheltered him from his own wild temptations and even went so far as to avoid pulling her stockings up high when he was looking. Lolla kept the attic nice, with the floor clean and no ashes left in the oven and the bed made up. Before he had had to buy his own food and other necessities of life himself, but not any more, and it worked out so much cheaper to eat the main meal at home instead of out at a café. And every mealtime now there was a plate, a knife and a fork laid out for him, whereas before he had to dig them out from a drawer. And now and then Lolla could be really nice to him and trim his hair and beard so that he didn't have to spend money at the barber's. It was good of her, since she was probably only telling the truth when she told him he wasn't able do anything for her. Fair's fair.

But he was declining, his heart was playing up too, and less and less remained of Captain Brodersen. In the autumn when he caught the flu' he took to his bed one afternoon.

Write a letter to Abel, he said.

She wrote to Abel.

But I did send him the money for the motor-boat?

That's all taken care of, said Lolla.

Where's the receipt?

She dug out the piece of paper and showed it to him. But it was an ordinary receipt for money paid in: Received today the sum of. The sum was there alright, but it had gone to another payment against the forged document.

He nodded, so he'd paid Abel and done the right thing.

Won't you see the doctor? asked Lolla.

He thought about it: It's not as if we don't know what it is, it's a touch of flu'. No, it's not worth bothering the doctor. Go and look up in my 'Doctor At Sea' book about heart trouble.

48

She didn't do that, instead she put her coat on and said: I'll be back in a few minutes. Then she tucked him up and left.

She returned with the doctor. Influenza. Prescription. Advice.

After the doctor had left she tucked him up again and went out to the chemist's to pick up the prescription medicines.

You're not to mention the silk scarf, he said from his bed.

I'm not going to that particular chemist's, was her reply.

He wasn't pleased with her when she came back, she could have looked it up in his medical book and saved the expense of the doctor. She gave him pills and drops, heated enough water for two hot-water bottles for his feet, thawed him out and made him sleep. He only dozed for a few minutes, but he said thanks for the hot-water bottles and that he was not feeling too bad now. Look up under heart trouble.

She read about heart murmur, about how the walls of the chamber of the heart get thinner and thinner, about paralysis, he listened closely and recognised it all. We used camphor and naphtha for that on board, he said. You've been out buying a lot of rubbish for influenza, but for that we drank boiling hot toddies.

Lolla watched over him and sat and carried on reading to herself from the medical book. He spoke, but it made him breathless, so he kept quiet most of the time. How does the sixth prayer go? he said. I know all the others.

She looked surprised: You mean the sixth commandment?

Not that. The sixth prayer. Forgive our sins or however it goes.

She realized he was getting mixed up and read aloud the fifth prayer. He repeated it a few times: We had the Lord's Prayer on board too, that always helped. But that probably doesn't interest you?

Oh I don't know about that, she replied, a little embarrassed.

The morning wore on.

Will you go out to the corridor for a bit, he said.

Lolla went out into the corridor and stayed there. She heard him moving in the bed, heard him talking, as if he was praying. Then he fell silent. She remained where she was a long time, uncertain, cold too, but she didn't want to disturb him.

When at last she looked in he was standing half on his head in the bed. He'd been trying to kneel and had toppled over forwards.

49

VI

ABEL WAS INFORMED BY TELEGRAPH OF HIS FATHER'S DEATH,
but he was in no great haste to travel. The months passed, and if he
responded at all to announcements and calls to attend meetings of the
beneficiaries of the will it was only to answer that he was doing just fine
where he was and felt no call to travel home.

But things must have been pretty tough for Abel one way and
another, because he wrote that he had neither clothes nor money for his
ticket.

No clothes and no money for his ticket . . . and him the son of a
wealthy man!

Money was sent, but Abel didn't come. He replied that he would
wait until the spring. The weather was nice and warm where he was,
and the life he was living suited him well. He had a donkey for a mount
and grew sweet potatoes and fished in the Ridge Streamlet and gutted
the fish and wiped his hands on his trousers and cooked the fish and ate

the fish and the sweet potatoes and apart from that he did nothing. It was so good, and since his wife's death it was all he needed, he wrote. But he might come in the spring if he got the chance.

More money was sent out to him.

In the middle of May he arrived. He was alone. His wife was dead.

Practically the same scenes on the quay when the coastal boat docked as eight years ago. The grown-ups and children gathering, people and boxes ashore, people and boxes on board, and the bell ringing for the third time.

Abel walked down the gangway in a brown ulster and carrying a suitcase. He eyed the gathering a little uncertainly. He probably recognised quite a few of them, but he didn't greet anyone and made little out of his arrival. He was clean-shaven, but aside from that he looked scruffy, his tie wasn't straight and his shirt dirty.

One of the workers on the quayside addresses him: Well, well, is that you, Abel?

Yes, he answers. Before I used to go home to the lighthouse, but not now.

He strolled slowly up into town, stopped and admired a small new public garden, looked at a fountain statue, stopped at the Seamen's Home and went in . . .

And this was the second time he came home and was so greatly changed. Not excessively changed. Not unrecognisably so and to the point of madness. But changed enough to make him different from what he was before, and different from others.

He signed in as Abel Brodersen, Norwegian citizen, 26 years old, previous address Green Ridge in Kentucky. Occupation was left blank.

A small room with an iron bedstead, a bowl for washing, table and chair. A hotel notice on the wall, flies in the window, doors missing from the top of the stove . . . an average sort of seaman's room. When they realized that it was Captain Brodersen's son, the one who had been so much talked about in recent weeks, they offered him a larger room. No. A room with two windows and a view of the quay and the approach and the lighthouse. No. Kind people who only wanted to help him, but he set no great store by it. After he had eaten his evening

51

meal together with the other lodgers he went up to bed. No, there was nothing special about him at all.

In the days that followed he visited various offices and announced his arrival. Robertsen the Customs man called in on him, was fatherly to him and gave him advice on all manner of things and told him that he'd bought his motor boat. Yes, it was in good hands, painted and well looked after, a few repairs done on the engine, that was only to be expected after so many years. Drop in and see us, Abel, when you've a mind to, you remember where we live don't you . . .

Lolla came. She was still wearing black and distinctly more reserved than in her younger days. She didn't call Abel's attention to the fact that they were now related to each other, and do you remember this time and that time, nothing like that, she sat in the chair and spoke about his father: a rare man and a fine death, *compos mentis* to the end. Abel asked her straight out and smiling how she came to marry his father – after all he was old enough to have been her grandfather? Well, said Lolla, and she told him openly and honestly that she hadn't been able to 'think' of any other way, everything had gone wrong at home, and there was a document in the bank with Captain Brodersen's name on it, even though Captain Brodersen had never in this world signed it, it was a forgery, they could've been severely punished for it. So she had no choice . . .

None of this was of any great interest to Abel. He said with a laugh: Well that makes you my stepmother! Funniest thing I ever heard!

That changed the mood between them and she carried on in lighter vein: Your father needed me to look after him, I cut his hair and cooked for him and did the washing and cleaning. He was all on his own and no-one to turn to, old as he was, think of that. He liked me and thought I was a good housewife, we got along just fine together, imagine! It wasn't like Lolla to talk so much, she was uneasy and chattered away as though she never wanted to stop going on about it.

Abel: Well I don't hold any of it against you, Lolla.

She blushed furiously and then slowly her pallor returned: Oh but you could do, she said. I've become part of your life now, and your inheritance too. But it's good of you, not to hold it against me, I'm glad you don't, and I'll show you – I don't want much, only what you think is fair. Let the lawyers do what they have to do, I'll give you back whatever you want. It wasn't like Lolla to be so impulsive.

That's fine, he said. Olga's married, I heard?

It was almost as though she'd been struck, and it took a few moments for her to catch up with him: Olga? Yes, married a long time ago. I was in service with them for a while. I didn't address her 'du' like the way we used to, I thought it would be too familiar, but she asked me to say 'du'. Nice people, both of them. They don't have children. She lent me books to read, she's so kind.

But not married to the one everyone expected, I hear?

No, she wouldn't go up to Finnmark and Rieber Carlsen had to go alone. Then she married young Clemens in a hurry – not because they had to, far from it, but I suppose she wanted to get the whole thing out of the way, God knows. They often go down to the wine-bar.

It would be nice to meet them, said Abel.

Yes, that's where they go. They don't drink anything, that's not why, but she's got nothing to do and she's bored, she can't find any rest. Sometimes they dance. Five Negroes play there.

Abel: If you want to come along we could go there.

She was surprised: It wouldn't be proper for me yet.

Oh?

And you probably shouldn't go with me.

Oh? No, you're too young, stepmother, he said with a smile. It could well be you're right, people would talk.

For a second time she blushed a deep red. In the old days Lolla never blushed for anything.

And besides, he said, I don't have the money to go either.

She laughed: That won't be a problem for long. You've got plenty coming your way.

Can you let me have something now?

She gave him what she had and said he should go and get more himself. Where's your luggage, your clothes? When she heard that he didn't have any clothes she clapped her hands together. He excused himself by saying that where he came from they had so few clothes because they were all as poor as each other. Maybe so, but he needed

53

clothes here, so she gave him motherly instructions to get along to the tailor that very same day.

At the door she turned, as she had done that time at his father's, and said: I can see you need smartening up a bit.

He drifted along to the wine-bar in the evening still wearing the same clothes, sat down by the door and drank a beer or two. The Negroes played and people danced on the oblong dance-floor, same thing here as everywhere else in the world. Olga was sitting with her husband away over to one side and he didn't see them until they came dancing towards him. Hello, Abel! said Olga. He stood up and bowed, and then they were gone.

He paid in a hurry and left. Once outside he smiled to himself and said: Well, there was nothing there to run away from.

He drifted around town for days, and once he'd got money and new clothes it was easier for him to go wherever he wanted without having people staring at him. And it was also as though he took a little more pride in himself and had come alive again.

He spent a lot of time down at the sawmill. Old-fashioned machinery powered by water, but in full working order. Ah but it didn't pay, too many people, not enough speed. He knew about sawmills from Canada and noted with interest that even those in the olden days were pretty clever at inventing new machinery. But they made heavy work out of it. He met Lili. She was married to Alex, but was still working in the office and had been promoted to chief cashier. They had a little girl. Abel visited them, the house was small and neat and they had a bit of garden. Alex was just a labourer at the mill, but the pair managed very well with their house and child and garden.

Funny – from his secondary school days Abel still felt a tenderness for Lili, she was still gentle and kind-hearted, and her name was mild too, like a sheltered climate. Lili.

But he couldn't be bothered with Robertsen the Customs man and his family. Hospitable but boring people, pushy. They were always talking about how Abel's father had enjoyed visiting them, that never a day went by without a visit from him. And they wanted to know about Abel's plans, did he intend to settle down at home? Who was it he'd

54

been married to? Didn't he have a picture of her? They gave him good advice, it was all wrong for Lolla to have come between him and his father as regards the inheritance, what was he going to do about it? Best get a solicitor, but not young Clemens, he wasn't much good. When Abel left Robertsen showed him out and started talking about a certain document in the Private Bank: Lolla's father had taken out a loan on the strength of it, but never in this world had old Captain Brodersen signed it, the thing was a forgery—

Yes, Lolla told me, said Abel.

What – that her father had forged it?

Yes, something like that.

Well I never! cried Robertsen.

It's all sorted out now.

Yes, it's sorted out alright. It was sorted out by her marrying him. So, Lolla told you about it? But at least now you know what kind of people you have to deal with . . .

I see you're doing some building, Abel said, to get him off the subject.

Yes, call me crazy if you like! It's for the girls, they're grown-ups now. Don't you think it'll be a fine big house? But it'll be dear too, so I need help. Your father was going to guarantee for me, but then he died . . .

No, he wasn't going back to the Robertsens any more. Four wretched lives under the one roof, stupid, self-centred and gossipy. The daughters were a waste of time. When he told them his Kentucky wife had French parents they exclaimed: Imagine, so she could speak French! They both came to him with their Poetry Albums and he had to write something in them and sign his name underneath.

But there were many place outside of town where he could go and lie and be away from everything. It was not that he was overcome by laziness, but in Kentucky he'd acquired a taste for the carefree, much as a drinker does for his whisky. He made a mess of his new clothes on the compost heaps down at the market garden, or in the white dust of the granite quarry, but that didn't bother him. Nothing finicky about him, the whole man was indifferent, often unshaven, and those small hands with the supple fingers that could bend way over backwards, those thief's fingers, he took no special care of those, he would just wipe them clean on his trousers. In her motherly way Lolla advised him to get a second outfit, two more outfits, and be like everyone else. Something light and grey would be suitable for the summer, he could wear a black band on his sleeve. Do it, Abel!

How's Tengvald getting on? he asked.

Tengvald, said Lolla with a laugh. He did the right thing when he broke up with me way back then. Aftewards he married Lovise Rolandsen and they were a good match. They've got seven or maybe even eight kids now they wheel around the streets.

So they have a hard time?

Oh they manage. He's a journeyman blacksmith and when his father, ancient old Krum, dies, he'll inherit something. But eight children . . .

I was going to pay him a call in his smithy the other day, said Abel, but I'm too disgracefully well-dressed for it, I didn't want to show my face there. Are you coming with me to the tailor's?

They went to the tailor's and chose the material. It was fun for him to make the choice, a brown outfit and a grey outfit. Silk lining, said Lolla, that's what young Clemens has. And a spring coat, she said. Right, and now let's go and get a hat.

They went off and bought a hat, two hats, one grey and one brown. Shirts, she said, ties, socks. How are you for shoes? Got a watch in your pocket? I saw, by the way, a gun on your table, what d'you need that for?

He'd been allocated two bank books, not outrageously excessive sums involved but healthy enough, about the same in each bank. We'll take one each, he said.

She wouldn't accept that.

We'll have one each!

Yes but I get paid a regular amount each month. That's the way it's arranged.

Oh be quiet. What do I need the gun for? I just brought it along with me. Where I come from all we wore was a shirt and pair of trousers and a gun. Lolla, you've no idea how much more natural it feels than a lot of clothes. You should've seen Lawrence when he travelled naked once to Mexico, came back again dressed, got drunk and gave away everything he owned. End of that. Now let's go and buy something with your cheque book too.

No! Lolla shrieked in the middle of the street.

Come on! he said, and his eyes darkened – the easygoing and nonchalant Abel turned dark in the eyes.

All I need is shoes, she said. Work shoes. Because I've got a pair for best your father gave me.

VII

HE VISITED OLGA ONE MORNING. IT WASN'T A STATELY HALL-
way with stained glass windows and oleanders in tubs, just a porcelain sign
saying Clemens Solicitor, and his office hours. A maid opened the door.

The lady of the house, he said, and stepped inside.

The first thing he sees is her sitting there reading a book and raising
a pair of extravagantly dreamy eyes, she's got the short hair and the
cigarette and the overalls, and the fingernails painted red. We're so
modern and so empty-headed, our neck is so thin and we have no breasts.

Is that you, Abel? My husband's still at the magistrate's office—

Abel, blushing like a girl: I just wanted to . . . You said hello to me
at the wine-bar . . .

Aha, so this is a Visit, Olga's probably thinking. Please, do sit
down! Yes, I recognised you again at once, of course you've changed a
lot, but you still look like yourself. So now you're home again. Will you
be staying?

I really don't know.

A lot of things have changed since you left. How long ago was it?

Must have been about eight years . . . But now he didn't care to sit any longer making idle talk with the lady, his shyness was gone and he said: Olga . . . so you went and got married.

What . . . ? she said.

It just seems so strange, to think about it.

She regained her composure quickly and smiled – she was, after all, a lady: Indeed I did marry. We all do. You got married too, so I heard.

Yes. In the end.

Do you think I should have waited for you? she asked with a laugh.

No. I had no chance.

No.

I couldn't bring myself to speak up last time I was home.

Yes, but Abel, it wouldn't have done any good either, she said tenderly.

No, he said. But it should have.

Silence.

You're a strange one. Shouldn't we be talking about something else?

Yes, we better had. But it's so hard to think of something else. It's been twelve years now since you and I were so young that we could talk to each other.

Yes, you're strange, Abel. The world would still have gone on turning if we'd never seen each other again.

Silence.

Actually I came –, he said, as he searched through his pockets one after the other. Ah here it is! I just came to give you something. Here. Look at this.

What? Why, no . . .

A small thing, he said persuasively.

A bracelet. What makes you do such a thing?

Abel smiles feebly: After all, I cheated you out of a bracelet once before. Don't you remember?

Oh that! Childish nonsense. No, I can't accept this, she said and handed it back to him.

You can't?

No. Thank you, Abel, but you must understand – something as expensive as that – anyway as you can see, I wear a wristwatch.

He wrapped the box up neatly in the paper again and put it in his pocket. He stood up and bowed.

Don't take offence at me, please don't. Couldn't you take it back?

No.

Did you bring it over with you?

From Kentucky? No, no. I didn't even own any clothes over there.

Ha. My God but you are a one, Abel! She gave him her hand: But it was fun seeing you again. It's such a bore my husband wasn't home, you two do know each other . . .

I'll put it on Jesus, he thought on the way home. It's not long now to Whitsun, then I'll put it on Jesus' other arm!

And then he stopped caring about the bracelet, about himself, and everything else.

As though it were a matter of indifference he told Lolla that he had tried to give Olga a bracelet he owed her from childhood, but since she wouldn't accept it he intended now to give it to someone else.

Was he testing Lolla out? He wasn't that cynical. And Lolla gave no sign of wanting the bracelet, she didn't even ask for a look at it. However she did seem afraid that Abel had gone and made a fool of himself.

They're upper-class people, she said, both her and him, and they've got enough as it is. Her father owns a lot of shares in ships, and people say he practically owns the sawmill now. And then there's all his shares in the milk boat, the *Sparrow*.

Yes, but that sawmill can't be making a profit, Abel was probably thinking. Aloud he said: Out there they saw one log in the time it should take them to saw ten.

What drive Abel has, Lolla was probably thinking. Aloud she said: Well, you would know about that. I remember you writing from a sawmill in Canada.

I was so hard-working and efficient in those days. Long time ago now.

I'll bet you could work hard now if you wanted to.

No. All that business of making an effort, I leave all that to others now. Let them get on with it.

60

Silence. Lolla seemed uncomfortable. What was all this about? What's going to happen to you, Abel? she asked in her motherly way.

She thanked me, he said, speaking his thoughts aloud. She would probably have accepted it too if she didn't already have a wristwatch.

They're rich, Lolla said again. Her father owns the chemist's shop too. I just hope you didn't offend her, Abel!

I don't think so. I'd been planning to do it for twelve years.

Lolla had become another girl now that she was able to afford it, another person. Pretty in her black dress, less flighty with her nostrils, a respectable widow. But Abel, you should have seen her those times she set off for town at night in your motorboat! Now she'd vacated the attic and was living with her mother in the house on the beach. It was the proper thing for her to do, cheapest too, the only option, the thing any upstanding person would do. Lolla was quite something alright. From her time in service at the Clemens' she'd also got into the habit of reading and had read many books.

She said to Abel: You should pay a visit to the cemetery. I don't know where your mother is, but your father's got a cross.

You must show it to me, he said.

Why didn't you write and answer his letters?

Don't ask me. I was busy with Angèle.

It would've made him very happy.

No, Lolla, I couldn't have written anything that would have made him happy, not the way he saw things. So I didn't bother. I'll visit his grave a lot instead.

Well that's not exactly the same thing.

No, he said.

He'd got into her head now and she asked: Was it really such a bad time with her?

With Angèle? No, no, it was good. She was wonderful to me. I sank to the bottom and she was there too, we both lived at the bottom. So did the people around us. Everybody walking around on the bottom, some carrying maybe a bottle of milk or a cob of corn to eat, others just walking about and feeling the cold, no-one making their way to see Angèle and me. After six months or a year a letter arrived, brought by a Negro who couldn't read it, so I just put it down and I let

61

it lie there. You probably think it's awful to have just a few clothes and not much food, but that's not what matters, together we were blessed, we were like animals. We lay down together in our ruination and we slept together. When we woke up we said nothing, just got up and walked, when one got up and walked the other followed along behind. We belonged together on the same path and we followed each other. Now and then I made her happy with one of the farmer's hens. He was so mean he used to keep watch. Once he shot at me, and after that I didn't dare anymore. It didn't matter, there were enough fish in the Streamlet, and in the autumn fruit all around. And I planted a bushel of potatoes.

Lolla said sadly: Couldn't you have got away from it all? It isn't good to be a wild animal.

Oh yes, it was good.

You worked so hard in Canada.

Yes. Long time ago.

You don't think it's good to work hard?

Some work hard and stick at it, he said: We had that farmer nearby us. A wretched little farm of forty acres, but he was hard-working and wanted to better himself and have eighty acres. Once we heard scream-ing from the river near his place, and Angèle and I went to see. It was just the farmer with his Negro worker, he was killing the Negro with a hoe because he wouldn't work. But as soon as we arrived the Negro had witnesses to his self-defence so it was the farmer who got killed.

How terrible!

Was it so much better to be hard-working and want to better him-self? Angèle and I, we didn't want any eighty acres, we had enough.

Her name was Angèle?

Yes. Pretty. Like a little prayer. She was a Catholic.

And then she died. Was she pregant?

She was. But that's not what she died of.

Lolla tried to be as motherly as she could. But now and then her eyes took fire and her nostrils quivered. Wine always made her restless, he didn't know that and he visited her at home once with a bottle of wine. It was all too stupid, she wanted to cuddle, she wanted to kiss his hand, and she took her hair down. The mother sat there, talking quietly about her fate, with a husband in the Azores now. Abel left early and he never gave Lolla wine anymore.

He sat listening to the service on Whit Sunday. A lot of familiar faces, psalm-singing, organ, sexton in black, priest in white. He sat in the organ loft so as to be close to the staircase up to the steeple and the door leading into it. There was just a hook for a lock.

When the priest left the pulpit and the organ started up he used that deafening moment to open the steeple door, slip in and pull it closed behind him. If anyone were to come along and ask what in the world he was doing in there he would explain that he couldn't stand the bellowing of the organ. Everything planned down to the last detail.

No one came. He sat on the stairs for a while and then climbed up. The stairs went up only part of the way, then there was a ladder. But at the top of the ladder there was nothing but a great chaos of poles and beams and pillars and ropes in all directions and on top of each other. A maze-like structure of timbers, he might almost have said a lion had made its den here, it was a lion's den. In the middle of all this a kind of platform for the bellringer to stand on when it was time to ring the chimes, and above the platform the bells. Two bells, the bigger one the size of a barrel and with an enormous club for a clapper. Above the bells a crisscrossing of wooden struts and supports that rose all the way up the interior of the spire and disappeared in the darkness at the top.

Silence. He hears nothing but a soughing through the vents on the sides of the steeple, and the only thing to watch out for the swallows. He sat down on a beam. It was very dusty, but that didn't matter. What he had to do now was wait for the church to empty.

Suddenly an avalanche of sound fills the steeple and the bells sway. He leaps up to save his ears, to save his life, he looks down towards the ladder and considers flight, he falls over, breaks his fall and ends up sitting on a cushion of clay and stone. He sticks his fingers in his ears again, but it hardly makes any difference, the bells sway back and forth, the whole steeple is shaking. Presently he gets used to it, he sits there and does nothing more about it, that racket from hell coming from those holy bells.

63

When they finally come to rest and fall silent he takes his fingers out of his ears then sticks them in again, takes them out and sticks them in again, he's a deaf as a post and in his whole being feels as though he's down in some dense chasm. Strange state, comical, he says something but hears it only with his mouth, he smiles and imagines that he can hear the smile too. But there's no suggestion at all that he's dead. He stands up and has a think.

Gradually his hearing returns, and he starts to make his way down. On the steps he stops and listens out for a while, nothing amiss, but he can't be too careful, people usually stop for a chat in the cemetery and he mustn't be seen through the windows. His whole plan is nothing but a damned stupid idea – but then it was stupid to visit Olga too, just as stupid. And now damned if he's going to hang around here any longer like some common burglar, he's been up the steeple but at least he didn't steal the bells.

He pushes against the door, but it doesn't open. What? He pushes harder. No. Some itchy-fingered person passing by must have placed the hook into the eye. He could easily break the thin door open – he's dealt with worse doors than this – but he's afraid of being heard by the widows and mothers pottering about the cemetery and tending the graves.

He examines the door and can just see the hook in the gap between the door and the jamb, but he doesn't have a knife, nor a sliver of wood, nothing slender enough to push through the gap and release the hook. Maybe he can find something up in the steeple, in the lioness' den, she might have left a hairpin or a pen-nib, the lioness, hah! But presently he manages to push the eye all the way out. It made an unnecessary amount of noise as it fell to the floor, and he listened out again. No, nothing. So he puts everything back the way it was before he leaves, pushing the eye back into place and hooking the latch into it.

Empty church. Jesus standing there on his usual shelf, but without a bracelet. He's going to get a new one. An idiotic notion, but Jesus is going to get a new bracelet. Abel steps up and slips it on him, arranges it nicely, considers the overall effect, then steps back down again. It's all over so quickly that he can hardly believe it, and from down below he again considers the overall effect.

He had already worked out which window to use for his his getaway. Of the few that opened this one faced the quietest part of the cemetery, but there was an old woman sitting on a white bench and looking over this way now. He recognises her, she's the widow of old skipper Krum, who finally died, now she's watching over the fresh grave. Abel has to wait.

Takes another look at Jesus again, and suddenly he realizes something: But of course, he's got *two* hands. So does Olga have two hands. She could have worn the wristwatch on one and the bracelet on the other – or even both on the same wrist. Was he an infant? It was hard to believe he was a grown man!

The widow sits there.

He was reminded of the time twelve years earlier, when he couldn't get out the window. Poor so and so that I was, so little and so terrified of the dead, all night long. God bless me, at that age I didn't know that you can get in and out through windows—

The widow sits. That obstinate and headstrong old thing sits there grieving over a husband she treated badly enough while he was alive. There must be some other old woman sitting nearby who can see her or she would have left by now. She's Tengvald's mother, journeyman blacksmith Tengvald, who did something with his life yes, became a journeyman blacksmith with his eight childen. Poor old Tengvald, he used to have those expensive sliced bananas in his packed lunch so even he could show off in front of a person who was only from the lighthouse. Poor so and sos, the lot of us . . .

The widow has finally left.

He opens the window just a touch, so it won't glint dangerously in the sunlight. Once he's on the ground he tidies up after himself and closes the window behind him.

VIII

AT THE SEAMEN'S HOME PEOPLE SAID RIEBER CARLSEN WAS booked to preach at the church the next day. Rieber Carlsen had just got back from Finnmark, such a talent, and now he was off to Germany with a scholarship and on his way there stopping off to preach in his old home town. It was in all the papers, they told Abel – hadn't he read about it? No.

The town was proud of Rieber Carlsen and got ready to put on a good showing in the church. His schooling and his studies had necessitated the sale of his father's last part-share in a ship, but what did that matter, now that he was the town's shining light? Such a gifted man. At the moment he was working on a dissertation on redemption – had Abel really not read about it in the papers? No.

But there were plenty who had. The church was full, said Lolla, even though it was only the day after Pentecost. And the parish priest was wearing white, but Rieber Carlsen wore only an ordinary black cassock because he didn't have the chasuble with him. And what a sermon, Lolla exclaimed, there wasn't a dry eye in the church.

I remember him well, said Abel.

Lolla: It must be funny for Olga, for young Fru Clemens, I mean, to sit there, and see him, and listen to him.

Was Olga there?

They were both there, the husband too. That's what I mean, it must have been funny for her. He's so famous now everywhere and she could've married him.

Rieber Carlsen only stayed a short while, but it turned that he had paid a Christian call on Olga on the third day and they had conversed in a friendly fashion. Yes indeed, and Rieber Carlsen did not give the impression of being offended that she'd broken up with him. He told her that Finnmark was a fine place to settle down, that flowers grew there, that the people were fine and the scenery magnificent. Of course there was the disadvantage of the long dark winters, but then the cultured families had their books, and as for him, he had his scientific studies to pursue . . .

On Delivery, Olga had said. I read about it.

On Redemption yes, he had answered, so nice and understanding that she didn't feel all that embarrassed, just blushed a little. And he helped her on by adding: That is, of couse, the dissertation I'll be submitting for my doctorate – if I manage it. In any event, there's a huge amount of study involved.

Oh goodness me yes! said Olga.

That's how the meeting went, and Olga herself made no secret of the fact that she had called redemption 'delivery'. She put the story about herself.

On the other hand, it was more difficult to understand how a great number of other things got out. Lolla had heard that Lili – the one who worked in the office and was married to Alex – was expecting a child, though it was five years since the last one. Okay, but she had also heard that Abel saw quite a bit of this Lili, when the opportunity presented itself. Well, what of it? But did you ever hear anything like it! But it was what Lolla had heard, and it was a disgrace, and God knows if there was anything in it . . .

It was true Abel spent a lot of time at the sawmill, and maybe it was mostly on account of Lili. But as it happened the chemist stopped him one day when he was out there and got talking to him. The chemist himself, sole or nearly sole owner of the whole place, got out of his car and even doffed his hat.

He'd heard that Abel was knowledgable in the ways of sawmills, moreover he knew, as everyone did, that Abel had inherited quite a bit of money: would Abel consider getting involved in the business? Things were not going as they ought to be out here, less and less profit with each passing year, there must be something wrong with the way they were doing things. Let's sit here for a minute or two, said the chemist, seating himself on a log.

The fact is, he said, I'm no expert in this field, but the majority of shares have been transferred to me and like a fool I've hung onto them so as to lay off as few workers as possible. We fortunate few owe it to the others to do our bit. Might you, Brodersen, be willing to invest a little, so that we can get things going again? Our order book is full and we're buying buy up whole forests for shipping, our credit is good and all the rest of it, and we saw and sell and keep at it the whole time, but it just doesn't seem work out . . .

What Abel liked about talking to the chemist was that he didn't have to answer his questions because the chemist presently talked them away himself, perhaps because he was afraid of outright rejection. Abel wanted nothing to do with the old sawmill, but he wasn't required to say so in as many words.

That's a nice car you have there. A good make.

You're know it?

Yes.

Very expensive, said the chemist. But to get back to the subject of our conversation: You could be business manager, what do you say to that? Even as we speak we could be finalising a good deal for forestry in Pistleia, but we don't have the money. We already owe them money and we can't get the forest on credit, that's the position. If you, Brodersen, would join us and put things right here and there it would restore their confidence in us. It would be a catstrophe for us all – well, if things don't work out. And then there are the workers who need the mill, it's all they have. Now you, Brodersen, you've been in Canada, you know the business, I gather—

It was quite different there, said Abel.

Yes I'm sure it was, a bigger operation, electricity. I don't know about such things.

The old chemist was an honourable man. He had always thought a little too highly of himself and liked the idea of being a philanthropist, though he couldn't afford it. Apart from that he was fine, he meant well.

Abel said: I'll spend some time out here and take a look around, if you like.

Thank you, said the chemist.

But his spending time out there and taking a look was resented by the leaders and the foremen who had been appointed by the board. Abel spent three weeks out there and got tired of it, and he was someone who quickly tired of a job anyway. But his three weeks out at the works hadn't been entirely wasted: with a mention of Abel's name and a bold hint that this moneybags and leading expert was now a part of the concern the board was able to raise the loan for the forest in Pistleia. It meant the saws could go on cutting all through the summer.

Why did you give up your job at the works? asked Lolla.

Do you happen to know if Kjørboe is still alive? asked Abel, changing the subject.

I'm pretty sure he is. Why do you ask?

I just wondered. Because Krum's dead now.

By now Lolla was wearing black with white trimmings and black and white gloves. She looked really good, dignified, she spoke nicely and she didn't pull up her stockings. A great change had come over her. She didn't go into service again, no, but she cooked and washed and sewed and mended and looked after the house on the beach, she put flowers in the window and she made it homely there. Her mother blessed her.

She said: But why did you give up your job at the works, Abel?

Abel said: I wonder how they're getting on in Kentucky right now.

He drifted around town, did nothing special, often looked scruffy in his new clothes but didn't seem to care, nothing seemed to bother him. He was well-liked at the Seamen's Home, he took care of most things on his own and didn't ring if the maid forgot his room, didn't mention it if the coffee tasted bad or the milk was sour, was polite, courteous.

He went to the wine-bar and said hello to the Negroes, found himself a quiet corner and ordered a beer.

A lady's been enquiring after you, said the waiter.

Who?

I'm not supposed to say. She only wanted to know if you came here now and then.

Abel smiling: A lady who asks after me can't be all that much of a lady.

You wouldn't say that if you knew who it was, said the waiter.

He sat on for a moment, then abruptly seemed in a great hurry, paid and left. By the door, on the way out, he bumps into both her and her husband. Abel says hello and tries to pass, but she says: It's Abel – looking relatively clean!

His eyes darkened and he answered: Never mock a man you don't know, Olga. After all, it might easily be me.

Oh goodness me, you aren't cross with me are you, Abel?

That isn't possible.

Do you two know each other? she said to her husband. No, dear Abel, it was just a joke. Come on, join us for a while! She took him by the arm, and they sat down. They greeted various people. We've just had a glass of port at home, she said, and we thought we'd come down here. It's good to see you, Abel, I've been asking after you, you're so different from all the others. You aren't cross with me are you? It was just a joke.

What are you two having? asked Clemens.

Wine, said Olga. Just a bottle between the three of us.

Yes we knew each other when we were growing up, said Clemens politely. Though I was actually several years older.

I remember well when you came home during the holidays, said Abel.

You can bet we remember you, said Olga, without a trace of contempt.

Why would you remember me? I was a student, I came home.

Yes, you wore your tasselled student's cap and you went ahead and made something of yourself. Not like the rest of us. Rieber Carlsen made something of himself too, he just preached that sermon in church. By the way, she said, did either of you notice that the Jesus in the church has got a new bracelet?

No answer.

You don't answer, but it's true. The last one was removed or stolen, and now he's wearing a new one. It's a miracle. If it happened in Lourdes people would say he was calving bracelets.

Ha ha , Clemens laughed, you're witty!

Only one person in our family is witty, she said, and that's you. Your health, Abel!

Well I'm damned, Abel probably thought, and he manipulated the situation so that the husband drank the toast with them. She's no better than she ever was, he thought, she's lovely and she's wicked. What her husband needs is a good stick.

She ignored him. She only had eyes for Abel.

Shall we dance, Abel?

No, I can't.

You can't? Have you never learnt?

Clemens decides he needs to smooth things over: I'm sure he's learnt quite a few other things, Olga.

Thanks for that elucidation. This is a good waltz, see how many there are on the dance floor! Oh they're singing now, God what soft voices they have, those Africans!

Do you *want* to dance? asked Clemens.

No thanks. I only said that to make up with Abel.

No no no, there's nothing to make up for.

I remember you used to have such soft hands – let me see.

Abel hides his hands under the table: I don't like to show them right now. I was out at the market garden earlier on.

Is that where your clothes got in such a state?

That must be it. Are my clothes in a state? I'll go out and get the doorman to brush me off, he said, and he stood up.

No, sit down. Don't let it worry you. Are you going in for market gardening now?

Oh I don't know about that. Why market gardening? No, I was just helping out.

Yes but you do intend to settle to something?

I've settled to so many things.

You've got to make something of yourself too, you know.

I thought of going to the Maritime College.

That's a good idea, she said. Big ship, captain and owner. But in that case you better get a move on, it takes quite a time.

I made a sort of start in Australia. But there's not much left now.

And when you do I'll sail with you, she said. Where shall we sail too? I mean, where would you like to go?

I don't know. Someplace or other in America maybe. I was married there.

People here say she was a Negro.

No, he said. But what difference would it have made?

Oh well really, I'm afraid I must—

Clemens: Well, they certainly make good music over there.

Yes, they're from Kentucky, said Abel. My fellow-countrymen. In the evenings we used to sit and listen to the Negroes singing.

Olga: Did you only have the one wife?

Olga, really! said Clemens, and shook his head, laughing.

She laughed along with him: Aren't I allowed to ask? Abel and I know each other so well, we even kidded people on that we were sweethearts when we were at primary school. D'you remember that, Abel?

You must have a good memory.

Isn't that right? So your intentions towards me were never honourable?

Clemens laughed at this nonsense, perhaps mostly to please her. Abel started to feel sorry for him, she was acting as if he wasn't there, and hadn't they once all been together in everything? Had the times turned bad? He was of medium height, with a parting, oil and scent in his hair, his hands small, wedding ring, watch chain, laughed with his own teeth, a good-looking and good-tempered man with nothing special about him. He was married to Olga. They had no children.

Abel wanted to work him into the conversation and said: When

72

you came home in the holidays – you'd been working really hard, you looked so pale and tired.

Well, we kept at it alright, especially around examination time. Were we pale?

I seem to recall Rieber Carlsen's face—

Oh, him! But he read all day and all night, aiming to be a professor. The rest of us just wanted to avoid being too bad.

You got a good grade, said Olga, being friendly to him for once.

Yes, he said. But it was luck. It happened to be something I knew a bit about.

I don't know much about it, said Abel, but there must have been a lot of somethings – were you that lucky every time?

Abel probably doesn't know how modest you are, said Olga.

Modest! said Clemens dismissively. No, the only thing that mattered to us average students was to pass the exam – and get the girl we were in love with.

Olga suddenly nodded to a gentleman in the middle of the room and made her way over to him. They didn't stand there talking, they just started jazzing right away.

Clemens smiled: she doesn't like to hear that.

Why not?

Well, the fact it, it wasn't her I was in love with – in those days.

She knows that?

I told her.

But does Olga really care about an old story like that? asked Abel.

Perhaps not. No, perhaps she doesn't. Olga's above it all. She took on the lady in question as a maid in our house after we got married.

What? Abel almost exclaimed, but managed to stop himself in time. His brow furrowed in thought. Both men fell silent.

The music stopped. There was clapping, and it started up again. Sing! shouted Olga up to the stage.

The things we're capable of at that age, Clemens went on. Something so remote, so impossible, and yet so real, you just can't get over it.

We usually manage to get over it in time, Abel suggested.

Perhaps. Shall we try the wine?

73

They drank and fell silent again.

No, we don't get over it in any other way than by burying it deep down. It stays with you, because it was the first time.

Abel, thoughtfully: Yes, there's something about first love.

Have you had a similar experience?

Sort of.

Of course there's something about it, said Clemens. Hmm, it must be the wine that's loosening my tongue. But if that girl were to come through the door over there now, it wouldn't be a matter of indifference to me. Not even now.

But in heaven's name, asked Abel, how did you cope with the fact that she was the maid in your own house?

Same way as I coped with everything else. Ever since the time I was a young student and came home during the holidays. By not revealing myself, not by the slightest word nor gesture.

Abel exclaimed: Well that's what I call self-control.

Yes self-control is something we're good at at home. Father and mother, my two sisters who were very young then, all of us, born self-controlled.

You couldn't just have gone ahead and got engaged to the girl back then?

Engaged? Out of the question! Even just admitting I was in love would have been considered an enormity.

So then there was something wrong with her?

Yes. Lower class. Wrong class. And she had the reputation of being wild, she was a pretty strong character. But that didn't matter to me. On the contrary, it was probably the thing that mattered most to me at the age I was then.

And didn't the maid ever realise you were sweet on her?

Never. And if I were to tell her so today she would be astonished.

Abel shook his head, smiling: Such things have a way of forcing themselves out through the cracks.

Never. Out of the question. What you should be asking is how my wife dealt with it.

She knew about it?

Knew everything. I think that was why she employed her as a maid.

74

It didn't upset her?

Clemens answered a little uneasily: A bit, perhaps. During those months it was as though she loved me more. She always liked me to take her arm. Dear dear, this wine! I'm boring you.

Absolutely not! said Abel.

But don't you think it was somewhat arrogant of my wife, of Olga, to employ her?

Abel thought about it: I don't know. When she knew that your self-control, your unnaturally strong self-control, held you back in every situation . . .

Yes, of course, that's right. And, in the final analysis, Clemens concluded – it doesn't usually turn out well if first love turns into engagement and then marriage. So it shouldn't be something to cosset. Here's Olga now! Forgive me for having talked so much nonsense. I'm absolutely fine.

Olga came back, accompanied by her partner, who bowed to the table and left.

I owed him a dance, she explained. Is there a glass of wine left? You recognised him, I expect, Abel? Gulliksen the shopkeeper's son, we do our shopping there.

I know him. His name is William.

Very ambitious people with a large business. But they didn't give more than a hundred kroner towards the new water supply, and I know of one father who gave a thousand. But that doesn't make the one any the less respectable than the other. Have you seen that little statue, Abel? Water comes out of it. Oh listen to me talk! It's the wine.

You're radiant, said Abel.

Well then you radiate a bit too.

Clemens smiles: He doesn't get the chance.

Did you hear me telling the Negroes to sing, and they did?

I should think so too.

I'm not so sure about that, Abel. They don't owe me anything. Now they're singing again! Ahh, and now the saxophone! It looks so good over there, all that black amongst the brass, black and gold. But what you said about being married to them . . .

75

Have you seen them close up? asked Abel. Everything about them is velvet, the eyes, voice, the skin – velvet.

Yes but married to one? And people say they smell. But alright, we'll sail to your Negroes when you get to be a captain. Thanks for the company, Abel! she said and stood up. We're off home now to our little ones. Have you paid? she asked her husband.

No. He reached into his pocket.

No need to bother, said Abel, I'll be staying on for a bit.

IX

MONTHS PASSED.

He drifted around, drifted around and found places where he could be at peace. Since it didn't look good to be wandering about to no particular purpose he bought himself a rucksack so that at least he had something to carry. Day in and day out, week in and week out he wandered about and did no work and made nothing of himself, no. The market garden was a quiet spot, and in the rucksack he usually carried a little food that he gave to a couple of the apprentices out there, they were always hungry and grateful for it.

He wasn't content. It was an unfamiliar feeling, to be drifting about and yet not feeling half-dead at the same time. If he had felt half-dead it would have been another matter. It was no use hunching his shoulders and pretending he was cold, he was struggling hard, his clothes were too good for that. Lolla might have been good to shiver away a life with, but in the first place she was his stepmother, and in the second place she had become a lady. But once upon a time she would definitely have been wild enough to waste herself completely. Lili, the cashier, the houseproud, was out of the question. She could only be his earthly lover.

People went on about how he ought to make something of himself. But why? Everyone made something of themselves, but it was only the same something as the all others, not more. But it felt highly unnatural to be walking around a gentleman of leisure with a black band around his sleeve and all the buttons on his clothes and every seam neatly stitched up and not a single tear.

A tile fell from a roof and almost killed one of the town's important men, Fredriksen, the man with the house in the country and the motorboat with the mahogany trim. Abel drifted on out to visit the family and asked if might be of some small service to them. In some surprise the lady of the house thanked him for his thoughtfulness, but she didn't know – didn't quite understand—

Well, Abel could bring along two lads from such and such a market garden and keep the garden free of weeds while Herr Fredriksen was laid up—

The lady still didn't understand, they had someone to do that, a gardener. No, she thanked him for thinking of them, but—

Why should he put himself forward and get involved in anything at all? Weeds in the garden indeed – it was October already and the nights frosty, Fru Fredriksen had good reason to be surprised. Olga had been surprised too that time he turned up and said he had a little gift for her. In general he had no luck at all in trying to make himself useful. Like the time he worked for three weeks in a bookshop and stationary store, but it didn't much interest him. Or the day he walked into Tengvald's smithy and they wouldn't give him work to do. You're surely not thinking to take the bread out the mouths of those of us already here! said Tengvald.

But of course he wanted to make something of himself, what nonsense it was, to suggest anything else! He was himself tired of his false position, a tramp and a gentleman at one and the same time. It was probably already too late for the Maritime College this year, but he was patient, he could wait. In the meantime there was always something or

78

other for him to be getting on with. Robertsen the Customs man came to him and asked straight out for a loan and Abel told him straight out no. That Customs man, with his busy ways and his wife and his daughters – no! But as for Lili's mother, the woman who took in laundry for the workers at the mill, he set her up in business selling waffles in the market place. Sometimes he would go down there and buy up her whole stock of waffles and then give them away.

One of the lads who lodged at the Seamen's Home came in and said a worker up at the sawmill was in trouble. The lad couldn't bear it any longer, standing there watching and no-one could help.

Abel made his way to the sawmill, and already a crowd had gathered there. One of the foremen stood with a great coil of rope doing nothing with it, the chemist had been roused and came swishing up in his car, he jumped out and shouted and wrung his hands. The saw had been stopped, but there was a godawful roaring from the waterfall and the manager and the office staff swarmed about all shouting different bits of advice. There was total chaos. There was Lili sobbing, holding her little girl by the hand as she hurried about from one place to another. A shawl covered her swollen belly. It was Alex, her husband, who was in trouble.

It was the big logs from Pistleia – they'd been careless in letting them through the sluice and one had got stuck at the bottom, just by the intake to the saw. Others had jammed against it and piled up, what they call 'mushroomed', into a mountain of timbers as high as the falls themselves.

Alex had gone down to the bottom with his boathook and actually managed to clear a few of them away, but he must suddenly have realised that with each timber he pulled clear the danger to himself increased, and now he was standing at one end of the bottom log with a mountain of logs looming over him. Alex was as smart as the next man and realised that it was only the weight of his own body that was holding that last trembling timber in place and preventing the mountain of timbers from collapsing. He was standing quite still and waiting to be helped. His face was pale. He was holding one hand cautiously raised as a signal that he daren't move.

Abel weighs up the situation, calculates, measures with his eye. A breath of life must must have stirred somewhere in his dulled brain, some memory of work and skill and daring in Canada.

The foreman with the rope and the manager have decided to use the rope to winch Alex up. Winch him up.

Abel stands and listens: Winch him up? When the men doing the winching don't have anything to stand on?

They can stand on top of the timbers, four men, begin to haul at a signal – and at the right moment jump back to safety.

Quite. But three seconds after Alex has been lifted from the timber he's standing on the whole lot will start to move and five seconds later it'll sweep away both him and the men.

When then how could they rescue Alex?

From the water, said Abel.

Oh yes. They'd already thought of that. But apparently Alex couldn't swim, or else he wouldn't still be standing there.

He can swim alright, I know him. And if it was just a question of diving in he would have done that at once. But he knows the avalanche will reach him even before he's swum the first stroke.

The men shrug their shoulders. They don't take kindly to Abel since he time he spent up there looking things over at the sawmill. Mockingly they ask if he intends to save Alex by boat.

It gets more and more crowded, family members arrive, people from the shops and offices. Olga's there, shivering nervously and clutching her husband's arm. Smith the photographer rushes round taking pictures for the magazines. The chemist is here, there and everywhere, wringing his hands: They're not doing anything, they'll wait until he's squashed flat! The chemist goes right up to the foreman and says: He's down there, waiting – aren't you going to try to winch him up?

The foreman jerks his head: *He* says he can't be winched up.

Who? You, Brodersen? Well in that case, you think of something!

Abel: If I'm allowed to do this by myself.

The manager and foreman snort: We won't say a word!

There's a breath of life moving through Abel, he takes the coil of rope from the foreman, hurries down to the water, pulls of his jacket, hangs the rope around his neck and sets off swimming.

It isn't far, fifty metres at the most, some current, but it's deep, clean water. Those watching on land see how, on his way, he picks out a timber from among those floating around, and drags it along with him, as though he wants a timber to stand on himself – and why might that be?

What happens now can be followed in every detail from the shore: He gets Alex very gradually and with infinite caution to vacate his place on the log and slip down into the water, one limb at a time, as you might say, compensating for the change in weight by gradually sliding the top of his own log onto Alex's. Precision work, carried out under the threat of death. That the slightest alteration in presssure on the timber at the bottom would have meant death for them both was clear a few minutes later when the mountain of timbers collapsed.

They were free. But because the timbers were slippery with water they didn't trust them to stay in position. Only when they had lashed them together, with the greatest care, did they swim away.

Cheers from the shore.

They were more than halfway to the shore when the timbers collapsed with a thundrous roar. Abel was swimming with the end of the rope in his mouth, and all it took to disturb the weight was the slight turn of the head he made to look back. Smith the photographer took another picture.

It was too late in the year, but he was still determined to make the effort to be a somebody and he went to see the principal of the Maritime College. Why should I be doing this, he probably thought, but he went anyway.

He came away deeply dissatisfied. Abel thought that the schooling he'd already had in Australia meant that all he would need was a Norwegian supplementary. Fair enough. But a cursory oral examination, a couple of questions, were enough to persuade him that he had either forgotten what he had once known or else never learnt it at all. He shook his head and left. But it wasn't his intention to give up, absolutely not, he proposed to begin again at the beginning. But here, in his native town, he really couldn't go back to school again, as old and big and tall as he was now. He would have to get away.

He made up his mind. It was serious now.

It became clear that he intended to leave taking nothing with him but the clothes on his back, but Lolla persuaded him to take along a change. He could certainly do that, he conceded. As she was packing he asked her some questions:

You know young Clemens don't you?

Yes, Lolla answered, surprised. I was the maid there.

He's a lawyer.

I know. What are you getting at?

What I'm getting at, said Abel, is that you could have got young Clemens to deal with that forged document in the bank and sort it out.

So?

But you said you had no alternative but to marry my father.

Oh I see. Don't you think I didn't ask Clemens? Of course I did. But he wouldn't do it.

Why not? asked Abel. He could well have afforded the first payment.

No doubt he could. But he didn't want anything to do with it, he said.

Did he say that? Were you two good friends at that point?

Not exactly friends, no. But they were good people to work for. Olga especially. He was always decent and kind too, but Olga was special towards me, always said please to me, even though I was a servant. And all the books she lent me to read. Once Clemens took away a book she lent me, he said it wasn't right for me, it was a dirty book.

Do you call in and see them now and then?

No. Well I did visit once and sat in the kitchen. Olga let me in, she probably thought I was visiting the new maid, but I wasn't. I haven't been there since.

Silence.

No, Abel, she said as she resumed packing, I had no choice but the one I made.

But it wasn't a good thing to do.

Why not?

Because you threw yourself away.

I could have thrown myself away worse, she said. I came out of it just the same as I was when went into it.

To get youself married like that! And to my father. How old was he – a hundred?

Do you hold it against me?

No, not for a moment. Although, Lolla, you could have been good for me. Someone to give up on everything with.

Lolla thought about that for a moment and said: I don't understand what you mean. I could have been good for you?

Yes. Someone I could have given up on everything with.

She packed, picked up shirts and socks, put socks and shirts down again. Well is it too late for that now? she asked.

Surely you can see that?

Yes, she said.

Silence.

He began talking about something else: that he should have sent some money to America, but now he wouldn't have time for it before he left.

But Lolla didn't want to change the subject, she repeated that she'd come out of if just the same as she'd gone into it, not changed at all, hardly—

Abel: It's money I should have sent long ago, but it never happened.

You don't believe me, I can see that. But hardly different at all—

Yes yes yes , Lolla. I really should have sent it.

Finally Lolla listens and asks: What is this money?

To a man named Lawrence.

Are you in debt to him?

No. Yes. He's in prison, so I have to send him something.

Lolla thinks it over: Well of course it's none of my business, but you should be careful with your money, Abel. It's not that easy to get it back again.

No.

You spent those three weeks in the bookshop and didn't ask for anything. But then you didn't get paid for those three weeks up at the sawmill either?

Abel smiles: I wouldn't have taken a penny from them even if they'd offered it. They're broke.

And now that you live in the Seamen's Home you have to pay for everything all the time.

Yes but, Lolla, I couldn't have accepted anything from them up at the sawmill. They have no money, no stock, they've got nothing.

I've been thinking, said Lolla, that it would be cheaper for you to live at my mother's.

What? said Abel.

Yes, down on the beach. There are four rooms and just the two of us.

Abel shook his head and said no.

Lolla: No, you could well be right, I only mentioned it. There would only have been talk. I'm standing here thinking this here is an ugly old suitcase.

I've got a new rucksack, should I take that instead?

For your shirts?! No, but this is a shameful suitcase to go travelling with.

My my, how refined you've become. Is it young Clemens who's instilled that in you?

He hasn't instilled anything in me. I only noticed when I was brushing his jacket that it was silk-lined.

Did you notice when he was undressing what kind of underwear he uses?

Of course I know, I was the one who washed it. I washed both his and his wife's. She had the lovelies, sheerest underwear, and I wasn't to scrub it, just move it backwards and forwards in the tub.

Really, and his?

Yes his was top quality too. But I'll tell you, what you bought is just as good quality.

Well then that's alright then, Lolla.

The only problem with you is the suitcase. I could go out and buy you a new suitcase.

Be quiet now and let's finish. Put this in there.

What d'you want this for?

Shove it inside one of the socks.

I can't see what you need a gun for at the Maritime College.

*

84

And so he went away. He meant business this time. He was in no doubt that it was too late in the year, but he went. Because he meant business this time.

He stayed away the whole winter and came back in May. Wrote not a line nor gave any sign of life but, being his stepmother, Lolla found out from the bank that money was regularly being sent to him, he had enough to live off and more.

And yet he came back tired and scrawny, he looked like a man who hadn't eaten much. If only his father could have seen him in those rags he came back in, and that he didn't have his best underwear with him. He'd handed it in to the laundry then left without picking it up.

Naturally he'd had another disappointment, but it was no great surprise, it wasn't the right time of year after all, he had left it too late before leaving. Now he was back once more in his old room at the Seamen's Home, living out his days as before, regretting nothing.

He explained everything to Lolla: Went straight to the principal of the big college, didn't even wait one day, said why he was there and got his answer. Oh yes the principal was very fair: I understand you're a man who wants to make something of himself in life, said the principal, so now let's see! He asked me a few questions about ordinary seamanship, it was a piece of cake for me, said Abel. Then he began to ask questions about what I had learnt from the books. It was all in English, I said. Well, tell me in English, said the principal, all quite fair. I told him what I'd learnt from the books, and it wasn't a lot. How much could it be after taking just a couple of quick exams in Sydney? And he understood that. It's a pity you don't really know enough of this, he said, what if you took some tuition? Yes I will, I said.

But it was a blow for me to be told straightaway that I didn't know anything and I said so. He admitted that and he was good about it. Think about taking private tuition, he said, I'll get you a good tutor, I promise you that!

But why couldn't I have known enough theory from the books to enable me to be able to begin at once under this principal? It was unfortunate. He wished me well, shook my hand firmly when I left. But because things hadn't worked out well for me I lay down in my lodgings and just thought about it. There was a young student in the same lodging house who'd already got quite far in the course, we talked together, and I realized that it was impossible for me to catch up with him because I was eight years older and I'd been married and all the rest of it. No, so I just lay there and gave up the idea. It was a crying shame, the way things worked out for me.

After Christmas and the New Year I began to see things in a different light: that it was a pointless life to be going around regretting things, and that things were better in Kentucky. I could have written to Lawrence and sent money and cheered us both up, but I didn't. I felt so miserable and wretched that when the young lad arrived with a message from the principal that he wanted to see me I almost didn't feel like going. But then the young lad gave my clothes a brush and walked all the way there with me and waited outside.

And what the principal wanted was for me to get started straight-away!

Funny how some people are. Even though he was a commander in the navy and the principal of the college he was actually more like a father to me, so I promised to do everything he asked. He wrote down a list of books for me to buy and on the way home the young lad and I went and bought these books, so I was all prepared and as far as I was concerned I was ready to go.

But it all went wrong, I didn't send for the tutor, and what I read on my own in the books didn't amount to much. So in April the tutor came of his own accord and asked what was happening. Yes well, I said, I'm on for it. Then let's get down to it straightaway, he said. He was the thorough type, he began at the beginning, and I learnt a lot in a couple of hours. It was encouraging for me to understand his explanations, and when he gave me some homework and said he'd be back the next day I was very pleased.

So now he came every day, and I was really getting the stuff learned. But it started to get very difficult and technical, and I thought again of the days in Kentucky, how good they were compared to now. The tutor would have none of it, he got very strict with me and gave me even more homework to read for the lesson the next day. I know I would have done it had it been the principal, but for this tutor, no, so the next day I was just even more apathetic. This won't do, he said. No,

I said. Shall we end this? he asked. It doesn't seem to me as though I can learn this, I said. Right! he said, and off he went.

By that time I was nothing but skin and bone, Lolla. You wouldn't expect me to have to do all this stuff at my age. When he started with me I just about knew the names of a few of the instruments, and I knew the compass best, I'd done so much navigating in my time. But at my age, as a science, navigation is a nightmare. You've got both a celestial and a terrestrial navigation, see, and they're both of them incomprehensible conundrums to work out and do the reckoning for. The one calculation after the other until your eyes begins to cloud over. You don't understand the first thing about it, but you're supposed to work it out. That's what you've got your compass and your chronometer and all the instruments for. But then, once you've finished your calculations, then the instruments themselves aren't correct either, so then God help us you have to work out the deviation on the compass and the chronometer too – the whole thing is unendurable!

Lolla has been sitting patiently and listening to all this.

Abel shivers and makes a show of grinding his treeth. How are things in town? he asks.

She realises that he has been struggling, that he's been trying as hard as he can, but she's deeply upset and asks: Yes, so I suppose you'll try again in a while?

No, he answers.

Silence.

Then what do you want to be now, Abel?

What I want to do now? Well what do we do, those of us who don't do much?

Yes, but what will you do now?

After a while he answers: Why don't you, Lolla, get some water, and water the geraniums here in the study? They don't look as if they've been watered since I left.

X

HOW WERE THINGS IN TOWN? NOT GOOD, NO.

The sawmill at a standstill, Pistleia Forestry Company demanded their money and didn't get it, the banks wouldn't help out any more. For a couple of months the business struggled on, then came bankruptcy and collapse.

It was hard on the workers. They had lived for and from the works, sons following in fathers footsteps, some married with wives and children, some with houses of their own, others who only rented. Alex, married to Lili, was – on paper – the owner of his own little house with its garden, but he owed much too much on it, and now Lili had given birth to their second child, this one a girl too, a little angel, but it meant one more mouth to feed.

It was bad news for everyone at the works, from the manager and the foreman down to the little boys who occasionally ran errands and got twenty-five øre for it. It was worst of all for the chemist. Painful to think of all he had to put up with. All those worthless shares in the business, all the bank loans he was personally responsible for, it was no joke, he lost his shares in the milkboat, the *Sparrow*, all he had left now was the chemist's shop and the car. But worst of all was that he and the board were accused of having acted dishonestly. What happened was that the manager went with a small deputation to the Pistleia Forestry Company and told them that a wealthy moneybags and a top expert in the field by the name of Abel Brodersen had joined them, and that from now on everything would be different. Later it emerged that this Brodersen didn't even have an official position at the works, he had just spent three weeks there looking things over. But it was on the basis of this false information that the big timber deal had gone ahead. And now the manager was saying that owner had been aware all along that he would making this claim. It was all very unpleasant.

The chemist accused of dishonesty! To look at him he didn't seem to take it that badly, he still wizzed around in his car. But of course, everyone knew that he was no longer a bigshot and a wealthy man, and it was almost pathetic to see him swaggering about now.

And what were all these former sawmill workers supposed to do? Nothing. There were no other sawmill-owning chemists the workers could turn to, so for as long as they could they lived off their last wage-packet, and after that for as long as Gulliksen, rich Gulliksen the storekeeper, would give them credit.

But when poverty comes in the door, love flies out the window. Disharmony arose in many a home, including the manager's. He and his wife had fallen in love with each other in 1912, and that was a long time ago now. She'd given birth to four children and now her hair and her skin were both tinged with grey. His hair was grey too, and thinning, but there was a slight curl to what was left of it, people still referred to him as 'the Engineer', he still carried a stick and wore his hat at an angle. They stayed together to avoid scandal, and for the sake of the children, but they were without happiness. They argued bitterly about waste in the household, about the husband's smoking, about the wife's hats, she owned three times the number of hats her husband did. Recently the wife had discovered that he was repulsively snub-nosed, added to which he was starting to develop a potbelly. She sometimes kept up her bickering all the way to suppertime, and said not a word to him at the table, but once they'd gone to bed they could shout goodnight to each other through an open door. Because they were together.

The living rooms of the workers' homes echoed to the sounds of quarrelling and fists on tables, and not often of wild dancing and of roofs being raised. The chap who'd been foreman in the drying room was by no means the worst, but he was furious because someone had misplaced his flat hat. After he'd turned the place upside down and finally found it in the crib, where it had got wet, he had every reason to give vent to a few long howls, but he restrained himself, his face foolish and unrecognisable with the effort. He looked at his wife.

She was an ordinary town girl, maybe a little too ordinary, in the past she'd done the odd thing or two for nothing or for money, depending on the state of her heart or her pocket. But for the most part she'd stayed true to the one who became her husband, and in the early days they got along with each other well enough. They had even agreed to get a little religion together. But once the saw stopped turning and the wage-packet stopped coming in a lot of things fell apart, he lost his desire for her and she felt the same way about him. Now he was off out to hunt razor-bills, he'd been promised a place in the boat and contributed to the whipround for a bottle and all the rest of it. But the wife, who never got to go along, was strongly opposed to all these razor-bill hunts and these whiprounds for a bottle.

As though he wanted exact clarity on the situation he asked: Has my flat hat got wet?

You can feel that for yourself, she answered.

Mm. Did you put my flat hat under the baby so I wouldn't be able to use it?

Ha ha ha, no.

What was the idea, laughing at such a time? Suddenly he jams the soaking wet hat down over his wife's head and holds it there. Ha ha ha, he says.

She's not afraid of him at all, she leaps at him and scratches away. No point in doing that either, nor was it especially religious of her to start cursing. She forced the cap into his face and screamed at him. That did it.

90

He went over to the corner where his shotgun was, and at first it looked as though he just wanted to pick it up and look at it for a while. He said nothing, and that was the scariest part of it. Nothing in the world is quite as long and thin as the barrel of a shotgun, and she let out a gasp. Oh my God! she said. Her tone had changed completely and he realized she was very afraid. As she watched he turned the barrel around and started preparing himself to leave this world. To do that he would need her help to fire the shot, but she wouldn't do that, far from it, what she did was run over to him and turn the barrel aside. What are you thinking of! she said. I'll wring your cap out for you and it'll dry on the stove in a minute! What did he say to that? Nothing. He put the shotgun away again and waited for his cap to dry.

In every home trouble, because there were no more paydays and no more security. Up to now husband and wife had got along pretty well with each other and with the children, they kept the show on the road, they had raincoats and overcoats, watches and wedding rings. Now all this was gone, and peace of mind with it. Just when they should have been wonderfully tender and friendly to each other they screamed and shouted over the slightest thing, they dug up the past and accused each other of so many sins they might as well have been devils. The children heard it all.

Things went wrong in Alex's household too. After he'd been laid off at the sawmill for a while he got drunk one evening and began accusing Lili of living a sinful life. He'd kept quiet about it long enough, now he was going to speak out. Ever since a certain someone had come back to town without his mate's examination Lili had been acting all funny again, hanging around him and flirting, it made people sick to see it, the way they flirted with each other: Was there never going to be any end to it?

Lili neither denied nor admitted anything, she replied that she didn't understand a word of what he was saying. Ah, but Lili might well have understood some of it, that wouldn't have been asking too much. She was absolutely not one of God's children, she was a wild child. The placid Lili had been awakened, after all these years of faithful marriage, only now had she been awakened to the real pleasures of the sensual life. Previously it had only been a matter of doing her marital duty, emptily and patiently, but now she was desperate. She loved often and ecstatically, and she made no effort to hide the fact that she was more or less crazy for it.

It was strange that no-one had caught them at it. They didn't carry on in houses where there were people, they were never seen in the local woods, and they couldn't get inside the church. Only one possibility remained: on board the *Sparrow*. The little white steamer that berthed at the quay every other day after its forty-eight hour journey was the very Garden of Eden in which they could hide themselves away. But was that really where they did it? Enough people kept an eye on the *Sparrow*, including Alex himself, and Lolla, and the daughters of Robertsen the Customs man, as well as others who begrudge them their pleasure. But no-one ever saw them there.

Alex starts talking like a book, trying to assert himself: So you fail to understand a word of what I'm saying, mm? I am talking about a certain person who doesn't have a mate's examination, now do you understand? Do you deign now to understand my words? Drunk, that's what he was.

Lili smiles mockingly.

Furthermore I am talking about this child here, he says and points towards the youngest. To begin with she wasn't there, do you understand that, you wretch? Wasn't there. And then she arrived from out of a clear blue sky and she was your angel – see? But was I the one who sent her?

It seems particularly important to him to get an answer to this question, but Lili smiles. He bellows it straight at her, but she smiles. And he wasn't the type to sit there and wait for her to be done with her smiling, he stood up. Stood up.

Ah but a really wild girl doesn't give up easily, she can go on smiling all day and all night, and he has to sit back down again.

Lili took it smoothly and didn't answer. It was a false silence, but it seemed natural. She was the one who had paid down whatever had been paid down on the house and garden, she'd been the cashier and had the good job, her husband had only been a labourer and dealt with logs. Could she affford to smile at the babbling and the half-dead eyes of a drunken man? You bet she could.

He didn't stand up again, he nodded and said well well, she would soon see! He wouldn't say any more, but she would see! Her – along with certain other people!

After he'd fallen asleep in the chair she took the little one on her arm and her big sister by the hand and went out. She left the children with her mother, the waffle-seller, and walked off on her own. It was evening now, and she had an appointment.

There was a maze of narrow alleyways down by the vacant lots, they weren't really navigable, but she lifted up here, and there she stepped over whatever it was that stood in her way. In the darkest of the alleyways was one hidden-away shack with a sloping roof, old Captain Brodersen had rented this shack to keep all his surplus furniture from the lighthouse in, and it was still standing, with all his curios from far-off lands, and beds and chairs and tables and all the rest of it. Lili went inside, and she stayed inside. And all the while, a close watch was being kept on the local milkboat, the *Sparrow*, until far into the night.

Abel couldn't be blamed for what happened, he would have preferred not even to have been involved at all. And as things turned out it was no great tragedy, just a bit of naughty playfulness, a case of a bit too much being said.

He met Olga and her husband in the street, and he didn't notice anything special, they were both their usual selves, her maybe just a touch more neurotic than usual. Her father had fallen on hard times and lost his reputation, not that it left Olga silent. Talking and talking away without saying anything, witticisms and gossip, a tapestry of broken threads: There's Abel! I haven't seen you for a year, Abel, and now I'm going to take a close look at you.

Don't do that, said Abel. I'm no better looking than I ever was.

You're worse. Why do you always put yourself down all the time?

Olga, really! said her husband with a smile.

She took Abel by the arm and walked along with him. I hear you're not going to your college?

No.

So then you won't be a captain?

Not a captain nor anything else, it looks like. I'm too stupid.

93

That's terrible that you're not going to be a captain. Now I can't sail away with you.

No, now you'll have to think of something else.

Such as what? Now I've lost my pin-money too, father needs it himself, they've picked him clean.

Well, you always found a way out in the old days, Olga!

Silence.

Who are that couple walking here in front of us? she asked her husband.

It's Robertsen the Customs man and his wife.

Of course you'll make something of yourself, Abel, what sort of nonsense is that. Everybody wants to be somebody.

That's right: everybody wants to be somebody, just not me. I don't want that. No will-power.

Why does everybody always have to *be* somebody? Clemens asked hesitantly.

Olga replied brightly: Because people have drive in them, Rieber Carlsen said so in his sermon.

Clemens: Well there's some truth in that. Perhaps especially as regards climbing up the social ladder.

Oh why are that couple walking at exactly the same pace as us? Olga said impatiently.

The men smiled, and Clemens replied: They're walking along a public highway.

They've turned round and seen us. And now they're altering their pace so that it's the same as ours.

We can overtake them.

No, she said. That would mean they've obliged us to notice them. I'll tell you what they're doing, they're gloating over me.

What?

Yes. I've noticed it in a lot of people of that class recently. They want to make me understand that now that father has lost his money then we're nothing any more.

Abel wanted to join in the conversation but he failed to make things any better: He built an extension to his house last year and now it's twice as big.

94

Yes that's social climbing, Olga said with contempt. Clownish, she said. What does he want with a bigger house?

They came to a taxi-rank and Abel said: We can drive past them.

Yes! cried Olga happily. Thanks, Abel.

They climbed in.

Clemens asked, laughing: And where are we going?

Past them, said Abel, laughing too.

Way past, said Olga. To the Fredriksens country place. Past the Fredriksens. The Fredriksens should get the chance to see that we're out and about. We can say hello.

Why? asked Clemens.

They whooshed past, past the Robertsens, who simply ceased to exist, and headed towards the sea again. Passing the Fredriksen's mansion she asked the driver to drive slowly, telling him there was a sick man lying there. She went out of her way to make herself visible, but no, there was no-one to see. Drive to the Valhalla! she said. Where's the Valhalla? asked Abel. The lido, didn't you know that? It's new since my time. No more bathers there now, it was too late in the year, but the restaurant was open. They told the driver to wait, entered the large, empty room and found themselves a vacant corner and ordered coffee and sandwiches. I'm starving, she said. You speak for us all, said her husband.

Olga: I'm sorry there was no sign of Fru Fredriksen, I would have waved to her. They're really marvellous people. Can you remember, Abel, the time we were in their vegetable garden and stole those carrots? Christ, it was a lifetime ago. Marvellous people, the best I know. And him, not a consul or a general agent or any of *that* kind of rubbish, just plain Fredriksen. Imagine, that slate falling off the roof last year and knocking him senseless, and he's still not recovered completely yet, but his wife keeps saying he's better, she's so patient. And even though he was so ill he bought up all my father's shares in the *Sparrow*.

Yes, said Clemens. He'd been after them for a long time too.

Yes. But you know why, don't you? It was nothing to do with a longing for the sea or wanting to make money from the shares. See, Abel, he's got a brother who's the black sheep of the family, Ulrik Fredriksen, the Captain on the *Sparrow*. You probably know him?

95

No.

Captain of the *Sparrow*?

There was no milkboat nor Ulrik here in my day.

Yes but it ties up at the quayside every other night. Have you never been on board?

No.

Someone said they'd seen you. With a woman. But Ulrik does nothing but party like a madman on board, and now his brother wants to get him away from it, he wants him ashore, he's bought a nice little smallholding for him. But Ulrik doesn't want to go ashore. So that's why Fredriksen's bought up all the shares he can get hold of, so he can make him go ashore.

Where was this Ulrik before?

People say he was in Africa. The black sheep. He still has comand of the boat, but neither life and limb nor his cargo are all that safe. Fredriksen's worried.

He's supposed to be a good Mate, said Clemens.

The coffee and the food arrived.

You're a tonic, Abel, getting us out like this. You're a nobody and you don't want to be a somebody, but there's so much you can do. Last year or was it this year you saved a man's life. We stood there and we all saw it, it was all so safe for us there on land, but I was crying when everybody cheered.

Oh yes she did, said Clemens, crying into my coat and shouting hurray.

Ha, *you're* a fine one to talk. You wanted to get up a party for Abel and you put your name down first on the guest list.

You exaggerate, said Clemens uncomfortably.

But you were nowhere to be found, Abel.

I didn't know about it, he said.

Nonsense, you hid yourself. We spent three days looking for you, then we got tired of it. That's when someone thought they might have seen you on board the *Sparrow*. Now what is all this about you actually *not* being on board the *Sparrow* with a woman?

I do assure you . . .

Okay. I'm sorry for wittering away. You two sit there and don't say anything and I say far too much. I didn't meant to be horrible to you, Abel, she said, and put her hand on his, forgive me! And now I'm sorry too for getting upset about Robertsen and his wife. Don't they have a perfect right to walk along the same street as me without me bothering about them?

All three of them laughed.

No I talk too much. By the way, your Negroes have left, Abel. But I'm talking too much.

Clemens: Actually, they left last year.

Yes, but can't I say it this year? I suddenly remembered how much fun it was in the wine-bar.

How about a little wine now? asked Abel and was about to ring the bell.

No no no! Olga interrupted him. There's no atmosphere here, just daylight and white paint. And no music. And we aren't boozers. And anyway it's not the same anymore.

Oh really?

No, it's not the same here anymore.

Abel, teasing: And what is it that has changed so much for you, Olga?

The pin-money. That's to say: my husand and I are having a dis-agreement.

Silence. Clear and cold silence. Frost.

Clemens had turned pale and said: Yes, that's quite true, you do talk too much, Olga.

Well I didn't say too much just then, she answered.

I'm not at all sure that Herr Brodersen wants to hear any of this.

Abel and I are old friends.

Yes, I think it's dull here too, said Abel and stood up. Wouldn't we be better off finding another wine-bar, even if it doesn't have Negroes?

They left and drove back. There was no more arguing. Passing the Fredriksens Olga signalled with her flashlight, a window on the first floor opened and two hands waved back for a long time. That was her, she said, she's so sweet.

They stopped at the Bellevue.

97

Clemens said: You must excuse me, I'll have to leave you now.

Aren't you coming in with us? asked Abel.

Do you mean we can go in without you? asked Olga.

Clemens turned towards Abel and answered: I need to take look at a case I've been asked to handle.

Have you got a case? asked Olga.

Goodbye now! said Clemens, and left them.

Left standing on the pavement the two of them looked at each other. The following subdued exchange took place:

Then I don't suppose you can either, Olga?

Hm. So you don't think the two of us can go in anyway?

No.

She offered him her hand, thanked him for the company, and hurried after her husband.

Abel offered to get her a cab, but she just walked off.

Poverty in through the door, is what he probably thought as he went in.

A small orchestra was playing. Right now a little Schumann, then Beethoven, Schubert one after the other, sweet favourites. All very quiet and still.

Lolla sits at a table with her mother. He greeted them but had no desire to join them, if that was wine they were drinking Lolla could become annoying and start wanting to flirt.

She stood up and he was obliged to walk over to her. What a woman, incidentally, she knew how good she looked dressed in black with something white, and the white gloves.

I've been looking for you, she said.

Do you want something?

Yes. We're drinking chocolate, do you want a cup?

They sat down, but he said no thanks to the chocolate, he'd just had coffee and a sandwich.

Where have you been? You don't look at all good.

Just exactly what Olga said.

Have you been with her?

Her and her husband. We were in the Valhalla.

I'm sorry I didn't find you before you went out. I would have smartened you up, said Lolla.

Her mother sat there silent and remote and said nothing. A pity about her, hard for her, grey head and dull eyes, a smile for a kind word. Once even she had been young.

Abel said to her: So, I see you're out dancing today too. The old woman smiled and shook her head at her own foolishness: It was Lolla who brought me along.

Yes and whyever not. I suppose your cactuses have finished flowering now?

Yes, but they're still pretty. We've got two in each window and the big one on the table.

In Kentucky they grew wild, Abel murmured to himself. What did you want, Lolla?

Did you guarantee for Robertsen? she asked.

What? No.

They said something in the bank yesterday, and it made me so afraid.

You and that bank, Lolla!

They were asking if you were here, if you hadn't left, if you were planning to leave. No, I didn't think so. Because they said they had a document from Robertsen the Customs man with your name on it. It had been defaulted on, that's what they said.

Silence.

What do you say to that?

I haven't signed anything.

What are we going to do, Abel? He must have done it himself.

I suppose he probably did, said Abel, indifferent.

But Lolla was on her way up, she was a lady now, looked after her name, that old forgery of her father's might surface again, Robertsen would protect no-one, he was the worst social climber of the lot.

What are we going to do?

I'll go and speak to Robertsen, said Abel. He doesn't live far away.

Lolla, pleading: Yes but, Abel, dear Abel, please don't let people find out!

No. Wait here and I'll be back.

The music stopped, and as he was leaving the jazz began. Outside the door he came face to face with Robertsen the Customs man.

I saw you go in here, I've been waiting for you, said Robertsen.

And I'm just on my way to the police to report you, said Abel.

They got straight to the point. Robertsen cheeky, shameless, and reckless too:

Oh yes you did too sign it, you can't get out of it. You sat there in my living room and you signed it. Look at the girls' Poetry Albums, and look at the promissory note – the name is exactly the same. And while we're on the subject – same ink!

Robertsen looked Abel straight in the face when he said this.

They walked a short distance away until they came to a bench.

Abel said: You're not afraid of being arrested?

Ho ho, said Robertsen, let them come!

You won't be saying that in an hour's time.

You're trying to frighten me, but it's you lot that are afraid. And Robertsen expanded on this: He'd been out walking with his wife today, and he was well aware of Abel and the fine company he was keeping, but had he shown any sign of being afraid? Not much!

They sat there talking like that and they had opposing views on the matter. Abel called Robertsen an uncommonly lowdown rogue, Robertsen didn't agree.

Abel roused himself from his habitual indifference. He called him a thief, a robber, a scoundrel, he was, by God, no better than an animal! Robertsen got angry and said now he was being insulting.

A dog! said Abel, as though finally arriving at a round sum.

Shut up, I won't have this, said Robertsen, and I don't want to hear any more about it. Ask anyone you like and they'll tell you who I am.

I think you're losing the plot here, said Abel.

Not much I am. You're forgetting that forged document Lolla had to pay back.

What does that have to do with you?

It'll come out one day.

Yes, but how does it help you?

It helps me this way, that you two are no pair of god-fearing bible-bashers either.

Abel said: What do you suppose they'll say at home when the police come for you?

You daren't touch me, said Robertsen.

Abel got up and walked away.

Robertsen stayed sitting for a moment before he ran after him: Where are you off to?

You're a dog.

Don't go that way, Abel. My wife's standing waiting for me down there.

Abel walked on.

The wife made out it was a surprise meeting and joined them.

Robertsen was still blustering: He thinks he can frighten me, but he won't get far with that.

His wife is already a little uncertain: Isn't there some other way of dealing with this?

I'll get the lot of them in trouble, said Robertsen and puffed himself up in front of his wife.

Abel: Take you insane husband home. He's about to be arrested.

The wife broke down and started sobbing: You wouldn't harm us would you, Abel? The girls are sitting at home with the blinds pulled down, they daren't even go out!

Robertsen, angry: Don't stand there crying in the middle of the street, good grief. I am a public official, everybody knows who I am.

You can't want to hurt us that badly, Abel, you're not made of stone.

Oh yes, just you wait and see.

I told you all along this would go wrong, his wife whimpered. She glowered at her husband.

Yes, but aren't you the one who kept telling me to build an extension?

Me? she cried. You said you would be getting promotion soon and you needed a bigger house.

I've never heard lying like it – it was you who said those exact very words!

Abel walked on. The wife ran after him and grabbed him by the arm: Abel, you mustn't go. It would cost you nothing to cover this at the bank.

101

What? Abel gaped. I don't want anything to do with you.

But the wife said that they'd sell the boats, and a lot of other things, they'd pay him back, and the husband joined in, admitting that he shouldn't have started on the extensions, but his wife and daughters gave him no peace . . .

Don't believe him, said the wife.

Abel was hardly listening anymore, he'd slipped back into the great indifference to everything. Why allow himself to get upset by such meaningless people? Nothing to be gained by it. He saw now that the way out of it was to go to the bank and pay up and get rid of the business once and for all.

Go home, he said. I'll sort it out.

They thanked him, they took his hand, even Robertsen offered to shake his hand.

When Lolla, deeply uneasy, asked what had happened Abel answered: Naturally I sorted Robertsen out.

Thank God! But, Abel, can we be certain it's alright?

Nothing will come out. The whole thing's over and done with.

Joy flickered across the old woman's face.

No doubt about it, Lolla understood what Abel had done, as she looked down she said: It's too bad I can never be anything for you, Abel.

Why is that? he asked abruptly.

She replied meekly: I'm just saying. You do so much for me.

XI

TIMES WERE GETTING TIGHTER FOR EVERYONE.

In the months that followed, with cold and snow, people had nothing to keep them busy. There was nothing. They went around working out all sorts of big ideas, but nothing was done. The only one with any initiative was Alex. In the month of February he left his poverty-stricken home and set out in search of work.

It was early one frosty morning. He carried a bundle of food Lili had made up for him, and she followed him part of the way. They didn't talk much to each other, fate was out hunting, it was hard on their heels. Alex was a by no means unreasonable man, but if he was to be forced to go out wandering through the world then at least he would do it angrily. Lili tried everything she knew to sweeten him, but no luck: I told you I would show you, didn't I!

Yes but Alex, it's not my fault that you don't have any work.

He was not about to remind her at such a time of her guilt in one thing and another, but he strode out and kept lengthening his stride until she could hardly keep up with him.

I can't keep up with you, she said.

Did I ask you to come along and waste my time?

No no, she said, and thought it best to drop it.

They had reached the small forest on the edge of town. He took his jacket off, lay it down in the snow and said: Sit down.

She misunderstood and protested: What do you think you're doing?

He untied the bundle and shared out the food: There – eat.

Me? But why?

You've more need of it than I.

She ate to please him, wept and ate. Things had been alright with them again recently, Alex wasn't so bad, he'd come to mean so much to her, he would do alright. But now that she was able to enjoy herself with her husband at last, now he was off. Don't you think it would be better if we just went back home again? she asked hesitantly.

He didn't reply.

Don't you think? Because that way at least we're together.

Just be quiet will you. Haven't I got enough on my mind as it is?

Funny he could be so angry just when they were about to part from each other for life.

You must write, she said.

Write? What makes you think they have a postal service that far away?

Lili alarmed: Oh my God, Alex, where are you thinking of going?

That I do not know. But out, into the wide world.

More tears, more emotion. But apart from that they made no agreement to be faithful, not to forget each other, that they'd sooner die, no, no words that implied forever.

You're sitting there freezing, she said.

Eat! he said.

No thanks, no more, she replied, and carefully wrapped up the bundle of food again. And that was it, she stood up, brushed the snow from the edge of her frock and said: I have to get home before the little ones wake up.

When some distance had opened up between them she called out: Don't stay away too long!

But a man who had once been manager of the sawmill didn't have the option of leaving home with his food wrapped up in a cloth in search of work. In vain he scanned the Situations Vacant columns of the Oslo newspapers looking for jobs, or else he drifted around town, still the Engineer, with the cane and the hat at a rakish angle, only now people didn't think he was important any more. Things had changed.

He'd started going down to the quay and taking trips on the *Sparrow*. He'd started doing it rather a lot, but what was he neglecting thereby? Nothing. He and Captain Ulrik got on reasonably well together, they were both a better class of person and were able to converse together. The Engineer didn't need to pay for his ticket, because he'd paid so much over the years when he'd travelled with the business, now he enjoyed the benefit of having once been a powerful man. He still pretended there was some purpose behind his trips, that a certain piece of forestry in a certain location was of particular interest to him. Then he would disembark and wait until the next day and join the *Sparrow* again on her return journey. The whole thing was a trip out to the country for him, an outing all on his own, without the family. During the actual boat journey it was usual for the Captain to provide something to eat and drink. There was no shortage of either.

Ulrik Fredriksen was actually a farmer and had grown maize in Africa, but he had enough seamanship to navigate the *Sparrow* in and out of the bays and headlands on her route, and for that matter there wasn't a man on board who wasn't familiar with the waters in those regions anyway. And now they wanted to remove him from his command by force. But Captain Ulrik had his own supporters, people who wished him well, perhaps mostly to spite the powerful brother out at his country house whom nobody liked. Anyway, there was no getting rid of Ulrik. Maybe he was the black sheep of the family, but the people on his route liked him, and he looked good too, even though he was greying, and had a blue scar on his forehead. They wanted him out in the country? Ha, they might as well have ordered him straight to bed

105

and have done with it! Maybe if it had been an ostrich farm – but pota-toes and barley, no thanks! But an ostrich farm now, that was something else, because those big, heathen camel-birds,well, they weren't chickens and they weren't mice either, you better believe that.

The Mate knocked and entered. He announced that Ananias was ill.

The Captain: Ananias, what's that?

One of the crew. He's ill.

He's probably just eaten too much.

He says it his stomach.

Exactly! See here, said the Captain, and dug out a half-bottle with a drop left in it. Give him a shot of this and let him turn in for a while.

That was Captain Ulrik's way of dealing with things.

And he was not averse to talking about women either, and other enjoyable matters, and he made no secret of the fact that he'd been engaged once or nearly, and that was the only time he'd ever really wanted to get married, he said.

The Engineer asked what went wrong.

It was me. Me unfortunately. She didn't say no to begin with, but then he was such an idiot, he didn't make a move on her – even now, today, he still regretted it. What else could things do but go to pieces when he was such an idiot? And next time she said no.

And I had such a good hold on her! said the old roué, regretting it again. I should've done what I didn't do.

Maybe it's still not too late, says the Engineer, flattering him.

Now? It was twenty years ago, and anyway it was in Natal. It does-n't bear thinking about! But Ulrik Fredriksen came alive at these old memories and damned if he'd given up hope completely: The only thing might be if I took a trip out there to see her. Maybe she's not mar-ried anymore.

Was she married?

Yes but that wasn't the point. There are other things to consider here. It all started when I ran into a hotel to escape a sudden squall, and she was just on her way out. Young woman, listening to the music in the foyer, English, pretty, so I took to her at once. The weather frightened her. I reached out and I grabbed the first umbrella I could

106

from the cloakroom and I said: This is yours! Mine? she said, smiling, and looked at me. I left a pound behind on the counter for the loan and walked out to a taxi with her. I am so grateful to you, she said. I'm the one who should be grateful, I says and I climbed in after her. *I never saw your like!* she says in surprise. To begin with she was a little reserved, and she got worried about her violin when I moved in closer to her, but then we started talking, and by the time we got to where we were going we'd done a lot of talking, and she didn't turn me down when I said I had to have her at any cost. I really meant what I said, and it was the worst case of being in love I've ever had, what you might call a kind of exaltation. Her cheeks went all warm and she got restless in the seat, if I just touched her hand it went right through her, her sex was all over her body. There's a lot of them like that, it's not that uncommon. She didn't want to let me come in with her, so I said it right back to her: *I never saw your like*, and I want to marry you. I am married, she said. What difference does that make? I said. No, she said. And on the stairway she said it as well, that it made no difference. Take good note of that. We came into the house, it was full of the most appalling animals and birds and there was an atrocious smell. A mad dog greeted us at the door, screeching birds in cages, three hedgehogs, a tortoise lumbering about on the floor, there was an ape sitting on the sofa. Did you ever hear the like of it, and maybe there was a snake or two there as well. I got so distracted by all these ugly beasts that I started talking too much about them instead of about her, and the mood passed off her. Damn those bloody animals! I know she would have left her husband, but then the next time I brought it up she said no. What I should have done, straightaway I should have chased that monkey off the sofa.

Hahaha! the Engineer laughed.

Yes, those were the days, says Captain Ulrik. Do they have that kind of wild and exciting life nowadays? Have you seen, in your own neighbourhood, a fight over a girl, a real one? Jesus, once I got a nasty scrape here in the forehead from a bullet, but it healed by itself. Now my brother gets a tile landing on his head and he's sick for years from it. Me, I just have this scar, it shouldn't be blue, but some dirt got into the wound, and right at that time I had no money for a doctor. Makes no odds now, the chief stewardess here, the *trisa*, she says anyway that it makes no difference if it's blue.

No, what does that matter.

Not that I care that much what *trisa* says, I don't want her thinking that. She's got some very unhealthy ideas. I say to *trisa* that we should have some children. No, she doesn't want to. But what kind of woman is that who doesn't want children? Who's supposed to come after us then? I ask. Dammit, soon there won't be a healthy person left in the world. In fact in general, that *trisa* has such an unnatural way of thinking that I'm going off her. So as far as I'm concerned she's welcome to that lame chemist. Do you happen to know if he has a wooden leg?

No.

Well then there you are, she's welcome to have it away with a wooden leg as far as I'm concerned. Ha.

One of the crew came in and said that a couple of passengers had started fighting on the deck.

Send them to me, said the Captain.

His usual way of making peace was to give both of them a real roasting and follow it up with a good drink and make them shake hands. There were some who took advantage of Captain Ulrik's unusual methods and would fake a good knife-fight just for the pleasures of his peace-making.

One was a wheelwright from town, the other a farmer, both of them old men and not much to look at.

The Captain put his cap on his head and stood up in front of them in all his gold threads and shiny buttons. He said, with dignity: Bow to your Captain, you possoms!

The two rascals hide their smiles and bow.

Now what is all this?

He's cheated me twice with bad wheels, says the farmer.

They were not bad wheels, says the wheelwright.

Oh indeed they were, disgraceful! is Captain Ulrik's decision. Don't you think I know that type of wheel! You've got to keep them soaked in water the whole time to swell them, or else the spokes fall out. Do you hear me? The spokes fall out. As far as I can see the problem here seems to be that the wheels have not been soaked in water. This man here has no water on his farm, look at him, he can't even spare a couple of drops to wash his face. What a pig! But on the other hand I ask myself this: What the hell is a wheelright from a workshop in town, what the hell is he doing on my boat and in these waters?

I'm travelling around looking for orders, said the wheelwright.

For wheels like that? mocked the Captain. I don't want to hear another word about it. Have you no shame! Here – drink this!

They drank, got another glass and drank again. They took hold of the door handle, said thank you, and pretended to be about to leave.

Stop! commanded the Captain. Did I say that you could leave? We're not nearly done yet. Here you are falling out over a few sticks of wood, cartwheels, for all I know just wheels for wheelbarrows, I'm ashamed of you. Why are you bleeding?

He used a knife.

So then there must have been some gorgeous girls or sweethearts you were fighting about? If there is to be murder and bloodshed on my decks then I want it to be for a proper reason, do you hear me? I won't stand for brawling, you're disgracing my ship, I'll put you ashore on some rocky little island. Here – now drink, and shake hands with each other! That's it.

But the Engineer wasn't much cheered up by this interlude, he was getting closer to town and to home and he knew what would happen: his wife would take the children and go down to the quay to meet him and pretend he's been away on a business trip and bought timber for the sawmill and now he was returning home to his loved ones. And they stood there waving from a long way out, and once again his wife had the chance to show how she and her husband were sticking together. But the moment he crossed the theshold and was inside the house she wouldn't say another word to him.

The Captain went up on deck. The Engineer gathered up his thick folder of documents and followed him. A glance towards the quay. A long sigh. I'm shivering! he said.

The Captain: Didn't I just tell you? Soon there won't be a single healthy person left in the world.

The Engineer waved in the direction of the quay, but he looked as if he was grinding his teeth. It's painful for him, sort of half-drunk from the Captain's cognac and with his pockets empty. Someone on deck taking up a collection for something, whatever it is, the Captain contributes, the wheelwright and the farmer are friends again after their drams and they give too, the Engineer has to pretend he hasn't seen, he ransacks his folder in search of an important document, surely he can't have mislaid that important document?

The Captain understands and tries to help out: Have you lost something?

Ah no, here it is, thank God! says the Engineer. Once again thank you and goodbye! he says and holds out his hand. His eyes are a dead blue, he's a little drunk too and so a little pathetic. In the old days he would willingly have chipped in, but not any more. Thank you so very much!

It just occurred to me, says Captain Ulrik – Bring your wife and kids on board. The *trisa* can lay places for all of us—

Lolla's there again, just recently she's been there every evening. She stands watching with interest as the white ship comes alongside and is moored. She's wearing a coat with a fur collar and she's a lady, it wouldn't occur to her to wait in a crowd with the others, but apart, and on her own. Lolla knows how to carry herself, if someone says hello she answers, but she doesn't say the first hello. She pays no attenton to the Robertsen women.

When she leaves the quay she walks back via the Seamen's Home or somewhere near it in order to meet Abel . . . She knows roughly the routes he takes on his walks and always has some business with him. For God knows how many winters now he's been going around in that disgraceful grey-brown ulster from America and generally looking worse and worse in his clothes. Spring's on the way now and once icy March is out of the way here come April and May, Abel ought to be ready for it in plenty of time and have a new outfit to wear, it's been a long time since the last time. Lolla knows what she's doing, the day might come when Abel has to be appear in front of a board of directors and make a good impression.

I'm glad I bumped into you, Abel.

Is there something you wanted?

No. I was down at the quay and just happened to be walking this way.

Did you take my gun? he asked.

Me? No.

It's gone.

Do you suppose I would go up to your room and take your gun?

No. But it's gone.

Well you don't exactly have a proper suitcase with a lock, said Lolla.

They passed the tailor's and Lolla pointed to the light spring clothes displayed in the window. Abel just shook his head and said: In Kentucky all we had were the clothes we stood up in.

Do you prefer grey or brown?

I don't know.

Because if you like that grey *there* I could go in and give the tailor an order.

Abel, relieved: Yes, you do that, Lolla.

He's got your measurements from before, so you won't have to go through all that again.

Okay. And let me tell you that I have never seen more handsome grey clothes. But there's something else, Lolla: Alex has gone.

I know.

Left his family and home.

Yes, well, it isn't your family, Lolla said curtly.

They couldn't pay the mortgage and now the house is to be sold.

Well the house isn't yours either, said Lolla.

No, you're right there. And I don't know how you're going to take this, but I had to pay off the arrears on the house.

What?

Yes, what else could I do? They had no house and nothing to live off. Alex is hiding out somewhere or other and sends nothing home.

Lolla: What does this actually have to do with you, Abel?

Well . . .

You'll turn yourself into a tramp.

Abel said nothing.

111

Did you at least get the papers to prove the house is yours?

Yes, said Abel.

Let me see.

Abel: Of course I covered myself. What do you take me for?

Let me see. Do you have them on you?

I was just on my way to fetch them. They're all ready to pick up.

I believe things like that have to be announced in public, said Lolla. Who arranged this business for you?

Yes who was it now? But everything's in order.

You must know who drew up the document?

Of course. Yes, it was Clemens. Young Clemens. Agh, I can't understand how you can be bothered to be so efficient, Lolla.

Young Clemens, said Lolla. He's not up to much from what I hear.

Him? Son of the Chief Magistrate and all that?

Oh yes, good family and a good man. But all the same . . .

He's got a big case, he was telling me.

Lolla, unimpressed: All that is, he's trying to get Pistleia to drop their action. I haven't heard anything about him having another case.

Abel grabbed his chance: It sounds as though you don't like Clemens?

Like him? I worked for them, they were good people to work for. If you please, Lolla, she always said. But I had little to do with him. On the contrary, once I asked him to fix something for me and he wouldn't do it.

And is that why you're angry with him?

I'm not angry with him at all. Though I do think he ought to at least be able to greet me in the street. She always nods, but not him. I did once work for them after all. Alright then, Abel, you go and fetch those documents and I'll go in and see the tailor now . . .

But Abel couldn't figure out a way to get Clemens to understand the whole business. He didn't lend out money against a security, or invest money in houses with gardens. That wasn't what he did. Lili would be puzzled by the legal side of it and Alex would have to be fetched back from his hiding place to sign.

It was all was so complicated that in the end he abandoned the whole idea of going to see Clemens.

XII

THE FACT THAT HE HAD NEW CLOTHES AND LOOKED SMART
about town led to nothing. Lolla must have made a mistake, he didn't
get called in to any board meeting where he had to make a good
impression. So sure, Abel was smart now, but why carry on being
smart? Anyway, he wasn't a man who took much care of his clothes, the
summer passed, and the light grey clothes weren't the same light all
over, in fact they weren't even grey all over. And now it was autumn and
he had to wear other clothes, and that grey-brown ulster from America
again.

But things worked out. Everything works out. Though sometimes
they work out sideways.

Lolla started worrying about his bank balance, it had definitely
been suffering. Not so that he was on his knees, and he wasn't worried
about it himself, but Lolla had certain things on her mind. Year in and
year out he lived in that Seamen's Home with all its daily expenses, he

could have lived more cheaply with her in the house down by the beach. And what had been the point of saving Alex and Lili's house for them?

How's things, Abel, everything alright?

Sure, everything's fine.

But you have to keep on paying for your board and lodging, and you're not earning anything.

No.

How long is that going to go on?

Abel: What annoys me is these clothes you tricked me into buying in the autumn and the spring. They're too costly for me.

You can't mean that, Abel. Everyone has to wear clothes.

We didn't have any tailor's bills when I was in Kentucky.

You'd be a good-looking man if you took more care with your appearance, said Lolla, and blushed. You've got warm eyes.

Abel pulled a face and insisted again that it was the last time he would be laying out for a lot of fancy clothes for himself. And now someone had taken his gun too, that was a real blow. He could get another gun but it wouldn't be the same, this gun was the one Angèle had been shot with. That reminded him, he should have sent some money to Lawrence, who was rotting in jail in America . . .

Haven't you done that already?

That's right, I did do it!

How much?

I don't know. It mustn't be too small an amount.

You've done it *already*, Abel, cried Lolla. I remember you doing it.

Have I done it?

Yes. I was with you.

Well then! But it was too little. You made me send too little. Think about it: he's locked up, he needs a new lawyer, he needs witnesses, all of that costs money. He won't get far with just his two bare hands.

Just don't go making a tramp out of yourself, said Lolla.

Silence. Abel sat with his hands clasped. Suddenly a breath of life seemed to waft through him and he said: In the spring I'm going to find something to do!

Lolla silent for a moment: What? Will you? But that's wonderful, Abel, do it, do something! That's the most wonderful news.

Good intention, blessed intention. Spring came, then the summer – and nothing changed. Abel carried on living at the Seamen's Home and let time drift by. The whole town was still and unchanged too, the only difference was people dying and people being born. The waterfall rushed on, but the sawmill stood idle, the coastboat sailed, thirty tourists visited the town, the odd fishing boat came by and picked up a load of cord wood for the Vestlandet, the *Sparrow* plied her route, and Captain Ulrik couldn't be got rid of – nothing changed. And Abel wasn't up to any more breaths of life wafting through him.

What d'you say, Lolla, there's a whole lot of junk and knicknacks my father left, what's the use of all that?

Why do you ask?

It's in a shed. We could turn it into cash.

Yes we could, she said thoughtfully.

And you'll get half of it.

Lolla angry: I certainly do not want any half of it.

Be quiet. Isn't that right? It's just standing there, we could turn it into hard cash. You'll get half.

I'm telling you, I don't want any half of it.

Be quiet.

Lolla almost crying in her indignation: I don't want either the half or the whole of anything, do you understand? I get my regular monthly allowance and that's enough. And by the way, there's something I haven't mentioned to you yet: when your father sold the motorboat he asked me to send the money to you, but that was never done. I was paying down the debt to the bank at the time, so I used the money.

Are you angry? I've got a feeling you're sitting there and getting angry, Lolla. How can you be bothered? Be indifferent to everything and everybody – that's the way to make time pass.

Yes, and the days and the years pass. And we don't do anything. And so our whole lives pass.

Abel nodded: I once thought of doing something, but not straight away. And if a thing isn't done straight away it can still be done next

115

year.

Why not do it now?

I don't know. Right now, with the summer nearly over? I've always thought it should be in the spring. Some spring or other.

Lolla shrieked in her distresss: For God's sake, Abel, you're letting yourself go completely!

Abel smiled: Don't get so worked up, Lolla.

Autumn already, with cold winds and swirling dust.

Olga appeared in front of him on a street-corner. She looked dusty and agitated.

Good morning, Abel! Let's find a bench somewhere.

Are you tired? Wouldn't you rather get a cab home?

No, let's walk to a bench.

There's so much dust swirling about.

Daren't you talk to me? she asked. After all, it really isn't all that often, I think probably two years since the last time. How are things, Abel? You look good. I'm a mess, I've been out for hours and now I'm on my way back home. Don't I look terrible?

Not if you took off all that powder and paint, Olga.

Remember a bracelet you once wanted to give me?

Which you wouldn't accept, yes.

A gold bracelet. I would accept it now, she said.

Now?

Yes. I need it to bring some glamour into my life.

I'll go and get it for you, said Abel.

Oh will you? Dear Abel, you're so kind! I was walking along and thinking that because it's actually really my bracelet, I would ask if you would go and get it for me.

Abel nodded: If it isn't gone by now.

No. I've been to church many times over this last year and I checked. So you understand what I'm saying, Abel? That I'd be happy to accept it now?

Yes. For some reason or other.

For a particular reason.

Abel had nothing against being set this particular task and made

116

his way up to the church with a light step. The moon was on the wane, going down, it looked as though it was lying on its back and sailing backwards against the clouds. Not a bird, not a single person in the churchyard, a hooting now and then from the vents in the steeple. Lovely evening now. If he met someone at the gate and they asked where he was off to he would reply with an almost roguish little twinkle: Wouldn't you just like to know?

He's familiar with the place, goes over to the window and tries to peer through the pane to check if the bracelet is still where it was. Impossible to see it so far away and in such faint light. He casts a glance across the graveyard. No Widow Krum sitting there grieving as she was last time, she's dead now. No-one sitting there now, it's autumn and the wind is chilly, it's an appropriate evening.

He starts to drill. He only has a few tools with him, a drill and a jemmy to prise the catches off with. It's soon done, he's good with his hands and has probably overcome tougher windows in his time. Then he pulls himself up by his arms and slides in sideways. Takes just a couple of wriggles of the hips, child's play. The heist itself is child's play, it's so ludicrously easy to climb up and take the bracelet and climb back down again that probably Olga could have done it by herself.

As he's about to wriggle out through the window again someone's standing outside. He sees right away who it is, she's still wearing the same clothes as earlier in the day and she's still agitated.

Neither one says anything until he's back on the ground, then they whisper: Did you get it? Yes. She puts her arm under his and walks out past the wall with him.

Here you are, he says.

Goodness me how heavy it is! she says. I'd like to give you a kiss for it, if you want.

No, it was just too easy to take it. You could've done it yourself.

The moment passed for her and she said: We forgot to close the window.

No. It's better if it's open and on the latch. That way it won't swing up and down, up and down.

Right then, so we're finished, she said. Thanks, Abel!

Abel: Why did you show up like that?

I felt sorry for you. I didn't want you to be alone when you did it. For my sake.

I don't understand.

Yes, because if anyone had come . . .

They walked in silence down the hill leading up to the church and parted company outside her door.

But the following day she turned up at the Seamen's Home and went up to his room. Her appearance astonished him and he clumsily offered her his only chair.

Can you lend me two thousand kroner? she asked.

Abel gaped: What? Yes, with pleasure!

You will? she cried, and threw herself down into the chair.

She was very agitated, but lovely and unpainted today. She was wearing the bracelet and jingled with it, made it very visible. Why all the agitation? She stood up, sat down again, held out her hand to him for no reason, laughing and whimpering at the same time. Nerves. Hysteria. And her words snatched.

I'm ashamed of myself. You see, I've known for a long time, and he can't afford it. It was my fault, so I had to do something. I went to see Fredriksen. No. That was yesterday. No, he said. Went to Fredriksen then back again. No, because he'd bought the shares in the *Sparrow* from my father and had nothing left. That wasn't true , but he said he had nothing left. That was yesterday, when I met you. Then I thought about some rings and about the bracelet, but unfortunately it won't be enough. And it's all my fault. I'm so thoroughly ashamed, as God is my witness. Sitting here, daring to ask you . . .

Abel: What's going on?

The tax people are at his office. But it's all my fault, he could never say no to me. Then I became poor, my father became poor, and we borrowed from the firm. I covered it up. Maybe I did it a bit crudely, I got into a bit of debt to someone I know, but I didn't really feel that ashamed about it, it's now I feel ashamed . . .

Take it easy, Olga! When is the audit?

Immediately. Could be any time now. Fredriksen wouldn't help, he's in bed ill and he wouldn't. I've never heard anything like it, he's going to do die soon, but he wouldn't do it. I begged him . . . no. The last time we managed to clear the debt, but then we did it again and borrowed again. Then I thought maybe some rings and the bracelet and stuff like that, but it wouldn't amount to all that much, I was told. They looked at it and wouldn't give any more. I really don't want to sell it either, I said, that's not why! But of course it was why . . .

How much do you need altogether? Calm down now.

He says two thousand.

Is that anything to get all upset about?

Isn't it? Oh, Abel, bless you!

Do you want to sit here and wait or come with me?

Come with you. No I'll wait here. Will you be long? Of course I'll sit here. I don't want to get in the way. I want to lie down, she said with a glance at the bed, just lay down for a while. Can I? She took off her hat and put it to one side, took off her coat.

You're really upset, Olga.

You see he'd never survive it, and it would be my fault. I'm so fond of him, I love him and want to help him as much as I can, but I just don't want to get any deeper in debt than I already am. Actually he says that it isn't my fault, but it is. All of it. He's too upright to do anything wrong, too decent a person, not a stain on him. It would kill the Magistrate, put his mother in her grave, and his sisters – the whole family are like that. And he says nothing himself, sits in his office and carries on working today as he did yesterday with this hanging over him, and not a word. Actually his conscience is clear, because it's my fault. From the start, the whole thing. I was too expensive, I bought everything I saw, I got whatever I pointed to, never counted the cost, the latest fashion in clothes, the wine-bar, three months of horse-riding lessons . . . Excuse me, Abel, I must just lean back a bit. That's it, better now. You're smiling?

Yes, but I'm not going to say why.

Are you smiling at me?

A bit, yes, I'm sorry. You're on your knees, you suppose, but at least you're going down in style. The latest fashions, you say, wine-bars, riding lessons. And all your jewellery isn't even worth two thousand!

You're right, Abel, sort me out!

No. It's just that you're getting far too worked up, you exaggerate.

119

He'd never survive it, you say – he'd almost certainly survive it, Olga. But right now you're almost beside yourself, it's no joke, your husband's in trouble and you love him. But if only you could see all this as the nothing it really is. That's the way I do it.

Abel puts on his hat and nods.

Are you leaving? She jumps up from the bed again and exclaims: I want to go with you anyway. You shouldn't have to do this on your own. And they'll think it's for a house again, for Lili or whatever her name is. It doesn't matter if they see it's for me. That's how far gone I am . . .

Hush, Olga! Do you want me to tuck you up nice and warm?

Yes please, tuck me up in my coat . . .

When he returned from the bank she was sleeping. Not easily and not deeply, but all the same a good nap. She woke up, was wide awake immediately and rose from the bed.

Did you go? Did you get it? Oh, bless you! It's a loan, Abel, I'll have money one day, I know that'll happen, I'll have a lot of money one day. Everything points to that. But at least I want this audit out of the way and not getting mixed up with other things. Poor thing, he'll be sitting there and suffering now! What time is it? I have to meet him at the office, and it's a long way.

Won't you take a cab?

No no, you've done enough for me! She throws on her coat and hat and she's ready. Don't I look terrible? Have you really no mirror?

Yes, that small one. But you look lovelier than ever. No paint, lovely.

Thank you again, Abel! She gives him her hand and leaves.

He noticed that, as far as he could see, she was wearing her hat back to front, and he calls after her.

Yes, she answers, I do it deliberately. Usually they buy the same hats as me and copy me – now I want to see if they wear their hats back to front and still admire me like they used to.

Bailed out, honour and life saved. God knows how she explained the money to him, maybe that her father was wealthier than anyone imagined, maybe that a certain family jewel had come to their rescue.

Once she'd primed him for her explanation he was too decent a man to enquire any further into it, and in too much need to spurn the help.

The rescue had a good effect on young Clemens. He pulled himself together and settled the case with the Pistleia Forestry Company: 1. It was not proven nor could it be proven that the sawmill was complicit in the false pretences offered in the matter of the timber deal. The manager was a well-respected man, but having lost his position he had understandably succumbed to a depression in which it seemed reasonable to him to place the blame on the Board. 2. Since what was effectively the sawmill's only shareholder was now completely broke nothing would be achieved by any potential verdict other than the disgracing of a decent man.

The Pistleia Forestry Company mumbled and grumbled about young Clemens' presentation of the facts but dropped the case. It had dragged on for years . . .

For some reason or other it now became a matter of urgency for Abel to sell the furniture and the knicknacks in his shed. He busied himself with it for several days and got a scrap-merchant to come along and look at the stuff and give him a price for it. The deal was almost done but then got held up when Abel demanded payment in cash. The scrap-merchant looked at him in surprise: How could small change like this be so important to a man like Abel Brodersen?

People think I'm rich, said Abel. But that's not the case.

The weeks and months passed and he let the matter lie, his old indifference had taken hold again. At his lodgings they sent him a number of reminders to pay his arrears, but he ignored them. The people running the Seamen's Home were considerate with him because he'd lived there for so many years and because he was the wealthy Abel Brodersen, but in the end they sent the bill to him via his stepmother, via Lolla.

Right then, said Abel. Today is the day.

He went to another scrap-merchant and took him along to the shed with him to look over the stuff. But now Abel withdrew from sale a lot of the stuff that he didn't want to go: the bed, sofa, chairs, table, a couple of paintings of sailing ships. Because he didn't want to leave himself completely bereft, he said.

Well, said the man, that doesn't leave much.

No, Abel agreed.

And I won't be able to get rid of the ostrich eggs and seashells and poisoned arrows. All the old skippers who might have been interested in that kind of stuff are dead and gone now.

I've got a couple of second-hand suits up at my lodgings you can have.

Well that's more like it, that's the kind of thing that sells. But now let's have a look at what you've got here. We won't itemise all these little things here, we'll just agree a round sum for the lot.

Abel showed him a box with no lock and key, finely worked in brass and with an intricate locking mechanism in its base.

Well, said the man, maybe Fru Clemens would have bought something like that in the old days, Olga Clemens. She used to call in on me now and then on the lookout for curios, and fancy embroidery and suchlike. But now she's got nothing left to pay with.

After they were done at the shack they went up to the Seamen's Home. The two used suits were good quality and clinched the deal, the man made him a good offer for the job lot . . . to be paid in three months time.

Same thing all over again: Abel couldn't wait. Once more he explained that he was not wealthy.

Then I'll give you a promissory note and you can get the money from the bank, said the man.

By now Abel had lost interest in the whole business. He said: You go and get the money

The man left, came back with the money, took the clothes and away he went.

Abel let out a sight of relief. Puh – all this bother just to pay his board and boarding, it was like giving it away to strangers. What did he gain by it? And when he went down to the office and handed over the 'good offer', they just looked at him. It was almost nothing.

The rest tomorrow, said Abel.

But not tomorrow, nor the week after either. Not until the people at the Seamen's Home once again resorted to his stepmother Lolla.

Are you short of money? asked Lolla.

122

He smiled: You've got troubles of your own. I'll pay tomorrow.

Of course, Abel had paid off the house for Lili, married to Alex, but now she'd begun borrowing on the property and eating away at its value. What choice did she have? Her husband was gone and she heard nothing from him, and her mother the waffle-seller couldn't keep the lot of them fed.

The bank was helpful to Lili, in the end they gave her a bigger loan on the house, then Abel turned up and borrowed from the loan. As someone who'd once done accounting herself Lili must have thought the whole business was crazy, but Abel smiled. He'd paid off the bill at his lodgings now, and they had enough to see them through the next few months as well, spring was on its way again with its light nights, they were comfortable and warm in the house and life was good. In the evening they put the children to bed in the little bedroom while they used the bed in the living room.

Early one morning they woke to the sound of someone padding about outside the house. Lili jumped up out of bed and had a look. It's Alex! she hissed.

Abel started pulling on his clothes, but it was too late, the front door shook and Alex was standing outside shouting: Come out of there!

Abel went out just as he was. He carried his shoes in his hand.

It was daylight already, and they stood there a moment looking at each other. Alex began swearing, it wasn't like him. He didn't say a lot but his words were angry and full of threat. And now I'm going to shoot you! he said.

Abel bent forward to put on his shoes.

Didn't you hear me? I'm going to shoot you.

You're an idiot, muttered Abel.

There was a bang.

Abel straightened up and said: I believe that gun you're shooting with belongs to me.

Alex fired again, and this time his aim was better. Abel groaned: Ouch! What the hell are you playing at?

Lili appeared in the doorway and called out to the two of them: Are you shooting? Who fired the shot?

123

Him, said Abel. With my gun. He's the one who pinched my gun, I was telling you about it. Terrific guy, eh?

Get out of here, Alex said.

You're forgetting that he saved your life once, said Lili.

Alex jumped up and down and shouted again: If you don't get out of here I'm going to shoot you dead!

Neither of them made a fuss about the wound, but since Abel was bleeding profusely from his right arm Lili ran inside to get something to put round it. She made a dreadful mess of it, being one of those people who can't stand the sight of blood.

No, *above* the wound, for Christ's sake! Tight! Pull it hard! Ouch, it's come loose again!

Lili, at a loss, shouted to her husband: Can't you come here and give it a good pull?

No, answered Alex.

Abel: I'm no good with my left hand, otherwise I would do it myself.

Alex *do* come here and help us! called Lili.

No, said Alex. But he put down the gun and came anyway.

Get away! said Abel. He took one end of the bandage between his teeth and managed to bind up his arm himself. That's it. He picked up the gun from the ground and examined it: It's mine alright. You thieving monkey, you're nothing but a lowdown yellow-belly!

Go inside and get your clothes, said Lili.

Yes, that's right! shouted Alex after him. Tidy up after yourself, you dirty wifestealer!

He did once save your life, said Lili.

They continued to talk about Abel after he had gone. Alex was sober and his talk was ugly. To begin with he refused to enter the living room. After him? he said. No thank you, I won't. And even after he had entered the living room he walked around, sniffing and looking out for anything Abel might have left behind.

What this? he asked. Are these his underpants?

No, Lili said at once, they're mine.

So you've started wearing men's underpants?

Lili: I've had to make do with whatever I could while you've been away. Things have been tight . . .

He pulls off his jacket and stands with it in his hand for a moment while he thinks over her answer: Were men's underpants cheaper? He gave up. Instead he asked her: Has he really been living here with you?

Lili said nothing.

Has he, I'm asking you?

Lili: Well you weren't here.

Alex digs deeper, prods, wants to know more, wants details. Lili answers now and then.

How often has he been here?

No, no often. Practically just only this time. This once.

Abruptly he goes and opens the door to the small bedroom, peers in and backs out again: How many are there?

Lili says nothing.

I thought I saw three?

But you weren't here, Alex.

He sat down. Sitting down seemed to do him good. I thought I saw three, he said.

You never came back, she said.

Can you explain to me why there are three?

Lili: Doesn't Lovise Rolandsen have children? She's got nine now. D'you think her husband's the father of all of them?

Why wouldn't he be the father?

Tengvald? she said. He couldn't father a sparrow!

Alex thought about it: Well then I guess your friend is a little different from him, that's what it looks like.

Don't say that, Alex, and don't mention him any more. You're the only man for me, Alex.

He visibly softened at this, but he had to reject it as empty talk, lies and falsehoods: D'you think I've got the time to listen to stuff like that?

I've cried and waited and waited so long for you that it's affected my mind.

The hell you have. And by the way, he said and puffed out his chest, you've no need to think I've been going without either. There was a fair few of them after me.

Oh I don't doubt that, said Lili.

125

Oh yes, but I didn't insinuate myself into married women and their families, like that repulsive lecherous friend of yours.

No, you're right, I don't understand how I could have done it. Because he's not a lot more than nothing to me.

Didn't you tell him you were a married woman?

Of course. And that the only man I loved was my husband! Lili went along with everything now. She moved in close to him and starting taking off some of the clothes she'd thrown on. You must be tired, Alex, she said, don't you want to lie down?

Not with you, he said.

No, of course not. That's not what I meant either. I'll sit here quietly and not disturb you.

I'm just wondering whether I ought not to leave again once I've had a sleep. Just go out into the big wide world again, he said as he took off his clothes.

Lili started to whimper, but Alex remained hard and magnificent for a long while after he'd got into bed.

Are you cold? he asked at last.

No.

Listen to me now, don't sit there freezing! he ordered, and he made room for her beside him in the bed.

XIII

ABEL HAD A WOUND IN HIS ARM AND DIDN'T LIKE TO BE SEEN in the street wearing a bandage. He had another wound too, from the first bullet, but that could be left to heal itself. He socialised with the guests and employees at his lodgings and talked to them. They told him a lot of things he didn't know, right now there was an incredible rumour going round, a hair-raising rumour, and he had to ask Lolla if she'd heard it.

Oh yes, Lolla had heard it. Lolla heard everything, she missed nothing. But this whole rumour was nothing but disgraceful gossip. Young Clemens and his wife who were so fond of each other and always stuck by each other, wherever one of them went the other was there too? Don't you believe a word of it, Abel!

Did they never fall out with each other?

No, never. Good people, wealthy people. And even if they're not all that wealthy anymore they're still good people, the wife is the loveliest person I know. And the Magistrate's whole family – how do you think they would deal with such a scandal!

They say it's young Gulliksen.

Yes and that's nonsense too, said Lolla. These Gulliksens – no, no-one can tell me there's any truth in that. Don't I know William Gulliksen? He was after me once too.

Filthy rich, people say.

Yes and that's the only reason. At heart he's a lovely person, and always well turned-out. He wasn't up to much before, but he's got a grip on himself. Although I don't know – they aren't cultured people. He tried to get me drunk once.

Did he, says Abel, without interest.

And tried to kiss me.

Silence.

Lolla looks sideways at him: Oh there's quite a few been after me. But the one I care about doesn't care about me. So here I am.

Abel: Do you think it's him or her who wants the divorce?

Lolla far away: Divorce? Neither of them.

That's the thing about wealth. Wealthiest in town, I heard.

Well – Fredriksen out at the manor house is still the big chief! Lolla voices a thought: Can you understand why Fredriksen can never get his drunk of a brother away from the *Sparrow*?

What? Is that any skin off your nose?

Yes it is, it tears me up. That lovely boat in the hands of Ulrik Fredriksen and his *trisa*!

Have you got shares in the *Sparrow*?

How could I have? But it would be a good investment. I hear the *Sparrow* gives six percent, year in and year out. That's more than the bank gives.

Abel yawns: It bores me, this with my arm.

What's actually the matter with your arm?

A boil.

At one point he was a little worried there might be trouble about the bracelet. The papers had reported the incident under the headline 'Church robbed', and it was much discussed at his lodgings: How could

128

people be so wicked! A wonder they weren't struck down by lightning! He would have advised Olga to be seen with the bracelet as little as possible for a while, but she was nowhere around. Anyway she'd manage just fine if anything came up – after all, she could get women to wear their hats back to front. Why should he get involved?

It was of more concern to him that at his lodgings they had started presenting him with a weekly bill. A funny business, it was as though they didn't trust him. He paid the first two with a smile, and when the third came he also smiled but said he hoped he would be able to manage it tomorrow or soon after. And when another week passed with no payment he was evicted. All very curious.

But it was best that way, this fuss over payment was disagreeable. He packed his things, his arm had recovered now and he could carry them, all he possessed of earthly goods.

And right then little Regina arrived, Alex and Lili's daughter, she brought a note from her mother: was Abel in a position to help them, because now they were broke again?

He jotted down his answer, short and sweet, on the note: Yes of course, later on today. You'll find me in the shack this evening.

But little Regina wasn't finished.

She was a big girl now and had lately been wandering the streets down by the harbour and visiting the rooms in the Seamen's Home selling copies of religious pamphlets to the sailor boys. Once Abel had bought 'God's ten commandments' from her, now she was selling 'The Silent Comforter', a whole pile of them. She kept a percentage of the sale.

So Abel bought 'The Silent Comforter' as well and put it on one side.

You should hang it up, she said.

But there were no nails or hammer or whatever.

She felt around for a moment and said: You can always hang it on a safety pin, but I only have one safety pin, and I've promised that to the man in number 8, if I can persuade him to buy one.

Strange kid that Regina, a pretty face but just at the moment not a tooth in her head.

Won't he buy? asked Abel.

Oh yes, I'm sure I can persuade him. Promise to come if I scream. What?

Well, he wants me to sit on his lap.

Abel thought it over: Then it probably isn't worth going in to him. Oh yes, I'll talk him round.

Strange kid. She didn't want to lose that sale. He offered to give her a krone not to go, but that didn't satisfy her.

She was gone just a short while and then whispered through the door that she'd talked him into it.

It wasn't too bad in the shack now that the scrap-merchant had cleared it out, it was starting to look like a living-room, in Abel's view. He might think about buying a heater for his living-room.

He could never be evicted from here, the shack belonged to the railways and it had been abandoned for ten, twenty years. Old Brodersen had paid rent on it because he was such a stickler for things like that, but Abel paid no rent nor was any asked.

Up to now he'd been getting his food from Gulliksen's, young Gulliksen never said no to him. Abel's needs were so few, he was used to going without.

When Lili came by that evening having a good time and that kind of thing were not on her mind. Far from it. She talked about Alex, he'd taken the whole thing very well and had quietened down now after she'd promised never to cheat on him again. She had no need to either, Alex was enough of a man, no problems there. And what about it, Abel, can you help us?

Of course, he said, and he showed her his food. Just take all you can carry.

Lili stammered: Yes, but—

Oh yes, everything you can carry. I'll be fine.

But that isn't it. Don't you have money?

Abel smiled: Money? No.

Lili speechless.

Maybe a couple of kroner, he said and dug into his pocket.

Lili: A couple of kroner, what good is that? The bank wants interest, regular payments. I've got several small loans and then that last big one.

They were both silent for a while. Abel said: The bank can wait. Because I don't have any money. I had to pay my arrears at the Seamen's Home.

The quick-thinking cashier in Lili woke up: But wait, isn't it a fact that you borrowed money on my loan?

Abel gaped: Right. Well, that is—

Then can't you pay me back that?

Abel thought about this: Not right now, he managed to blurt out. Not this evening.

Well then, when?

Later. I've got a few things to sort out first.

When she left she took along with her most of the food, but it really didn't matter to him. He had a place to be, so to speak his own house, what people called a 'furnished apartment'. Still lying about in odd corners were a variety of things the scrap-merchant couldn't be bothered to take. He found a knife in its sheath, rusted all over but it could be cleaned, an alarm-clock he might be able to repair, a saucepan with a hole rusted through the bottom, a defective paraffin cooker, a broken tin candlestick-holder, some old nails in a box, a piece of knitting his mother had started on – worthless things being eaten up by rust and moths, they meant nothing to him, though he recognised them all from his childhood at the lighthouse. His father kept everything, couldn't bear to throw anything away, and his mother always ill and unable to tidy up.

But living among thick dust and broken pots didn't bother Abel one bit, in matters like that his demands were simple, and he didn't even need to lock his door to feel as though he were at peace in his own home. His humour was good and he lived a life of simple well-being. The floorboards moved up and down, and there wasn't even floor everywhere, but he didn't even try to straighten things up in the house, or clean the windows, or put his candlestick-holder on the table in an attempt to make the most out of what he had. He had a good-sized window with six panes in it, one of them was gone now, but it didn't matter. Directly outside the window was a high embankment that carried the railway line, if he wanted to see the sky he had to squat down. On three sides he was hemmed in by shacks, with the embankment on the fourth. It was good,

good to feel hemmed in like that and not have much room, he didn't hear all the bellowing of the age, of the newspapers, of the people, he wasn't curious, he wasn't reading over anyone's shoulder.

Then how could any news from town ever find its way down into his hidden-away nook? Oh, but it could. Now and then he would take a stroll through the streets, sometimes he sat on a bench down by the fish-dock and talked to people, with the average, decent people of the town, a postman, a custom's man. He sits there and chats, smoking away on his pipe.

Young Clemens passes by on his way from the office. Though Abel is on doffing terms with him he prefers to look down and offer no greeting.

Clemens makes the approach: No, no, don't get up, it's just that it's such a long time since I've seen you. You well?

Yes, replies Abel, tolerably well.

Clemens is carrying a black briefcase, as though he's on his way home to do some more work. His hair is longer than usual over his ears, he looks older.

And you? Asks Abel.

Yes thanks. You know, one day at a time.

Olga well?

Yes, Olga has trouble with her nerves, but apart from that . . . It's the time of year, I've heard of a number of people who suffer like that. Sorry for disturbing you. Shall I say hello to Olga?

He doffs his hat and leaves. Clothes nicely brushed, crease in his trousers, a neat man. But then there was that hair over the ears, and there was something subdued about him. Had something happened? At least he was a man who could carry a burden without panting in people's faces.

I hear he's getting divorced from his wife, whispers the postman.

I've hear there's nothing in it, answers Abel.

Oh yes. That's to say, it's the wife.

She'll probably change her mind.

She isn't used to living on a law clerk's wages.

There's a lot live on less, says Abel.

That's true enough, but . . . They left on the *Sparrow* this morning. Who left?

132

I was out with the mail at six o'clock. Gulliksen was first to arrive and went on board. Then she came. Said they were just taking a trip.

Abel wasn't interested in any more gossip and said: It's a very common thing to take a little trip to the country on the *Sparrow*. Go on board in the morning and come back again next day in the evening. He yawned and stood up.

What do you get up to during the day? ask the postman.

Not a lot. I've just fixed a cooker that was just lying round.

Do you cook for yourself?

Yes, cooking for myself now.

Not living at the Seamen's Home any more?

No, I'm living in a shack, down by the vacant lots.

The postman: I'm sorry. I'm only asking in case I get any letters for you.

I doubt there'll be any letters for me.

He took a haddock back with him from the dock, and a can of paraffin. Sure he could cook the haddock himself, he could fry it himself too, if he wanted. It had been an easy matter for him to repair the paraffin cooker and mend the holes in the saucepan. That time the cook fell overboard on the Spanish Main he'd cooked and fried for a whole ship's crew. No problem there.

He made his own days good. After dining well and sumptuously on a fish or a piece of calf's liver he could doze for a long time, he had a bed with bedclothes he could lie down on, as well as a sofa. And come the spring he would definitely plant a bucketful of potatoes on the embankment in front of the window. He'd done that in Kentucky.

During the course of that winter Lili often called in and asked for money. But he had no money. Those who owed him didn't pay up, and he'd actually had to sell quite a few things just to have enough for his daily needs. Gulliksen the grocer asked for his money too, and then stopped giving him credit. That wretched Robertsen the Customs man never did sell his boats and pay him as he'd promised to. There were a couple of other outstanding debts too that Abel, for shame, couldn't bring himself to claim. Given the circumstances, how could he afford to give any more to Lili? She complained bitterly about it, Alex was unemployed, the bank was on at her, they had even had to beg for money from her mother, the waffle lady.

They sat there and discussed things and the mood was glum, and there was no talk about having a good time together and suchlike, no, Lili was crying. To comfort her he reached out and tried to hold round her, but at that she reacted like a furious child and cried out No at the top of her voice. What do you take me for? said Lili.

She stayed away for a month, and when she came again it was only to show him a letter from the bank.

He read the letter and said: No, this is all wrong.

Wrong? Do you understand just how wrong it is? They're selling the house!

Sit down, Lili, calm down.

Sit down? On the sofa, you mean? So you can sit down beside me?

Abel gaped.

I know you, she said. But never again, do you understand? Never again! But she sat down on the sofa.

Abel said with a smile: Alex must have worked some kind of miracle on you.

Yes he has, she answered. But it's this other thing we've got to talk about.

It was the same thing over and over again, one of them was in need, and the other could do nothing to help.

You sit down too! she said angrily. You stand there wondering and wondering if you dare sit down beside me but I don't want you too. It was different when you paid off the mortgage on the house and had clothes and food for us, I would need to have been some kind of monster not to be good to you then. And anyway, Alex wasn't around then. What, you're smiling?

I didn't smile.

Oh yes, you smiled. And it's true, we did begin before Alex went away. But is that all going to be all my fault now too? She howled and threw herself down on the sofa.

Completely uninhibited, wild talk, some of it unreasonable, some of it truthful too.

I would like so much to help you, he said.

At once she was on her feet again: So you really can't? That's mean! You borrowed from me, you sat waiting for me to come back from the bank and borrowed from me. And now they're selling the house. Can't you see what it's doing to me?

It's not my fault, he said.

No, but what use is that?

Abel said nothing.

And you can't borrow money on it?

No – not a second time, he said, and looked at her. He said it like that so she would have time to think it through.

But Lili didn't think it through, she said: That's so shabby. After all we've shared together.

I cannot! Do you hear me, Lili? So many thousand? I don't have that kind of money . . .

After she left Abel took the table by the window and carried it down to the scrap-dealer, then he went back for his bedclothes and all told he got a fair price, fifteen kroner for the lot. Now that winter was almost over he had no need of duvets and blankets on his bed, and anyway there was always his trusty grey-brown ulster from America. He had no more need of a table in the living room than he had of cloth on the table.

On his way home he found a useful chest he could use as a table, and straightaway he had the idea of painting it. He had these great ideas now and then. Replace that missing window-pane. Buy a heater for the living room . . .

He gathered up the notes and put them in an envelope. See here, he said, as though he were talking to a messenger, see here, take this money and give it to Lili!

And since he had no messenger to send he went himself.

Alex was in the living room. He was lying on the floor in his shirtsleeves with no shoes on, playing with the two little ones. He sat down in a chair, showed no sign of unpleasantness, far from it, he was friendly, it was amazing. How are things? he said.

Abel looked around. Here too there was quite a bit of furniture missing. There wasn't even a clock on the wall. Where the rose-painted corner cupboard had stood there was now a mark on the wallpaper.

Where's Regina? asked Abel – so as to avoid asking for Lili.

If she's not out shopping then probably with her grandmother, said Alex. She often visits her grandmother. Did you want a word with her?

No. Yes, it's just that I've got something for her.

Alex looked dull, dulled by years of hard times and no work. He had never been a particularly unusual person, just a bit better-looking than the average man, with his long eyelashes and his cupid's bow lips. He could have had one of Captain Norum's daughters in his time, but Lili got him.

D'you recognise these two? he asked.

Abel looked at the two little ones and said: They've grown.

The funny thing about them is, they hardly ever cry.

Really.

Just the odd whimper. Now Regina, she howled and screamed. Those two there are completely different.

Abel said: They're mine.

Yours? No!

It's true.

No, yours? Never in this world!

Abel wanted to hand over the notes before Lili came. No purpose could be served by hanging around here.

If you were to come and claim them you couldn't have them, said Alex.

Can you deliver this to Regina or to Lili, whichever you like.

Put it down there. I've grown fond of them, see. They can hardly stand up, but they come and hold on between my knees. Hold on tight! I tell them. On tight! they answer, and hold on. Then they look up at me: What am I going to get them to do now? Spit on my trousers! I say, just for fun. And they spit and laugh. Because there's nothing they enjoy more than making a mess. I've heard it said that all children are like that.

It's just a small amount, said Abel. It's all I have.

Alex went on: I suppose you know the youngest is a boy?

Yes, I heard that.

His mother thinks he's my favourite, but that's nonsense. I make no distinction. But Regina, she's too big and grown up now.

*

Lolla had been out searching for him dawn to dusk and so far he had managed to avoid her. She knew he was living down in one of the shacks, but there were so many of them, each trader had his own. She wanted to see him and she left messages all over the place that he should go to the house on the beach, but Abel didn't go. The postman found his shack one day and delivered a letter to him, Abel was just lying there. There was no proper street outside or path, he was more or less enclosed by planks you had to climb over, and some barbed wire you had to wriggle under, what he usually did was sneak along the railway line and down the embankment, though that was strictly forbidden. It took a lot of cunning to surprise him in his lair, but Lolla managed it one morning, just as he was on his way out of the door.

I've been looking for you, she said. I've no idea where you are from one's year's end to the next. Have I offended you in some way?

To calm her down he made a joke of it and said: I've got news for you, someone told me that Ulrik Fredriksen has resigned from the *Sparrow*.

I know that, she said.

So now you're happy I suppose?

Lolla wasn't in a joking mood: I can give you another bit of news – your house is going to be sold.

What?

That house you paid off for that Lili.

Oh, that! said Abel.

They're advertising it now. And you knew nothing about it?

Abel: They surely can't just sell the house?

Oh yes they can. For three or four bad debts.

Abel said nothing.

I suppose it's them who've gone and eaten up your house?

Abel: Strictly speaking – it was so long ago – no of course it isn't them who've eaten it up.

Well I've been to the bank and it wasn't you who was doing the borrowing.

Me? No. Why would I want to borrow?

No. So now it's a question of whether that IOU you have is in order.

137

Oh yes, said Abel, it's in order alright.

Do you have it?

Lolla, it was such a long time ago, said Abel. I don't know, you're so thorough. But from one thing to another: D'you know why Ulrik Fredriksen resigned?

Lolla just looked at him and didn't reply.

Long silence.

Lolla appeared to come to some agreement with herself, not that she gave a few ponderous nods, but she did press her lips together. She looked round the shack: an empty room now, empty bed, a paraffin cooker, pots and pans, some fish leftovers on a chest beneath the window. She caught sight of her own letter and picked it up. You're not thinking of staying here? she said.

No.

No, you're not?

Just for a while, a few days. Just for fun. But actually I am thinking of doing something. I sit here and I'm working really hard at it, this business of trying to be a somebody.

Yes yes yes.

In the spring, I said. Don't you remember me saying in the spring?

Yes I do – that was two years ago.

Abel furrowed his brow: Was there something you wanted?

No, I'm leaving, she said and stood up. But she didn't really want to hurt this simple fool, this piece of human flotsam from the depths of Kentucky, she wished him well, wished him much too well. Can't you come and live with us in the house on the beach? she asked.

My dear Lolla, he said, you don't understand my sense of fun. I want to stay here for a while. I'm going to paint the place. Do it up.

There was no future in it so Lolla dropped the subject: You wondered why Ulrik Fredriksen resigned. Well, it was because his chief stewardess was leaving. She wants to go ashore, so Ulrik wants to go ashore too. Handed in three months notice.

Abel was only half-listening.

That was the only thing that could have got him to go ashore. He's

138

finishing the first of June. And yes, I admit it, I'm glad he's leaving the *Sparrow*. But does anyone know what he sees in that stewardess? He can't seem to do without her.

Who? asked Abel.

Who? Alright, I'm leaving.

Lolla had several things to do. She visited the tailor and ordered two suits in the same sizes as before – one was to be dark blue and with a double-breasted waistcoat. The buttons she would provide herself.

At three o'clock she went to see young Clemens in his office at home.

XIV

NO DOUBT ABOUT IT, LOLLO KEPT UP WITH ALL THE NEWS IN town. Now she'd just heard that Olga had moved back home to the chemist's, but she didn't believe it. Decent people didn't do things like that, she reasoned, and if Fru Olga had done it then she must have had her reasons, but she couldn't have any reasons. The only thing might be that young Clemens was impossible to get along with. But then, he wasn't.

She would be cultured and courteous and sensitive, but she was not going to enter his office like a former maid come to do his dusting. She had worked out what she was going to say.

She greeted him and said with a smile: Now I know you turned me down once before and wouldn't help me, but—

She stopped right there.

Won't you take a seat, he said and pulled out a chair for her, even though it was already pulled out enough.

She sat down and went on: But today I'm here on behalf of some-one else.

He was taken aback. Had she perhaps come with a message from his wife? She and Lolla were good friends. It was quite possible.

I'm here for Abel Brodersen, she said.

Ah, Abel Brodersen, I see. Hm. No, about that other time, Lolla – may I call you Lolla? – there was a reason for that.

I'm sure there was. It was probably too vulgar for you.

Ah, so that's what you think! He got to his feet and said: On my honour, that was not the reason! And when he sat down again, he was blushing. Now, what was this about Abel Brodersen?

It was like this, and like this: What was the position of the house out by the sawmill in which Abel had security. What about the docu-mentation? His security?

Clemens looked blank. He furrowed his brow, looked up under B in the ledger. Nothing, no Brodersen.

That's what I was afraid of, she said.

He's getting me mixed up with some other solicitor.

Yes, he's got mixed up.

There's something strange about Brodersen, said Clemens after a silence. He's different from the rest of us. I have a feeling that in some way or other he's his own worst enemy.

I just don't understand him, said Lolla.

Nor do I. Myself, people like me, we're simply too normal to understand him.

Do you think there's something wrong with him? He mentioned that he once got sunstroke in America. Perhaps that had some effect on him? D'you think something's wrong with him?

In what way? No, at least, not as regards his intelligence. I really don't understand it, I've only spoken to him a couple of times. He was very friendly, it was a pleasure to be in his company. Olga knows him, ask her, they've been friends since childhood. Olga isn't here at the moment, but I'm sure you'll run into her.

He's not interested in getting on in the world, said Lolla.

No. But is that really so absolutely necessary? Does he find it a cause for unhappiness himself?

141

I don't know. It's degrading for him.

Is that what he feels?

I don't think so.

There, you see! Most of us achieve the little we do because we're so normal. He's from some sort of border region quite unfamiliar to us.

Lolla blushed and said: It's a comfort to hear you say that! After all, I've become quite close to him, in a way we're – I mean—

I know, said Clemens when she stopped.

It isn't natural for a young man not to want to be something, to achieve something.

No. Not from our way of looking at things. He might also have suffered some kind of setback, something that broke his will. Or more likely sapped his energy, because my impression is that he does have willpower of a sort. He wants to do what he wants to do.

He was married in America once, do you think that might be what did it?

I don't know. It might be, but I don't know about such things, I'm a solicitor.

If she dragged him into the gutter with her?

The gutter? asked Clemens. Did they live in the gutter?

Yes. The way he talks about it. They lived like trash.

For how long?

I don't know. Several years. It was an absolutely awful life. And then she was shot.

Did they fall out?

He says no, he was so besotted with her. He's still got the gun, and he speaks so warmly of her. It doesn't make sense.

No, said Clemens. He seems to be avoiding me recently, I don't know why. Does he drink?

No, not even that, said Lolla. He's just apathetic and doesn't care about anything. Now he's living down in one of those shacks by the vacant lots.

Surely there's no need for that?

No, not at all. But it's what he wants.

Then perhaps it's merely that he wants to seem a little out of the ordinary?

Oh if only it were that! But he's not the type that wants people to notice him. Well, forgive me for taking up so much of your time, but I feel so worried about him.

Don't go just yet, Lolla, there was something . . . I wanted to ask if you couldn't come here and stay?

Total silence.

Run things for me, he said.

Run the house? she managed to ask.

Yes, run the house. I told you Olga isn't here – no, her nerves, it's the spring, she wants to try living at home at the chemist's for a period. So I'm a little bit of a mess right now. I need someone.

I can't, she answered.

I thought of you, he went on. You're familiar with the place and could arrange everything just as you please.

Lolla shook her head: There's something else I want to do.

Ah, he said. Well then, please do forgive me!

You see I can't, she said and stood up.

He stood up as well: No, it was probably a bit too forward of me.

No, no, no you mustn't say that! I still remember how good it was here. And all the books I could borrow – and just everything!

Listen, would you like to borrow some books now?

Lolla: I couldn't, could I?

Couldn't? Go right in, you know where they are. The newest ones are on the bedside tables.

She went out, stayed out a long time, very long time. When he peeked in she was standing there looking at herself in the mirror and fixing her hair. She'd really helped herself, came back in with a lot of books and put them down in front of him – would he help her choose?

Won't you take a seat again, he said. I'll find some paper to wrap the books in.

They packed, their hands touched, he didn't seem to mind, was actually looking for it – those big, sensual hands of hers.

Then when she was finished she got up, stood there uncertainly and didn't leave: May I ask you about something?

Yes, anything you like.

I'm so worried about that boy, d'you think he could hold down a proper job?

Well – that depends. What sort of job?

I hardly know whether I dare say this: as Captain of the *Sparrow*?

Silence. Clemens thought about it for a long time. Let us sit down, Lolla. I did hear that Ulrik Fredriksen is leaving, but that isn't necessarily the end of the story. Abel Brodersen has spent a long time at sea, he told me that once, but that isn't necessarily the end of the story either.

No. He isn't a Mate, he couldn't learn it, he says.

Ulrik Fredriksen wasn't a Mate either. So as regards that . . . But he had a brother in a position to give him the job. That was the deciding factor. So it's really a case of whether Brodersen has anything similar?

He's the majority shareholder in the boat.

Clemens leaned forward: Is he really? I thought that was Fredriksen out at the manor house?

Abel bought up Fredriksen's shares.

Ha ha! said Clemens. That's wonderful, that is at least of great significance. Fredriksen might perhaps also give him his personal support?

Yes, he promised me – or rather, Abel.

So then that's more or less it.

So perhaps he might get the job. But can he keep it?

Certainly. Anyway the ship already has an unusually good Mate. What's his own view?

He doesn't know anything about it yet.

Clemens was surprised: In that case how could he have bought the shares?

Er – through a third party, of course, said Lolla.

Clemens didn't want to pursue this any further. He thought for a while and said: Then it's probably best that he gets the whole story in one, now. That you drop the bomb.

Lolla: That's what I was thinking too. That's what I was hoping.

That he'll get a short sharp shock that'll set him on the right track. You're right, Lolla, that's good thinking.

In that case, will you put in a good word for him?

Me? he said. That wouldn't help. I'm nothing.

144

At the door he offered her his hand in farewell, though it was not called for.

I'll be back with the books, she said.

Yes, whenever you like. Come back, exchange them for others—

She pondered things over as she walked homewards. Clemens had seemed so strange, not surprising really, since Olga had gone off and left him. Three times he'd asked her to take a seat, as if he liked seeing her there. A good, kind man. Apologised for having offered her the housekeeper's job. Olga had no reason to leave him.

But Lolla had other things to think of. There was much to be organised on the occasion of a certain great day. She'd already got a lot done, laid her plans, stuck at it stubbornly for months and years, in a fashion sounded it out with Westman and a couple of the other members of the board of the *Sparrow*, and finally paid a visit to the tailor's – yes, she'd got a lot done, she was content.

The biggest *coup* was the shares, damned if that wasn't a *coup*! She knew very well she had to have the majority, without that she was powerless. And luck was on her side: Fredriksen out at the manor was more than willing to get rid of his shares at once as a way of cutting off a possible avenue of retreat for his brother. I must tell you, I'm a sick man, I need to turn everything into cash, he said. Oh, but he was a hard man to bargain with.

Look here, Abel must have your majority shareholding, and here's what he can pay for it, said Lolla, and took out her bankbook.

Fredriksen looked at it and said: Well that won't do. That's less than par. No, that won't do.

Sick as he was, and with hands like a corpse, he was still greedy, still clear-headed. Fru Fredriksen sat in a chair by the sickbed with furrows in her brow.

How many shares will you sell for what's in the account? Lolla asked straight out . . .

Fredriksen did the sums with his eyes closed. Then he pulled out a bunch of keys from under his pillow, held them out to his wife and said: They're on the left! Puh, just the least thing, my head goes to pieces. And me who always had his health! Who would've thought it?

145

After the shares had been counted he did the sums over again with his eyes closed to be quite sure, to be fair to her. Here you are, he said, I'll hold on to these seven, apart from that you can have the lot. It's daylight robbery.

That's above par!

Even so, it's daylight robbery. I would be stupid to sell at par, the boat makes six per cent and might even go up to eight.

Lolla: What did you pay the chemist for his shares?

What? asked Fredriksen. That was different, the chemist had to sell.

Lolla didn't dare push it any further, she picked up her shares and left. The wife showed her out.

The wife had sat there with a frown on her forehead in there, quietly shaking her head but never saying a word. The wife out at the manor house, known for the goodness of her heart. She had made it clear that she disapproved of her husband, yes, had it been up to her she would have let the shares go for next to nothing, that's the kind of lady from the big house she was. She had actually said nothing, only shown the visitor just how different she was from the man she was married to. Lolla was expecting a whispered word or two once they were alone in the corridor, and yes they came, those whispered words came: He's such a miser, it's nothing to do with me, as God as my witness! Having covered herself like that the wife probably expected a thank you in return, but Lolla just left. She liked the husband a whole lot better than the wife.

Lolla hurried to the bank, borrowed a small amount on the shares and returned to the manor house. Here you are! she said. And here you are, said Fredriksen back at her, there's six here – I'm retaining one for the voting rights, but that still makes you the majority shareholder . . . Swiftly done, basically fair enough, but in the end barefaced robbery. Fredriksen took care of his margins again, lay there in bed and earned himself a couple of thousand, but promised to give Abel a good reference – had heard of him, he'd saved a man's life up at the sawmill, knew his father—

Fru Fredriksen wasn't there this time around.

Now Lolla makes her way home with the parcel of books under

146

her arm and thinks back over the whole business and smiles. She has almost forgotten the business of the security in the house that Abel had once saved, it wasn't worth brooding on that anymore, the money was lost. Ah that Abel, worst of all to himself and a riddle to others. It pained her to see him waste his life so contentedly. He didn't complain, he smiled, but it hurt to see him smile. The offers she made to move into the house on the beach were always turned down, he mustn't be allowed to throw any more money away, the purchase of the shares would see to that. Abel didn't think in money, he had no understanding of it. So now there he sat, in a shack down by the vacant lots.

Lolla would arrange for the great rehabilitation, she would raise him up to a position of power and authority. The day was coming.

Now why so much kindness and concern for a stepson? Lolla herself was the only one who knew the answer to that.

Anyone else would have grown tired of struggling with the man, but she wasn't tired. Some anonymous nobody living in a shack, a nothing, a clown – it must have been something pretty strong for her even to notice his existence at all. Well alright. But as for any other reason she might have had – she could justify herself in the eyes of others: she was simply looking after her own interests, wasn't that obvious? Once Abel was captain, she would be stewardess on board the *Sparrow*. Nothing in the world would suit her better. No, she didn't want to be housekeeper for young Clemens, she had other plans, she wanted to be stewardess on the *Sparrow*. Be the hostess, with people under her, be the lady of the salon with only the Captain above her, be somebody. Many would envy her, strictly speaking she wasn't related to the Captain, but they were family, she was his stepmother, mother, she was in a powerful position. Lovise Rolandsen, Tengvald's wife, would like to be in her shoes. In the Robertsen household the girls would be fuming with envy. Let them fume—

Whatever else Lolla might be hiding in her heart – so she hadn't got mixed up with this Abel and his shack for his sake, but for her own. She was after a job and a livelihood. Clear enough. Fact.

It was not unthinkable that her short experience of life as a wife and then an unnatually young widow had been an embarrassment to her. The whole thing was a little comical, something to smile about. In people's eyes she'd been married but not wed, and after that a kind of serving maid to a dead old man. None of this suggested distinction, nor did it call for a fur collar on her overcoat.

Things were going to change.

When she got home there was a letter waiting from Olga: same request, different direction: the wife asking her to keep house for the husband. A letter written in haste, a rushed pile of rapid thoughts and hyphens, but not lacking in concern for the husband: He had no proper help – sorry for him, sad to think about. Couldn't do any more herself, it was over – but Lolla, you know the house inside out and please I'm asking you do it!!! He hasn't asked me to write this – but I feel for him, and since I left he has no-one. Don't whatever you do forget the oleander in the middle room – anyway, you know all about our house – Yours Ever, Olga.

Lolla indignant on behalf of young Clemens: Heard the like of it, leaving such a decent, kind man? She would say so to her face when she met her, even if Olga had once been her mistress—

She has a few words with her mother about something or other then goes out again. She's preoccupied, more restless than she needs to be, she goes up into town and buys some gents' underwear. June the first is still weeks away but she buys the gents underwear today, so she can make a nice job of embroidering the name and the number on it.

II

XV

AND TIME PASSED AND ABEL MADE LESS AND LESS OF HIMSELF. He didn't plant potatoes as he'd planned to, no, he went to the railway people and asked for permission to dig in the embankment but didn't get it. It left him free and not having to do it, so he felt no guilt. He was wretchedly poor by now, but he had a roof over his head and the odd fish to eat when he was lucky. Sometimes he was seen: Are you stealing my fish, you bugger? – You can have it back. – No,you have it!

And one day at a butcher's on the edge of town: Can I have this little piece of liver for my cat? – Have you got a cat? – Yes and a dog. – Where d'you live? – I live down by the vacant lots. – There are no houses there? – I live in one of the shacks. – You're a queer one! You can have the liver.

Life became more and more unreal, some inner truth was gone from it. He probably wouldn't have been able to put up with it had he not been used to it from his years in Kentucky, but now his days seemed almost unbelievably good and cosy. In the winter when the nights were blessedly dark he went out walking in the countryside and found both carrots and potatoes in cellars, now the nights were lighter and hampered him in his business. But life goes on, it was spring and summer in the world, lovers walking in the woods, and Abel had just had a tremendous piece of good fortune: he'd found an unlocked goods wagon standing on the tracks directly above his window. It was evening and quiet, no traffic. He made a hurried inspection of the wagon, and it was a simple matter for him and a real pleasure to jog down the embankment carrying a crate of tinned food. Couldn't have been closer, and no transport costs. When he got down into his room he read on the crate 'Norwegian salmon'. Lucky sod, nothing to compare to salmon. But what if there was meat in the wagon too? They canned all sorts of stuff at the factory, little sausages he'd heard of, meat balls. He's no longer lethargic, his head is working flat out, a moment later he's up by the goods wagon again, creeps in and reads on the crates. Salmon, salmon. It's full of other stuff too, so he has to clear things out the way, wood-products, chairs, hides and furs, gravestones from the stone-mason's. At last he finds the cases with the cocktail sausages and pushes one over to the doorway.

A man sticks his head in, redbearded from the eyes downwards.

Good, you're keeping your eyes open, Abel says to him.

What? How?

Aren't you the watchman?

I wasn't that far away, says the man and laughs maliciously.

Then you probably saw the fella who ran off with a crate?

Did someone run off with a crate?

Towards the market garden, says Abel and points uptheway.

The man looks uptheway: I was only just – dammit – I was just down at the quay for a minute. What was in the crate?

What do you think? Gravestones?

And what are you doing in this wagon? the man enquires suspiciously.

Well I'll tell you: he threw his knife at me, he could've killed me. I'm looking for the knife.

The man climbs in and he starts looking too.

By now Abel has eased his knife out of its sheath and says: Here it is!

Give it here! says the man. This will be handed over to the police.

You do that! That monster! He could've killed me

I'm wondering which crate it might have been.

There's nothing to wonder about. Go get your inventory and go over them.

They climb out of the wagon.

The man: Yes but there are so many inventories, one from each business. I'll have to go through the whole wagon.

Yes, and then the station-master will find out about it.

So what? Think I'm scared of the station-master?

You left your post.

I went down to quayside – dammit, I was hardly gone at all, way less than an hour. I had to see a man about something.

Abel gets ready to leave.

See here, says the man and hands the knife back, I'm not reporting it.

What?

No, there'll just be a lot of fuss. I'm not doing anything. You won't say anything?

Me? No.

But things didn't always go so smoothly, sometimes he was treated to a real mouthful and suffered humiliations that might have persuaded anyone else to stay at home.

Sometimes he strolled along to the railway station, when the trains were arriving or departing, and looked up the waffle-seller. He had, after all, in his good days equipped the woman with a wagon and basket and some start-capital, and now he walks up to her, cheeky as you like, and just takes a few of the waffles, his excuse being that he just wants to check the quality of her goods. The first time the woman put up with it with a smile, but when it happened again she protested: Hey, hey, don't empty the whole basket! The woman's anger didn't upset him too much, but if little Regina was there helping her grandmother it bothered him the way she looked up at him in surprise, as though she didn't recognise him from the time he bought 'The Silent Comforter' from her.

Down but not desperate, rarely really desperate. He didn't suffer, he was empty, alive in his easygoing way and kept himself afloat. Nor was he dull-witted. It took quite a bit of thinking to stay afloat, real creativity to work out his nefarious tricks, and pulling them off required all his concentration. Sometimes he managed it, sometimes not, could go either way, luck could change.

But there were many worse off than him.

Alex came to see him – Lili had probably shown him the way. He was shaven and clean.

We're up to our necks, said Alex. Soon we'll lose the house.

Look, are you hungry? said Abel and treated him to salmon.

This is good stuff, said Alex and ate. He looked around. There was nothing there, all the same he said: Lili thought we might be able to move in with you?

Here?

We've got our own bed and table and chairs, so it wouldn't be any bother to you. I see you've not got a stove. I was thinking if you had a stove we could've sold ours. That might fetch a bit. But I see there's no stove here.

Abel said nothing.

There's bags of room here, Alex went on, and we can fix that hole in the window. There's only four of us, Regina spends most of her time at her grandmother's. I don't see why it wouldn't work out, and naturally we'll bring our stove and install it.

Abel: Be quiet! You talk and talk. This is nonsense about selling the house.

You think so?

They won't be able to sell it. There are no workers left with the money.

Alex thought that over and said: I don't much care what happens, it's the children and Lili. I could happily go off travelling far and wide again all over the world, but it's no good, she's expecting another one any day now, it's like everything happens at once. But how about that Lovise Rolandsen with her nine! Some people just can't control themselves.

154

Shut up, d'you hear? Eat.

I can't eat any more. Don't you have a bit of bread?

No.

Alex wipes his oily fingers on his trousers and takes a piece of paper out of his shirt: It's my pleasure to show you this reference. You won't find many better than this.

Abel read it and said: Yes, and what good is this?

That's what the Engineer said too: what do you want with a reference? he said. I've got references too, but I still can't get a job, he said. Well it won't do me any harm to have one, I said and I got him to write it.

Yes it's a good reference, said Abel and yawned.

Alex chuckled to himself: Ha, he wouldn't've written the way he did if he'd known everything.

Really?

I'm not saying anything. All I'm saying is that his wife is full of energy. A mother of four and still she's crazy. You won't believe this, but while he was writing the reference she sat there giving me the eye and making signs to me just like when we were young.

You knew her before?

Yes, both before and after.

Then the children are yours.

No, she says, not all.

Abel: You're bragging because you're so handsome and irresistible. But you weren't enough for Lili.

Wasn't I enough? asked Alex. I was enough alright, but I couldn't get excited about her all the time she was sitting in that office so blue and skinny.

Just shut up with this rubbish, Alex, I get so tired of listening to you.

I guess I'll take what's left home for the kids, said Alex and shoved the tin inside his shirt front.

Lili came later that evening. She was calmer than the last time and smiled slightly: I heard you had salmon?

Abel lifted up a loose plank and retrieved a tin from under the floor.

155

Oh a whole tin! I got such a craving for salmon, can you imagine that? I'm definitely going to buy myself a tin when I get the money.

Abel: You can't move here, it's out of the question.

Is it really? We'll bring our furniture and the stove.

You and Alex don't understand at all. We're not even allowed to have a fireplace here.

Oh, said Lili and was silent for a moment. Do you have anything else besides salmon?

No. Maybe you wanted syrup with it?

Ha ha ha! Lili laughed. But seriously: there's room enough here, and you've got the paraffin stove to cook on.

Abel tired: Do what you like.

Our bed can go *there*. And I want a curtain.

Do what you like, I'm telling you.

There's no need for you to move out if we do.

Well . . .

No, not if I have a curtain up. But I don't want anything to do with you. Don't go getting any ideas.

No.

Because I won't.

Babble and chatter. Abel got up from the edge of the bed where he was sitting and stretched.

She looked at him and said: You don't shave. Did you see how smart and clean-shaven Alex was?

Yes you have a handsome husband. But now you better go, Lili. Coming out here so late it might start people talking.

Alright then. I just feel sorry for you, Abel. Are you all on your own here in this shack?

A cat comes to see me now and then.

Alone day and night, she said. And you sleep on that bare mattress? You had such fine underwear once upon a time! She stood up and felt the mattress, prodded it to see if it moved up and down, then she turned round and put her arms around his waist: I feel sorry for you, you're alone day and night—

Footsteps outside.

156

Alex! she said. Why does he bother? He knows I'd never be untrue to him.

It's warm in the sea already and the sun is shining. Abel washes his shirt in a stream, rinses it and hangs it on a bush to dry. Then he wades into the sea.

That's all it takes, he sets off back home well pleased with himself and determined to repeat the piece of bravado often, absolutely and definitely. The world is alive, the grass is growing, people are laughing, Abel puts his nose in the air. He's no older than Alex, who is handsome but vacuous, Lili was so strange, the way she held him round the waist. It had been a long time since the last time.

Lili was right to say he was unshaven. For a long time now he'd been plucking the hairs out of his beard with a rusty pair of pliers, but it took an age.

He finds a barber's down by the market garden, enters and says: You're not doing anything, you might trim a little bit off this beard.

Certainly.

Yes but this that and the one thing and the other – but I can offer you this knife for your trouble.

And just who are you?

Sailor.

Aha, on shore leave and flat broke. Sit yourself down.

They carry on talking while he's being shaved, Abel has to tell him whose son he is . . .

Really, old lighthouse keeper Brodersen, I remember reading in the papers that he was dead. A respected and capable man. But you never amounted to anything?

No.

Isn't that a bit sad when you think about it?

What did your father do? asks Abel.

My father? He was a teacher and a sexton in these parts. Mayor for many years. I'm not a patch on him, no.

Then I'll say yes. It's rare for a son to match his father, you almost never hear of it. But they boast of the father. Your son will hear the same thing: he's not a patch on his father!

157

But I'm nothing much, says the barber, so I hope that all three of my sons'll be more than I am. And don't think I'm complaining about my lot, I'm not. I'm a trained professional, I've got my own business and I don't owe anyone anything.

Abel nods: Just exactly what my father would have said.

Well what more can we say? Every man gets what fate deals out to him.

Abel: My father couldn't have lived for a single day the way I live year in and year out. He didn't have the potential in him for it. He had the potential in him to be a respected man, something I don't have. What he had was the potentional to live out a life anyone else could have lived out here on earth in exactly the way they would have lived it, if not even better.

Maybe the barber doesn't quite get all this, but he says: You're a big talker. As though you're something completely different from what you appear to be.

Will be, says Abel, will be something completely different. I've made up my mind about that. I've just been waiting for the right time of year to get started.

I see, says the barber, indicating with a bow that he's finished.

D'you want the knife?

No, no. Where d'you live, where d'you hang out?

Down in town. By the vacant lots. I live in a shack.

The barber shakes his head.

Oh it's not that bad. It's summer now.

I'm just standing here thinking – that's the funny thing, we can all find ourselves on our uppers. You're very welcome to a razor blade to fix yourself with. I've got so many I can't use in the business any longer. Sit down again a moment and I'll adjust it for you.

They carry on talking while he does so.

You've got two chairs here, d'you need that?

Oh yes. Especially on Saturdays when people want to look their best for Sunday. Or for that matter any special day. Then I'm run off my feet, my eldest boy does the lathering and I cut the hair and trim the beards.

If you had an enemy I suppose you could easily kill him in the chair?

158

That never happens. An enemy would go to another barber.

D'you cut hair for many women?

Not many. Most of them go to the ladies hairdresser.

Sound, regular thought-processes and commonsense answers. An everyday life without fate, without disturbances. The family lives above, now and then they drop something up there with a loud crash, but it doesn't matter. When it's time to eat the son is there to relieve him, and if a customer comes the boy can already shave a farmer or a fisherman, but if it's a gentleman with a cane and gloves then he rings upstairs for the father. The whole thing hums along wonderfully well.

Abel accepts the blade.

It's really nothing, says the barber.

For me this is a blade that has come into my hands by a piece of real good fortune, says Abel, determined to make a big thing of it. I'll keep hold of my pocket so it doesn't fall out on the way home.

A few days later he helps the chemist and Olga when they get a puncture. One corner of the car is up on the pavement and the chemist is standing there looking at it. People passing by but he doesn't ask anyone for help.

Abel! Olga calls.

Ah, is that you, Brodersen. I was unfortunate enough to land on the pavement.

It doesn't look too bad really.

Abel gets in and backs the car down. Olga is sitting beside him all made-up and stylish, fresh and lovely. You'll have to get out a moment, he says, I need to get at the tool kit.

Alright. I could have got out straightaway, but I don't like standing there and being stared at.

Your looks can stand it, Olga.

Abel! she cried, very surprised, are you flirting with me?

He jacked the car up and changed the tyre as the chemist stood there making small talk: That was a piece of good luck your coming along, Brodersen! See, I was going too fast to get a puncture, so I mounted the kerb. Thank goodness I didn't knock anyone down. Thank you so much, Brodersen, that's extremely kind.

Olga has her own chat with him on the quiet: How funny that whenever I get in trouble you're there to help!

Then you're not in trouble that often, Olga.

It's so easy to ask you. I did want to talk to you, but it's so difficult. My husband's alone now, you know that?

I did hear something.

Yes, alone. Can you persuade Lolla to help him?

That I don't know.

She's so good and she knows our place inside out. That way he wouldn't notice my absence so much. I feel sorry for him.

I could mention it to her.

Thanks. She told me no in a letter, but maybe you can persuade her.

Abel shakes his head: No, well in that case – I hardly ever see her either.

Olga: I see you're wearing workclothes, what are you doing?

Nothing. But I'm waiting for the right time to start on something.

That's right, Abel, you do that. You're not exactly a somebody, but you know so much. And so handsome and shaven today. Even though you're in workclothes! She removed a glove and took Abel's hand and held it, a hand with oil and sand on it: It's been so long since I saw you, you're looking well—

The chemist arrives and says thank you again: Won't you ride along with us?

No thank you.

I can drop you off wherever you like? No, you sure? You coming now, Olga?

See you again sometime, Abel.

She didn't mention the two thousand kroner.

XVI

A BOY ARRIVED WITH A PACKAGE FOR HIM, A LARGE BOX, NEATLY wrapped and clearly addressed.

Abel wasn't curious, he didn't cut the string, he started untying the knots. Inside he comes across a label – ah, from the tailor. So Lolla's been busy again.

He reties the knots he's unfastened and leaves the box there.

Later a package arrives from a shoeshop, and a large package from Folmer Henriksens & Co., Gents Outfitters.

This wouldn't do. He had a think and told himself he better run. In the doorway he met Lolla.

What was all this about, had she gone out her senses?

Get out of the doorway and let me in! said Lolla, taking charge. She was carrying another big package for him.

It took quite a while to explain everything, and since he was very doubtful a lot of it had to be explained twice.

I don't believe it, he said, but his eyes were shining.

He changed clothes while she sat there, stopping every once in a while and refusing to go on.

Get yourself ready, Abel, she said. You're coming with me, they want to see you.

He smiled and called it all a piece of nonsense. Are you trying to kid me I can sail the boat with no exam and no certificate?

Don't you think so?

No. Though I have been to sea a few times.

Ulrik Fredriksen didn't have an exam either. And he hadn't even been to sea.

All very curious! said Abel and thought about it. But the boat's insured with Veritas, at Lloyd's?

I don't know. It's only along the coast, with the milk churns. Do put your clothes on! I'm sitting here wondering how it is your body is so clean.

Me, who bathes almost every day the whole year round? Didn't you know that?

No, she answered laughing, I didn't get that impression.

Like a nice piece of salmon? he asked.

But Lolla had just eaten, and she was intent on getting him kitted out.

Abel: Did you know that Olga's left her husband?

Yes, she's a minx. A fine outstanding man like him!

She wants you to run the house for him.

How do you know that?

She told me yesterday when I met her. She asked me to ask you.

I'm not running the house for him.

You still hold something against him?

Me? I've never held anything against him. He's always been good and kind to me. But I'm not going into service with him now, Olga better believe it. I can't understand why she keeps going on about it when I already said no. It's as though she's got something else in mind.

What might that be?

I wouldn't know. I've spoken to him too, and said no to the both of them. But he took it very nicely, asked me three times to take a seat while I was talking to him, and let me borrow books to take home. If I've got anything against either of them it isn't him. Olga isn't behaving at all in the proper fashion. Did you ever hear the like of it, leaving a perfectly good man like that!

Again they talk about the matter in hand, about what lies ahead of them. Abel doesn't quite believe any of it yet, because there's no way he can figure out how she's arranged the whole thing. And even though she has explained everything she goes over it again gladly: what she said and did out at Fredriksen's place, the innocent little visits to the members of the committee, the hints dropped here and there—

Abel only half-listens, she's disappointed that he isn't more interested and she rushes on: But I didn't do it all for your sake, so there's no need to feel uncomfortable. I was thinking mostly of myself.

Oh.

Because once you're Captain of the *Sparrow* I hope it'll benefit me a bit too.

Oh, he said, in what way?

That Mr Captain Sir will make me Chief Stewardess on board the boat.

Yes with the greatest of pleasure! he burst out. Afterwards he laughed, shaking his head over the fact that he was already in a position to hire people. We sit here, he said, talking to each other like children.

Hurry and get ready, Abel! We're supposed to be there at eleven o'clock.

What do they want with me?

They want to meet you and talk to you, there's nothing odd about that. But now do you see why I don't want to keep house for young Clemens?

He noticed that the underwear was nicely embroidered with his name and asked who was responsible.

Me, she said.

He nodded his head, overwhelmed. But when he got to the fine stockings a devil got up in him and he said: These'll be good for hiding my gun in!

She was hurt by his irresponsible tone and said: Well, if that's what interests you at a time like this.

163

Lolla, I'm sorry, he cried out. It's just that I can't believe any of all this.

Now he finished getting ready as quickly as he could and looked so good, much too good, disgracefully good. Once they got outside he gave his cap a little twist to make it look more casual.

Lolla went with him to the office and waited outside. Was she sure there was nothing she'd forgotten? She should have tutored him a bit, because suppose he acted uninterested and indifferent the way he usually did? He went in there with his face unguarded – and yes, it was a good enough face, the whole man was good enough, but that open man and that unguarded face—

He was quite a time in there, whatever negotiating they had to do, she walked up and down the street a few times, back and forth, looked in the shop-windows and spoke for a while with a girl who was selling religious tracts. Lolla bought 'The Mirror of Faith'.

Where are you from?

From Saggrenden.

What's your father's name?

Alex.

Ah. Then your mother's name is Lili?

Yes.

Lolla pursed her lips and didn't want 'The Mirror of Faith'.

But you paid for it, said the child.

Lolla walked on a bit, turned round and said: Alright then, let me have it.

There was no point in being haughty, Abel was in there a long time, maybe something was going on, an hour had passed by now. What on earth were they up to in that office? Was it possible God might interfere and disturb her great plan?

She glanced at 'The Mirror of Faith' and found nothing there to stiffen her courage. It was hard to take. She began to walk around the whole block, at one junction she met the daughters of Robertsen the Customs man – was she really obliged to turn her gaze in the direction of these creatures? Don't be haughty, it was no fault of the girls if their father was a scoundrel. Good day! she said and hurried past them.

Maybe Abel had emerged by now and finding no sign of her gone his way? That would be a fine thing! She lengthened her stride. For shame she didn't dare to run, but she walked like a man.

There he was.

Ah, Abel, what did they say?

He seemed sobered himself by the strange thing that had happened to him, he shook his head and said: Well, yes, well it looks as though they're really going to let me have a go.

Lolla breathed out. Thank goodness! she said. Now do you believe it?

Yes. No, not quite.

What else could they do? You're the majority shareholder.

Abel: Well – that is actually you.

Let's not quibble about that. What did they all say?

Very nice people. They asked me a few questions, where I'd sailed, what kinds of ships, what flags. A few of the older ones had known my father, that probably had some effect, good worker, they said. The younger ones remembered that I'd sort of saved a worker out at the sawmill once. And on top of all that I had a real smart stepmother, they said, and that was far from the least impressive thing.

Me? said Lolla, blushing crimson. Nonsense!

They asked if I was familiar with the *Sparrow*'s route. Ever since my childhood at the lighthouse, I answered, and after that as a grown man with a little motorboat I had. No worries on that score. And anyway, there's not a man on board that doesn't know these waters, they said, and I'd be getting a good Mate.

Yes, yes – don't let's stand around here. Did you get a contract?

Yes. Three months notice with wages.

How much are the wages?

Well the wage is certainly good. I wasn't listening all that closely, but it's probably in here somewhere—

They both looked through the contract, and Abel said: Yes right, here – Wages! It's a long time since I worked for a wage. It feels strange to me.

June the first, she said.

Yes but they want to report to the Mate now, this evening, they said. Do you know him?

I've seen him.

It has a funny ring to it: the Captain to report to the Mate.

Slip of the tongue, said Lolla. Right then, Abel, now we have to go to the tailor's!

They walked to the tailor's. Uniform ready for trying on, the tailor pulled open a lot of the stitching and chalked and fastened with safety-pins. Lolla handed over the buttons with anchors on. June the first, very well, said the tailor.

They went to try on the hat, paid for it and took it with them in a box. And that was it done. They sat on a bench.

Abel: No it wasn't a slip of the tongue. I was to report to the Mate, they said.

To take over the logbooks and the accounts.

I'm to consult with the Mate if anything comes up. He's always been with the boat and he's unusually good. An older man.

I should think around fifty. A grey-beard.

They didn't mention Captain Fredriksen.

No apparently he just drinks all the time now.

They sat for a while, each in their own thoughts, and then a breath of life seemed to stir in Abel, and he said as though in astonishment: Yes, it really does look as though they're going to let me have a go!

She smiled and pressed up close against him. He took her hand quickly and thanked her, but he didn't dare make too much of it, because she was pressing so close. He cooled her down by asking: What's that little tract you've got with you there?

I bought it while I was waiting for you, 'The Mirror of Faith'. This cheeky little girl was selling it in the street. Well, I have to go now. I've got a long list of food to get onboard in good time. Here, Abel, this is your money.

He shoved her hand away. What money?

For the motorboat that your father sold. Now at last I can sort it out.

He took the money, but he said it was too much, it was all wrong—

In the end she said: And now you're not going back to that hovel of yours in your new clothes. We're got a clean bed for you in the house on the beach.

Thanks, but I still owe them up at the Seamen's Home, so I'll go there instead.

That evening she was there in good time before the *Sparrow* lay to. Abel kept everyone waiting. She saw Captain Ulrik waddling ashore with packages under both arms, moving out. Shortly after his Chief Stewardess came ashore, then the firemen and the crew, all carrying packages, dirty laundry or whatever it was. On board all was silence now, passengers, milkchurns and a couple of baskets of radishes delivered, and the boiler gone out. Only the Mate remained, pacing the deck, smoking.

Abel arrived. Big, calm, looking smart in his new clothes, looking alert for once. You here too? he said, not quite liking it.

I thought I might as well sign on straightaway, she answered.

They went on board and introduced themselves and said who they were. Quickly done, no nonsense.

Sorry if you had to wait, Mate! I met Captain Fredriksen on the street and he detained me with a long speech.

I wasn't waiting, said the Mate. I live on board. I sleep on board.

Two waitresses had now got themselves all made up and were standing close by ready to go ashore. Your new Chief Stewardess, the Mate announced, and Lolla said hello to them. Quickly and smoothly, the whole thing.

The Mate had a full grey beard and a few wrinkles, a serious sort of man, shabby but correct, with two bands on his sleeves. He showed Abel round topsides and below, the salon in red plush, the pantry with the mugs and trays and pans on the walls, the cabins in green – all the usual on board a local boat, in good condition, flower pots here and there, nickel silver in the buffet, electric light.

They sat down in the Mate's cabin as though they were already old friends. Abel noticed that the calendar hanging on the wall was seven or eight years out-of-date and was showing the right date, a day in winter. But apart from that the little cabin was in good order, clean and tidy, a few books on the shelves, the doorknob polished, a few shore-going clothes hanging on the wall.

They talked to each other about their lives at sea, the Mate very reserved, Abel very open: I don't know what you must think of me, Mate, taking this job without having any kind of qualification at all?

It'll work out fine, said the Mate.

It surprised me too they're letting me have a go. I suppose the only thing is I know distant water sailing.

You don't need anything else.

I'll be counting on you, Mate.

The Mate said: We're a man short. We've been sailing with one too few for the last three months.

Why?

Ha – we wanted to keep the berth open for Ananias who got a stomach ulcer. But now he's been sent to hospital and he's gone for good.

I've got a man, said Abel.

The Mate nodded.

A good man. I'll have him on board – when do you want him?

Whenever. Captain Fredriksen has two trips left before you take over.

It shouldn't be necessary to sail short-handed, after all the boat pays out six per cent.

Who says so? asked the Mate.

That's what I heard. Isn't it true?

The Mate says nothing.

A brusque man, a man of few words. Abel asked: Where are you from, Mate? You're not from these parts.

No.

Abel waited, but there was no more. Sorry for asking, he said, but I'm really very surprised that you weren't given command of the boat.

After a moment the Mate answered: There's no need for you to worry about that.

That put me in my place! Abel must've thought. As he rose to leave he said: Right then, there's nothing more to say for the time being.

As the Mate was showing him out he said: It could be we don't need the extra hand, there isn't enough work here for all of us. But the lads wouldn't put up with it. And since you've got someone—

Yes, I know a man, said Abel.

*

168

Everything went really well on board, not that you'd expect anything else. An experienced crew, a good Mate, and the Captain in a new uniform with gold buttons and three gold bands round his sleeves. Top notch. Abel could say to his helmsman: Steady as she goes, then leave the bridge himself and mingle with the passengers and be Captain of the ship. And five minutes later be back on the bridge again making sure the boat didn't end up in someone's potato fields.

It was past the lighthouse and along the coast the whole way. Abel wasn't the Mate, no, terrestrial and celestial navigation were beyond him, but he had more than enough seamanship to captain the *Sparrow*. He never needed to give an order, never a reminder, each man knew what he had to do and he did it to the very best of his ability.

During Captain Ulrik's time things did go wrong now and then, it wasn't unknown. He was a man who used unfamiliar methods and sometimes completely ignored the rules. As when one morning on the outward-bound trip he tossed an empty milk-churn ashore. The Captain tooted and tooted, but they'd overslept up on the farm and no-one appeared. So then Captain Ulrik got hold of the milk-churn himself and tossed it banging and crashing onto the stones. Sure it gave everyone on board a big laugh, but on the return trip the farmer stood there with his churn and showed him what a mess he'd made of it, so you better give me another one, he said. Some hope! said the Captain. Give me another churn! the man said again. Now it so happened they had a sack of flour on board that they'd forgotten to put ashore and as far as the Captain was concerned it was just a leftover. You can have this sack of flour, he said. You can't be serious, said the farmer. Oh you bet I am, answered the Captain. Heave the sack ashore, lads! he called to the crew.

See, that was good old Captain Ulrik's way of taking charge and getting things done on board. But it was all changed now, things were done properly now, nothing was left undone, everything was where it should be, not a bucket out of place not even for a second. There stood the farmers' milkchurns all neatly lined up in rows in the big ice-locker, and any water that leaked out from it was immediately swabbed up. Spic and span. All shipshape and tidy.

The crew's working days were good, with little to do and plenty of time off-watch, and they could go ashore and home to their loved ones in the evenings. There were two of them. But two weren't crew enough for a hand of poker, because the Mate would never join them, and the galley-boy was never free when they needed him. So they got the Third Hand to help them out with their poker: Alex, signed up by the Captain himself.

Why shouldn't there be three ordinary seamen when there was both a captain and a mate on this milkboat, as well as three men in the engine room? No danger of anybody being paid off here! After all, the boat paid out six per cent, everyone knew that, and that was almost double what most banks were paying out these days. So were these milk-churns the only cargo the *Sparrow* carried? Oh no no. She also transported a surprisingly large number of passengers to and from the town. It might be craftsmen and agents who had business inland with the farmers, or people simply taking a day off, or even couples so madly in love they had to find some forest where they could talk in private. The *Sparrow* was good for everyone, it had First, Second and Third class places on board, and those First-class tickets were a red that was a sight to see. On Sundays, when the *Sparrow* lay over, first this and then some other organisation might want to hire it for a pleasure trip with flags and gramophone music, and over the course of a year these incidental earnings added up to a tidy sum. And what about the mail, didn't the boat earn anything there? Sure, the *Sparrow* carried mail, and she delivered postcards to every town along the route, and was well paid for it too, the money just rolled in.

And what about the restuarant, and the Chieft Stewardess, the *trisa* – what about Lolla? Well thanks for enquiring, Lolla answered serenely when anyone asked, it's doing well. People who asked didn't know Lolla. Sure, she was starting out on a new career, but she'd brought along with her all her commonsense and her efficiency. Damned right the *trisa* was doing good business, even though her food was so good it outdid the hotels in town.

She did her shopping at Westman's. Of course, she had also received a brochure from Gulliksen's, but no thanks. Later on she got a whole letter from him, signed by young Gulliksen: they'd done all the provisioning for the previous *trisa* and hoped now to have the honour

170

of hearing from Lolla. But no thanks. Those Gulliksens, that William who'd run off with the wife of young Clemens, and him such a fine man—

No, Lolla got her provisions from Westman, that venerable old tradesman, where she'd also done her shopping during the time she was married to old Brodersen. Westman was perfectly alright, not exactly a wealthy man, but solid and in addition a small shareholder in the *Sparrow*. He was one of the board members she'd visited about Abel and now as far as Westman was concerned she was the greatest *trisa* of all the *trisas* that ever were.

The old man always served her himself. He gave her advice, he was on her side: Sure, I've got both porter and caviar, see for yourself! But to tell you the truth, they're not genuine enough for you. They're Norwegian.

Then you'll have to send off an order for the genuine articles. My stepson the Captain is very particular about that.

She walked around like a lady on board, quietly, nicely dressed, ladylike God knows where she got it from, unless it was from the books she read. She insisisted on the Captain's dignity and guarded it well. Captain Brodersen, she said, the Captain himself, she said. Are you still standing here after the Captain has rung? she might say to the waitresses. I'm on my way already, one of them replies, and off she flies. When she came back she said: the Captain just wanted me to take away the flowerpot somebody put in there earlier today. Or on another osccasion: the Captain asked me to say thank you for the cakes, but he doesn't eat cakes, I'm to say!

And now, finally, what about the Mate? As though anyone knew anything at all about him! Name of Gregersen, good references, even a qualified skipper, commanded ships and sailed the great oceans of the world. His references were old, and he seemed to have been without a job for many years before being hired by the *Sparrow*. It was Fredriksen out at the manor house who'd forced the choice through.

I don't know the man, said Fredriksen, but I've heard of him through a connection of mine. We're getting a first-class man.

These references are so old, said the others. Where has he been the last seven years?

From what I understand he was in another business.

He's commanded ships, why does he want to sign on now as a Mate?

That I don't know. Unemployed maybe, temporary unemployment.

They whispered about it among themselves: when Fredriksen out at the manor house absolutely insists on his brother being Captain then he has to have a real seaman at his side. The whole business was unusual, suspicious even, damned if it wasn't—

But no-one had any regrets about giving Gregersen the job. Perhaps there was something mysterious about him, but it didn't really matter. It wasn't as though he was an unknown quantity, on the contrary, news got out that he came from a good family, with influential relatives. But there was something mysterious about him, this working as a Mate year after year and even being grateful for it. Maybe there was something behind it all, maybe he'd done something, made a mistake, no-one knew. But it was Fredriksen at the manor house who had made the arrangment, to the satisfaction of both parts. Thank you for your faith, Gregersen had said.

And Captain Ulrik Fredriksen had sailed with him for several years without encountering any great disasters, though now and then the Mate had to cover for his Captain. But not any more. Brodersen was a seaman and didn't make mistakes, he used the whistle, he rang down to the engine-room, and when there was a storm and high seas past the lighthouse he hoisted the foresail. No question of mistakes.

It was hard for him to get the Mate talking. Brodersen was no great talker either, but he was articulate enough and could converse when the situation called for it. The Mate was silent. Did his work, kept himself busy at something or other, smoked and kept quiet. What did he have to keep quiet about? The Captain might say, just to be friendly: Fine weather north-east! And the Mate mutter something and agree, but not take it any further. Couldn't he have said – just what're looking for?

The silence was disagreeable, and the Captain turned to the people. He had no choice. It wasn't much he had charge of, just a milk-boat, but it didn't seem too small for him, more like just right for the talent he had. He made small improvements, even found how the

172

engine worked, perhaps even knew the engine best. Here on the *Sparrow* they had an old and cumbersome engine to drive up the steam-pressure, he was more familiar with the small, neat engines from America and Australia and he told the chief about them. He suggested they repair a valve that had come loose in its socket and was leaking oil the whole time. It's been like that since before my time, said the chief. All the same, the chief wouldn't ignore a Captain who knew about engines and he set about fixing the valve.

That way everything went along just fine.

XVII

BUT THEN THERE WAS A BIT OF AN UPSET.

What was Lili doing on board? Wasn't it enough with the husband, Alex?

She asked to see Abel.

The waitresses knew her and her reputation, they had nothing against a chat with her, a bit of gossip, they made time for what promised to be an attractive and entertaining little bit of entertainment.

The *trisa* strode up to them, she tutted: What's all this?

I was just asking to see Abel, answers Lili all, sweetness and innocence.

Abel? Do you mean the Captain?

Yes, I mean the Captain.

He's probably in his cabin. Can I give him a message from you?

What? No thanks. I've got a husband on board, but I don't see him anywhere. It's Alex.

Go forward to the crew's quarters and have a look there, you'll find your Alex there.

But now Lili wasn't smiling anymore, she probably didn't like the *trisas'* tone. Lili was no common sailor's wife, she'd been cashier in an office with responsibility for the big account books. Sure she'd known difficult times and nearly lost house and home, but now her husband had a berth, he paid off the house, bought clothes and food – who did this *trisa* think she was?

I just wanted to ask Abel about getting free travel, she said. Since I have a husband on board.

The *trisa* said: You can talk to the Mate about that.

Well how d'you like that, was what Lili probably said to herself as she made her way forward. The stewardess hadn't offered her anything at all, not a biscuit, not even a coffee. But really, so what? But the *trisa* was none other than Lolla, the woman who'd been married but not wed, ha ha.

She found Alex and gave vent to her indignation.

Alex smoothed things out: It all comes of you calling him Abel. The stewardess won't put up with it. Not from you.

Lili thought about it: I'm not interested in what she'll put up with.

Later she saw Abel on the bridge. Lili couldn't go up to him, it said 'No Admittance', and from her days at the sawmill she still had a respect for signs. But she stared up at him and nodded, she nearly waved, but he pretended not to have seen her.

Oh well really! said Lili, and almost cried.

In less than half an hour's time Abel came down. Steady as she goes! he told the helmsman and made his way down.

He took his round of the passengers, spoke here and there to people, came to Lili, stopped and said: So – you're off travelling?

Lili answered yes and didn't manage to say anything else, her anger had left her. She would never set foot on the *Sparrow* again, she was worth better than that.

But Abel was, after all, the same as ever, just a lot more elegant in his buttons and braid. He said: I guess you found Alex?

Yes.

Ask him to show you round.

175

Then he moved on and spoke to others. A few minutes later she saw him up on the bridge again.

It's the Captain's watch, said Alex by way of explanation. That's all he's got time for.

Lili disappointed: I don't care whose watch it is.

No, the whole thing was not what she was expecting, with coffee and cake and a glass of wine. Excuse me, but I'm not coming back here again.

As though Lili wasn't enough her mother the waffle-lady turned up later in the day. How about that? Wheeling along with her handcart, picked up the basket and climbed on board. Afterwards she stood by the railing and shouted down to Regina to go and meet the trains. Work hard now, Regina!

Waffles here! she said to the passengers. Anyone for waffles?

And yes, plenty of takers for waffles. They ordered coffee served up on deck and made themselves comfortable and ate waffles for breakfast.

Everthing went fine until the *trisa* arrived: What's all this? she said.

Waffles, said the waffle-lady. Eight øre each, you get four for twenty-five. You want waffles?

No, said the *trisa* and marched off.

The sales made inroads on her takings in the restaurant, but she let it go. She was a lady, she was the Captain's stepmother.

The waffle-lady wasn't as lucky with the Mate when he came along to sell her a ticket. Ticket? she said.

Yes ticket. How far are you going?

I'm just selling a few waffles, she said. I've never had to buy a ticket to sell waffles.

How far are you going? asked the Mate, getting ready to write it out.

How far? Just until I'm sold out.

The Mate stood there.

Where's Alex? she asked. He's married to Lili, my daughter. Go and fetch Alex!

So you don't want a ticket? the Mate said.

No, she said. It won't pay me to sell waffles if I have to buy a

ticket, you can work that out for yourself. Where's Abel? she said suddenly. Many's the time he's had a waffle from me. And praised the
quality—

The woman got away with it. But it was embarrassing for Alex.
He'd been on board since the middle of the summer and learnt the does
and donts of things, he would've prefered it if his family kept away, was
kind and courteous, a good man to have on board, didn't irritate the
trisa, didn't say Abel when he meant Captain.

What does it matter? said the waffle lady. Isn't his name Abel? I
knew him when he was a child, when he rowed Lili home in his boat,
he's had many a waffle off me. Don't be silly! And if that's the way of it
then I'm never setting foot on board this boat again.

Alex had nothing against that.

There were all sorts of people on board, even the chemist, that
madman. He had a woman with him but he'd fallen out with her about
something, the lady had discovered handsome Alex and was standing
flirting with him beneath an awning. The chemist paced around the
deck and was not a happy man.

And – as always – the blind hurdy-gurdy man was there too. He
sat there, tiny and hidden in a dark corner beside his instrument, blinking with his crusty eyes, fumbling with his fingers, smiling when
anyone spoke to him. Now he was even pretending to be lame as well.

Play something! they said to him.

He shook his head: Things aren't like they used to be. Captain
Fredriksen always asked me to play when I came along, he treated me
to drinks too, and the *trisa* gave me something to eat. Captain
Fredriksen himself sometimes even passed the hat for me.

What's that – have you done something to your leg?

Talk about unlucky! I can't see to look out for myself. It was last
month.

Is there a cut?

It's black. It's gangrenous, people that can see tell me.

Never heard anything like it. Whatever you do you've got to get it
seen to straightaway.

A lot of people know him and have heard his stories before. Once he was deaf and couldn't hear a thing – not until a few of them started whispering about lifting his wallet from his pocket.

But it must be a terrible thing to be blind and not able to see. He was born sighted, but it began to fail and he couldn't get work anymore. They burned a film off each eye with electricity – and after that he could see nothing at all, he said, after that he was blind. He could probably have managed some job or other, but no, he couldn't see, he said. An unhappy man. People felt sorry for him and bought him a hurdy-gurdy. Him and the hurdy-gurdy are both getting on now, but they keep moving, he usually gets his food and a free passage, a pair of shoes here and a hat to collect the money in there, he does alright, people don't feel as sorry for him now, he never has to sleep rough. When you get right down to it he's not far off being pretty damned good at getting by and providing for his needs just by travelling around with his instrument and his disabilities. Note how freely people talk in his presence, because he's only the blind hurdy-gurdy man. He knows how to use this, finds out about a lot of things, gets to know a little something about everyone. A character, a personality. Some people think he's got plenty of money stashed away somewhere. What's your name today? someone might ask, teasing him, because he's known to use different names, and sometimes claims he's the illegitimate son of a famous woman artist.

Once a few jokers made out they were planning to cut his face with a knife to test him out, but he jumped up into the air with a loud cry, like a magician. Hahaha, they said, so you aren't blind, you old fraud! I bloody well am blind, he said, but I can see shiny things when they glint in the light. But the knife isn't even shiny, they said. Well there you are, he said, now you know how blind I am!

The Engineer was seen on board too, the man who'd once been general manager up at the sawmill. He looked pretty shabby these days but still carried the briefcase with him as usual and walked with his back straight. No Captain Fredriksen now, no more being treated to a drink, not even a dram. He stayed on board as the ship made the stops, moving from one seat to another to avoid the draft, gradually freezing and turning blue. When Alex came by he said: Aha, so you got the job

178

with my reference? Yes, said Alex, being kind. My pleasure, said the Engineer.

He didn't have the money to eat in the salon, but of course the waffle-lady was on board . . . Four for twenty-five øre! As she was about to hand him his waffles he got all refined about it and stopped her: No no, let me pick them myself! Nor did he eat his waffles in front of everyone but crept away to the same dark corner as the hurdy-gurdy man who could see nothing. And really, they were such good waffles, with butter and sugar sprinkled on them, if only there'd been four more!

It was a good job he'd eaten them all up before the chemist came and sat down beside him.

Huff, it's bitter! said the chemist and sat on a crate.

Bitter! said the Engineer. You wouldn't have a drop of something?

No. But come along to the prescription room this evening. You know the way.

This evening? This evening's a long way off. The Engineer fell silent, he was probably feeling a bit sleepy after his waffles.

Him over there doesn't look as if he's freezing, at least not in that foot.

Life must have taught the Engineer something, adversity had changed him. He enquired politely of the blind man: Does your foot give you pain?

Gangrene. I recognise that voice, you're the man who had the sawmill.

Yes.

I hear the refinement in it.

The chemist, laughing: Well in that case I bet you can't tell who I am?

Things didn't turn out too well for the chemist nor his sawmill either, says the blind man.

Things didn't turn out well for any of us, says the Engineer.

Nor his family either, nor Olga. She was always so nice to me, at least a krone every time. And then it stopped.

The chemist replies: Yes well it isn't all over now, let me tell you, she's on top again now. He turns to the Engineer: I guess you heard this about William Gulliksen?

Don't know if I did.

That he's been fiddling his tax. They're making him pay back-taxes.

You don't say! Where did you hear that?

It doesn't matter, says the chemist, there's a lot more in the same boat as him. But the lady didn't like it, I understand.

Is she still living at home?

Yes. They're going to be married by the Justice of the Peace.

When?

Yes when? The problem is she feels sorry for that husband of hers. That clown. Sits in his office, nothing to do but sits there every hour of the working day. All he's got is his clerk's wage.

The Engineer: I don't owe him any thanks for one. He settled that Pistleia business by blaming me.

Well anyway, he's not good enough for her.

By putting most of the blame on me. But he was very considerate about it. He said I had an excuse.

He's a fair-minded man, no doubt about that.

I mean, he came and showed me what he was going to write.

Did he really?

And asked if it was alright. No other lawyer would have done that.

The blind man has been sitting there following all this closely.

But the chemist was not a happy man. And probably tired of the boring talk, he's heard it all before. He stood up abruptly. Was he also a crafty old fox with a plan? Seeing Lolla some way off, the *trisa*, he walked straight up to her, stopped, his short leg swinging, and bowed to her.

She looked him straight in the face and and cut him.

There are so many people here want to travel free, what are we going to do about it?

The Captain thought about it: You decide, Mate. The hurdy-gurdy man is probably in the habit of travelling free.

What about the Engineer? He hasn't bought a ticket.

No I suppose he hasn't. Do whatever you like, Mate. Perhaps he isn't travelling all that far.

There are others too. Some of them come up and ask to see Abel.

180

They must be people I know. I could pay for them, if you think that's alright.

The woman selling the waffles?

Yes many's the waffle I've had off her. Yes, I'll happily pay for her, says the Captain and dips into his pocket. If you think that's okay.

What? If I think – ? It's the *principle* of it, Captain.

Alright then, the principle. But you just do exactly as you see fit, Mate.

And doing exactly as he sees fit the Mate goes up to the Engineer and holds out a ticket.

What? But you know, Mate, I usually travel free.

Yes. But things are different now. New captain.

Ah, says the Engineer and fumbles in his pockets: I don't have – I didn't bring enough—

How far are you going?

The Engineer casts a glance at the landscape: This is my stop here, the next one. There's a certain little copse I'm considering buying.

We'll let it pass this time, says the Mate.

Shall we go in and sit down? the chemist asks his lady-friend. We've got a cabin, you know.

Are you cold?

It's bitter, yes.

Is it bitter, Alex? she asks.

Alex only smiles and silently declines to take sides.

The chemist moves on, freezing cold, jealous. It's cosy in his cabin, he finds an old magazine on the washstand, flips through it, throws it aside and rings the bell: Half a bottle of port and two glasses! he says to the girl.

To his great surprise it is the *trisa* herself who arrives with the tray. She smiles and is civil enough, certainly not embarrassed, but not without a certain reserve, the smile quickly disappears.

You bowed to me on deck, she says.

Er – yes.

I imagine you noticed that I did not respond?

Oh? Didn't you respond? Not even a twitch of the eyebrow?

No. You greet me in town as well, you stop and quite shamelessly bow to me the whole time I'm passing you. But I don't respond.

Yes, why are you so rude?

You know perfectly well why. You are to stop revenging yourself in this way, stop bowing to me.

Ah. And I'm supposed to take the hint.

You should do. But now I'm asking you formally please to stop doing it.

Well well! Oh listen, Lolla, stop all this nonsense, have a drink! He pours two glasses.

She shakes her head: Now look, it really was so many years ago – and anyway there was never anything between us. We were merely engaged for a while, but there was nothing between us. You are not to bow to me, there are people looking on who read something into it. The thing between us is over, please, oblige me in this! There was never anything between us, not really—

No. But was that my fault?

No. You were angry because I wouldn't—

Alright. Why are you bringing all this up again?

I just wanted a bit of fun, you said, just a little taste—

Alright, for chrissake! shouts the chemist. But then why did you come to me?

I came to you because after all, we were engaged. We got engaged immediately, remember, and after that I came to you. I was so desperate to get engaged, you would've preferred not to, but I wanted to because Tengvald had broken up with me and I was afraid of becoming an old maid. The outlook wasn't very good for me, in service out at the lighthouse and turning into an old maid, that was why I did what I did and sat with you in your prescription room and drank wine.

You've become quite the lady, Lolla. You probably don't even remember that I've kissed you?

Yes, because we were engaged, and a lot of things can happen. But now I'm asking you to forgive me for coming to you and to stop being angry at me.

The whole thing is such rubbish, says the chemist. Listen, can't you just sit down and have a glass of wine with me like in the old days?

No thanks, I'm going. I just wanted to ask you not to bow to me anymore.

Hah! he sighed in exasperation, took his glass and emptied it: I needed that, Lolla! So then, you want a complete break? I've got a bad reputation in town, so now you don't even want to admit that there was ever anything between us.

It's really not much to ask for, she says.

Revenge? What nonsense! It isn't revenge. But surely I have a right to upset you just the tiniest bit?

It upsets me. I'm not always alone when you stand there and start your bowing.

No by God you aren't! he says and laughs.

Both of them fall silent for a moment. She takes hold of the door-knob and is about to leave: Yes well, I guess I'll just have to put up with it!

Just a moment! Hm. If it's really so important to you, Fru Broder-sen, then I won't greet you anymore.

What?

I won't say hello.

That – that's good of you. It really is.

He dismisses it, acts noble and as if he's given her something valu-able without counting the cost: I might take exception to certain aspects of the way you describe our relationship. You've altered the time-scale and changed the story so as to make yourself appear the innocent party.

I did come to you at night, she concedes.

You rowed the boat all the way from the lighthouse to come to me. Yes.

Might that not have seemed to me a slight hint that you wanted something from me?

She says nothing.

But you didn't want anything from me. When the time came you ended it. But in those days my reputation wasn't as low as it is now. And as you say, it was many years ago. I wasn't a man you could throw aside just like that.

No, she concedes. But she is in no doubt that he is sitting there boasting and is after still more of her humble gratitude. She daren't owe him too much, that way he becomes a creditor and might come back to press his claim.

Him: I had a taste for the wild life, and it didn't get any the less from being in your company.

No, no, now listen here – goodness me! But now I'm just happy that you won't be bowing to me any more and not saying hello.

I can't say that it makes me a happy man.

You're doing yourself a favour too. You don't know how degrading it is for you to stand there greeting me.

Him, annoyed: Well, that's my business!

Yes, but you look so ridiculous. You're standing on just the one leg, you know. People laugh at you.

A hard look comes into his face, he turns pale and is about to say something. But then the door opens and his lady-friend is standing there.

Well I must say! his lady-friend exclaims.

The *trisa* squeezes past her and leaves.

What must you say? he asks.

I was obviously interrupting something – wine, two glasses—

Yes, and aren't there two of us?

Glasses filled and all that.

Yes – and awaiting you. Can't you bloody well see I'm the only one who's had a drink?

If I'd known about this I would never have come.

Stop this nonsense! Sit down and drink!

No thanks. D'you think I don't know she's your old sweetheart? She was quite worked up, the lanky old bitch. She must've waited until I wasn't around.

Be quiet!

You really ought to be ashamed of yourself: asking me to take a trip away with you, and then this.

Probably in the attempt to stop her in her tracks he said: Have you finished flirting with Alex now?

It didn't stop her: That lanky bitch! Married but not wed – but good enough for you. Christ! I'd rather be dead than be that tall.

184

You're just exactly the right height, my dear. Here's your glass, now let's—

No! she shrieked and grabbed the door. Get away from me! Let me out!

He had to use force to hold her back, to sit her down, to kiss her. It really wasn't all that difficult, she was small and round and not too wildly unreasonable and in the end she was helping him.

They drank their wine and everything was alright again, apart from the fact that the chemist was lost in thought and almost dreamy. He swaggered again, and acted as though nothing was really bothering him. His senses were probably dulled by the wine.

It isn't her I'm thinking of, he said – perhaps precisely with the aim of making his lady-friend jealous.

But the lady couldn't care less. She threw herself down on the other sofa and lay there and tugged her skirts down.

Since he wasn't getting anywhere he began a conversation about a fly: Yes, that's right, a fly had fallen down onto the tray and looked as if it had killed itself. Strange thing about all the half-dead flies on board ships, they come to rest in all sorts of odd positions. This one here is lying on its back and gives no sign of getting up again.

Can you see flies? said the lady.

Yes. I expect it's the same one I took a swat at when I came in and didn't hit it cleanly enough. Yes, I can see flies.

And the chemist, that old roué, had another shot at seeming thoughtful and dreamy. He doesn't give a damn about the fly and wastes no pity on it, he has other things on his mind. He doesn't look bad, his nose is a bit lumpy, he has thick brown eyebrows and a square chin, but his eyes are good and blue and direct, and his mouth is a lovely cupid's bow. His hair is a mess and he combs it with his fingers. Now and then his false teeth come loose and he has to work them back into place with his tongue.

Cheers! He drinks up what's left in the half-bottle and asks if she wants more? No. When he reaches out a hand to lock the door she opens it again. He locks it again, she opens it.

Yes, he says, you're right about her being too tall, Lolla. But all in all she has a fine body.

185

Does she indeed? Well you would know. So it's her you're sitting there thinking about.

No, no. And he turns all tender and faithful unto death and all that: You know that you're the only one for me. Please. He locks the door.

But she unlocks it again.

Going ashore with his lady-friend he looked pale and determined. He stands on one leg directly in front of the *trisa* and bows again.

As the chemist and his lady-friend take their little trip on the *Sparrow* so do others take theirs. It's an excellent boat, quiet, the cabins are comfortable, there's no more congenial spot for a little wine and lovemaking as the autumn goes by.

And people travel, each with their own business to attend to. There's Lovise Rolandsen just visiting some relatives in the next town. She's travelling with her husband Tengvald, the smith, and five of her children. And Tengvalds' presence made no impression at all on the *trisa*, the woman he'd once broken up with, no not the slightest impression. *Trisa*'s gaze lingered a moment over the man and his menage, then she strode off, all unconcerned.

After Christmas the *trisa*'s mother arrived and stayed on board for a few days. The Captain was friendly to her and sat her on his right hand side at table, and he allowed her to help herself first. Perhaps because he spent so much time keeping Lolla at a distance he was extra courteous and kind to her mother. And anyway, she was a likeable and decent person.

He asked her about her husband.

Thank you, he's well, living in a town called Ponta Delgada. Have you been there?

No, I've never been in the Azores.

Everything grows there, even coffee and sugar and all that type of stuff. It must be so fertile.

Isn't he coming home?

Yes as soon as possible, he writes. But he's enjoying himself and teaching himself Portuguese and lives just like them. He works in the harbour.

And what about you, is everything alright in the house on the beach?

Yes thanks, the woman answers.

She's so grateful, so kind and quaint now, she doesn't recall the man's crazy tricks, doesn't nurture old grudges.

She too was once young. Now she's dull.

XVIII

TRISA STARTED FUSSING ABOUT HOW THE CAPTAIN OUGHT TO get himself a new uniform. The worst of the winter was over now, it was best to do it in good time, soon it would be Easter and then everybody would be wanting new clothes.

The Captain smiled indulgently. The uniform he already had was good enough for a milk boat.

Yes but he should have another one, a change, for best.

No.

She was tiresome, Lolla, with her suggestions. How could he afford a new uniform when he not only had to help Alex pay the mortgage on his house but also put aside a little for himself every month?

Not that Alex was in any desperate need of help, he had his job and he had his poker and he was doing alright. No you shouldn't, he told the Captain every time, I've got a good wage and I pay and pay.

Yes but you've got a lot of children at home. And when I help out it means you can get it paid off that much quicker.

Yes but why does it have to be paid off so quickly? asked Alex.

The Captain: I have my reasons.

But since he'd begun to helping Alex out every month and wouldn't stop, it left him with almost nothing to put aside for himself. What was he to do? He needed money, a lump sum. He'd been over nine months on the *Sparrow* now, living aboard here for something like three hundred days and nights, and for what? Was it – surely it wasn't a waste of time?

The first time it occurred to him that he actually didn't belong on board he dismissed it out of hand, like a man. What would the owners say, what would Lolla say if he began to entertain such thoughts? And all the expensive clothing he'd paid for, and for that matter all the tiresome efficiency and concern he'd been showing for the past nine months? It was out of the question.

Later it was easier for him to understand that he'd made a mistake when he charged off to become Captain of the *Sparrow*. What was he doing here? Did a warm glow of pleasure pass through him at the thought of the life on board, where there was far too much food, and that taciturn and dour Mate, the milk churns, the passengers, the whole of the ship's unchanging and monotonous routine? It didn't make him feel good at all. Things had been different to begin with – things are always different in the beginning: when it was his Morning watch he was dressed and on deck in three minutes, glared at the weather and the compass as though he was bound for the Bay of Biscay, rang three bells down to the engine-room and set course – Steady as she goes! He gave it his all, he talked to the passengers, deposited empty milk churns ashore and took full churns on board, made the journey in forty-eight hours, came back and tied up at the quayside. No problem at all.

But was it reasonable to expect things to go on like that? He no longer felt the same urgency to get dressed in the morning, nor was the Captain's glance at the weather and the compass as fierce, he didn't feel in the mood for it. Nothing happened to him along the way, no disaster at sea with people crying out to God, the only thing was when now

189

and then he had to take action to avoid running down some fishing boat that drifted carelessly across their bows, since it was only the milk-boat, after all.

What about that tear in the sleeve of his jacket? He got in the way of a load of iron hoops clamped in a winch that were to go ashore. The Mate saw what happened and for an instant seemed to smile before he averted his eyes. It didn't bother the Captain in the least, the merest trifle, but for several days he'd had to turn this way and that to hide the tear from Lolla. He didn't want to be dependent on her, sooner ask one of the girls to repair it. As though that were really an option: the first girl would cackle away to the other one and boast about it, and the other one would let the *trisa* in on the whole thing.

By the time he showed the sleeve to Alex he must have already worked out his plan: Can Lili stitch me up again? he said.

Why not the tailor? said Alex.

No not the tailor, he'll just want to make me a new jacket.

But Alex, that handsome lad and husband, didn't seem to share the Captain's view. Alex had begun acting strangely, he didn't want Abel in his home and he didn't want Lili on board. Big changes in the course of a few months. Once Alex got his keep and a decent set of clothes on his back he shrugged off his shame and became a man, joined the union where everybody made a fuss of him. You're not to come aboard, he told Lili, no need for us to be acting poor! And Lili, who'd put on weight again and got new clothes and low-cut buckled shoes, agreed with her husband. Why should I come aboard, she said, because you come home every other night—

And yet – when Abel entered her living-room in his full uniform and asked her to patch him up she had to catch her breath and she blushed crimson. It probably felt a little strange for her, this was Abel, now he was a Captain, and there were gold buttons and braid on his jacket. Well I'll try! she said.

He sat there in his shirt-sleeves talking away naturally to her while she sewed. They've grown, he said, meaning the two little ones. They had got hold of his cap and were marvelling at it, each of them trying it on in turn. The third, the youngest, was sleeping. Abel asked if this was a girl too? Yes, girl. Lili couldn't understand it, why she almost always had girls. Still, she did have one boy, the apple of his father's eye. Yes I like him, said Abel. D'you think he looks like me?

Quite possibly something might have happened, but Alex arrived, hot on the heels of his Captain. To begin with he smiled and put a brave face on things, but he was hardly the ideal host, hardly even showed the proper respect. The mother told the children off for playing with the Captain's cap. Alex responded: Why doesn't he just take his cap off them? After a while Alex too took off his jacket. Disrespectful and very uncivilised. Then he stretched his arms up in the air and yawned gracelessly. Then he slumped down on the edge of the bed. The bed creaked.

Towards the end Lili seemed a little embarrassed by her husband, she'd given him a look once or twice, but apart from that she sat there and kept busy. Abel took no notice of his deckhand's behaviour.

Perhaps Abel was sitting there and thinking back. It would have been disgraceful of him to be sitting there remembering how that bed used to creak, but there were other things. Looking out of the window the steps were to the right, and at the foot of those steps he had once received two gunshot wounds. They had healed by now, but still there had been two wounds, from his own stolen gun. That was what hurt most, that gun had been sacred to him. Strange how scarring and age can cover all things and the events themselves increasingly be forgotten. In time things went wrong for all of them, but at least he had that shed down on the vacant lots to be in, they had wanted to move in with him and he wouldn't have it, but he'd treated them to salmon, to a little bit of stolen salmon. Their paths have crossed each others a great deal, but it's done them no lasting harm. And now here are Lili, Alex and the children, the situation is intimate, it's domestic again. On board he is Captain and master, here he's more like one of the family. And suddenly he asks Alex: What possessed you to break in and steal my gun that time?

Alex blinked and thought about it: Because I had no knife, he said.

Knife? What did you want with a knife? It's downright dangerous for a fool like you to have a knife and gun, you might kill someone.

Lili, deeply uneasy: It was all such a long time ago—

Yes but I spent a whole year looking for that gun.

Yes, it was wrong, she said.

Alex probably felt he had to do something and show how little it bothered him, he called to the two small children – the two little ones that with some exaggeration he called his own. Spit! he said.

In the cap? they asked, glowing with happiness.

Alex! Lili shrieked, beside herself.

What are you screaming for? he asked. Did you think – I'm not that uncivilised, am I? He pushed the cap across the table.

Abel took no part in this, didn't deign to, couldn't care less. A lot of silly behaviour ensued and the cap would have fallen off the other side of the table if he hadn't prevented it, but he couldn't start letting his deckhand get to him. Big changes in Alex these days, all his good luck had done wonders for his courage. And he and Lili had done well to get back on their feet again so quickly. The clock back in its place on the wall again, the rose-painted cupboard back, the chairs, table, the two flowerpots—

Where's Regina? he asked.

Lili answered: Regina's such a grown-up girl now she's gone into service.

There was no need for it, said Alex.

Lili: She's at young Clemens'.

Regina is? How is she making out?

Well, she's picked up a lot, a bit here, a bit there, mostly from her grandmother. She can bake waffles and suchlike.

Alex snorts: Ha, fry up a piece of liver and a few potatoes for the master!

Yes, Regina's a clever girl, said Abel. She once sold me a copy of 'God's Ten Commandments'. All of you, you're all clever. I can see how you've got back on your feet again, in every way.

Lili with sudden warmth: Thanks to your help, Abel!

Oh, that! I had to pay back what you thought I'd borrowed from you. Don't you remember that?

Lili lowers her head and is silent.

But Alex isn't silent: Did he borrow money from you, Lili? Then that's quite another matter! It was probably you who kept him going while I was away that time.

Oh do shut up, Alex! she said.

Now we see! Because I couldn't understand anyway how you'd eaten up the whole house by the time I came back.

Lili screams: Be quiet Alex, do you hear me!

Abel continues: And it's important to pay off the mortgage. Alex there doesn't think there's any rush, but he knows nothing about it. There's no telling how much longer I'm going to be with the *Sparrow*.

What? Lili asks quickly. You're not resigning?

Abel didn't answer. He wanted to give Alex a shock. But Alex sat heedless and invincible on his bed and didn't begin to tremble.

Lili again: You're not resigning?

I don't know.

Then Alex said: If you do resign, I can still stay on just the same. I'm a member of the union and all that.

The jacket was ready and Abel put it on. Like new! he said. Not a stitch showing! Now look here, Lili – for your trouble—

You'll take nothing for that, Lili! said unshakeable Alex.

But on board the following day Alex was polite and respectful again. It wasn't his living room, and his wife wasn't around either. Perhaps he'd had second thoughts during the night, perhaps he'd talked over a couple of things with Lili.

Good morning! he said and touched his cap.

Good morning, replied the Captain. Go up to the chart room and get everything spic and span.

Aye aye.

Clean the windows too.

Aye aye.

And the ceiling light bulb's gone, replace it.

Aye aye.

Nothing but deference the whole way, the Captain could hardly get a word in.

Abel was expecting someone, the whole boat was expecting them. *Trisa* and the two girls had shaken and brushed every cushion in the salon and in cabin number 1, the big double cabin. And no flies there,

193

oh no, nothing but a flowering begonia in a pot on the table, and brand new bars of soap for the washstand.

At seven they arrived. The Captain didn't greet them because he was on the bridge, but he bowed deeply and straightaway rang down to the engine room. *Trisa* greeted them and in defiance of all the usual conventions extended a personal welcome: Welcome, ma'm!

Olga, said the lady.

Alright, Olga, welcome!

Trisa showed the couple to cabin number 1, opened the door for them and stepped back. They stayed there just long enough to deposit their hand-luggage, then they took a stroll around the milk-boat.

They were married now, married by a Justice of the Peace, but that was quite a few weeks ago. This really wasn't a honeymoon trip, just a quick visit to the neighbouring town because Gulliksen couldn't spare the time for more. The couple were elegantly dressed in furs, the lady hardly wearing any makeup at all.

When the Captain came down from the bridge and made his rounds among the passengers he conversed in a natural and straight-forward way with Olga and her new husband. Gulliksen seemed a little arrogant, a little familiar, perhaps he was recalling the time he had denied this Captain Brodersen credit for his groceries and was now determined not to seem embarrassed about it, quite the contrary. Abel didn't appear to think you could blame a shopkeeper for something like that, for he was as friendly and nice to Gulliksen as he was to all the other passengers.

But Olga was another matter. When he greeted her she removed her glove eagerly. They gossiped away like two old pals, shook each other's hands and smiled. He stood with his head bared the whole time.

My God, you're absolutely radiant! he said.

Yes well I am a bit radiant, she returned. It's such fun to take this trip now that you're Captain and you've come up in the world. So there you see, Abel, what did I tell you! I said so all along, even when every-body else disagreed with me and you most of all did. See, I knew you, that you could do it if only you wanted to—

She made too much of it, Gulliksen left them and strolled on. Maybe she was embarrassed in front of Abel: the last time they met had been in a restuarant and her name was Fru Clemens and her husband had been with her, now she was here with a new husband she didn't want anything said about it, just wanted to talk it all away: Yes and how are you, Abel? It probably feels a little strange for you, but oh if you only knew how happy I am to see that you've found your proper position in life. Listen – I bought that brass box of yours from the scrapdealer.

Ah, that!

Really strange, no key, secret. And I'm not going to show the trick to anyone. So if you want to write me letters, Abel, then I'll hide them in there, hahaha.

I'm needed up on the bridge, said Abel.

Alright. We'll meet later.

She stayed with the *trisa*. Perhaps she felt a little embarrassed with her too, after all the *trisa* had been in service in her previous home, cooked and washed and dusted, and now the *trisa* was her hostess on board a steamship. Quite a big change. But it didn't prevent them immediately casting aside all restraint in typical female fashion, no subject was too embarrassing to bring up, ha, they talked about everything.

Olga: Yes I can see Lolla, when you had this waiting for you, you could hardly consider keeping house for Clemens.

Who has he got now?

Oh I really don't know, but someone mentioned he has a little girl, a young girl.

Well that can't be good for him.

I don't know. Her name's Regina and she's the daughter of a member of the crew. But she's been to Confirmation and she's smart for her age. But I don't take much interest and don't ask. I'm sure you understand, Lolla, I can't worry about that sort of thing now. I've got my own life to live.

Yes.

I'm somewhere else now. But it's worked out well with this young girl, she's religious and she was in the Salvation Army. Sometimes he opens the door to the corridor so he can hear better when she's in the kitchen playing the guitar and singing. She's got a lovely voice, he says. Well that's what they do. But as I say, I can't remember who it was told me, probably I heard it on the phone, I hear nothing and I don't ask.

Naturally Gulliksen wouldn't put up with it either. Yes yes, my God, everyone has something. It's been a hard time.

How did the judge and his family take it?

Dreadful. The wife took to her bed, both the daughters came home, the judge wanted to resign. Wrote the letter and sent it off—

Lolla interrupts: Then what about – I mean, what about young Clemens?

Well it would have meant trouble for him. But his sisters managed to intercept the letter and the judge withdrew his resignation. That was the good thing about it. But there's no limit to what I've had to put up with. I've no honour, no heart, no understanding of people, his sisters tell everyone I'm mad. I don't know, I'm not the only one who's ever done something like this, am I?

I'm sorry, Olga. Well now you've got what you want, but will he manage?

In what way? You mean on just his clerk's salary? I really don't know, I told you. In the end that was all we had too, the clerk's salary. But now listen to this, it's very strange. He had quite a large bill outstanding at Gulliksen's from before, from my time, I mean. I was the one who kept piling up the credit – but now Gulliksen won't cancel the debt. I've asked him to but he won't do it. Quite the contrary, he's sent a letter of demand to Clemens. It made me feel awful, because Clemens didn't even really know about it. But he started to pay it off. Tiny amounts, almost nothing, no use at all, hardly noticeable. I saw him once when he was making a payment, just caught a glimpse, then I hid. Oh God, he was standing there at the counter, handing over a few coins . . .

Olga gives a stifled cry and throws herself face down on the sofa. Her back heaves, she bites the cushion to calm herself, Lolla strokes her. It lasts for a while, and then Olga, still lying on her face, starts talking again: Imagine, he's standing there, he's taken off his hat, his hair is a bit long, he's got his briefcase under his arm. And he pulls out a few coins with his lovely hands and puts them on the counter and asks for them to be written off against the debt. Completely innocent, you know, it's almost unbearable. And the boy behind the counter is polite, he thanks him, he gives him a receipt. And then Gulliksen got tired of all this small change, says Olga, turning over and sitting upright, he handed Clemens a pile of bills to collect: Let's get this sorted out, you're a lawyer aren't you, get distraint, show them you mean business. But can you imagine Clemens levying a distraint, Lolla? No. It didn't come to that either. So apparently he spoke to Regina about it, the young maid. I don't know anything about it, but he must have spoken to her. And Regina goes over the bills and she takes them with her and off she goes. Incredible, but that Regina is clever, she's unbelievable, in her time she's gone out into the streets and the harbour and up to houses and sold biblical tracts, and she's sold waffles for her grandmother, so she's a real businesswoman and she doesn't take no for an answer. And she comes back with the money, really quite a lot of it, people knew her and they they gave her money, some the whole lot others just something on account, and Regina's given them a receipt. A strange young child, a real rock. Gulliksen's thrilled: If you carry on like this, he says to Clemens, you'll get not only your percentage but I'll pay you for your summonses and your court appearances, even if you don't serve a summons on a single person! Wasn't that marvellous? Gulliksen told me about it himself, but it's all so complicated. It works out better for him to do it that way, he says, rather than take it to court and get a bad name. Actually the debtor is supposed to pay the collection costs, but Gulliksen is shrewd about money and says in the long run he makes more from paying them himself. Why? Because of course now he gets the money straightaway, whereas if it goes to court and settlements and distraint then he'll have to wait forever to get it. Business and trading are just one big science, Lolla, he explained to me how it pays to get the money straightaway and not have to wait for it. Money is expensive, he says. I don't understand, I mean, he's rich. But whatever it all is, it was lucky for Clemens to get that help with collecting the bills and now Gulliksen's given him a lot of new ones, a whole pile of new bills to collect.

Lolla distractedly: Clemens has been kind enough to lend me books, and every now and then I return them and borrow others. Then we talk together a bit, just about the books, of course, and the different things that happen to the people in the books.

What is it like there now? asks Olga.

197

Your house looks just like it always did – his house, I mean. Just as neat and tidy in the living room, and the oleander in the middle room nice and green. Yes you've no need to worry about anything there.

Me? It doesn't bother me in the slightest, what's it to do with me? My home is elsewhere. No, I'm sorry, but really, Lolla.

I didn't mean to—

My sweet, it wouldn't be at all strange if you did have an opinion on it all, I did live there once, after all, I went to bed there and got up there. But just not any more. The last I heard – I don't know who it was told me – but now he's handling two big cases for Fredriksen out at the manor. It's actually Fru Fredriksen who engaged him, to get things handled properly, because Fredriksen himself is so slow now. Cerebral hemmorhage this time. And proper cases are really Clemens' strong suit, not debt-collecting. Some problem with a will, I think, the wife thinks she's being done out of something, that she hasn't got enough, I don't know. And the other business is something to do with that Ulrik, the Captain, something to do with him having a wife away over there in Africa. Can you believe it? But Clemens is being paid good money to get it all sorted out.

Silence. Both women listen to the footsteps in the corridor.

Ah, so this is where you are! says Gulliksen.

He might be a little embarrassed – at least he should be – in front of Lolla, the same Lolla whom he once tried to get drunk and kiss and all that. But he's all self-assurance now, doesn't let that old story bother him, he's on top of things, cool: I've been looking for you, Olga.

I couldn't see you, so I came here, answers Olga. I'm just telling my old friend here how well we get on together, that we're never apart, and that you've been trying to educate my bird-brain in the mysteries of your science of business.

Well you've plenty to talk about! Apropos, Fru Brodersen, I took the liberty of sending you a letter some time ago, perhaps you never received it?

Oh yes, I received it.

You won't bring your custom to us? The previous stewardess bought everything from us. We both did very well out of it.

I've always dealt with Westman, so I'm staying with him.

198

Yes, I was merely enquiring.

Silence.

Olga defusing the situation: Yes so that's what we've been sitting and talking about. And most of all how good it was of you to take me along on this trip, even though you have so little time. I'm as happy as a little child – but now Lolla, I have to tell you, I'm starving.

It's all ready, said the *trisa*, and left.

Ready? How can she know what you want? he asked.

Just a little second breakfast. She was my maid once.

Oh yes, that's right! he exclaimed irritably. There's no getting away from the past.

They arrived early at the next town. Gulliksen had business and went ashore straightaway, his wife put her coat on too, but since her husband was long gone by that time she changed her mind and remained on board. She spent a long time with the Captain in the chart room.

I'm not going to put on any kind of pretence for you, Abel, she said, I'm here with a new husband.

Congratulations! he said.

Yes, yes, congratulations! Imagine, I got a letter from Rieber Carlsen: Congratulations! That's the second time he's had to congratulate me.

Oh yes, the one who preached in church. I recall something about ambition—

Now don't be like that, Abel, Rieber Carlsen is pretty well-known and he's a great man. I was pleased to get his letter, he's so gentle and so serious, it was supportive, I felt as if I wasn't completely alone. But I can see he's worried about my eternal soul and all that.

Alone – you? With a rich and powerful man like Gulliksen to support you?

I don't know if you're being serious or not. But I'll be straight with you: I couldn't do without the pin money. That's why I did what I did. I'll put up with a lot to get that money.

Abel thought about that and said: I suppose you need the pin money for quite a lot of things.

Yes, don't you think? she answered, grabbing at this. Now you're being nice. That's exactly what I've been saying, that there are lots of things I need pin money for so I don't have to do without. But what do men understand about that?

No. We don't paint our fingernails red and our eyelashes black.

Exactly! Aha. And I supppose you'd rather see me with my hair in braids down my back while everyone else has theirs short?

Let me look at you now, you're so wonderfully unpainted today, Olga, he said and switched on the ceiling light.

Yes. And it may well be I had my reasons for that, since I knew I was coming on board.

Well I don't suppose it was for the benefit of me and the Mate.

Abel, why don't you get married too?

You're right, I should really have someone at home to take care of the milking and the chickens and mend my stockings.

I'm being serious.

I've been married, he said.

That was a piece of nonsense. I'm the one you should've had, Abel.

Yes, you probably were. But I had no chance.

No.

And anyway, I would only have lost you again if I had won you.

Yes, if you couldn't keep hold of me.

Hold of you, Olga? With what? You're impossible to get a hold of. You're like that electric light there. A fire created just for the eyes, for the vision. Maybe there's a tiny amount of heat in it, but it's not like the heat of a fire.

Not like with a stove, exactly. But I do try, in my fashion, to be held onto, she said quietly. Did you notice when we were out together that time – with Clemens, I mean – that I didn't call him by his first name?

In the restaurant, yes I remember that.

Not one single time. I just said You, so I didn't have to say his name. I saved that for my new husband, they both have the same name, they're both William. Of course, he wasn't my new husband then, but I saved it for him. I wanted to do that for him. Do that much for him.

Abel blushed furiously and tried to hide it by being casual: Very nicely done, I think.

Olga flushed: Oh, Abel, it's so kind of you to say that. No-one else seems to think it matters.

Oh yes, very nicely done. But – if I can say this – it's not – I mean, there's tenderness in it alright. But not the other thing. It's not the heat of a fire.

Olga complains: I've worked hard on that too.

Silence.

Around her wrist there's a bracelet he recognises, but apart from that she isn't wearing a lot of rings and suchlike, she's modest in her jewelery. Suddenly he feels for her. This is Olga, with whom he was once so desperately in love, the only one for him at school, and in town, the only one in the whole world. He laid his hand on hers.

What is it?

Nothing, he says and takes his hand away.

No, what was it, Abel?

Nothing. Just a moment I forgot to remember to forget.

Ah, from childhood. You're so different from the way you usually are, you look so lovely when you blush, even the way you talk is different. Completely different! She leans over the table and scratches at a little stain he has on the lapel of his jacket, she takes some spittle on her finger and rubs the stain away.

Yes, she knows what tenderness is

Abel: I was about to say poor Olga, just a moment ago. It was just right for what I was thinking at exactly that moment. But I'm glad I didn't say it.

She says nothing.

Because there's no need to feel sorry for you, is there? You've got what you wanted.

Oh yes. Indeed I have. We get along very well together, don't think any different. He's so smart and clever, his father leaves everything to him now, and he's kindness itself to me. No, no-one could say I got the worst of the deal. Did you think maybe I regretted it? Please – we knew each other a long time before, while I was still married to the other one. I knew what I was doing. There's no reason to say poor me.

Whoa! he said, as though reining in a runaway horse.

Olga: Now tell me a bit about how brilliantly, you, Abel, are doing.

Me? Why? I'm not doing brilliantly.

Oh no?

But I do as you do, I put up with it.

You've got a good position. You've become somebody – oh it's so good to see you getting ahead! I used to feel for you before. Don't be angry with me, but I asked Gulliksen to give you a job at his store.

Abel laughs: You didn't, did you?

I did. Are you angry with me?

What did he say?

If only I could remember. But anyway, nothing came of it.

I owed him a bit at that time.

Yes.

Yes, you say, you mean you know about it?

I mean, you did, didn't you, owe him a bit, I mean? He didn't mention it.

So that's what you did, Olga, you asked him to give me a job.

You must admit, you were a pretty sorry sight in those days.

I was happier in those days. Happier than I am now.

Nonsense. You'll get command of a big boat soon, then I'll sail away with you. To your Negroes, remember? But of course, you've forgotten that I was going to run away with you.

Trisa arrives and announces that supper is being served.

Right, thank you. But can I wait a bit? My husband's still in town—

He's back.

Ah! cries Olga and springs to her feet.

On the return trip the next day Olga never left her husband's side the whole time. It was as though he wanted to keep her all to himself. But just before she disembarked – while Gulliksen was paying the *trisa* – she got the chance to say goodbye to Abel alone: It had been such a pleasure to meet him again, now that he'd come up in the world. She wished him all the very best. She often thought of him.

They stood close together and spoke quietly.

Suddenly she said: You're wearing the same collar as you had on yesterday.

Can you tell?

There's a smudge on it, probably coal-dust. But it doesn't bother me. It's just that you're Captain now. Well okay then, I better be going ashore. Goodbye, Abel! It's been a marvellous trip with you and Lolla, lovely weather and dead calm, the white gulls following us all the way out and back again. I slept like a log last night. It's the sea air. I'm going to make this trip again—

Small-talk, chitchat, Fru Gulliksen was in no hurry to go ashore.

I'll still have this soot smudge on my collar tomorrow as well, he said. It doesn't bother me.

Gulliksen called: Are you coming, Olga?

Yes.

She didn't mention the two thousand kroner.

XIX

EVIDENTLY THE MATE THINKS THERE'S SOMETHING WRONG with his mouth, some kind of blister or other in his throat, and it leaves him even less inclined to conversation than before. He is extremely taciturn, and so whenever Abel feels like a conversation he turns to the men in the engine-room and the crew. They're not much interested in him, but he is the Captain after all.

They discuss the fact that the *Sparrow* has been hired for an outing tomorrow, Palm Sunday, it'll be a big occasion, with flags and singing and music. Three organisations have pooled resources for the hire of the boat, the Master Craftsmen, the Association of Small Traders, and the Local Government Officers. So not just anybody but a group of solid and respectable citizens with an average wage of around four thousand kroner a year, more or less.

Trisa and her girls are going to be kept busy, they expect every cabin to be booked. Robertsen the Customs man applied in good time for cabin number 1, the big double, for himself and his family, but the *trisa* said no, she didn't like him. Robertsen the Customs man, the cheat, the rascal who wanted to report her and her father for forgery, the whole thing had cost Abel a lot of money . He can have number 7, the bell there is out of order and there's something wrong with the lock. And I don't even know if he can have number 7, the *trisa* concluded angrily.

But when the next day dawned and the three organisations came streaming aboard the *Sparrow* with their flags and gramophones the double cabin was still not taken. Robertsen peered in, registered that it was empty, and went to see the *trisa*.

Why can't I have number 1?

Because it's taken.

There's no one in there at all. So which cabin am I getting?

Trisa checked in her register: 7.

The Customs man made his way to number 7 in a sour frame of mind. He sniffed, checked everything and went back: Am I to tell the three ladies in my party that that dog-kennel is our cabin?

That's number 7.

The bell doesn't work.

It'll be repaired by next Palm Sunday.

The Customs man stood there as if he'd just been clipped round the ear. I'm not having number 7, he said.

Trisa calmly removed his name from the register.

Damn that damned Customs man. Now the *trisa* had two vacant cabins, and it was her responsibility to see that they were occupied. But not everyone was as pompous as the Customs man, the majority had no desire to go to the expense of renting a cabin. What use did they have for a cabin? The idea wasn't to sleep, and if they were cold they could always go and sit in the salon.

She managed to rent number 7 to a young couple who perhaps wanted to talk to each other in private. But she couldn't get rid of the double cabin and didn't dare to advertise it openly. And who could she offer it to anyway? These were just middle-class people – hardly even that. People like Robertsen and his wife and daughters, not even someone from Westman's grocery store to make a fuss of in the cause of good business relations.

One way out of the dilemma would be to lock the double cabin — and she did so immediately.

Things proceeded as usual on such outings, with music, and singing and dancing on deck between the refrigeration room and the winch. The coffee counter was already doing a lively trade, there was the popping of corks from soft-drinks bottles and the shrieks of young ladies getting hit by the corks. The atmosphere was good.

The *Sparrow* was not carrying milk churns, but the Captain made his rounds as usual and kept an eye on things. He conversed with some of the passengers, nodded to others, shared a joke here and there. He met one old acquaintance and stood talking to him for several minutes, the barber from up near the market gardens who had once shaved him for nothing and even presented him with a open razor. Abel had long ago made his way up to the little barber shop and paid, but he had been wearing civilian clothing at the time and said nothing about being in command of a steamboat, so today was the first time the man saw him in his uniform and looking so magnificent. It was a source of great astonishment to him: I can't get over it! he said. Are you alone? No, I'm with my wife and three boys. That's them over there. Abel greeted them, decent people, good faces, friends. He went up on the bridge again.

I want to do something for them. I'll treat them to dinner, he thought and rang down from the chart room. Probably a breath of kindness passed through him, a tremble, a piece of foolishness.

Trisa arrived and asked what he wanted. Yes, he had an order. But the thing was, he had to be careful to phrase this order more like a request, because *trisa* could be strict about stuff like that, she might object. She could be remarkably insolent to him, that *trisa*.

Yes there's just the five of them, the man, his wife and the three boys.

Again! said *trisa*.

Again? What d'you mean? I'm talking about now.

He didn't realize how lucky he was to have the *trisa* to keep him in check, it was by no means unusual for the Captain to order dinners for strangers on his account, and his wage wasn't as big as all that. She was the level-headed one, not him.

Both tables are fully booked, she said.

He saved my life once, he said.

No, your memory's playing a trick on you, it was some other family who saved your life. About a month ago.

The Captain gave the matter some thought: I'm the one who pays for it, he objected.

Yes, but it's so stupid of you.

That's them standing down there, he said and pointed through the window.

Trisa without looking: Anyway, they'll have to wait until later. Then we'll see.

The Captain thought about this: I really would prefer if they didn't have to wait until later.

The same goes for a lot of people.

Yes but for this family to have to sit and watch while others get served – as though they weren't every bit as good as them, or even better.

Who are these people? she asked and looked out.

Man wearing the grey hat with a black band round it. He's wearing a white necktie, he's a master barber, a decent, respectable man.

Which is his wife?

She's down there too. Standing by the winch.

That's a very strange hat she's wearing.

The Captain is offended: The lady wears whatever hat she pleases. I've never heard anything like it. Affluent family like that—

Really? says *trisa*. Where do you know them from?

It's a long story. I'll tell you later.

Well anyway, they're going to have to wait.

I said no, Lolla! They can eat in my cabin.

In the Captain's cabin? cried *trisa*.

Yes, anything the matter with that?

Not as far as you're concerned. But it's just not done. You're so casual, you walk around wearing the same uniform for a whole year and daub yourself with soot and oil – and you don't care at all. What's that there – have you ripped the sleeve of your jacket?

No, he said curtly.

Who mended it?

And they're to have beer with their meal.

Answer my question.

Yes, they're to have beer with their meal.

To put an end to it *trisa* said: They can't eat in the Captain's cabin. It's better if they use the double cabin.

He seized on this: Wonderful! Go and tell them, that man there with the white scarf round his neck. And coffee, remember the coffee afterwards! Be nice to them! And beer!

But *trisa* had been right to try to restrain him, how right she had been. Wasn't this the very time when he needed money, a lump sum of money? Whatever it was he needed it for, he needed that lump sum. The bitter truth of the situation dawned on him.

When he came off watch he visited Robertsen the Customs man. He was sitting in the salon with his family and making fun of the *trisa* for that prominent family she'd rented the double cabin to: They must be really important people, not even overcoats in this cold weather—

Abel removed his cap and sat down. The girls had nothing against that, they invited him to join them on the sofa, but he declined. He addressed himself at once to Robertsen:

You remember my putting up some money for you at the bank?

For me? said Robertsen.

To cover a note forged by you?

Robertsen turned to his wife and daughters in astonishment: I don't know anything about this.

Well, now I'd like to have that money.

I'm sorry but you must be getting me mixed up with someone else.

Is it not the case, Fru Robertsen, that you promised to sell the boats and pay me back?

The wife: Don't involve me in this. This is my husband's business.

My my, haven't you and Lolla come up in the world! Here I come aboard with my three ladies and we get offered a dog-kennel of a cabin like number 7. I shan't forget that in a hurry.

I would prefer it if you wouldn't forget to pay me. I need the money now.

What on earth is this money you keep talking about? Is it money that's supposed to cancel the forged draft that Lolla once had at the bank?

I don't know anything about something cancelling something else, and Lolla has never had a forged draft at the bank. She did, however, pay off a draft forged by her father.

It's the same thing, said Robertsen. And that I should owe you anything when it was you who paid to keep things quiet about that document of hers – oh no. Ha ha, I don't think so.

Then there's still a chance you'll be arrested.

Ha – who's going to report me?

Me.

But my dear Abel, in that case you would need proof. It isn't enough just to say that it's not your signature.

We'll soon see about that. In the meantime you can just carry on living like the dog you are.

I will not be insulted by you.

Isn't there some other way of settling this? says his wife quietly.

And by the way, you can thank me for your having your job, Robertsen went on. Because if I'd applied for it I would have got it, not only do I have a mate's ticket but I can provide tiptop references from the Customs service. Oh yes. So I think you can be pretty pleased I didn't stand in your way.

Again the wife said a few conciliatory words, that things like this were so unpleasant, much the best thing was to reach an accomodation—

Don't take his side, please! Robertsen shouted at her. Please remember I am a civil servant and I can speak for myself. Don't worry about that. I'm a public official.

I only meant that—

Be quiet, I said! And what would have happened to your father all those years you were away, Abel, if I had not kept open house for him?

That's true, Abel! said the wife.

Robertsen, beside himself: Don't sit there fawning on him, do you hear? Let me tell you, Abel, that your father came to our house every day and enjoyed himself there and got thick pea soup just like we had at sea. And always coffee afterwards and a smoke – with my tobacco. I

209

didn't keep any accounts, I'm just telling you the facts—

I'm reporting you this evening, said Abel.

The *Sparrow* wasn't going any further, she tied up at the quay and was to spend two hours there. They were in a bay, the town was big, with shops, a telegraph station, a lawyer, a doctor. Most of the party went ashore here, waving flags and singing patriotic songs, making their way up to a monument close to the church, where Robertsen was to give a speech.

A spring thaw had set in and the track was slushy with puddles and the procession jumped and sang as it made its way, sang and jumped along the way.

Several other organisations were already assembled at the monument, with banners waving, even though the person commemorated by it wasn't especially famous – a colonel from the days of the Swedish war. Yet the day wasn't a completely fabricated excuse to go on an outing and celebrate, because the colonel was a hundred and fifty years old, or something like that.

A man was already standing by the stone delivering a speech, wasting time, moving nobody. Robertsen the Customs man shifted his feet and looked at his watch, the ship was due to return to town again at a scheduled hour and as soon as the podium was vacant he pushed his way forward: Ladies and gentlemen! But he didn't move anybody either . . .

The sun shone, but it was sinking low in the sky. The crowd was getting bored and cold. A man making his way down from a forest path attracted their attention. He was leading a cow along on a rope. Whoa! he cried in a loud and unembarrassed voice to the cow, and stopped. He carried an umbrella under his arm in the sunlight, wore a sunshade on his head and a starched white shirt-front with neither collar nor tie. A horse-blanket had been tossed over the cow so that it wouldn't feel the cold.

Whoa! he cried again, loud and unembarrassed, as though to make sure everyone recognised him. But it was hardly necessary, almost everybody had already recognised him and many went forward to greet him. It was Ulrik Fredriksen, Captain Ulrik, formerly of the *Sparrow*.

Out for walk?

210

Out for a walk yes. I've just walked from home, I live back over that way, got a farm. What's all this about a party? I heard there was going to be a party here?

We're just here on an outing.

On the *Sparrow* then, I guess? Mind if I join you on your way back to town?

Yes, can't see any problem with that. Sure the Captain himself can come along with us!

It's quite possible they were making fun of him. He looked a bit strange in that outfit, no collar but the starched shirt-front, and the umbrella tucked underneath his arm. The cap was the one he wore when he was Captain on the *Sparrow*, with the braid and buttons removed.

But I'm damned if I know what to do with the cow, he said.

Are you taking her to the bull to be served? they asked wickedly.

No, I want to sell her, he replied. I heard there were going to be a lot of people here so I though I'd come along and try and sell her.

What's wrong with the cow?

Wrong with her? No, my brother gave me a little farm with cows and horses, but he's not well and doesn't understand what I say to him. And it's no good talking to his lady-wife, she's against me. But what use is a farm to me when they won't give me any money? So, I have to sell the cow.

Captain Ulrik seemed subdued, his bravado and his arrogance not as they had once been. It suited him well enough and didn't make him pathetic. Quite the opposite in fact, he seemed more upright, like a man who has 'seen the light'. With his open answers to all their questions he created a sympathetic impression, people wanted to help him. Mathisen the butcher was standing over by the momument listening to the speech, so they fetched him over to take a look at the cow.

He asked how old she was.

Three years, that's what they said at the farm.

Why did he want to sell such a young animal?

At home they say she milks on only three teats, one for each year, but when she's four years then she'll milk on four teats, that's what they said.

The crowd roared with laughter.

I don't know, he said, embarrassed.

Shame. They'd been making fun of him back at the farm. Mathisen bought the cow, pulled out his big wallet and paid for it.

Ulrik thanked him. He looked happy and relieved, and he generously declined an offer to return the horse-blanket. The butcher hired a man to walk the cow overland to town.

After Robertsen the Customs man had finished his speech and everyone had given three cheers, he organized the march back to the boat. Again they sang. Captain Ulrik went aboard a moneyed man.

He called on the Mate and sat in his cabin.

Still the same year! he said, indicating the calendar on the wall. When's it going to change?

The Mate didn't answer.

I said, when's it going to change?

When the time comes.

Ah you're full of nonsense! He rang and ordered wine. It arrived with two glasses, but the Mate didn't drink. Just nonsense yes. And how do you and him get along together?

We get along alright.

Yes but how?

The way you and I did. We keep well out of each other's way.

Well that's just dandy! sneered Captain Ulrik. He'd drunk several glasses by now and was beginning to be more like his old self. Like dumb beasts and mutes, he said. I couldn't be doing with it, I resigned. When I think about it, month after month, year in and year out, you not saying a word – and your calendar that never moves – it's as though you're not allowed to move it for ten years. What's it supposed to mean?

My mouth is hurting so I'm not able to discuss this with you.

I don't care anymore, but many's the time I used to think to myself: Maybe he's lost his human rights for ten years? Is it any wonder I thought that?

The Mate did not reply.

Well regardless, it was unpleasant, and I didn't want to carry on anymore.

Well no, of course, your *trisa* left.

212

Trisa? I've got no connection whatsoever with that tramp of a *trisa*. Nix. Anyway, the last I heard, she was letting herself go along with some chemist, d'you know about that?

The Mate didn't answer.

D'you know anything about it, I'm asking?

He was on board not long ago, with another lady.

You don't say! cried Captain Ulrik. He was interested.

The Mate looked at his watch and didn't seem much interested in this line of talk. Look here, can you see anything in my mouth? he said and opened wide.

What am I supposed to see? That's a revoltingly ugly hole, I have to tell you that. But mine's probably just as ugly.

Look down the throat, said the Mate.

Yes, it's brown and blue.

It's sore.

Ulrik: Take a look now at mine and see if it's the same. I can't believe it's the same.

The mate looked and said curtly: No. I just can't understand what that is in my throat. Maybe I ate something poisonous. Sometimes I get like a long, stabbing pain.

You should have it seen to.

Soon I won't be able to get any food down. Not that I have any appetite anyway.

Well we each have our own cross to bear. She wrote to me you know, cried out to me, missed me so much and all that. But you say the chemist was here with another woman?

About two, three weeks ago.

So he's dropped her. By all that's holy it sounds as if he's dropped her! Doesn't it sound like that to you?

So what if he has dropped her?

No, of course – you have to be so mysterious and not know any-thing. I shouldn't've started selling off my cows so as I could afford her. There was no need for it. I should've just sat and waited at home and she would've come back to me.

Quite possibly, said the Mate and looked at his watch.

Then I won't try to meet her this evening. I'll sleep on board tonight and sail back with the boat early tomorrow morning. Don't you think that would be my best plan?

Someone said I should try lemon juice for my throat.

Or cognac, said Ulrik. There's nothing better for the throat than cognac. It's what I'd use for everything back home on the farm, except that it's so ridiculously expensive, so I haven't had any for quite a long while.

What do you do on your farm?

Do? Put a man like me on a farm? I quit!

What will you do now?

What will I do? If milady out at the mansion house keeps going on at me the way she does then I'll show her—

The mate looked at his watch and left . . .

Each man had spoken of the things that mattered to him. Did they hatch some plan together, plot some evil? No they didn't, but they were both in a bad way, nothing was going right, they were unhappy with themselves and unhappy with others. How're you doing? I'm not doing at all, it's a pain just to be alive. No, they didn't rage and curse, they were calm in their helplessness, they looked down each other's throats.

At the quay Captain Ulrik paid for the wine and bought another bottle to take ashore with him. He didn't come back to spend the night on board. We change our minds. Every man has his own cross to bear.

Captain Abel was decisive in a quite different way: as though the whole business were slightly contemptible he went to the police station and reported Robertsen the Customs man. So pressing was his need of money.

214

XX

DISQUIET BENEATH THE SURFACE.

The Wednesday before Easter young Clemens joined the milkboat. He must have had some reason or other to go onboard, and he made no secret of it: he wanted to know something about Africa, about Natal. He thought Captain Brodersen might be able to give him the information, but Abel hadn't travelled in that part of the world, America and Australia, that's where he had been.

Then I beg your pardon, Captain!

He sat in a corner with Mathisen the butcher who was travelling to fetch back a cow that had run away in the night. They sat together for a long time. Clemens was well turned-out and smart, his hair was trimmed, he was wearing new galoshes and gloves.

When Lolla passed by Clemens got to his feet and greeted her, they knew each other and spoke a few words together: This is the first time I've travelled with you, Lolla. – Welcome aboard! – There was something I wanted to see the Captain about, that's why I'm here.

Once Lolla had gone he explained things to Mathisen the butcher, so that there would be no misunderstanding: I called the head stewardess Lolla, because she used to be in our house – work for us, I mean. We're old acquaintances.

The hours passed, they had a nice sheltered spot and wouldn't find a better one. Cozy to sit here, doing nothing, smoking. They watched the goings on at each port of call, otherwise they just sat there observing the seagulls and the scenery, conversing now and then. The weather was blustery, with small gusts of snow that whirled in off the sea.

When the Captain was relieved he came down and joined them. Talk turned to the cow that had run away.

That was a helluva trick she played on me, said Mathisen the butcher. It's Easter, I need the meat, the cow should have been slaughtered yesterday, but she's run off home.

Ran all the way home from town?

Yes we could hardly believe it, but I got a phone call telling me she'd turned up at home. I bought her just this last Sunday from Captain Ulrik. A fine young animal, but he wanted to sell her, she was only milking on three teats, he said. Which by the way was not true, we milked her on all four teats when we got her home, somebody was having him on, because he knows nothing about that kind of stuff. Well, so we put up the cow when we got her home and gave her a feed and all that. And the same thing yesterday when she was resting after the walk to town. But you know what, in the night she slipped her tether and got the door open and away off home she ran.

Incredible!

I've seen something similar a couple of times before. Animals have such a good sense of direction that even if they reach a town by sea they can run back home by land. And even though they don't get mash and molasses at home like I give them, home is where they want to be.

It's the love of home, said Clemens.

God knows what it is, but they want to get back to where they grew up.

The Captain: And now the cow's going to be slaughtered anyway?

No, said Mathisen, almost embarrassed, I've traded her off as a milch cow. She was such a lovely animal . . .

Oh that's alright then.

Yes well, my wife kept on at me. So, Captain, if I can prevail on you to take the cow back with you when you sail then she won't have to take that long overland trip for a third time.

I'm sure we'll manage that, said the Captain.

I spoke to the Mate, but he didn't think there was room.

There's room alright.

Mathisen the butcher went ashore to see to his cow.

The Captain: Remarkable, that story of his!

Clemens, after he's thought about it: It's a well-documented fact – I've heard it from others besides him – animals are homeloving, they want to be home. Even wild animals have their territories, their patches, their homes. Often they'd be better off somewhere else, but they want to be where they came from. In spring the salmon and the trout head back up to the spawning grounds where they began life themselves. The migratory birds nest where they were born themselves. I remember one particularly striking example from my own childhood home: when all the nesting boxes were full there was one pair of starlings that made their home on a wretched little wooden tray stuck on the wall. One year the tray with the nest fell down. It was carefully returned to its place on the wall, and back came the starlings.

They probably had no option.

Plenty of options, there were thousands of tiles, she could have found them a splendid space beneath one of them. But best of all, the starlings came back to that same nesting tray the following year, year after year, wretched little home that it was. Then one year, just after Christmas, in plenty of time, the tray was removed and a nesting box hung in its place. As an experiment the tray was moved over to another wall, but wouldn't you know it, the starling found it and started using it again! And all summer long that new nesting box stood empty.

What was special then about that tray?

The base was a narrow bit of wood, and on the sides and over the top it was covered over with oilcloth It was a hovel of a nesting box, dreamt up and knocked together by a little boy. But it became a home.

Isn't that what you call instinct?

Yes it's love of home, the voice of the blood. I don't know all its secrets, but it's beautiful. In the middle of the confusion and doubt in which we humans wander, that's the way life reveals a will and a purpose: Life itself gives us the love of home, it isn't an invention.

The Captain is silent for a while, then unexpectedly he asks: Then what do you say about a man who dreams of nothing but, who is sick with the longing just to get away from his homeland for ever?

Did you say for ever?

Yes I did, for ever.

I'm no expert, answered Clemens. But might it not be that he is – as you yourself put it – *sick* with the longing? That this is a measure of how unhealthy and unnatural he is?

He has no roots here.

None? But of course he has. The language, for example, his native language, where he understands everything that can be said, and can say whatever he wants. That he spends a long time away from home, and when he returns the sight of it reduces him to tears. That he feels a bond with fellow-countrymen whom he meets abroad, that he is seeing them for the first time and yet knows them, recognises them, feels as if he links arms with them. I've never travelled, this is just something I've read about. But you, you have travelled.

The Captain: I don't know anything about all that.

Naturally Clemens spoke to a purpose: And if he finds himself lying at death's doorstep in some foreign hospital then he will wish he could return to his homeland to die. If his thoughts turn to God then it isn't the same God as the one here. God here was known for his goodness, that in itself was a medicine for the sick, the very intensity of it. *Herregud!* he says. He doesn't say *mon dieu*.

The Captain: I have been speaking of myself.

I see. You do have roots Captain, the very best, that's exactly what you have here. But somehow or other, some of them may have been severed.

The Captain shuddered: Just look at how it's snowing – and right now there's a warm sun shining in Kentucky! But as though he regretted having been so open he stood up and said: But you wanted to know

218

something about Natal. The Mate will probably be able to tell you what you want to know. He's on the bridge.

Then he left.

Yes, Clemens had business here on board and it was important to show that he hadn't forgotten it. He waited until dinner, when he had the Mate sitting beside him at table. But as things turned out he didn't get any information from him. The Mate was in a bad mood and his mouth was bothering him, it was painful for him to swallow, he winced each time, it looked as though he was swallowing by the sheer force of his will.

Excuse me, Mate, I hear you've been in Natal?

I've been to many places. Which Natal?

You know, Natal. In South Africa. Is there more than one Natal?

At least two. A city in Brazil and a country in Africa.

But the town of Natal, in Africa?

The town of Natal in Africa is called Port Natal. In fact it's not even called that any longer, they call it Durban.

Clemens apologised: Unfortunately I seem to have forgotten everything I learned at school.

What did you want to know about Port Natal?

I have a case pending there and I really need to know a little bit about how things are. For example, if necessary, how would I get there?

Just get on a boat.

Long journey?

Yes.

Clemens realised that he was bothering the Mate and he fell silent.

And now the Mate succumbed to the distraught bitterness of his mind. He was a sick man, he was wracked by pain, everyone at table saw how he flinched and swallowed as though he had fire in his mouth. He turned to Clemens and said: And now I suppose you'ld like to hear about the Natal in Brazil?

Clemens stared at him.

Well, I've never been there, said the Mate.

Clemens said nothing and finished his meal. No, he didn't want to know anything about Natal in Brazil, maybe not about any Natal anywhere in the world. His mission here onboard had been absurd.

After dinner he remained in the salon. He found some newspapers and a magazine, but rather than read he spent the time observing the *trisa* as she moved about while the girls cleared the table. Without being asked the *trisa* brought him coffee and cakes. You're welcome to smoke here too, she said, we'll open the windows afterwards. She was so solicitous. Sure, she was Fru Brodersen -but she was also Lolla.

He started to talk to her: I must ask you again to forgive me for having asked you to come and keep house for me.

No, no there's absolutely no need—

It was stupid of me. When I see how you're suited now

I believe you've got a really good girl now? Lolla blushed, checked herself and added: I don't remember who told me.

It was probably Fru Gulliksen, he said quietly and correctly.

Lolla said nothing.

Yes indeed, Regina is good. She's young, but she's very mature, very efficient. But there's no telling how long she'll stay.

I think she should stay a long time. Good position like that.

No she'll probably go and get herself engaged one of these days. And then I'll be back where I started. But won't you sit down and join me, Lolla? Here in your own front room, he added with a smile.

Lolla sat: I saw you talking to the Captain. I'd really like to know, what sort of impression did you get of him?

Clemens responded with another question: How did he take it, didn't it come as a real shock to him to be appointed Captain?

I don't know. Probably at first yes. But things don't last for him, it doesn't excite him much anymore. I can't get him to take the job seriously and appreciate it, he's still wearing the same uniform as when he started, and he refuses to go to the expense of a new one.

It didn't appear to be this Captain Brodersen that Clemens was really interested in, he said: Yes, he's a strange one alright. And what about you, Lolla, do you like it here?

Yes I like it.

What are you reading at the moment? I've got quite a few new books.

I don't get much time to read these days.

Me neither, he said. I've got a couple of awkward cases just at the

220

moment. That's what brings me on board here today, I thought I might be able to get some information about Africa.

Yes it was outrageous the way the Mate spoke to you. But he's a sick man, he has a lot of trouble with his throat.

I realized that, said Clemens. But you must come and see these new books, Lolla. He took her hand – such a big, sensuous hand, and pretended he wanted to take a closer look at her bracelet: Doesn't that strap pinch? No? It doesn't stop the blood circulating? This right here is an artery—

He didn't take it any further, let go of her hand again. But it was something, after all.

Lolla returned to the question of Abel: So you didn't get the impression he was wearing his first and his last uniform?

No, why should I? No, he said nothing at all about that.

Because I notice he's beginning to get restless. He feels himself drawn away, he's being drawn away again.

Norsemen are a travelling people, said Clemens, probably hoping that would be the end of it.

But she persisted: It upsets me so much on his account. He could have stayed here and had a job and board and lodging for life.

Clemens comforted her: He's probably just not the type. But don't take it so hard, Lolla, God knows, perhaps he's happier out travelling than we are staying put. It'll work out, you'll see, everything does, for him as well as for the rest of us.

Since all she wanted to talk about was Abel he left her and went out on deck. Miserable weather, flurries of snow, the deck wet with melting snow, a dreadful day to have business on board the *Sparrow*. And yet, all things considered, by no means a wasted day. Not because the Mate later approached him with a sort of apology for his rudeness at the dinner table, that didn't make any difference. But Clemens felt a quiet satisfaction at being a somebody on board the boat, that people were respectful of him, considerate. When he needed to get by someone they always made way for him, and if he passed a remark about the weather he was sure to get a courteous response. These were not trivial matters for a man who for years had been no more than his father's deputy, who was not an especially good lawyer, and whose wife had left

221

him. He seated himself once again in that sheltered corner he had occupied earlier in the day, and he noticed that several of the others passengers seemed inclined to join him, though they did not do so. Damn but it was good to be something more than a nobody!

And then along came Lolla with his rubbers and told him to put them on, it was cold, and the deck wet – why she even bent down as though to help him. No my dear Lolla, absolutely not, what are you thinking of! But when he took the rubbers from her he managed to find her hand again, and that was something too.

A great day to be aboard the *Sparrow*.

No, there was no big deal about the Mate's apology. A man like that never asked to be forgiven, no, but he did offer a sort of explanation: the food had been so warm, he felt he was being burned alive and it made him irritable.

Oh that's alright, said Clemens. Why are you wearing that thick bandage around your throat?

Well, I don't know if it does any good, but I've got something wrong with my throat and I'm trying all sorts of remedies.

Diphtheria?

I don't know.

Let me take a look, said Clemens, standing up and showing sympathy.

No, there's nothing to see.

Well, I'm not a doctor, said Clemens, and sat down again.

Doctor! sneered the Mate. As if the doctors know anything. I won't even tell you what they say is the problem with my throat. He called out to Alex: Get the swab and get this wet mopped up!

They reached their destination and tied up, milk churns and goods were unloaded from the boat and then everyone was free, Abel was free. Clemens went up to the kiosk and bought newspapers, Abel wasn't the reading type, he got to talking with the men from the engine room. The evening passed. Clemens had number 1 cabin, the luxury cabin.

That night Lolla gave two short raps on the Captain's door and went in. The ceiling light was on, the alarm clock ticked, it was about two o'clock.

Didn't you ring?

Abel, without turning round: No.

That's odd, your number dropped.

Go to bed, he said.

Yes I might as well. So there's nothing you want?

No thanks.

Sorry I'm only half-dressed.

Go to bed, Lolla.

He hadn't turned round and hadn't looked at her, it was not the first time she had visited him like this. It was very solicitous of her, to go around in the night like that, checking that things were in order and everybody was alright.

On the return trip the cow came aboard. A young beauty, she was. She was a little nervous but walked up the gangway without protesting, and once on board she turned out to be a model passenger. Where should they put her? Here maybe – or maybe there? Why can't she have a cabin, some joker asked. They made a tremendous fuss of her, everyone stroked her and the serving girls came along with something to eat for her. What's her name? Klara, I believe, said Mathisen the butcher. There, didn't I tell you she was human?

Klara occupied the sheltered corner, and there was alway someone sitting there talking to her. They untied her once they reached the calm waters inside the lighthouse, and Klara wandered about and looked at the shore from the railings, her large, gentle eyes filled with visions.

Klara went ashore and Robertsen the Customs man took her place, storming aboard. He was searching high and low for someone, looked in the salon, the *trisa* was busy with something or other.

Where's Abel?

Abel?

Yes, where is Abel, that's what I asked.

Trisa didn't answer, just carried on with what she was doing.

Goat! hissed Robertsen and stormed off.

He discovered Abel in the Captain's cabin, naturally, Abel was at home. Robertsen might have thought of that if he hadn't been so wound up. He raged and he shook and he yelled: Abel would regret this, he'd pay for this! Unspeakable wickedness, to set the police onto a man who had done nothing. But just you wait, there'll be fun for all the family, Lolla had already been reported, he intended to report the whole family, her father had had a child with the serving girl before he ran off. And Abel would take everything back. Investigate a public figure, a servant of the state, outrageous—

Clemens wouldn't go ashore until he'd tempted Lolla yet again with his new books, she really must visit him one day and borrow as many as she wanted. Lolla thanked him graciously and excused herself, saying she had so little time to read on board, but just think, if only the Captain for once would pick up a book and start reading! But he didn't, the almanac was the only thing he read, he studied the almanac. No, she couldn't understand him at all. But what sort of impression did Clemens get of the Captain? Truthfully?

Yes yes, Clemens said, she was to be sure to remember about the books if she ever happened to be passing his way—

XXI

SHE DOESN'T SAIL ON GOOD FRIDAY. IT'S A PUBLIC HOLIDAY SO the *Sparrow* doesn't sail. But look, here's the big coastal steamer just arrived, all the big boats run on Good Friday, and every other day too, no exceptions. The milkboat's different, she doesn't sail on public holidays.

Restless in his idleness, Abel looks over at the coastal steamer and wishes he were on board her. Just the thought of it is enough to raise a breath of life in him, a joy that opens like a flower. He calls to the Mate who sits smoking by the engine: Has she rung yet? The Mate perhaps answers, but not loud enough to hear. Abel hurries over to him and asks, as though it's a matter of some importance: Has she rung yet? First bell, answers the Mate – and there's the second bell! The puff goes out of Abel: so what if the coastal steamer had rung her bells? He couldn't sail with her, he had no money. She rang for a third time. It was nothing, he said, only a letter—

A good chance gone. He'd miss the next one too. Nor could he get

225

away on Easter Sunday, when he would be lying over, and on Easter Monday he would be out with the milk again. There was no prospect of getting away until Whitsun. Whitsun was seven weeks away.

During that time the police called on him several times in connection with their investigations: Robertsen insisted that it was Abel's own signature, both his wife and his daughters had seen him write his name in their poetry albums, and then on the obligation. Same letters, same pen, same ink — here you are, have the lot examined! said Robertsen. And the police thought: If Abel's name was forged, then why would he go to the bank himself and pay off on the forged document? All very odd.

They kept on about it for so long that in the end he fell back into his old ways and stopped caring a damn about any of it. On top of it all Lolla found out about it and was extremely upset. How could he have resurrected that old business which he had sorted out himself long ago? It was an uncomfortable time for him.

He stands on the bridge in the weeks between Easter and Whitsun and captains the *Sparrow* and loathes and hates it. This has all been a deep disappointment to him, it has been a torment to him to have to maintain a show of order and a conscientiousness in regard to something that does not interest him at all. Then what did interest him? Hanging around maybe, passing the time? At a sawmill in Canada he was able to work, long ago. Even here at home he was once able to save the life of a man named Alex, long ago, an isolated incident, a puff of wind, then nothing.

Nor did life onboard present any particular challenge, none at all. Once established the daily round of idiocies was self-perpetuating, a minimal maintenance of the milk churns that were to come aboard and those that were to be put ashore. How could he endure that? The absence of risk that characterised the whole ship, provisions made in the interests of safety in every direction, this irritated him, the porcelain sign above every door to stop people getting lost, bells to ring, cushions, cushions everywhere. Not that he sought out risk and death, his indifference was too great for that, but a change would have been refreshing. On the big sailing ships there was rigging to clamber about in, on board here there were staircases with carpets and brass rails. No rigging.

226

But then wasn't the job an exact match for his abilities? Was he perhaps some great chieftain with sabre drawn and wild courage: Ho! Follow me, lads! No. But in all his insignificance he was not without character. That was something. He had a divine indifference towards how things turned out. That was something. He could endure, he could go without. He didn't cling on to anyone nor seek protection, for he was sublimely uncritical himself and had nothing which he thought worth defending. His weak ambition and average intelligence were his tools, as they later became his liabilities. But they were reliable and complete, and they made him, in his own way, a king. In their own way then: his kingliness.

Wind and weather a matter of indifference. Some slight change, a little engine trouble? Same old thing. Not to speak of matters of a quite different order, being shot at, for example. That time when Alex shot at him he was tying his shoelaces, and he finished tying them. He would have done the same again today, finished tying them.

He could of course have run off with the boat and stayed out all night, so that people had to set off in search of him – but no, he just ran these errand with the milk churns, from farm to farm, and then back home again in the evening.

There was a chart hanging in the chartroom showing the *Sparrow's* route. It was as unforgiving as a railway line, like a railway line it lay open to view and shameless, with no attempt to excuse itself. He stands on the bridge and realises that it's impossible to make a mistake, they cleave to the coast all the way, he's doomed to paddle the shallows. And when they see him coming folk say: What manner of steamer is this approaching? Ah yes, it's only the *Sparrow*.

Week after week on the bridge. Whitsun approaches. But so what if Whitsun approaches? He couldn't steal the money-box and run, for there was no money-box, only an accounts book. He could sell a few clothes to a second-hand dealer, but he wouldn't get much for them. And still that rascal Robertsen wouldn't sell his boats and pay him.

Today, once again, he arrives on the bridge at the last minute and hasn't given himself time to dress properly, with no collar on and just the jacket over his shirt. Doesn't care. It's the end of May, and mild.

No passengers, people don't travel just before Whitsun. Only the blind hurdy-gurdy man to help up the gangway with his instrument. He doesn't have a bad foot and gangrene today, but he's still as blind as usual, fumbling his way forward. His hands are absurdly small and fine-skinned because the lazy monkey has never worked. He has no objection to people noticing his small hands and assuming that he comes from a good family.

Lolla brings the rest of the Captain's clothes up to him so that he can change in the chart room. She's done this before, she's so correct and proper on his account, he's to look his best by the time they make the first stop. Everybody has their own little obsession, and Lolla is a lady.

Do you want me to help you with your tie?

No thank you.

She's offered to do this for him before and he's turned her down, he doesn't want her breasts so near him, to feel her breath in his face. He could scream. Not that it wasn't good breath, it was too good.

And here's a clean handkerchief.

Thank you.

And after this there's nothing left for her but to leave. She daren't bring up the Robertsen business again, which has been gnawing away at her, no, she even hums a little as she makes her way down the steps, as though she's in a nothing mood and has just been acting out of simple courtesy. And the Captain has thanked her and been courteous, what else could he do?

The hours pass, the long hours of the morning watch, the captain gets relieved, goes down to his cabin. Instantly the blind hurdy-gurdy man is on his feet and follows him. No fumbling, he sees like a hawk and he follows, he's in a hurry. He opens the door without knocking and enters. He closes the door behind him too, but to be as blind as possible he asks: Is that Captain Abel Brodersen of the *Sparrow*?

What the – ? Abel gasps.

The hurdy-gurdy man hands him a letter and says a few words about who it's from, it's from Olga, Fru Gulliksen. Then he's back out through the door again. Gone, no one is to see him here.

Ah that Olga – money and letters: I'm sorry this is only half of it –

228

if only I'd asked him for the whole two thousand before we got married – but now he's got me anyway and still he won't. But later – and have a good Whitsun, dear Abel – yours in haste.

Yes yes yes, of course, Olga was the only divine person in the world, she's lifted him high on the crest of a wave and there he sits. Hard not to tell someone, but he isn't crazy, he's smart and he hides the letter and the money inside his shirt. He smiles and makes the trip that day as though in a dream.

That evening, at the terminus, he seeks out Lolla and has a friendly talk with her. She's pale with worry, Robertsen wants to scandalise her name, he wants to destroy her. No no, says Abel, Robertsen can't do her any harm. And suddenly he asks, as though from another world: Can you remember, Lolla, if any money was sent to Lawrence that time?

Ha, I can see you've got matters of your own to be thinking about.

Well yes, because it's strange that he hasn't been released by now and written to me.

Money was sent.

Thank you, Lolla. You're so good at getting things done. See, they were talking about that cow, remember, the one that was so fond of its home, it ran away in the night, it wanted to get back to where it came from. What was it's name again?

Klara.

And they said it was something that was there in all healthy creatures, the desire to get back to where they lived as children. Right. But then what about Lawrence, I was thinking.

Lolla, provoked and despairing of him, covers her face with her hands. He smiles and for some reason he's in a good mood and pities her in her despair, he really does and he wants to help her out of it: Sorry, but Lawrence just came into my mind. He was Irish, but he came to Mexico when he was eighteen years old and he hasn't been home since. His roots in Ireland were cut.

How can you care about all that? Lolla sniffs and begins to cry.

Yes, because you see, he was the son of tenant farmer and was due to get married. But then she married the son of another farmer.

He has Lolla's attention: Why did she do that?

Well you couldn't blame her: she had to get married to the other man.

Ah! said Lolla.

So then Lawrence left Ireland and hasn't been back since. So what about his love of home?

Don't know.

Let me tell you a couple of things about Lawrence.

If you like, says Lolla patiently. She sees clearly that Abel is in another world, and though she's feeling low herself anything is better than sitting alone and brooding. Did he have it out with the girl before he left?

Yes. But as I say, she had her reasons, so he didn't want to stand there just being in the right. That's what he told me himself. God be with you! he said to her. God be with you too! she said back to him, and kiss me! she said. But he wouldn't, she looked changed to him already and her face ugly. Kiss me just once, she said. No he wouldn't, but God be with you! he told her again, and left her. She's written to him since, but he hasn't replied, he says.

Lolla: What does he look like, this Lawrence?

He looks magnificent, let me tell you. We met each other when we were young and kept up with each other even when our ways parted, and when we met up again after our letters we were pals again. To begin with he wasn't as good as me at the various jobs we took, but he was always the one who got us out of scrapes with the police because he was the good-looking one.

Were the police after you?

Not really. Very occasionally. But it didn't take a lot, you under-stand. When we were out and we had nowhere to live and no food and no money we might pick a lock or force a window, and once we were inside there were other locks to pick while we were looking for some-thing to eat. But that kind of thing was strictly forbidden, according to the police. But then Lawrence showed what he was made of, he would rip open his shirt to show how skinny he was. Look here, he said, even though we weren't actually the least bit skinny.

Lolla managed a smile. What a strange life! she said.

Once upon a time he'd been a solid type, a good Catholic, went to confession and was respected by everyone. He got caught up in a revolution in Mexico but escaped with his life, in Canada he joined the police. Still handsome, still neat, but he'd started to let himself go. When I met him in Canada I often took the glass out of his hand and emptied it, and he never protested. He stayed in the police for three years, because he was good at the job, but then he got fed up. We were in good spirits when we headed into the States, it was in the spring, and he got work in a cemetery laying turf around the graves. I started in a little factory stuffing spring mattresses. It wasn't right for either of us, though Lawrence was familiar with that type of work from his childhood in Ireland and he was expert at laying turf. After we'd been working a while and earned some money we bought a woollen blanket each and travelled across the States. In the spring we worked on a big farm, that was another thing Lawrence was good at, he was one of the best workers, he was the owner's right-hand man. There were ten of us. When the spring work was over we headed out again and came to Kentucky. We had plenty of money by this time and travelled for most of the summer, and in the autumn we got work on a farm again and saved for the winter. Things were working out for us. It was six months since we'd left Canada.

But Lawrence started drinking too much. I don't blame him really, we ended up in a black town and once we got tired of the blacks there was nothing else left to do in that town but drink. We put up with the blacks, they sang well and all that, but to have to put up with them from dawn til dusk if you're sober – ! Some of them had snow-white hair and beards and black faces, the complete opposite of us, to us they seemed like beings from under the ground, or the moon, and they didn't laugh, their mouths weren't made for laughing. For a while Lawrence had a black girl living in his cabin, she made the bed and cooked the food with a cigarette in her mouth and didn't care where the ash ended up . . . It wouldn't have bothered me, but Lawrence got tired of it and pulled her hair, and so she ran off and left him on his own again. He couldn't look after himself, he should have travelled on but instead he stayed put, just went to pieces, grieving and drinking and grieving, it wasn't a grown-up way to behave. And not even a priest to hear my confession, he said, I have to carry the burden all on my own.

So in the spring we left there and came to a white town. We got jobs and thought everything would be better, but Lawrence had got the habit. And on top of all that he got a letter from the girl in Ireland. He said he never answered her, but that was just his pride, because wherever we travelled there was always a letter waiting for him when we arrived, so she knew where he was. Her husband's left her, he said. That's too bad, I said. It makes no difference, he said, it's just some tricky business that leaves them free to do whatever they like. Lawrence didn't let it bother him, he seemed to have got over her, the only thing that bothered him was that he was the loser, the other man had got her. That made him bitter.

But it was stupid of him to drink so much, we talked about it, and he agreed to stop, and gave me his hand on it. Then he was off to Mexico again, he went to confession then left for Mexico. He was gone a year and when he came back he looked wonderful in his polished boots and with a velvet collar on his jacket. He was a strong, handsome man and hadn't let himself go any more, though of course he did a lot of crazy things when he was on one of his binges, because he had lots of money, God knows where he got it from. Well I guess we're all just people. I held down that job in the little prairie town the whole time, repairing cars and machinery, I didn't want to lose the job, so I didn't see much of Lawrence at that time—

Lolla listens to all this with interest. She says: He wasn't the right company for you anyway.

Abel: You think not? Then you don't know Lawrence. He was the best company you could ask for. He could be serious and god-fearing enough when it was called for, take my word for it. I don't understand how you can say a thing like that.

That's the impression I get from listening to you talk.

Let me give you one little example. We went to a dance-hall one evening, and we were sitting at a table eating with two women Lawrence knew. There was a couple at the table opposite who were annoying us, they were drinking champagne, the man was talking too much, nothing the waiter did was right for him and the whole time he kept repeating his name: My name is Clonfille, remember it! Then he's probably a French Canadian, is what we thought. Everything would probably have been alright, but the man had such an unbelievably loud voice he drowned out the music, we might have made something out of it straightaway but we didn't. But after you've heard for the fifth time that my name is Clonfille it gets to be too much, and on top of it all the man kept looking over at us because we had better-looking women. The waiter arrived with their food, nice food, good food, but it wasn't right, take it away, my name is Clonfille! God, he's so insistent about that name of his! said our girls. Lawrence said nothing, he dipped his face down and carried on eating just as insistently until he'd finished. Meanwhile our neighbour carried on, hitting the table and swearing, challenging the whole room. The manager stayed away, he didn't want to have to throw him out because he was drinking expensive champagne. But everyone should have known that Lawrence wouldn't put up with a man winking at his girls, it took a lot less than that to get him started. And so when the man was finally ready to eat and picked up his knife and fork Lawrence stood up and went over to him. He grabbed hold of his neck and pushed his head forward: Say grace before you start!

Lolla clasped her hands: Well I never!

So you see, that's the sort of person he was: Say grace before you start!

And did the man?

It took him a while. First he twisted his face up, and when he saw who it was he beat the table with his hand to show that he gave in. Once Lawrence let go of him the man stood up. Lawrence called him Pat: Out playing games again, Pat? Never mind, just you say grace! The man sat down again, smiled sheepishly and prayed. Goodnight! said Lawrence and left him.

Lolla again: Well I never – but who was this Pat?

Yes, who was he? No-one, maybe. Out of jail yesterday, a robbery last night, a party this evening and back inside again tomorrow. Something like that. Lawrence just said: An acquaintance from the time when I was a policeman. But now listen, Lolla, this is the kind of man Lawrence was: Later on he went over to Pat again and said: Now you dunk me just the same as I dunked you! Pat was sober by this time and wouldn't do it, but once he heard that Lawrence had been fired from his job as a policeman he did it. That's fair, he said, and gave Lawrence's head a real dunk on the tabletop. And afterwards they shook hands.

Lolla shakes her head: I don't understand that kind of life.

No, it wasn't exactly like the life here on board. Anyway – that was the night I met Angèle for the first time.

You met . . . Oh, her . . .

She was sitting at our table, kind and gentle, the best-looking of the two of them, best-looking in the whole dance-hall. I've never seen anyone to touch her. Lawrence was the one who knew her, but I walked her home. She went to bed and I sat on the side of her bed and didn't want to ask her for anything the whole night long, that's how pretty she was. We saw each other for a while and I bought her a little silk dress to wear when we went out, and after that she wanted to belong to me That's how it started. We spent so much time together that I lost my job at the workshop and then times were hard for us. As far as Angèle was concerned it didn't matter, and after we got married she was happy to come with me to that black town where I once lived with Lawrence and where I knew my way around. It cost next to nothing to live there, I fished a bit, planted sweet potatoes and at night I went out to look around and always found something or other. They were good days.

Yes, so you say.

So I say? Abel flushes and he exclaims: I want to go back there!

Lolla: *What* do you want?

Joke, Lolla, joking of course. But at least once before I die I would like to . . . I mean, there's a grave there—

On the return trip the following day there were only the ship's own people aboard, even the hurdy-gurdy man had gone ashore. It was the day before Whitsunday and the weather was good. Lolla planned to go home to her mother's place on the beach and stay there until the Monday. No point in asking where the Captain and the Mate were going to spend the holiday, they would be staying on board. One of the girls was going to stay to look after them.

The hours pass.

Who's that singing on deck? The *trisa* asks in surprise.

The girl runs out to take a look and returns: It's the Captain.

The Captain? says the *trisa* in surprise. How strange.

They tie up at the quay. The big coast boat hasn't arrived yet.

But Abel is impatient, he starts changing at once out of his uniform and into his ordinary clothes. Through the half-open door he asks if *trisa* has gone. The girl answers yes. But when Abel steps out on deck in his grey suit, almost unrecogisable in his finery, *trisa* is standing there. She gives a start: Are you going somewhere?

Abel manages to smile and is all innocence: Well yes, it's Whitsun isn't it? I thought I'd be the gentleman and accompany you into town, Lolla – with your permission? There's a shop I have to go to before it closes.

While they're in town he hears the coast boat whistle. I'm just going in here, he says, Goodbye, Lolla.

But it was his bad luck that the shop turned out to be a little grocery store, a place where you could buy soap, candles, eggs, oranges – what would Lolla make of that? He had to apologise to the woman in the shop, tell her he'd made a mistake, and leave. Turning his gaze up the street he sees Lolla standing there, keeping an eye on him. He darts into the next shop, a farm-store selling everything from children's toys to rope to boots, and by the time he comes out again Lolla has started to walk on, though she turns and looks back. And then he daren't wait any longer, he sets off running and doesn't even risk looking back to see whether she's following.

The coast boat rings her bell for the second time, then shortly after that for the third time.

Abel races on board the *Sparrow*, grabs the gun which is lying there wrapped in a pair of socks and races off again. It's too late, the coast boat has cast off, as usual she's backing out to make her turn, but a small boat might still reach her. A rowing boat. Abel has one, two, three of them lying in a row, Robertsen's boats, he runs to the first one, casts off and takes up the oars. The waters around him are surging and he reaches the coast boat as she's in mid-turn. A rope! he shouts, and shoving the rowing boat away with his toe he hauls himself up on board.

Once on deck he stands and looks back. Everyone has gone from the quay by now, only the tall figure of Lolla remains.

XXII

HE COULDN'T BE STOPPED BY THE POLICE, BECAUSE HE HADN'T run off with the takings, he'd just left. Maybe he'd be back soon, after all, he'd left all his clothes in his cabin, as if he was only going away for a Whitsun holiday and would be back on the Monday.

Lolla warned Westman and the others directors on the board of the *Sparrow*, she didn't hide the fact that she thought Abel was gone for good and what should they do? As well as being the chief stewardess on board she was, of course, also the majority shareholder, so it was a matter of some concern to her. The board would have to do something.

They waited the whole of Whitsunday, but Abel sent no telegram and he didn't come back. The *Sparrow* was due to sail the following day as usual, and there was no-one to take charge of her. They could probably have got hold of Captain Ulrik again, but having once got rid of Captain Ulrik they really didn't want him back, he spent too much of the time drinking. They would have to put Gregersen the

236

Mate in temporary command, and get Lolla to continue as chief stewardess.

Gregersen the Mate wasn't happy about it and objected: he wasn't well, his throat was bad and he had to gargle with cognac.

Yes, they said, but his throat would get better in the summer.

Well I hope so, said Gregersen, annoyed with them for having an opinion on what was, after all, his throat.

Then it's agreed, they said.

Not at all, Gregersen wanted to think it over first.

Yes, but the boat's due to sail early tomorrow morning, seven o'clock?

Gregersen, irritated by their persistence: I suppose I'll do it then, but not for long, remember that. You're arguing with a sick man here, and my throat hurts too much for me answer you. But alright then, I've said I'll do it. Who's going to replace me on the bridge?

One of the crew, they had thought, perhaps the most senior. They would leave that up to him to decide.

Well thank God for that! Gregersen sneered, his throat on fire.

So that worked out, everything does, Gregersen in command now, with Alex to relieve him on the bridge. Alex? He was the youngest of the deckhands, but he'd been making the trip for thirteen months now and no-one could teach him anything. On top of that he was polite and well-turned out and could be given the job of selling tickets to the passengers. Dammit, he was just the right man for the job.

They sailed, and the temporary solution got less and less temporary. The weeks went by, and nothing changed. Everything depended on Gregersen's willingness to carry on as Captain. And, strange as it might seem, he really did get better and better as the summer progressed, though it was hard to say whether it was because of the mild air or the regular gargling with cognac. He carried on in his post, and *trisa* and Alex carried on in theirs.

But naturally the situation wasn't entirely satisfactory: Gregersen refused to go to the expense of buying a Captain's uniform, no, not even a third stripe for his Mate's jacket, and that meant that Alex's chances of getting any stripes at all on his jacket disappeared. It wasn't that easy for him to collect ticket money from passengers wearing his ordinary civilian clothes, people sometimes turned awkward and refused to pay a man who wasn't wearing any stripes at all. And a new and difficult question arose: so far Alex had been taking his meals with the rest of the crew, but now his ideas got bigger and he wasn't averse to the notion of eating at the Mate's place in the salon. He was too polite to come right out and ask, but he hinted to the girls that he would like them to put his case. *Trisa* said no. The rejection came after Alex had been three months in the Mate's job and it hit him hard. He hinted that he was married to Lili, a lady who had once been the cashier at the sawmill. That only made *trisa*'s no all the more decisive: Lili, huh? And what about her? As Christmas approached Alex began to wonder if it might be something to take up with the union.

Ah, the whole structure was out of shape by now, nothing was where it was supposed to be: Gregersen didn't move into the Captain's cabin, nor Alex into the Mate's cabin. And what about the poker games, was it alright for Alex the Mate to sit and play poker with the crew? And ought he to put up with it when the old sailors Leonart and Severin made laboured fun of the Mate and asked him for his estimate of the height of the sun?

But of them all the one who suffered most was probably the *trisa*, Fru Brodersen. Before she had been the Captain's mother, even if only his stepmother, she'd been the lady on board. Now she was the *trisa* and nothing more. She was a well-read and well mannered and refined lady, an imposing figure , elegant, proud, dignified, she didn't mix with just anyone; but now things began to change. On the busiest public holidays, when it was crowded on board, people started expecting her – yes, her! – to bring the coffee or the half-bottle of wine they'd been waiting an age for. She listened to these absurdities and said nothing. If she didn't want to get involved in an argument with just anybody then she had to keep quiet. Now that she was no longer related to the Captain she had lost her privileged position. She was very uncomfortable. For both Gregersen and Alex their promotions had brought advantages in the shape of a wage-rise and heightened prestige – but what had *trisa* gained? She stuck it out until the late summer, then she went to see young Clemens.

*

She might well have turned to Olga for advice, but she turned to Clemens.

He was just the same as ever, affable, decent, looking perhaps just a little happier these days. He showed her all the books that were just waiting for her, more and more of them as time passed, he hadn't wanted to shelve them with the others until she'd seen them.

Her response to his loyal consideration was a polite thanks and a mild show of interest. She had come on other business, she hoped he would forgive her for bothering him, she didn't know if she might allow herself to share certain of her more private concerns with him?

But of course, of course. She really was looking a little bit down today, he said.

Lolla smiled: Well, at least he wasn't.

Him? No, things were going too badly, he'd had a few sizeable cases and already won one of them – an out-of-court settlement as it happened. So he wasn't complaining. But her?

Well – Captain Abel had, of course, left.

Yes, he'd heard that. A strange person.

Run off, she said, there was no other way of putting it. And now she was fed up with her work on board and tired of the whole boat, what should she do?

Clemens didn't misunderstand, it never occurred to him that she had come to offer her services as his housekeeper. Or did it? Of course it did. Indeed it did. For one brief, beautiful moment he felt it in his heart. He sat there, uncertain. Yes, we all need advice, he said. Then he added, dear Lolla.

Yes, but what should she do?

Silence.

Listen – would she perhaps like a glass of wine, now that she was here?

Lolla, blushing furiously: Did he – did he mean it?

But of course. She had offered him coffee and cakes on board, it had been so welcoming of her, he remembered it well. And since she was here anyway, he would fetch a bottle, he said. He stood up.

No, but he shouldn't have to—

It was nothing.

239

Lolla got to her feet too and followed him. She remembered from the old days where the wine was: But wouldn't he allow her to –?

They ended up doing it together, found a bottle of port with a drop left in it and Lolla brought it in on a tray. They nodded to each other and drank.

Yes, there were quite a few things around the house he had to do for himself now, he said. Regina had left.

Oh!

Regina had finally got engaged. The grandmother came now, the waffle lady. She made his breakfast every day. He ate dinner out and got his own supper from the larder.

Lolla shook her head.

Oh it wasn't too bad, he didn't suffer. But that wasn't what they were supposed to be discussing. Surely she wasn't thinking of leaving the *Sparrow*?

Oh yes, she was considering it.

I see, he said, and waited a few moments. He knew perfectly well that she hadn't really come in search of his advice, she had come looking for someone to talk to. And would it really be such a bad idea for her to leave the boat?

No, would it? she repeated. Sure, she had the job on board, it was something to do, it paid her wages, gave her a future and all that. But she just wasn't enjoying it anymore.

Did she have another job in mind?

She'd certainly thought about it. She didn't know if she was being too ambitious in thinking about opening a little shop?

Clemens, back to earth with a bump: A shop – mmhh – a little shop—

Yes, it needn't be more than a little dairy?

Mmh, that was certainly one option.

A dairy shop with a window display and a range of goods on the shelves.

Yes, but was there any point in being so modest? After all, she had a controlling interest in the *Sparrow*.

The shares weren't hers, she said. But she might be able to raise a small loan on the strength of them.

Of course she could.

It cheered her up to hear that he thought her plan practicable, and she asked whether Hr. Clemens would be willing to help her out at the start with the odd matter, business letters, the lease and so on?

With the greatest of pleasure.

She stood up.

Right, and now you must pick out some books for yourself, he said, and fetched a large sheet of wrapping paper.

She wondered whether she might leave that until later. Because if she was going to be on the move—

Quite right. That was silly of him.

He drank with her, they emptied a second glass, and he followed her to the door. When she gave no sign of offering him her hand he took it and said: Do come again soon. Oh by the way, Lolla, that oleander that was so well looked after in the old days – won't you take a look at it, now that you're here?

She went into the living room, looked the plant over, felt the earth in the pot and then returned to the door. He took her hand again.

She went to see Westman and they talked together. She was too cautious to hand in her notice immediately, but she hinted that she was getting tired of the *Sparrow*. She was going to train the older of the two girls so that she could replace her if needs be.

She was active again, full of energy, bustling about in seach of suitable premises, doing her sums. She didn't want to sell wine, but certainly cigars, baked goods and fruit along with the milk and eggs, tinned food, quality meat. A good neighbourhood was the most important consideration, nice people, upper class. She met Robertsen the Customs man and was no longer afraid of him, he didn't bite, on the contrary he greeted her, and that was because Abel had gone and the case against the Customs man been dropped. She met Lovise Rolandsen, married to Tengvald the smith, accompanied by four of her innumerable children, clamoring and rioting around their mother – and God knows, perhaps it was precisely having so many that made life bearable for Lovise Rolandsen.

Young Clemens had understood her so well and made things look

241

brighter for her, she could go on board again in a better mood than when she left. The Mate sat smoking by the engine-room door. Pity about him, he didn't even nod, something or other on his mind maybe, as he watched the sparrows on the dock with glazed eyes. He looked thin, yellow.

I was wondering, Mate, if we might not be able to cook you something that wouldn't hurt your throat so much?

The mate, dismissively: Why is that?

Well – so maybe it wouldn't hurt your throat so much.

I'm alright.

Yes, thank goodness, you do seem better now, I was only wondering if we might make something special for you.

Her friendliness has an effect on him, suddenly it affects him very strongly, he gets up and stands there. He turns his head to one side to hide the flush on his yellow face: I'll be frank with you, Fru Brodersen, it isn't worth it. But my sincere thanks to you.

Tell me, if you anything occurs to you.

Preferably not something hot.

Not hot no. We'll be sure to remember that.

It really won't make any difference, he said. It was better in the summer, but now it's getting worse again.

But can't anything be done? What do the doctors say?

The Mate snorts: The doctors? They wanted me in hospital last year. One after the other they said I should admit myself. I'm not doing that.

Not doing that?

No. Apart from that I'm in good shape, it's just this pain in my throat. Came on so quickly. Admit yourself straightaway, they said. It's urgent, they said. That was last year, and I'm still here.

Aren't you taking any medicine?

I smoke diligently. And gargle with cognac. I should be ashamed really, but look here, I carry this little hip-flask everywhere with me – like an alcoholic.

Doesn't it burn?

Like fire. It burns.

But you think it helps?

242

I don't know. But this is what I use now. No, I guess it doesn't really help. But it wouldn't help to get myself admitted either. Even last year they said I should have come to them earlier. I should have come to them even before I knew there was anything wrong. What's the point in having myself admitted when it's already too late? It's *cancer*, they told me! he screamed.

Are you married, Mate? We know nothing about you.

The Mate didn't answer.

I do feel sorry for you, she said at length.

Immediately he was brusque and dismissive again: For me? There's people a lot worse off than me.

Lolla didn't say any more. After she left the Mate sat down again and studied the sparrows. It must be awful, she probably thought. He'd stood there the whole time with his head turned aside, maybe to avoid breathing his cognac breath all over her. In the midst of all his woes he was a strong-willed and consistent man and there was perfection in his determination.

He's as prickly as he's ill, the crew used to say. They had something to say to him now, and they were all going in together. As the eldest Severin would be their spokesman, but Alex, who was now an officer, couldn't go along with them. That left just two, a deputation of two, Severin and Leonart.

They caught him at a bad time. He was sitting there and regretting everything he'd said to *trisa*, all that confessing, all that stuff she'd got him talking about, got him to turn himself inside out – damn her intrusive friendliness! He runs over to the railing and spits angrily into the sea, takes out his hipflask and gargles, pretends to spit it out, then sits down again by the engine room door. Damn her intrusive friendliness—

What do you want? he asked.

Well, said Severin, the same thing as last time.

The Mate stood up then sat back down again at once and it was almost as if he hadn't stood up at all.

Yes, what do you want?

What do we want? Well – now that Alex got put up on the bridge there's just the two of us left, that's Leonart here and me. We're a man short.

Talk to the owners, I told you.

But we have done, Mate—

Captain.

Okay then, Captain. We have done, Captain.

He notes the malicious repetition of Captain but asks: And what did the owners say?

They said they needed to hear it from the Captain if another man was needed.

The Mate gets up and remains standing: Another man is *not* needed, Severin.

Hm! said Severin. So you're not going to put in a good word for us, Mate?

No, the Captain will not.

That's all we wanted to know, Mate.

The deputation leaves. Muttering to each other about resigning, picketing. Hahaha, he won't be able to sail with two-thirds of a crew—

XXIII

YOUNG CLEMENS HAS DEVELOPED A HABIT OF SITTING ON A bench on the quayside and looking over towards the *Sparrow*. Now he's there again.

But back to the beginning. Where it began was two days ago, when he plucked up his courage and went on board to see the *trisa*. It bothered her that she wasn't dressed for the occasion, wearing a white apron that covered her from her chin to her shoes, because she was in the middle of cleaning and polishing and getting everything ready for when she left.

And young Clemens arrived. His behaviour seemed odd, different, as though he were playful, young, playing with fire. Fair damsel, he said to her. And yet he wasn't drunk – the very idea, young Clemens drunk! But then, the very idea of saying 'fair damsel'!

He'd been thinking about this idea of the dairy shop, it really wasn't quite the right thing for her. What she should do instead was marry him, he said.

He had to say it in that desperate way, or else he would never have got around to saying it at all.

She was lost for words.

It helped him to stare at the floor the whole time and carry on speaking: She was the one he should have had, her and no other. Thought about her for twenty years, loved her, sick with the love of her. And now here he was saying it for the first time, and he probably didn't realise how twisted his face was. He didn't even dare look at her face—

Have you come straight from home? Lolla managed to ask.

Aha, straight from home. But don't change the subject. What you mean is, have I made a few stops on the way here? Not a drop, smell my breath! But don't change the subject, I want to tell you everything—

He told her everything and a lot of other things all over again, talked for a long time, kept her there. The expression on her face changed many times, she listened to every word he said, sat there pale and interested. She promised to think about it.

That was two days ago.

Now she's made a trip with the milk boat and she's back again. Young Clemens sits on his bench. He catches a glimpse of her in the doorway to the salon, not that she waves, but she's dressed for their meeting and that in itself is a kind of wave. He hastens on board and finds her in the double cabin, the door left wide open for him, there she is. They throw themselves into each other's arms in front of the open door.

Then she must have thought and thought about it and in the end realised it wasn't such a bad idea. But it was a miracle and it was a mystery.

What will Olga say? she whispered.

He got over that easily enough, Olga had gone her way and he his. But his family, his sisters?

What about them? He was getting married! He got over that one too. He made no mention of the fact that he had once before been involved in a scandal, a divorce, and that the family must be inured to it by now, he said something quite different and much sweeter: Let's not change the subject. It was you I should have had, Lolla, you and no other, it's you I've longed for these past twenty years, more than twenty,

246

I don't know how long. It began when I was home during the holidays, I loved you, couldn't eat, couldn't sleep, loved you. You couldn't tell by looking at me, but that's how I was, I didn't plan it, it just happened. Remember when you were working for us, for Olga and me, you didn't know then either, I had no way of getting you close to me so instead I did the opposite, I pushed you away, I refused to help you with a forged paper at the bank. And then there I was, just a clown without you, days and months without you in my home. So now I'm here to tell you that you should marry me before you do anything else, so that finally at long last I have you.

She was listening, it showed on her, she sat with her mouth half-open and her nostrils fluttering the way they did when she was young. Now and then irrelevant things crossed her mind, Abel crossed her mind. What was he doing here now, but here he was.

What will Abel say?

Abel? he said, searching his memory. But my dear – he was your stepson.

Yes of course. It just popped out.

Don't change the subject, Lolla, don't put it off, I've waited so long for you. Abel? Ah, you mean the shares. Let them be his, whatever you like, and now you won't have to borrow on them either. I've got two big cases at the moment. My father retired and I'm not a law clerk any more, but I still get cases. The previous two worked out really well, now I've got two more. Don't worry about the shares, don't worry about anything, Lolla! And now I've told you just how much you mean to me and I've never spoken truer words.

Another irrelevancy: I'm a widow, she said.

He searched his memory: Oh, that! Sort of a widow.

Yes, sort of. Apart from that I'm still as much of a virgin as anyone, nearly—

That you've been married, yes. Everyone knows that. And in my own way I'm sort of a widower.

But it was complicated for more than one of them. Lolla and Olga, who had such similar names, and who had been so close ever since primary school days, well, now and then they started showing a little bitterness towards each other. What the hell did they have to be bitter about? Lolla maybe because the other had had him before her, Olga because the other had him now?

They met each other on the street and it was Lolla who was the uncertain one, diffident, almost as though she'd done something wrong.

What's this I hear, Lolla, are you married to him?

I suppose I am, answers Lolla with a feeble smile.

And how does he feel about that?

Lolla looks at her: What exactly are you getting at, Olga?

Please,forgive me. But have you noticed – he's a bit strange, reserved and aristocratic, and now with him getting one case after another it'll be quite a job for you to run his house and be his wife. But you're so wonderfully efficient, Lolla, I'm sure you'll manage it alright. But don't do anything where he thinks he has to take it up with you, he can't stand that. He goes into his shell and turns away from you.

Lolla wants to leave.

I see you're carrying a basket, are you going shopping? Don't you have a maid?

No, what would I want with a maid?

No. But in my case I'm so used to it I just can't imagine a lady without a maid. I have two maids.

Lolla pales at her own audacity: Yes, but then you do have to feed all the boys working at the store.

Do you know about that? It's my husband's arrangement, it's cheaper for the staff. My husband does so much for other people, but of course he can afford it, being rich. While I remember: whatever you do, don't make him wait for his breakfast so that he's late at the office. He's very particular about that.

That isn't until ten o'clock.

Yes, I'm only telling you because I wish you both well and I don't want you to oversleep. He likes his shoes well-polished too, but since you don't have a maid—

He'll get his shoes polished. You really should try to relax Olga, and stop worrying so much about my husband and I. Try, for example, to get a little more sleep at night—

248

Hm yes, but the fact is, I had him first, I've been married to him, I know him inside out.

I'll tell him you said hello, said Lolla.

What? Yes, do that. Tell him I've given you a couple of tips on how to look after him. That I wish you both all the happiness in the world. That I'm so happy myself and wish the same for everybody else. My husband has just offered me the choice between a long and expensive cruise or a stay at Wiesbaden, but I said no to both. I want to be at home with him, I don't want to be parted from him. I'm sorry for keeping you, Lolla. I can't get over it, you being married to him. It seems almost unbelievable to me.

It was you yourself who wanted me to go to him, Olga.

Well yes, that is true. Are you going to have children?

Olga, Olga!

I don't think he's particularly interested. I didn't want to get him used to the idea, and he never wanted to discuss it anyway. He's so reserved and decent, actually he's a sort of a doll husband. Ah but if you only knew Gulliksen. He's a William too. Now there's someone who speaks his mind. And on top of that he's such a hard-working and successful businessman, earns lots of money, he lets me have anything I want.

Didn't I hear that he had to pay a lot of back-taxes?

Olga stopped in her tracks: You knew that? You know everything. Yes, they really flayed him, but what's that to someone who's filthy rich? It's disgraceful the way some people stick their noses into everything and spread gossip! Forgive me, Lolla, I'm not referring to you, please don't misunderstand me. What was I going to ask you, wait a moment: What happened to Abel?

He ran off.

I only ask because it hurts me so much to hear that he ran off. He was so kind and good, I could talk to him about anything. Of course he was in love with me too, but we didn't let it bother us, it was only very occasionally I thought about him in that way. Such a strange person, but a real man alright, lots of children, or so I heard, bit of a rake. It's such a pity, there he was Captain and then ruined everything for himself. But actually, I sort of admire for him that too, he didn't let

249

anything in the world get to him and just threw himself away. It's so daring and uncommon. Yes but of course you can't understand that, Lolla, that's too much to expect. But it was me who should have been on board with him, it was too much for you. But anyway, I'm nothing special now either, although—

Right, said Lolla, that's what it sounds like.

I can see you're offended. You're such a goose, Lolla, to let yourself be offended so easily. If anyone fell in love with you I would be able to accept it—

No, accept it is exactly what you can't do. Goodbye.

They parted company, both bitter, both with pursed lips. Love and hatred had bubbled up between them, neither one felt good about it afterwards, both of them were hurting. And somewhere in town a good husband sat working in his office and knew nothing about it.

Lolla went to Westman's and filled her shopping basket. When she came out again Olga was standing there. She was crying, and didn't care who saw it: I followed you, I can't bear it, do something nasty back to me! Yes I did, be quiet, it was disgracful of me. I'm all torn apart, worse than I ever was before, do you remember before, Lolla? Do something bad back to me, do you hear? Or else you'll go around thinking I've been poisoned by someone, but that's not true, I'm happy at home, I'm doing fine. Please make him understand. He's not to imagine that I'm in a bad way and regret anything. He would have to be really mad to think that. I wish you all the luck in the world, Lolla, and forget everything I said. It was nothing, is that what you said? Oh yes it was something, but you're such a good person. Goodbye. Give me your hand.

She turned and left quickly, hunched over, walking rapidly, not looking up. In front of a large plate-glass window she stopped, used a handkerchief to dry her tears and wipe her nose, straightened her back and walked on, her carriage erect, smiling to all who greeted her.

Lolla walked home. She took a detour so as not to bump into the chemist again like she did yesterday. He was still doing that spiteful business of his, standing on one leg and bowing to her. It was the little revenge he took for being crippled and not looking like other people. But he was a person too, let him be.

She let herself in quietly so as not to disturb her husband in his office, didn't sing, of course, didn't whistle or bang the pots and pans in the kitchen.

How strange for you, Lolla, to belong here and for all these things to belong partly to you. It wasn't at all sumptuous, very modest, a pretty average sort of home. From her days here as a maid she recognised everything in the house, with now some of the glasses and the crockery smashed and gone, and the earthenware set incomplete, the two kitchen chairs damaged, but nothing that couldn't be made good again. The beds, the linen, the rugs a little worn, as before, but Lolla was an expert at repairs. She mended the curtains without taking them down. She was good.

A few weeks went by.

She knew that the crew of the *Sparrow* had handed in their notice and that at a certain hour on a certain day the boat would be picketed.

What of it? asked Clemens.

She had shares in it – well not her actually, Abel.

My dear Lolla, there's just us two. Don't worry about anything else.

He did not express his love in any more open fashion that this. He didn't call in from work to see her, but she was in his thoughts. She never bought anything for herself, it seemed to him, was there nothing she needed?

No thanks. For example what?

Didn't she want her mother living with them either?

No thanks, mother wanted to stay in the house on the beach with her cat and her cacti.

Lolla made no demands, she wanted to show him the difference between a good wife and – another type of wife. But even though she carried her own basket through the streets and did a maid's work around the home her bearing had become more distinguished. She didn't want anyone making a mistake about that. She would really have liked a canary, but she was afraid that might be lower-class. Should she go to church? Only if he wanted to and went with her. Dancing? Oh yes. But could she dance? Same as everybody else. Everybody learns it, if not at school then just by picking it up.

251

One evening they showed up at the wine-bar. It was something he wanted to do, an idea he had, something nice for Lolla. She took a trip into town every day, to the market or to Westman's, and always alone, while he just sat there and was no part of it. He wasn't blind to the fact. So now it seems he wanted to show people that he really was married to this woman, this queenly woman. And she was grateful to him for taking her. They danced, and no-one gaped at them, no-one whispered. Even though his reputation had been until recently only that of a pretty run-of-the-mill sort of lawyer, people had always respected him because he was so handsome and refined.

It's a long time since I've been here, he said as he looked around the room.

I've never been here before, she said.

Do you like it here?

I'm really enjoying myself.

Cheers, Lolla!

Like a party for them, the music seductive, the lights, the flowers on the tables, the wine.

There's Olga with Gulliksen, he said and waved to them. Quite a coincidence.

Lolla suspicious: They must've seen us coming in here.

Do you think so? Why would they follow us? No, of course they didn't.

Lolla allowed herself to be reassured, she watched the dancers, sipped her wine and enjoyed herself. It was an enjoyable evening. They stayed for a long time.

There were three men sitting at the Gulliksens' table with Olga and she was having a wonderful time, radiant as she talked. They were drinking champagne. Let them. But what shall I – Lolla – talk about? Clemens, my husband, says nothing. She would like to have had taken a carnation from the table and put it in his buttonhole, but she didn't dare.

That thing they're playing now is so pretty, she said.

I was just sitting here thinking the same thing, he said. He would have said that even if it weren't true. He was so courteous.

Her: I can't play an instrument.

He answered: Nor can I, not a note. But we can't all be musicians.

But you used to like to hear Regina play.

Who told you that, Fru Gulliksen was it I expect? I thought Regina had a pretty voice. But then so do you, Lolla.

He was so courteous.

They started talking about books they had read. That was fine by him, he was fond of talking about books, and Lolla could say such unexpected things, either that she'd heard others say or straight out of her own head. It was no more than ordinary small talk, nothing unforgettable, just whatever ingenuous, wicked, smart or stupid words the occasion invited to. Until Olga called out from her table over there: Cheers, Lolla!

They drank the toast. Lolla said: What was that about?

She's so impulsive, answered Clemens.

But we've already seen that they're drinking champagne.

Do you think that's why she did it?

They want to show that it doesn't matter to him if he has to pay back-taxes.

Clemens looked at her a moment and then smiled: You could well be right.

She slipped her hand over his. The effect on him was always sweet, he licked his lips. Perhaps they should leave? They agreed on it, why sit any longer. Once he'd paid he reminded her to return Olga's greeting.

Do you think I should?

Oh indeed you must.

It had been a marvellous evening and she thanked him for it, she was tender and snuggled up close to him and held him lover-like all the way home.

As they passed the little garden of roses and bushes by the fountain Lolla sudenly exclaimed: No, look at that!

A bumble bee resting in a flower, a red dahlia. Resting in the same flower a second bee. They're sleeping, cushioned in the petals. What a bed to have found themselves, what a night of wonder!

Clemens remained standing there. This was the kind of thing he

253

really liked. Not to wake the sleeping pair he spoke in a whisper about the wonder of the night. I shouldn't've said it, Lolla was probably thinking, I shouldn't've said it. Don't you think it's chilly? she said and took hold of his hand.

Of course it is! Forgive me!

They tumbled into the house and undressed quickly. Neither of them spoke.

XXIV

LOLLA HAD SHARES IN THE *SPARROW* – OR RATHER NOT HER, Abel did. It wasn't a matter of indifference to her what happened to these shares, she'd invested Abel's good money in them and she didn't want to see the value drop.

She went on board to find out what was going on. It was Saturday evening and the crew had already gone home. Her plan was to find out what was going on but nothing came of it.

Gregersen the Mate stood with his back to the engine room puffing on an empty pipe.

Good evening, Captain—

He barely turned his slack face in her direction and didn't respond.

I won't disturb you, I just wondered how you were?

Don't ask, he said.

She could see that he was at a low ebb, a pitiful shadow of himself, and she was afraid to give him the jar of honey she'd brought along with

255

her. She went inside to the girls. They were busy getting ready to go ashore so the conversation was short. Yes that's right, they were expecting the boat to be picketed once the crew left her. They didn't know what the mate intended to do, he was very ill, not speaking, not eating.

The Mate must have realised on reflection that he'd been unfriendly. When Lolla returned he told her politely with his broken voice that he couldn't complain, not really.

I've brought something for you—

He was on his guard at once: For me? Why?

It's just some honey, for your throat.

It won't help.

Try it, please.

It isn't just my throat now, I've got sores all over.

You know you really should get something done about it.

They say it's cancer.

There now. Let's sit down and talk about it.

I can't sit, said the Mate.

Why not?

I can't sit and I can't lie down, all I can do is stand. I'll stand til I drop.

Didn't gargling with cognac help?

No. I gave up doing that a long time ago, it just made me drunk.

Now listen here, Mate, you should go ashore at once.

Yes, he said.

Good, I'm glad to hear it's what you want.

He wavered: It's what I want, and it's what I don't want. And now he began to talk about the *Sparrow*: he had anticipated Abel Brodersen's leaving and entertained hopes of being appointed Captain himself in about six months time.

She seemed surprised: In about six months – but you're captaining the *Sparrow* now?

In six months, said the Mate. Fredriksen out at the manor house knows about it.

Then you really must get better.

The Mate continued: I could have bought up your shares, Frue.

Yes.

I had relatives who would've helped me.

Mm, hhm, that's good—

Then I got this business in my throat, said the Mate. And now it's all over.

Lolla: Wait, I'll go and get a cab for you.

You? he said doubtfully. I can do that for myself. But I don't know that I want to.

When she returned with the cab the Mate was still standing there. He had hooked his arm around a strap on the engine room wall and was hanging from it. He was exhausted and obliged to let this masterful woman arrange everything. She fetched a jacket for him from his cabin and a hat and let him change where he stood, she asked if there was anything he especially wanted to take. He gave no answer.

Realising that it pained him to walk she offered to take his arm, but he shook his head angrily. I could perfectly well have gone for that cab myself, he said.

They drove off. Unable to sit, he knelt inside the cab. That was how Gregersen the Mate left the *Sparrow*, and he never came back.

Things were back to where they had been several months earlier: the *Sparrow* was without a master. Again Captain Ulrik's name came up, but why always Ulrik, and why did they need a Captain at all? With the boat about to be picketed they hadn't much time to act and the members of the board voted to suspend the service with immediate effect. The *Sparrow* was just a plain milkboat, a motorised fishing boat could take over the route. Meeting adjourned.

But things didn't work out as planned: the crew of the *Sparrow* decided to take command of the boat themselves.

What on earth-?

Sure, I mean exactly what I say, Severin replied, and put it very simply: What did they need with a Captain? They were three experienced seamen, they'd been halfway around the world and they knew their business, they knew every rock and reef along the route, and Alex there who knew how to sell tickets, all three of them highly respected members of the union – they'd been led for so long, now was the time to do the leading themselves!

The members of the board thought it over. As if it wasn't enough to be a man short at cards the little boat would be plying the route between two towns with neither Captain nor Mate! Where would it end? But the board members were sick and tired of the whole business and to save any more trouble said yes. Only Westman the storekeeper raised his voice in protest. Westman, the matter has been decided—

How did it work out? Wonderfully well. Seven o'clock on Monday morning the *Sparrow* set off as usual and everything seemed quite normal. Severin, as the oldest, was sort of in charge, and God was with them on that first trip, and on the next, and on the following ones and protected them from bad luck.

It was getting late in the year now, with September already half over, the *Sparrow* plied her route and the crew now had a captains' pay to divide between them and profited by the arrangement. There was no longer talk of strike action. It was the time of the autumnal equinox, the weather wet and windy, or stormy and raining, with high seas out beyond the lighthouse, but the *Sparrow* sailed on, the picket line forgotten.

But then something happened. 'Let him that thinketh he standeth take heed lest he fall!' God probably thought, and let something happen. Alex, that vain peacock, was the one to blame.

Alex had taken to dressing up, grooming himself and shaving more often. He wore a stiff white collar with a watch and chain across his chest, and at their various stopping-off points he was always to be found in the chart room surrounded by papers, where people could see him, and that way he gave the impression he was more important than the others on board. It couldn't go on, it caused bad blood. Fair enough, Alex was a nice-looking lad and basically a decent shipmate, but he attracted dislike and envy on account of his behaviour. The Engineer's wife came aboard, the wife of the manager at the old sawmill – she came aboard, and that rascal Alex treated her like a personal friend, he let her travel free and spent time with her in her cabin and took all sorts of liberties. His shipmates made it their business to visit her too and asked if everything was alright, there wasn't a draft from the ventilator, but it did them no good, not a bit of it. So there was bad blood. There was muttering.

Then came the disaster of the captain's cap.

It took some time before relatives of Gregersen the Mate came aboard to collect his things after he died at the hospital. And, of course, among his clothing were the uniform jacket and cap, and for a very long time now Alex had had his eye on these treasures. One day he put the cap on and strolled about in it, even though the weather was stormy.

What the hell? said Severin and Leonart.

Alex said it was mandatory when he was ticketing.

His two shipmates couldn't find words to express their contempt. They looked as if they would spit at him, as if they would blow their noses and wipe the snot on him. But it was Alex's turn at the wheel and he escaped up onto the bridge.

He was well aware of the fact that he looked splendid in the uniform cap and the other finery today. And if he'd had any sense he would've kept his head low and walked on tiptoe until his comrades had got over their anger. But he didn't have any sense, he swaggered about and checked his reflection in the window and tilted the cap at a saucy angle. A saucy angle! Imagine that. He must've been crazy. There was no other way Severin and Leonart could see it than as affectation and snobbery. He isn't even a real sailor, they said to each other, just a labourer from the sawmill, just a logroller from the old days. Let's have it out with him.

They went up onto the bridge and put this to him. Alex was stubborn in his stupidity and refused to listen. Severin intimated that if anyone had the right to wear the cap it was him and nobody else, he was the oldest man on board and more or less the unofficially appointed leader.

You can't do the ticketing, said Alex.

And what can you do, you plank-carrier from a bankrupt sawmill? Whereas both Leonart here and me too, we're both fully experienced seamen who've sailed the great seas of the world, you landlubber.

I am a proletarian, shouts Alex.

They got nowhere. Alex stayed where he was, unshakeable, his cap at a saucy angle.

At the next stop he stayed up on the bridge and let the others do

259

the work with milk churns. There was a crowd gathering down on the quay, and Alex showed off in front of them, took out a handkerchief and gave the inside of the cap a wipe and then put it on again, at a saucy angle. There was a young girl standing down there looking up at him and handsome Alex couldn't resist it, he nodded to her. She returned his greeting and called him Captain: Good morning, Captain!

Severin heard it.

They cast off and sailed on. Out beyond the lighthouse the waters were foul, with breakers smashing over a couple of hidden rocks and the *Sparrow* rolling mightily. Severin went back up onto the bridge again. He had the key to his chest in his hand and he looked grim.

I hear you're Captain, he said, and made a grab for the cap.

Bad luck, you missed.

He made another grab.

Leave that cap alone! screamed Alex.

But Severin was raging now and used the key and already Alex was bleeding. They grunted and called each other the most unbelievable names, kicking and punching each other. Alex looked round, he probably wished there was a belaying pin to hand, but there was nothing. Suddenly he let go of the wheel, leapt forward and butted Severin. Right then the boat lurched and the legs went from under him, he tumbled over and pulled Severin down with him. It was sheer luck they didn't fall overboard but that didn't even occur to them, they were too busy rolling around the bridge and fighting.

The *Sparrow* was sailing herself. Nothing vague and sickly about you, my little *Sparrow*, you don't drift off into a trance, oh no, you stick to the route that's in your blood. Why, I'll bet you can find the way home all by yourself. Ah but the seas were mountainous and the wheel hung slack, and no one could tease miracles out of a milkboat, she turned beam-on to the waves and began drifting helplessly. The two men carried on fighting, they got to their knees but were knocked over again, and now Alex had got hold of the big key and was using it, both of them were bleeding, they couldn't see any more, a tooth went flying, they howled and they groaned.

Finally, down below, Leonart noticed the shuddering and juddering of the *Sparrow*, a deep rolling that was so unlike her. He climbed

260

topsides to see what was going on. What the hell? he exclaimed, but right at that moment he had no idea what to do.

The *Sparrow* was in a desperate way by now, when she wasn't on her beam ends the entire hull was flying through the air. The last of those hidden rocks was now just a few fathoms away from the bow and it was as though the boat had caught sight of that rock and didn't like it, couldn't stand it, was hot on the trail of it. Leonart got confused, he knew the rock should have been on the port side, now here it was on the starboard side. When he finally grabbed hold of the wheel and tried to straighten her up it was too late, he turned bad into worse and the boat ran up onto the reef. And that rock wasn't interested in giving way, no no, it resisted, it resisted irresistibly, it turned the *Sparrow* on her back and threw her.

Explosion! Smoke! Noise! Judgement Day! Cries to the high heavens—

Yes yes yes, alright, so that's what happened when the crew ran the ship on their own.

Were there any 'left alive to tell the tale'? Yes, all of them. They were seen from town and every lifeboat launched to save them.

But that wasn't the end of it. Now the hearings began. The police, the experts and the board members made their way out to the wreck, Smith the photographer went along to take pictures, young Clemens had his work cut out trying to reduce the charges brought against the owners and crew, and the insurance company flatly refused to pay out. The *Sparrow*, old and rotten, was condemned. It lay there, broken in two.

There was so much upheaval and activity in town that nothing was done to salvage what could be salvaged from the wreck. A cap was blamed for the wreck, but the cap was never found. According to witnesses it was a peaked cap with a badge, braid, and a gilded brass button on each side.

The storm had left the wrecked ship in disarray, along with everything inside her, the salon was upside down, the chart room and the refrigeration locker gone. Everything had been washed out of the Mate's cabin, all that survived was an old calendar still nailed to the wall. In another six months it would have been ten years old.

And a few days after the disaster the wreck sank to the bottom of the sea.

It was a disaster for the shares that went down along with the *Sparrow*. For people like Westman who had only a couple it was no great loss, or Fredriksen from out at the Manor with his single share. But for Lolla, who was the majority shareholder – well, not her, but Abel.

She wanted to sue the board, but young Clemens, her husband, advised against it. In his own way he was very angry with the board. He called them criminals, and coming from him this was tantamount to cursing and hoping they would rot in hell. But he advised Lolla not to sue. It's because he's jealous of Abel and enjoys the thought of him losing money, Lolla perhaps thought. But no, decency and a sense of fairness were his only motives. The board, he said, were just 'decent folk' trying to help the farmers sell their milk. They built the dairy and started the milkboat, didn't make a fortune from it but kept it going for the benefit of the rural communities. They let the *Sparrow* sail without a captain, that way they averted the threat of strike action. Not only that, the crew benefited to the tune of a whole captain's wage which they could share amongst themselves. For a long time things went well, but one day things went wrong, and they were censured and found guilty. In conclusion Clemens asked her if she didn't think they'd been punished enough by the guilty verdicts? And, in the final analysis, what did Lolla have to do with those shares anyway?

She didn't like it much, but she accepted it. When she reflected on the fact that she had once had a fat little bank account at her disposal and now it was all gone she didn't pity herself, but she didn't pity the town's 'decent folk' either.

And on top it all they had the gall to offer her shares in a motor-boat to transport the milk. They sent her a subscription offer in the post. Shameless. Her anger flared up again when she showed her husband the shameless proposal, and again she urged him to do something about that board. But no, Lolla, we mustn't, he said.

Impossible nobility of spirit! She walked off, bitter at heart. He followed and said he was sorry for opposing her. He was almost bashful, like he had been on the morning after their first night. He'd been just the same then. Though he was more accustomed to marriage than she was, he was the one who most shy in the morning when they looked at each other. His upbringing, she had thought at the time, his fine education. And he has that same shy look now. Look, he stands there, eyes downcast, trying to turn the whole thing into a joke: To think that you, Lolla, who are so sweet, can feel so vengeful!

But she had her good reasons, and moreover she was able to think it through: Once she had had a bank account. It was, strictly speaking, not hers, but she had had it. And for one reason in particular she had invested in strong shares – should she not have done that?

You've been very clever, he answered, but this time you were unlucky. And those shares weren't as good as people said they were. Two to three percent. I once handled the chemist's shares for him, so I know what I'm talking about. But they might've been just right for someone who'd lost his way in life, and who might have managed to get back on the right track again with their help—

Abel, said Lolla.

I was thinking of Gregersen, the Mate. Fredriksen out at the manor knew his secret.

What was that?

Clemens said: Don't let's talk about the dead, Lolla.

Impossible nobility of spirit! she was probably thinking. No, I shouldn't've bought those shares, she said.

No. As regards the *Sparrow* you were far, far more successful as the *restauratrisa spekulatrisa*.

She ignored the play on words: if I had been on board I would have refused to sail without a captain.

Yes but, Lolla, I'm glad you weren't on board. I'm glad that you're here, and that you're mine.

It was irresistible, he wasn't the type who said this kind of thing all the time. But she was compelled to reply: Not everyone is as glad as you are.

Ah, you mean – But then, of course, I never go home to visit my parents anymore.

263

That was true, it bothered her that she never got to visit her parents-in-law, that she was and remained an outsider in her husband's family. But there were other people too who were not on her side, though she did not include Olga among them. The town – the town was against her. She wasn't good enough for him.

It wasn't all good news, marrying above your station.

But then spring came, and a great many things changed.

XXV

ABEL CAME BACK IN MAY. ABEL? YES, UNBELIEVABLE, HE CAN'T have been thinking straight. No-one was expecting him, there was nothing that needed to be done, so what was he doing here?

When he came ashore from the coast boat he was carrying nothing but a bundle wrapped in newspaper under his arm, his clothes were shabby and he was unshaven, he didn't look like any kind of gentleman at all. That's why one of the longshoremen could say to him, wonderingly: What's this, are you still alive?

But he looked strong and hard, and he held his head high.

He went up into town and rented his old room at the Seamen's Home. He had no luggage with him so they asked him for a deposit. Later, he said, there's something I have to do first. It was tiresome the way there was always such trouble in getting the man to pay, because apart from that, Abel was the ideal guest. They said he could stay provisionally.

A breathing space then, a week spent doing nothing.

As he had done all those years ago when his arm was in a sling after the gunshot he hung around with the staff at the Home and got all the news from them. It was a year since he left and a lot had happened:

That's right, his old ship was now lying on the bottom of the sea, and the owners had been fined.

That didn't interest him much. How is Olga, Fru Gulliksen?

They didn't know, she was rich, snooty. Now and then they saw her in the street. They knew more about Lolla, a whole lot more, they could read him the whole novel.

After a week at the Home he still hadn't paid, so they evicted him and he drifted away. It didn't seem to bother him particularly, he accepted it.

He went to the old shack. It was still standing, untouched and dusty, just as before, as quiet as ever, a roof over his head. The bed was still there, the mattress a little chewed by mice but fine apart from that. It was now two years since he'd last been here, but it didn't smell bad, with the air that got in through the missing window pane.

Of course, during all that time, people had been inside, but since there was nothing to steal they'd left again. The paraffin stove was still there, along with a lot of other scrap-iron, and the ulster too, that indestructible grey-brown ulster, the loop had broken, yes, the heavy coat had slumped to the floor and lay in its corner looking like a pile of rags. That had saved it from thieves.

He was home. Straightaway he set about sewing a new loop on the ulster and hung it up. That done there was nothing else to do and he went out.

Sat in the sun, wandered for hours, didn't avoid anyone, met several acquaintances but paid them as little attention as they paid him.

In the market place Lolla stood buying cabbage from a woman, he went straight up to her, held out his hand and said: Congratulations, Lolla!

She took a step back and stared at him.

I should probably have greeted you first, but instead I congratulate you first. That's wonderful, absolutely the right thing to do. There's no one like you, Lolla.

Ha. So you're back?

Yes. A few days ago. Well, I had nothing to do out there either, so I came back home again. You're in good health, I see.

Her cheeks flushed, perhaps because she had so obviously put on weight. And you, she said, how are you keeping? No, I can't get over it. She finished her business with the woman and suggested they sit down on a bench. Abel offered to carry her basket but she declined.

It was only when they had sat down that she looked directly at him: Big changes this year, she said. Big changes for all of us. And you're well?

Yes. I'm well.

You disappeared. Imagine, I can hardly remember now. You ran off.

I just got so tired of everything. But what you've done, that's the most wonderful thing!

So you heard?

The lot. I'm so happy for you. You deserve it.

It's just a pity that everything didn't work out equally well.

Oh but it did, it's wonderful!

I've got something to tell you, Abel.

I'm holding my breath.

It's no laughing matter. It's about the shares.

I heard you were unlucky and lost everything, he said.

It was you who lost everything.

Me? he said airily. But who cares about the shares? You got a won-derful husband instead, you've married well, you've got a home, a position, all the blessings you could ask for. You shouldn't worry about the shares.

I can see you've not changed, she said, shaking her head. But it's a relief to me that you're taking it so well. But now you, Abel, should do something about that board and get what you've got coming for those shares.

Ha! he shouted, and clapped his hands over his ears. I've never owned a share in my life I'm pleased to say, they're there to be lost. But now tell me: how's Olga doing?

Olga? Well, she'—

Why do you stop?

267

I don't know anything about Olga. Where are you living? she asked.

Living? At the Seamen's Home, of course. To begin with.

I ask because I found all your clothes in your shack and I took them down to the house on the beach.

Were there any clothes there? he asked. Ah yes, now I remember. A lot of clothes, quite nice clothes actually. At the house on the beach, did you say?

I'll have them sent to you at the Seamen's Home.

What? Not at all, I'll fetch them. Nice clothes, I remember now, that's terrific. Once I start wearing them I'll probably be able to get credit at Gulliksen's again.

Lolla shook her head and gave up on him in despair: I don't get this at all. You don't even remember being aboard the *Sparrow*?

But of course I do. All your food, that dour Mate—

If he hadn't died of cancer he would have bought the shares. That way they wouldn't have been lost.

Imagine that.

Yes, you just yawn. Why did you disappear?

Stop being so severe, Lolla.

I'm just asking why you disappeared.

You wouldn't understand. Suppose it was to visit a grave again? For another sight of a giant cactus growing free? Angèle and I often went to look at them, they're stranger than other monstrosities because their monstrosity is their very essence. Same as Angèle and me. So we often went to visit them. And I wanted to see Lawrence again, a friend I once had. I told you about him, I don't know if you remember.

Did you find him?

Yes. But they'd already executed him.

Oh!

Yes. Taken him out and executed him. I arrived too late.

Oh, that's terrible! said Lolla and shivered.

Terrible! Abel repeated. But actually they do things in such a civilised way over there: first they sit him in a chair and then they kill him.

So that was the end of him.

He left a letter addressed to me, but I didn't read it.

You didn't read it?

What could possibly be in a letter like that that I didn't know before?

Maybe it was a message to the girl in Ireland?

So you remember her? Yes, I was wrong, I should probably have read it.

Do you still have the letter?

No. I left it there.

Oh! said Lolla irritably, everything about you is just so completely strange. Why come back again when you've gone to all the trouble of leaving?

Good question. Your husband once told me about a cow, and about some starlings that wanted above all else to be in the place they came from. I might say it was because of something like that. That's an unusual husband you have there, Lolla.

Yes, he is.

I had a long conversation with him once. He knows a lot.

Yes, said Lolla and got to her feet. It's time I was leaving.

Shall I carry your basket home?

No thanks.

I'll call in at the house on the beach today and fetch my clothes, he said.

He sat back down on the bench and watched her walk away, watched her swaying off down the street. Nicely dressed as always, body a little thicker now, dignified. In the old days she would have asked him to walk along with her. A good thing she was married now, she'd never find her way to his shack.

After he picked up his clothes he sold the best of them to the second-hand dealer and bought himself a brown suit, he looked good, smart, and he made his way up to Alex and Lili's home near the sawmill.

They were both at home, sitting at supper with their four children. There were four now.

All the chairs were taken but Lili got to her feet, blushing, holding the youngest in her arms.

Don't get up, don't get up, said Abel and sat on the bed.

So, you're back again, said Alex. That was well done, disappearing like that and leaving us all in the lurch.

Abel replied that he'd already heard the odd comment.

The Mate went into hospital and died, in the end I had to take charge of the boat. I made a pretty good job of it too, but on that last trip there was a terrible storm.

I heard all about it.

Lili: And you're doing alright, Abel?

I can't complain. But you aren't doing so bad either, meat in the middle of the week, I see.

Calf's liver, said Lili. So I suppose you've been halfway round the world since you were last here?

Just a quick trip to America.

Oh what fun it would have been to go with you! she said.

What are you doing back here again? asked Alex.

I don't know.

Lili answered for him: You'll find something to do. Not like certain other people I could mention.

Alex, angrily: I don't see as how you've been going without recently, have you?

Lili turned to Abel and said: We get a little from the welfare, that's about it.

Alex even more angrily: Have you been going without, is what I asked?

It's different for you, Abel, you never touch rock bottom. I can remember when we were really down and you gave us salmon. Imagine that, salmon, my favourite food. A whole tin.

They were still eating, but suddenly Alex stood up and pushed his chair away: I don't want you sitting on that bed.

They stared at him open-mouthed. What would Lili, the lady from the office, make of such behaviour?

Alex! she said.

Yes, Alex! he mimicked. I only meant, you should sit on that chair, Abel, if you're going to sit here in my house.

Abel moved to the chair: Actually I'm not staying, I just popped in. They've grown, the little ones.

Do you think so? asked Lili. They're all healthy, thank God, the eldest one here is a regular bear of a lad. The youngest is a boy too.

Abel gave each of them a krone. The little one put it in his mouth.

Don't let the nipper swallow it! shouted Alex.

They held out their little hands to thank him. A tremor seemed to pass through Abel as he took the tiny hands in his. And Regina, where's she? he asked.

The mother replied: Regina's on her own now, she's married and got a family already. Her husband's an engineer on the coast boat. Oh yes, Regina's done well for herself, she's got a good head on her shoulders.

She won't have anything to do with us, said Alex.

Well what do you expect? asked the mother. Get involved in our misery!

Alex had backed off now, he didn't ask her again if she'd been going without recently: No, why I was wondering what you're thinking of doing, Abel, is because maybe you could get me a job with you while you're at it? What d'you think?

I'll think about it, said Abel.

Oh yes, said Lili, do think about it.

Alex: I was a good hand to have on board, from what I recall?

Yes.

Did whatever job you put me to. And after you left and I was promoted to Mate and did the ticketing and all that, well I managed all that, I had it all in my head.

What happened to your front teeth? asked Abel.

Lili: Yes, have you ever seen such a sight.

It was on our last trip. Severin hit me with his locker key. Does it show?

Not at all, said Lili with a laugh. Makes you even better-looking.

Abel said goodbye and left. The afternoon wore on. He could have done with a nice bit of liver, but they'd never offered it, so he stopped off at a cafe for a piece of bread and a couple of smoked herring then went home.

In the evening, as dusk was gathering, a young man came in through the door and stopped, surprised and half-afraid.

Ha. Someone here, he said.

Yes.

There's not usually anyone here. What are you doing here?

I live here, said Abel.

That's funny. There was no-one here before.

I came back a couple of days ago. I always live here. What are you doing here?

Me? Nothing.

Everything here is mine, said Abel. The bed is mine, I left it here while I was away. I used that chest as a table.

Alright alright, said the lad and left.

He was disappointed, thought Abel, watching to see where he went. Turned out he had company, a light dress disappeared with him.

I must get a lock for this door, he thought, or they'll rob me of everything I own.

The next evening, after he'd been sitting out in the sun for a long time, he came home late and met a couple on their way out of the shack, a girl and an older man with a full grey beard.

Abel wanted to ask what they'd been doing in his shack, but his question might have been misunderstood so he said nothing. Instead he just grabbed the ulster, which the man was carrying off with him, and said: That's mine!

The man held on to it and said: It's as much mine as it is yours. Very reluctantly he finally let go of the ulster and said: You're welcome to it anyway, it's not much of a coat.

As they walked off the girl whispered: I told you you shouldn't've taken it. That it belonged to someone—

Abel caught up with the couple and stopped the girl: What's that you've got under your coat, miss? No, you're not getting away with that!

Leave the lady alone! warned the man.

That was very silly of you, miss, to try to steal my underwear.

Don't stand there lifting up the lady's clothes, I'm warning you! shouted the man.

Look at this, shirts, underpants – why, you can't even use this stuff!

The girl began to whimper: I said all along we shouldn't. It belongs to someone, I told him—

272

Then why on earth did you take it? It's men's clothing all the lot of it.

Her cavalier intervened and started getting aggressive. Abel grabbed him by the shoulders and forced him up against the barbed wire fence. When he returned the girl had gone. She had run off up the embankment to the railway line.

I really must get a lock for that door, thought Abel.

But he never did anything until the need was really pressing. He left it until well into the next morning, even took a walk and bought himself a bunch of carrots from the market-place before he began to get really worried about his property. The first thing he checked for after he got back was the gun.

He knew where the lock was, in that old crate from the lighthouse in which his father had stored all manner of scrap iron. The lock didn't work but it was easy to repair. He could do anything with his hands, even using the most primitive tools he could repair engines, could tin and solder. That loop he'd sewn into the ulster to hang it up by, it wasn't just ordinary thread or tape, it was a bit of brass chain that would last forever. When he couldn't find the key to his padlock he filed a little piece of nickel to shape that would open and close it. It was clearly not the first time he'd ever made a picklock.

XXVI

ABEL'S MEETING WITH OLGA.

Finally he found out the places she frequented: the homes of other merchants, a couple of families in public life, and the homes of the fashionable and vivacious, places where she could feel wealthy and modern and appreciated. What did he want of her? Nothing, just to meet her. It was Olga.

He was looking his best, and with the thought of her in mind even washed and starched his yellowing collars from his days on board, and he made a point of keeping the encounter casual and friendly, waving and calling to her: At last!

It affronted her slightly, he was neither her brother nor her husband. Good morning, Abel! she said. You greet me as if we'd seen each other just yesterday.

Forgive me! I did it on purpose, I planned it.

Ah. Yes, you're very strange.

I wanted to make it informal, I wanted to avoid all that smacking together of hands and all that You here, Abel? and all that Why did you leave and why have you come back and I'm lost for words—

She nodded: That bothers you. I understand.

Yes it bothers me. Because actually I really don't have any particular explanations, and in your case I wouldn't even make a very good job of lying.

You're looking well, Abel. Why did you say 'At last'?

I've been looking out for you for nine days. Ever since I got back.

We can't stand here, said Olga. Do you want to walk me home?

Yes thank you.

Well I didn't actually mean . . . Where are you living?

Nowhere.

Well then, can't we go to your place and have a chat?

We could go to a wine-bar.

I daren't, she said. It's not that, no one would forbid it, but . . . Do you really have no fixed abode, Abel?

No. Just a shack down by the vacant lots.

I remember those shacks. Once I was on the roof of one, and you were standing down below, and I jumped down on top of you. Perhaps you would show me your shack?

It's no place for you. I would carry you there, Olga, but it's no place for you.

Then walk me home. To my door, I mean.

I will, thank you.

She glanced at him sideways as they walked: You're looking well, wherever it is you've been. Have you heard about Lolla?

Yes, everything.

It doesn't mean anything. It doesn't bother me, but it doesn't mean anything. Now she's filling out too. I have no children, Abel.

He said nothing.

I said I have no children.

Yes indeed – I mean indeed no, you have no children. That's good, and it's bad.

Exactly! she said. The first time I didn't want any, now I do want them but he can't. It's ridiculous not to be able to. Wretched.

Maybe it's not such a bad idea not to want to.

But now I do want to. I'm not at all sure it would make me ecstatic with happiness, but I'd like to try it. Can you understand what I mean?

You don't have time for that kind of thing, Olga.

I don't have time? What sort of nonsense is that?

You've got all your hobbies to cultivate, he said. You've got your makeup to put on, and your hair to curl, and your pills to take, and dresses to change, you've got to weigh yourself, and cigarettes to smoke—

Do you have a cigarette?

No. Just a pipe.

Everything you say is true, but I would have time. You're so hard on me, you monster. Is everything about you so perfect? Are you never in doubt? You just list all the bad things about me, but there's a good side to me too, there really is. I can be warm and tender too, but you don't take that into account.

Oh but I do, he said. I haven't forgotten it for a single day in over thirty years.

She stopped and looked at him: What's that supposed to mean?

Even from when we were children, he added. Then abruptly he changed the subject: Strange how late the spring is, it just won't rain. Here's a bench, how would you like to sit down for a while?

It was quiet all around them, just a few small birds singing in the trees, a little chilly, the buds on the lilac bushes in the park behind them only just starting to show, a late spring.

Shortly after they sat down a young couple came along and sat on the bench on the opposite side of the path.

Oh why do they have to sit on that particular bench! said Olga.

Let them have it.

What was I going to say, Abel – so, you never amounted to anything anyway?

Here we go again.

No, I'm not going to go on about it. But, Abel, you had the boat and the good position and all the rest of it, did the devil get into you?

I guess so, he answered with a smile.

276

It would be dangerous to be married to you. One fine day all that's left behind of you is the proverbial pile of ashes, ha ha.

But no one's married to me anymore.

Were you married?

By the priest.

Well, let's not talk about that. But I was supposed to go on a trip with you one day, didn't you think of that?

Oh no, he answered. I had no chance with you.

Because you spoiled your own chance.

By not making anything of myself? I can see where you're going. But at least I'm not confused like you, I don't brood on things, I'm calm, I'm nothing, I'm vanished, nameless.

You're always overstating things. But to put it in words of one syllable, you've got no drive. That's it.

Quite right, I don't follow the pattern. I'm satisfied with one meal a day, after that I make do with a lick of sunshine. Why should we make something of ourselves? That's what everyone does, and they're no happier for it. They make all that effort to rise up in the world, but where's the reward? Their peace of mind is gone, their nerves are frazzled, some drink to help them get by and it only makes things worse, they think they have to walk on high heels wherever they go, and me who lives in a shack, I feel sorry for them.

I've never heard you so articulate before.

Abel smiles: I've had years to work out my speech.

What's almost worst is that you just smile about it all. But you must admit, it's quite a comedown from being Captain on the *Sparrow* to your life in the shack. A degradation.

That's how you're bound to see it.

When did you become like this?

Like this? You mean when did I begin to be mature? It was a long time ago. It started in childhood. I started out with no chances at all, and that's how it began. I was rootless in foreign countries, and that matured me. And then I married Angèle, and that liberated me completely, thank God. I'm doing fine. Now let's discuss you for a bit.

Me? I'll never pass! Can you understand why that couple there don't move on?

Let them be.

They know perfectly well who I am, and you're so nicely dressed, so they ought to show us some respect.

Abel smiles: Shall we leave?

No. We aren't the ones who should leave. What were we talking about? Maturity, you say. One meal a day? God help us! I can tell you're struggling, and when you say you want to live like that it's because you don't have the drive for anything else.

What if that's a talent, Olga?

She looked taken aback: A talent? My, we are eloquent today, I've never heard anything like it. A talent? Well, maybe you're right, and none of it would matter anyway. If only it wasn't you, Abel, who was going to the dogs.

It sounds strange to you, he said, but when I sit out in the sun I don't need much food. In the tropics I saw how they lived one day at a time, from hand to mouth, live on almost nothing and sunshine. Millions of them. You don't hear anything there about getting on in the world, they don't think in terms of money and food and furniture, their lives are simple, they use flowers for jewellery. It was such a sight to see them, so good for the eyes to see them. We sailed out to the islands and stayed there a while, we had nothing in our pockets they needed, they didn't want to buy anything from us, and they didn't beg. We went inland, they danced and laughed, they were friendly and gave us fruit, they were beautiful and brown, almost naked. We were there two nights—

Not days? You reckon in nights?

Yes we were there days too.

Yes yes yes, she said impatiently. Listen, Abel, you've spent nine days looking for me, you say. I've been waiting a year for you. Now don't misunderstand me – but you're the only person I can talk to. I can say whatever I like to you. Great God in heaven, she burst out, if you would only take proper care of yourself! I don't suppose you've got any money on you now, have you?

Some.

I still owe you a thousand kroner. It's terrible—

Don't think about it.

278

Don't you ever save anything?

No, he said.

Well in that case you won't have anything for later on. You had an inheritance, you could have been one of the big shots in town if you'd held on to what you had. And I would have been able to take that trip with you.

My father saved yes. I squandered my share of it as soon as I could. Lolla was smarter, she invested her share. But then she lost it. So now we're both as broke as each other. No, I don't save.

That was just bad luck about the shares. You're not interested in having things, owning things. I can't image a life of going without, I can't live on nothing. I want to be able to want things, and then to get them.

There's nothing I want.

You've no-one to save up for anyway—

And you do?

No. Stop getting at me! You've got no-one to save for, you're alone, it's twisted you. I save a small amount so I have something for later – no I don't, that's not true, I'm in debt, God, I can't talk to you. It's natural for people to save a bit and not spend everything they have.

That's true. All of us, we think we've got to get something out of this world, to squeeze as much out of it as possible, long for more – and then die.

Now you're being nasty!

But what does it lead to, Olga, all this stockpiling of things? Haven't you seen for yourself what happens: the children or the grandchildren spread it to the winds after you, and the whole thing levels out again. Then their children start saving up in their turn. Don't you find it all just a bit absurd? It's just not interesting to hear people talk to me about how I don't save.

You've got no drive, she said with a nod.

And now tell me about yourself, Olga.

You're abnormal, that's what you are.

Abel, irritably: All you people with drive, you don't get that far either. You get a bit rich, a bit arrogant, and a bit envious, and that's about all. My old school pals haven't done all that much better than

279

me, I wouldn't trade places with them. There was a man on the *Sparrow* with drive. He kept his mouth shut tight, made his grim way to the top, he was a Mate, they made him Captain, he wanted to own the boat—

Is that the one who died?

Yes. And then he died.

Silence.

And even you, Olga, with your drive – now you've got a little blue vein showing up here by your temple—

I most certainly have not—

Oh yes. A sweet blue vein, pretty, lovely.

Why do you say it like that, you don't love me.

Oh but I do, he said. Then changed the subject: You must be freezing.

Yes. But I want that couple to leave first.

Come along! he said, and without more ado he stood her up.

She went along willingly enough. To defer to that couple! she said. What must they think? Shortly afterwards she said: I liked it when you grabbed my arm and walked off with me, Abel. It gave me a thrill. Where are you taking me?

I'm taking you home.

I don't want to go home, she said. I've hardly had a chance to talk to you. I'll come with you to the shack.

Oh no you won't.

Oh yes I will. We can't talk out here in the street, no-one can. I want to come with you and see something other than a home with tables and chairs. She took his arm, took his arm there in broad daylight, and squeezed it.

Abel: What if we meet someone?

She had an answer for that: You keep us out of danger. You can do anything.

A few brief words, his orders. She clung tightly to him, and he walked on in desperation. They sneaked along narrow alleyways and hidden shortcuts down to the railway line and from there down the embankment to the shack.

Oh this is so exciting! she said as he opened the door with the picklock. Oh! Why this isn't a hovel at all! Are these the terrors you boast of? You've got light, fresh air, a bed even! Well I never! She was praising the room to be kind, and as a way of excusing her presence there: You can never call yourself down and out with a place like this. It's fun being here. I think I'll take a seat.

He folded his ulster as a blanket for her in the chair and sat on the bed himself. Presently it dawned on him that they were here together, that they had both been very reckless, and that now it was a question of how to get her away from here without being seen.

Dear Olga, why did you want to come here?

Olga: We can't always explain everything. You can't explain why you ran off and then came back. I want to talk to you, you're good to talk to. You see, Abel, she said suddenly, things haven't worked out the way I expected when I got married again.

Silence.

It hasn't worked out the way either of us thought. What do you make of that?

Abel shook his head.

I don't go wandering about town because I'm desperate, she said. I haven't come here because I'm desperate and want to flirt with you. But I don't know what to do, I needed to talk to you. How do you think I can stay away from home as long as this? It's because he does-n't care. That's right. I fuss, he says. I fill the place with my nerves, he says. There's something in it, to a degree he's right. I wish I wasn't like that. But then am I supposed to hang myself? No fear. I show my claws. I become a witch. Look at Lolla, off she went and got married to my ex-husband. It's a bit odd, she was our maid, she did the cooking and the laundry.

You wanted her to look after him.

Because I thought – well, since I had left. But that it would lead to their getting married? No. And now she's pregnant too. Okay, they're married now, they can travel about and come and go and do whatever they like with each other. I have no children. Maybe it would have helped, but he can't give me one. So what am I supposed to do?

Abel thought about it: I don't know, have you thought of adopting a child?

One of yours?

Olga!

I'm sorry! No, that wouldn't work. I need to be a mother myself. But there's no chance of that?

Oh don't, I know that. But I wanted to talk to you, because you know so much. You're the one I should have had, Abel, I'm sure of it, we should have had each other, from all I've heard about you. You were going to take me away with you on a trip, you know.

Ah yes, that trip.

No, you mustn't say it like that. But yes, well, I suppose it is too late, I'm where I am now. But back then – if you'd come and just whisked me away – because I'm the one you should've had. I got another letter from Rieber Carlsen, there's a man with drive, soon he'll be a bishop I expect. I told him all about you and me, and he writes back so nicely, that I must abandon all thought of you since I'm already married, ha ha. I don't know, what he writes doesn't seem to help me any. Am I boring you?

No, Olga.

No, she wasn't boring him. But the way she spoke it was as though she spoke of a love of some kind, and he didn't seize the moment, didn't grab it, instead he was suspicious: maybe she would lead him on, a long way on, and then leave? What did he know – an unhappy woman, time on her hands, passionate, tender, hysterical? Sure he could make a pass at her, and if necessary put up with the rejection and the loss. But that would be such a pity, because this, this here, this was Olga—

I recall the time you whirled through this town like a waltz, he said.

She looked surprised: Was it so long time ago? Yes I suppose it was. The years pass. Now we're so ancient, but there's breath still left in our bodies. So you remember the time when I whirled through the town like a waltz? That was back then. Those days are dead and gone.

I was thinking it was so different from how depressed you are now.

Yes, I am depressed. But what do others do? What did you do yourself? Did things always go well for you?

No. Not in the end.

Tell me about it, teach me something, she said and took his hand.

Ah those hands of yours, they're like velvet, you can bend the fingers over backwards, but they're strong enough alright. Take it away! she said, and gave his hand a push. Why did you wander off like that and get married? Was she pretty? Did you get caught? Couldn't you get away?

Whoa!

Alright. But couldn't you get away?

I didn't want to. It was a good time. We had good times together.

On one meal a day?

No, there was much more than that, sometimes far more than that. But that wasn't what it was about. When I fished in the river we suffered no lack of anything. There was always maize and swede to be had somewhere or other around the farms, so we cooked up a broth and sliced it up and that was our bread. I grew into that life, until I couldn't imagine any other way of being.

But you say yourself, it went wrong in the end. So things didn't work out any better for you than for me.

That was because of Lawrence, a friend of mine named Lawrence. He knew her before I did, and when he got back from a trip to Mexico and heard that she was mine and we were married, he went looking for her. It was all on account of him. She got shot.

Were you there when he found her? What happened?

Yes, I was there.

Suddenly Olga said: What, you found them together. And you shot her?

Me?

When she looked into his face she grew afraid and backed off: No, I didn't mean – of course not—

He was the one who shot her.

Silence.

Right. I see. So then I suppose you took some kind of revenge on him?

Yes. That is, I didn't. There was chaos everywhere, she was lying there, dead. So I forgot to shoot him as well, then it was too late.

Him as well. He noted his own slip of the tongue, moistened his lips and gaped, his mouth wide open, all his teeth showing, an animal's mouth.

But then you met him again later? she asked, pretending not to have noticed.

Unfortunately no, he never got out of prison again. Some of us tried to get him out, and I sent money from here, but it wasn't much, so he never got out. In all the months and years since I've been carrying that gun of mine around, waiting for him, he could've shown up anywhere. I wanted to give him a chance when he did, there would be a gunfight. But now the gun's no use any more. D'you want to see it? he asked, and got up quickly from the bed.

No! she screamed to him. No, I said no!

It was lying wrapped in a pair of fine socks, beautifully maintained, lovingly looked after. Now he breathed on it and stroked it.

Olga: Why is it no use anymore?

Lawrence is dead. They'd executed him years before I went back over.

Quite right too! said Olga.

Oh now I'm not so sure about that, he answered. Lawrence was a damned good bloke. But he came along and ruined something for me. I never stop thinking about it. It was a double murder: my wife and my child. Three lives, including his.

Yes, three lives.

I don't know why I brought the gun back with me. Do you want it?

Goodness me no! No, just get me out of here now. It's getting dark.

XXVII

APART FROM THAT, NO-ONE VISITED HIM IN THE SHACK, ONLY Lili, who came often, stayed a while and then left. In the beginnng she'd been faithful. But Alex, her husband, had grown lazy again and stopped keeping an eye on her. Lili wasn't lazy, she was alert, she was awake, and she was crazy. Before it had been Lolla who brought him news from town, now it was Lili.

And some of the gossip he picked up himself on the fish-dock, or when shopping for a carrot and some potatoes at the market. A stall-holder told him one day that Robertsen the Customs man had been shot. Along with two other Customs men he'd been chasing after some smugglers who fired on him, wounding him badly. Yes, accidents and madness, that was all the news, the papers were full of it. Schultz at the market garden had fallen through one of his own glass roofs, cut himself to ribbons—

Abel had an inspiration and he acted on it right away, went straight from the market to the Custom's house and had a talk with the supervisor. There were consequences. Robertsen's absence led to a series of promotions through the ranks and a vacant space at the bottom. Abel put in a good word for Alex. That was his inspiration.

Well – yes, said the supervisor, I've already had a few people here. What was that now, weren't you suing Robertsen?

Abel: I dropped it.

Why?

Abel gave an account of the whole business. Phew, quite a strain for someone who didn't care a damn, but the supervisor had the patience to hear him out. I need to know a little bit about my staff, he said, and I'm interested in what you've just told me. It's noted, along with certain other things I've heard about our friend Robertsen. Not that it'll do much good, his union is very touchy. Just for the record, could you let me have all this in writing?

Yes.

Not that we'll necessarily have any use for it, I hear that Robertsen is very badly wounded. This man of yours can come here at ten o'clock tomorrow morning.

Thank you.

That evening Lili came to the shack. She brought more news from town: a young girl had been robbed in the woods last night. There was only ten kroner in her purse, but wasn't it incredible how low some people could sink? Robertsen the Customs man shot and lying in hospital, it was too dangerous for them to try to remove the bullet and the surgeon held out little hope. And, on top of all that, breakins, robberies, car crashes—

Is Alex at home?

I suppose so. Why do you ask?

He's to present himself at the Customs house at ten o'clock tomorrow morning.

Lili gaped : Is it about a job?

That depends, but they're a man short. He'll have to start at the bottom.

You're an absolute angel, Abel!

*

286

He didn't see any more of Olga. It was June, she'd probably gone out to the country. They had a place in the country, a car, their own driveway, Lolla had seen her in town with Volmer the dentist, or was it Folmer? Whatever.

Lolla was approaching the birth now, she didn't bother him anymore, didn't ask questions so that he didn't have to answer. Hadn't he once been obliged to give her every last detail about a house of Lili's that he had been paying the mortgage on? Good God, it was a trivial enough business, just a little house near the sawmill – but was the loan secured, Abel? Are the papers in order, Abel? In the spring, when he came back home, there were still vestiges of her concern for him and he had to explain to her that he'd returned to Kentucky to look again at a certain kind of cactus that grew there. But then why had he come back? Wouldn't you just like to know that, Lolla?

All over now, Lolla had other things to think about. She looked ugly now, she really did, but still beautiful from her inner contentment. Of course, there was this business about not being accepted by her in-laws, but it took more than that to get Lolla down. And now she'd even got a canary. What? Yes, Clemens himself had bought it for her one day. So that if anyone should come up to her and say it was lower-class she could always say: Maybe it is. But there it is, and my husband likes it.

Lolla had settled down.

Olga, on the other hand, would probably never settle down. She didn't drift helplessly around with each passing breeze, far from it, she was Olga, won't say a word against her. But she was eaten up by restlessness, she'd become eccentric. Down at the place where she bought her clothes they said she was no longer as exquisitely particular about the underwear she bought – and what might be the cause of that? Had she lost just a little of her self-esteem? Not at all. She was strong-willed in her changing tastes and if it pleased her to do so she might well buy herself a cheap dress. They tempt her with the costliest dresses: Oh, if madame will just look at this one! She answers: No, I want *that* one, there. Have it sent home to me!

She could buy things that were displayed on the counter that everyone had seen. And the very next time it would be nothing but silk.

Her time passes until five o'clock. It's Saturday, but she doesn't want to go to the place in the country, she wants to try on a dress she's expecting, she says. Fine by her husband, so long then! The dentist is already sitting waiting in the car, the dentist often comes out to the cottage in the country with them.

She wanders, wanders about outdoors on her own, restless and discontent. What's to do at home? An empty house with tables and chairs, old Gulliksen in the living room, founder of the family business. Most of the time he's in his shirt sleeves and slippers. Now and then judge Arentz calls in for a chat with him, but the judge is an old man too and all they talk about are the times, the economy, the business down on the ground floor. Olga doesn't understand a word of it.

She leaves that empty home, comes to the railway line and slants down the embankment towards the shack. The evening sun is shining, but she makes her way down to the shack. It's locked, the door is locked. In broad daylight she makes her way up the embankment again, annoyed and reckless, she can't be bothered to hide the fact that she's wandering about in this area. For a while she sits on a bench in the little park, and then it's seven o'clock. She heads off again, straight for the railway line and the embankment and the shack. The shack is locked.

Abel has a lot of places to be, Abel can't always be at home. He has to go off in search of food, of the lick of sunshine that keeps him going, and whatever else he does he absolutely must get hold of a can of paraffin today for his stove, or he won't be able to cook anything. It's not that easy for him, no one's laid the table, no cook, no housekeeper, so no, he can't always be at home. And most of all he can't be home for Olga. He sits inside and he knows it's her, because her footsteps are different from Lili's, but he doesn't open up. It's a bizarre situation: he doesn't open the door to Olga! Now listen here, he says, as though someone is listening to him, she sat here in the chair and she spoke of love, she leant right over and took hold of his hand – if that was an offer then it was an extraordinary offer. And then to not accept it! Now if only it had happened to *me*! he says and smiles.

Tomorrow is Sunday, and Olga attends church because she knows the priest's family. Her husband isn't with her, he's still out at their place in the country. There are quite a few people out there, three cars, but all

288

is peaceful, all is quiet on this Sunday morning, so everyone must be fast asleep. No they are damn well not fast asleep. Some are deep in the woods whispering and giggling, and when the van from the hotel arrives with food for the party they have to sound the horn to call the host, William Gulliksen.

Not a bad-looking guy Gulliksen, tall and dark-eyed, but with a very crooked nose. You didn't notice it from the side, but there it was and it was the only one he had. In addition to that he was a pretty shrewd businessman, a bridge-player, and a smart dresser with a good head for alcohol. This evening he was due to leave for Oslo on business and stay away for three days. He usually enjoyed these Oslo trips, he was alone, Olga had only travelled in with him the once.

The party at the country place was over now and he drove back into town. It was a warm day, the dentist was sleeping in the back seat. Gulliksen treated the sleepy man tenderly and dropped him off at his office. Then he drove home.

Olga wasn't there. She'd probably spent the night at the priest's house as she'd often done before. Didn't bother him at all. He packed his two suitcases, the shirts, the dinner jacket and the patent leather shoes, and he was still at it when Olga returned.

Good morning! he called cheerfully, his mood good and jokey after the all-night partying.

Good morning. Are you going away?

Yes, didn't you know? I thought I mentioned it.

It's too bad I wasn't here, I could've helped you pack.

No thanks, there isn't much to pack.

Olga: I heard at the priest's that the Customs man who was shot died this morning.

Oh really? he said, and wondered if there was anything else he should be packing in his suitcase.

The priest had been to see him. He'd been up all night before preaching the sermon today.

Gulliksen smiled absent-mindedly and was still preoccupied with his own business.

They also told me that Fredriksen out at the Manor has had another stroke.

Gulliksen found that more interesting: I've lost count of the number of strokes he's had.

The doctor said that this would be the last.

Gulliksen looked at his watch: I must hurry. The coast boat hasn't rung yet has she?

Olga went to the kitchen and called for someone to take the suitcases downstairs.

Well, goodbye then! he said, without taking her hand. I'll be gone three days.

Yes yes, she said. Enjoy the trip.

Gulliksen called a farewell to his father through the door and hurried down the steps. That was his leaving. It wasn't as if he was going on a long trip.

Olga went into her room and sat down and began to scribble something. From the street below came the sounds of the blind hurdy-gurdy man, surrounded as usual by children. She heard Gulliksen drive off to the dock. She scribbled and wrote, finished her letter and went down with it.

The first thing she did was stop the hurdy-gurdy man and give him a five-kroner piece: Will you deliver this letter for me?

Then she noticed old Gulliksen leaning out the window in his shirtsleeves watching her: It's to Lolla, to Fru Clemens, she said loudly. A recipe I promised her.

The blind man nodded and said okay, unscrewed the barrel from the organ and set off. It wasn't the first time he'd run an errand for Olga, he ducked into an alleyway, put on glasses and looked at the letter. The blind old man was probably just doing it for show and saw nothing. He stood in thought for a moment, puzzling, looked at the letter again, then headed for the railway line, then down the embankment to the shack.

Locked.

He made his way back up to the railway line and paced up and down there for a while, everyone knew him, he could go wherever he wanted. Finally a man came and made his way to the shack. The blind man followed him and knocked on the door. When it opened he said: Are you Abel Brodersen? I can't see. He delivered the letter and left.

Abel wondered if maybe the thick envelope contained a thousand kroner, but there was a photograph inside, and a few scribbled words: I'm alone and I have to see you – I'll try to find you later today because I absolutely have to see you!! The enclosed is from the days when I was a waltz in town if you'd like it. If not then no harm done. I beg you, please be there when I come – it will be so empty to go back home again—

He had shaved and swum in the sea, his shirt was still wet, and since it was her then it was probably best to change it. Afterwards he sat down and studied the portrait. It had been taken some years ago, between the first and second time he had come back from sea. She was young and lovely, in the full flower of her beauty, a good portrait, it looked as though she was sitting talking to someone. But why had she sent the picture to him before she came? Was it to get him in the mood for lovemaking?

For a long time he waited, kneeling so he could keep on eye on the embankment above, and when she came he ran towards her and embraced her tenderly and spirited her away inside.

She wore no makeup at all, her skin was warm with small brown flecks that were sweet and small. She threw her arms around his neck at once and kissed him, missed him, searched again and found his mouth. More! she said.

He felt her sinking to her knees and sank down with her. More! she said. Take me to bed – kiss me more—

She came back again next evening and was the same again, deliriously and happily the same again. This time he was not as overwhelmed as he had been before and he was able to please her.

Afterwards she stayed for a long time, talking to him in her breathless way, in bursts: You and me, imagine, how strange, if only he knew! He left for Oslo yesterday and he'll be gone three days. It was clever of the blind man to find you, but he always gets where he's going. Abel, will you be angry with me if I say something?

No, no, no.

No, I prefer to wait until I'm leaving, because you will be angry. No, just think of it, you and me, Abel. Now Rieber Carlsen can stop writing his letters. You know he's going to be a bishop soon, well he can stop writing me letters now, there's no point any more. I'm so glad, I'm so happy about everything.

Finally he managed to get a couple of words in: You're so wonderfully bold, Olga. And if you were poor and an outcast and wretched, would you come to me and still be mine?

No, she said and shook her head. Oh no, I'm not so bold. Haven't you noticed that I need people to respect me? I hold myself back.

Yes but, Olga, what about when he finds out what's happened?

We'll sort that out between us. Don't you worry about that.

Strange, he said.

Olga: Don't be angry with me, Abel, but I won't lead a gypsy life with you. I just won't. You would just drag me down into the dirt.

Abel smiled : Well I didn't actually mean – you take me too literally. I just don't understand how you'll deal with it, living at home, how you'll make it okay with him.

He isn't stupid. He won't want to make himself ridiculous.

Ah, it's like that.

You won't be named, she said. No-one will be named.

Is that all he asks? If it were me I'd do a lot more.

Yes, you'd use the gun, said Olga and got up.

Quite possibly.

That's what you did when you shot her.

What?

Oh yes you did, you were the one who shot her. I take that for granted.

Abel gaped: You take that for granted?

Three lives, she said. I mean, you're a killer, not a doormat.

Listen, Olga, I wasn't firing at her. If my aim had been good enough there would have been just the two lives, his and mine.

How come he got the blame?

He said it was him that did it.

Olga thought this over: You shouldn't admit that, Abel. It makes you seem cowardly.

I had a score to settle with Lawrence. He was so good-looking, did whatever he liked where I was concerned. It was the fourth time. But don't let's talk about it, he said. He stood up too.

No, this doesn't change anything for me. You missed, but you did shoot. That's twice, she said, her eyes shining, twice I've been with a killer. That's really something!

He paled, his lower lip drooped, he said foolishly: Was that why –?

Don't be angry with me! It was exciting. I know I'm a bitch.

So it was for the thrill?

I knew you would be angry. Now I wish I hadn't said it.

Before you leave, Olga: Wouldn't it have been more or less the same kind of thrill for you if you'd managed to hook the bishop?

No, Abel, she said sadly, it would have been you, come what may. Then this came up, and it excited me, it's true. Three lives, I thought, and it was Abel! It's been on my mind these last few days, it got me excited. But it would have been you, regardless. Kiss me before I go.

He probably felt humiliated and wanted to reassert himself, because he asked: Do you want to do it again – now?

Now? she said.

Yes, for my sake? Not for the thrill of it?

It's getting dark already. Of course it was for your own sake, you know that. So, you won't you kiss me before I go? But that makes it so ugly. No, don't come with me, I want to be alone.

XXVIII

BUT TIME PASSES, IT PASSES WONDROUSLY. IT'S NOT MOVED along by some visible hand, and still it passes, never seen anything like it, in the twinkling of an eye it's the autumn.

There are certain disadvantages to the autumn, it's strangely cold, there isn't much sunshine, nor is there always enough food. But the times themselves seem to be getting worse too, fishermen have never been so particular about every last haddock as they are now, nor the butcher with a slice of liver. But Abel had one advantage over others: he had no need to gather wood for his home, because he had no stove to burn it in. That's right, no stove. Not even a pane of glass for his window.

He had reverted to the simple way of life and become rather eccentric, it didn't bother him that much to feel the cold on his skin or go a day on an empty stomach. Consider the others, look at Fredriksen out at the manor: in his miserliness and greed the lowest of the low, and dead now anyway. Abel happened to catch the funeral procession, a forest of high hats and every manner of transport imagineable. The chemist arrived just as everyone else had come to a halt, came whizzing up. When we are the chemist we don't drive our car along in step with the others, oh no.

It was good to be at home and not have much of a social life, Olga nowhere around, Lolla out of the picture, with only Lili left. It left Abel ever more silent, until he hit on the idea of talking to himself. That worked out alright too, more and more it was as though someone was there with him: Why don't you lift up that loose floorboard one more time and see if there isn't a tin of salmon still left there? Nothing there, did you say? A poverty-stricken house then, bad planning – shame on you! And while we're at it: why don't you block that hole in the window with a pillow? Maybe a blue silk pillow?

Life wasn't as difficult as some people thought, it was more that they made it difficult for themselves. Say for example that he sat down on a bench, by that little fountain, and someone who'd been sitting there before him had eaten bananas and shoved the bag under the bench. He picks it up, it's full of peel, but even the peel of a banana is not something to turn your nose up at.

Or say he calls in at a local cellar cafe and says: I just want to warn you that I saw a mouse squeeze in under your door. A mouse? the proprietress shrieks, picking up her skirts. There it is! he cries, pointing. The proprietress doesn't see it, but she opens a door and calls the cat. Abel nods and walks on, taking with him a little piece of sausage, a reward to himself for warning her about the mouse.

He was lucky too on another occasion when he went looking for work at the market garden. Sure enough, Schultz himself had fallen through the greenhouse roof and hurt himself, Abel spent a week there and had all he needed to live on right between his hands. The only drawback was that it made a mess of his clothes.

So life is very often a simple business.

And Alex is doing just fine. Things had improved for him, he had a steady job and all the drive he needed to dream of wearing a new Captain's cap. As yet the wage wasn't that good, but it meant he could come off the social security and was in a position to pay for his two front teeth so he could be handsome again.

But actually Alex was a pretty dubious sort of guy, not really such a great guy. Did his job okay and was appropriately sweet and stupid when times were hard, but as soon as he got back on his feet again he showed a vulgar side and stuck his nose up into the air. More than once Abel got a taste of his meanness.

When Abel had something to cook then he had to use his paraffin stove, but a tin of paraffin wasn't enough to see him through a whole autumn, and right about this time things were especially hard for him. So one day he took his piece of calf's liver up to Lili to get it cooked. Lili was her usual sweet and kind self and said: No, look. I've got something much nicer for you! And straightaway she heated up the frying pan for a piece of steak, a slab of pure beef! And while they were waiting for it to cook they got carried away again. Not that it mattered, when Alex returned home unexpectedly and marched into the living room he found Lili already standing by the stove and Abel over at the window, so nothing could have happened. But the suspicion was there.

That's quite an entry, said Lili.

Where are the children? Alex asked, for something to say. I see you're back in my living room again, he said to Abel. I'm beginning to wonder when you're going to stop it.

Lili minded the frying pan and just said: Shame on you, Alex.

It smells good in here, he said. What's happening? A party, some kind of feast? He crossed to the stove and took a good look: That's steak, unless I'm very much mistaken?

Yes, said Lili, that's what it's like when people can afford things.

Alex turned crude: I don't see why I should feed every hungry mouth that turns up on my doorstep.

Lili acted astonished: What are you talking about? It was Abel brought this piece of steak here to me and asked me to fry it for him.

That was a blow to Alex. The only thing he could think to say was: Well, that uses up butter.

But Abel handled the situation wrong, he said Alex could have the steak. Give me something else, Lili, haven't you a bit of calf's liver or something?

But she wouldn't hear of it, her heart was too big for that. When the steak was done she took it out, and once it was cool enough she put it on a plate and wrapped it in a piece of paper and said: Here you are. You can bring the plate back another time.

Alex interrupted: No, it would suit me a lot better if you never came here again. It leads to nothing but trouble.

Lili: Well in that case, I'll come and collect the plate from you myself, Abel.

This was even worse, but Lili looked determined – and who can outjump a lamb in spring? Alex said nothing. He followed Abel outside and threatened to shoot him dead if came back again. You know we carry guns, we Customs men? he said.

That was Alex for you.

Robertsen, however, turned out to be a different class of man altogether, a man of honour, honest to his last penny.

November is known for its ugly, raw cold and its unpleasantness. Nothing good had ever happened to Abel in November, at least not before this year. The priest stops in the streets and says hello: Are you Abel Brodersen? Ah good, I've been looking for you. I won't trouble you to come along to my office if you'll allow me to ask you a question here: Did you get back the money you once deposited at the bank for Robertsen the Customs man? You didn't? That's what I was afraid of. But now three boats and a number of other things have been sold so that you shall be paid what's owing to you, and I have been asked to ensure that this is done. How much was it?

Abel tried to think, then shook his head: I don't know.

Well, said the priest, the bank knows. I'm sorry for troubling you. What is your address?

The bank perhaps, said Abel. It could be delivered to the bank.

Good! The priest said goodbye and walked on.

Some November! It was a tidy sum, sixteen hundred wasn't it, or was it six? A fortune at any rate, more than enough. His mood was bright as he made his way homewards, things had been tough for a long time now, the cold was probably the worst, eating well didn't stop the cold, when the sun didn't shine either. So – he would be getting his money after all? Unexpected development. Miracle. And truth to tell I was angry with Robertsen and reported him to the police and called him a dog, but I was wrong, Robertsen the Customs man was at heart

297

a man of honour. And that priest a very nice chap too. Straight and to the point: You'll get your money.

He walks tensely back and forth in front of the bank a few times the next day, he doesn't go in but shows himself outside, he stands there reading the various posters and looking at the foreign banknotes in the windows. On a handwritten note he reads that Hr. Abel Brodersen is requested to call at the bank. He does so, signs his name and walks away, bulging with banknotes. Life is simple.

Now you might suppose that a man with no drive would just tear those notes into pieces, toss them to the wind and trample them underfoot. That's not what he did, he must have learnt his lesson. He had a few small debts to settle, and a bill to pay at the Seamen's Home that was so small one big note covered it. He needed to go to Lili's and give her something for the steak and the rest of it, plus he owed small sums at a few of the basement eating places – small debts the lot of them.

On his way to the Seamen's Home he suddenly bumps into Olga, walking along with another lady, both of them in furs. He greets them and the other lady returns his greeting, but not Olga. She looked at him, but didn't respond, didn't acknowledge him.

Strange. She might at least have nodded. Because with that she had destroyed a beautiful image he'd had of her, a portrait he'd been carrying around for thirty years. So she might at least have nodded. *Was* it Olga?

Let's see now, he says to himself, was it maybe the clothes? She looked you up and down but didn't nod, she held herself back. But something can be done about those clothes, a lot can be done about those clothes, though it might be expensive. And along with the expense is the bother of getting used to the new clothes, because the buttons are never in the same place as the old ones were, because every tailor practises his own branch of buttonology. And how about the pockets and the lining? Pathetic, you just can't get hardwearing clothes anymore and that's the truth of it. That week of mine in the market garden ripped everything to shreds.

He went to the tailor's and got himself a fine winter outfit, called in at the Seamen's Home, went to see Lili, paid up at the basement cafes. But in the evening he said to himself: What difference is there between today and yesterday? What do I have now that I didn't have before? A few clothes. When he went to bed that night he covered himself with the ulster and the window pane was still missing.

People took more interest in him now, they acted surprised when they met him, and said hello. They studied his clothing in surprise, here was a gentleman, a man of the world. Tengvald the smith greeted him, the postman greeted him. Smith the photographer detained him respectfully and asked whether he was interested in having a good photograph taken of himself taken? Yes I am, said Abel and there and then went right along with him. It might be fun, he hadn't done this since his first trip to sea – ah but you probably don't remember the days when you had your photograph taken and gave your picture away to the girls in the big seaport towns. And the girls were so grateful for the picture, they kissed it and said they would get it framed – and then left it behind on the bar room tables—.

Smith the photographer said: Forgive my taking the liberty of mentioning this to you but you have something on your hat. What might that be?

Abel takes a look: Those stains? I don't know, fruit juice maybe. I worked a week at the market garden in the autumn.

If it's fruit juice then you'll never get it off, said Smith the photographer, and as politely as he could suggested a new hat.

Of course he should have bought a new hat at the same time as the new clothes, but you can't think of everything. I'll buy a hat and gloves, he said.

Now that he was looking good enough to meet Olga again he never met her. He often walked the streets on the lookout for her, but he never met her.

He met the widow of Robertsen the Customs man. She was wearing black, with her hair newly permed and a thick layer of powder on her face. It's not often we see you, she said to Abel and let her eyes wander over his new clothes. She knew well enough where the money came from, it came from her, and she didn't hide it: Such a lot of money for me in my bereaved and defenceless state, but it was his dying wish and with the bullet in him and all I couldn't refuse it. But he should never have got the priest involved in it, what business was it of his? They've got the man who shot him and he'll get years for it so his death wasn't in vain. Will you be popping in to see us soon, Abel? Now that you can afford to buy such nice clothes for yourself you ought to take the girls out one evening to a concert or something because they're in mourning. Your father never missed a day at our house as long as he had the health and strength for a visit. Do you want me to say hello to the girls?

Everywhere you looked, people were insane.

The most tedious thing about being a man of means was the enforced idleness. He no longer had to worry about where on earth his next meal would be coming from, he had more than enough clothes, a roof over his head, a bed. Not having always known these luxuries meant Abel had a hard time dealing with it all, so now here he was with his stupid riches that just made him lazy. What did he have time for? What didn't he have time for? He passed the time alright, he'd become a natural layabout. But now everything bored him. He might just as well go down the dock as anywhere else.

The *Sparrow*'s old berth was now taken by the motor-boat that transported milk to the two dairies. A big, ugly monster of a thing, with lines like an old galleass, a working boat without mahogany, without brass, oiled and tarred where she should have been polished and painted.

Abel went aboard and said hello to his old crew from the *Sparrow*, Severin and Leonart. This is a great honour, Captain, they said. How about this devil's barge of a thing compared to the *Sparrow*, eh? they said. She doesn't even have a name, just a number. A porridge bowl on calm seas, a disgrace. They praised Abel, saying that if he'd carried on as Captain things would never have turned out as badly as they did, never in a million years, that's our humble opinion. Stick a Captain's cap on a log driver and let him take the wheel? But the owners paid for it alright, and serve them right.

It doesn't look like such a bad old tub, said Abel.

Bad? Jesus Christ, she's got no nose, all she has is a gut. And Captain, the day you buy a new boat we'll be there, ready to serve under you. Count on it!

Abel answered that he didn't have anything to buy a boat with, at

which they looked him up and down and said: Well you certainly look
as if you do, Captain.

It was on the way back from this idiotic trip to the dock that he met
Olga again. But before that he came across a familiar figure pushing a
pram along, Regina.

She blushed, innocently and brightly, her eyes shining. She was so
grown-up and nice-looking, and now here she was wheeling her little
girl along, a child already big enough to sit up in the pram. A smart
girl, that Regina, in her time she'd sold waffles and copies of 'The Silent
Comforter', now here she was a happily married wife and mother at the
busy heart of her life.

They talk together for quite a while, Abel being almost twice her
age is somewhat paternal. She tells him that her husband is a bright
young man and an engineer on the coast boat. She's reluctant to admit
that he's only the second engineer, and she's certainly not going to confess that he's a fireman. Abel gathers that they can just about manage on
his pay. But she proudly reveals that he's on board the *King Roald* itself,
the biggest and finest of all the coastal ferries! She's made several trips
with him, but not since she had the baby. But we'll go with daddy again
when you're a big girl, Selma! she says. The child has probably heard
this so many times before, she understands and waves her arm in the
air. When you get to be a big girl, yes, says the mother, smiling.

Abel digs out a note and says: Buy her a dolly.

Thanks, but she has a dolly, her father gave her a dolly.

This is for another one.

Oh but that's much too kind. Thank the man, Selma!

The child gives him her hand. He can't hold a child's hand, it
makes him silly and sentimental every time. A child's hand is so sweet.

Then he says goodbye and walks off into a completely different
world.

Olga is sitting in her car, heavily made-up. The dentist is driving,
they've pulled up outside a florist's and are waiting. The car door is
open.

Abel greets her, and after a slight pause she nods twice and smiles.
It's the clothes, he thinks. Not you, but your clothes.

301

She detains him: Good day, Abel. I'm just on my way to see Lolla. Ah that Lolla. It's a boy, isn't that wonderful! I thought straightaway of flowers, I thought I would. Will you be going out to Lolla's?

Later, he said.

When the bouquet arrives he doesn't expect her to pick out one little flower for him, though God knows he has a brand-new buttonhole that would be an ideal place for one. No, he's of no interest to her, she doesn't even offer him a lift, she keeps him at a distance. No secret handshake, no special look, nothing, nothing special just for him, only sensation, and then more sensation.

XXIX

BUT THE WINTER WAS HARSH, AND IT TOOK A LOT OF FOOD JUST to keep the cold at bay. The money shrinks, Abel needs shoes, work shoes, Lili needs shoes. He has no talent for managing his money and has not learnt from experience, he lends money, lends money to Lili from his fortune.

It's the truth, Abel, the two little ones, you know, God they're so big now, they need proper clothes, and so do I, Abel, a few clothes to keep me decent on a Sunday. He's just given me this pullover, because he couldn't for shame show himself in it at work any more, and it keeps out the cold alright, but it's not quite the same as a coat trimmed with grey fur like the one Lovise Rolandsen's got.

Let's go and buy that coat, Lili.

That was the last time he was able to afford something.

During the four worst months of the winter he eked out a wretched existence, scrounging a meal here and there, doing a day's work when he could get it, petty thieving and burglaries carried out at night. He still looked respectable enough in his clothes and could gain admittance wherever he wished. He didn't complain, other people weren't much better than he was, they had more to live off, sure, but then he a talent for doing without.

He was right there. He had a talent for doing without.

There was Lolla, hadn't she known her share of trials since that fine marriage of hers? For a start she wasn't welcome at her inlaws. But never mind about that – Clemens never took her out with him as he had done with his wife Olga. Sure Lolla had put on weight and the pregnancy and all that, but that wasn't all her fault, was it? She was still Lolla, with all her warmth and spontaneity and her capable ways. When Robertsen the Customs man got shot and died she was pleased in her healthy, strong way, but her husband shook his head over her. What was the point of that kind of delicacy? They were out walking, and the chemist had stopped in front of them, his short leg dangling, and bowed.

What's this, what's the meaning of this? Clemens finally asked. Why did he always make such a show of it? Do you know him?

I used to know him, answered Lolla.

Ah, you used to know him. Well I would greatly prefer it if he would desist from that malevolent little charade of his. That's the third or fourth time now I've had to put up with that.

I've asked him to stop, but he won't.

Oh it's like that, is it, said Clemens. He didn't step forward and use his malacca cane on a poor wretch like that, he just regretted the fact that his wife had known such people in her previous life. Clemens withdrew into his shell and kept himself to himself.

Lolla wasn't happy. It was more fun in the days when she borrowed books from her husband and returned them, and was given others, when she sat and talked to him of Prince Myshkin and Jean Valjean. Now he was almost on the point of thinking of his wife Olga again. Tears and despair. Her face was so much prettier, she was a wittier conversationalist, she wore make-up and was what they called *chic*, but she wasn't much good at the other stuff, really not much good there, you could see it on her, no breasts, flat, ha ha, once she even started wearing her hat back to front, just for something to do—

Then everything changed, the child was born, a boy, a marvel. Had a mane of hair which fell straight out, but then more hair grew in to replace it, and a grip like a two-year old, a good loud crier and hungry for his mother's teat.

During the first few days the mother was less than enchanted with him. She'd set her heart on its being a girl and had already given a lot of thought to the name. There could be no question of calling her anything like Rosamunda, which was the only name that really suited her, but her father wouldn't have it. And when it turned out to be a boy they might as well call him Ola for all she cared.

Clemens wasn't exactly a great hero the first time he saw the child, he flushed and grew flustered and daren't carry it in his arms. The mother knew better: You've got to hold him! Later, he answered, and headed for the door. Right now I'm in the middle of a big case.

Later, that's what he actually said!

And as a matter of fact it was true, he was in the middle of a very big case: The sawmill still owned the waterfall, and it was to be sold to a new factory, Clemens was handling the deal. A lot of money was involved. It would put the chemist back on his feet again.

Three weeks later it was concluded. According to the newspaper reports, Clemens had negotiated things brilliantly.

While all this was going on he used to sneak into the room after work, take a long look at the boy, and then sneak out again. When the wonder cried there was a terrible commotion, with Clemens urgently calling for the mother and the nursemaid: You're leaving him on his own, both of you!

What are we going to call him? asked the mother.

Damned if I know. I have been thinking about Hannibal.

That's a bit grand, she said.

What's grand about it? he retorted, offended. I think it suits him. And some people are called Alexander.

A sweet problem to be faced with. Clemens came out of his shell and played his part in it. Strange how things had changed. Bethlehem wasn't the only place a child had been born.

Listen, he's crying again!

Now really, just calm down – that was the canary.

She smiles. Ah that Lolla, good at everything, born to it, woman and sweetness. He wants to give her something he forgot about, amazing really, the ring, the wedding ring, completely forgot about it. He comes home with it one day in a box. But it falls flat, ha ha, it gets as far as the second joint on Lolla's finger and gets stuck.

The present that pleased her most right about then was an invitation for her and her husband to the house of the new judge and his family. So the old judge would just have to sit there and put up with it! But Lolla misunderstood, the old judge didn't just sit there. He and his wife were members of the upper-class, alert and protective of their status: once they heard that William Clemens and wife had accepted the invitation they turned down theirs, offering influenza as an excuse. They protected what they were born into.

Yes, each busy protecting his or her own, always busy! Abel protected nothing, and yet still he lived. Lili often visited him, stayed awhile, then left, she didn't see any signs of need there. And she too had things on her mind: just suppose I could get my old cashier's job back at the sawmill now that they're turning it into a factory! I want you to put in a good word for me, Abel! Alright, said Abel. She read all the stories in the newspaper: That bookseller you used to work for in the old days, he's gone bankrupt. Clemens is handling it. Strange how things turn out: Remember his daughter from school? Her name was Eleonora and she got pearl earrings for her confirmation. She married a bank manager in Oslo. Then he did something wrong and went to prison and then he went off to South America and disappeared. And now the father's gone bankrupt. You might almost think it wasn't worth while wanting to be anybody other than yourself, Abel. I know wouldn't swap with anyone, not if I could get my old job back.

Abel sensed that someone in town was thinking about him, probably some outsider or other. It was definitely not Lolla, he was nothing to her now, no longer his stepmother, now she was Fru Clemens. But one evening when he came home a pair of new, thick socks were hanging on his door. They looked as if they'd been bought at a farm-shop. Silly notion, he didn't need socks. If he ever became truly sockless he had the brightly coloured pair with the silk stripes in which he kept his gun wrapped. Another evening there was a parcel of underwear that he had no need of either. What was all this monkey-business about?

He tried to get Lili to confess that it was she who had hung the stuff on his door, but she swore it had nothing to do with her, she was as innocent as a newborn babe.

Take it if you can use it, he said.

Hm, it's not something you found somewhere is it?

No, it was hanging on the door.

Because they get so worried out about where people get things from, and if I took that it might make me a receiver of stolen goods. I daren't, Abel.

Please yourself.

Don't be angry with me. She told him that the blind hurdy-gurdy man was dead. A peaceful death in the hospital. They found twelve thousand kroner on him, under his shirt, taped to his skin. Ever hear the like of it? And now all the money was to be divided up among his relatives, people he'd never seen and didn't know about, according to the paper.

Strange paradoxes of life.

But after the hurdy-gurdy man's death there were no more packages left hanging on Abel's door.

And yet still there was no doubt about it, someone out there in town had him on their mind. Sometimes he was approached in the street by women who asked him to make them a brass chest like the one Olga Gulliksen had. Sailor's wives, maybe, they needed a chest like that, with no lock and no key, he could for example leave it at Gulliksen's store and pick up the money there.

Yes, said Abel.

Maybe these women had got together with an idea to help him make some money. These old biddies, so determined to do good, at his expense. They had no idea themselves that they were offensive, that he held his nose when he was around them. Now that they'd reached the age when the sex-life was gone they turned instead to religion, charity work and politics, they did a lot of cackling but laid no eggs, even tried to crow too, but couldn't get the hang of it. The old biddies of this world, what was left for them? Religion, charity and politics. Well, just so long as he could keep out of their way—

One of the priest's daughters wanted to know when she could have her chest – in a couple of weeks time? Maybe a month?

Yes, said Abel.

An offer communicated to him by Clemens seemed a little more realistic: I believe, he said in his courteous way, that you were once kind enough to help out Fru Fredriksen at the mansion with some gardening. Might you be able to do so again?

Yes, thank you.

She wondered if you could get some men and move a couple of large trees for her?

Yes, I can do that.

She will be pleased. Might you be able to start work soon?

Tomorrow, said Abel.

He went home with the intention of selling some socks and some underwear. That should be enough to pay for his packed lunch.

Where did you get these from? asked the second-hand dealer.

They were hanging on my door. I found them when I came home.

I daren't buy this, said the second-hand dealer.

Abel: I don't want it, can I leave it with you?

No, take it with you.

As it turned out he didn't need a packed lunch, food from the kitchen was often brought out to him, coffee and cake, things like that, and the lady herself sometimes came out for a chat with him, a vivacious woman. Two horse-chestnut trees were to be moved, they were blocking the view of the sea. The lady found something to sit on and talked for a long while about her husband, and Captain Ulrik, and about herself.

She was probably about fifty, heavily made-up and with eyebrows plucked so that just a faint line remained. She was full of praise for her husband, a lightning-quick businessman and a noble soul, but she was his second wife, and very much younger than him. She would rather not have talked about his brother Ulrik, but in fact she talked about him often and told stories about him.

Abel worked all he could when the lady wasn't chatting away to

308

him. He dug a deep ditch around the trees, secured them with steel hawsers so they wouldn't blow over, then filled it with water so that the earth and the roots would freeze together into a moveable mass. Now and then the lady asked if he didn't want someone to help him with the digging. No thanks. And she seemed well content to him have there on his own so that she could talk freely to him: Yes it wasn't always easy, he was sick and bedridden for years, and I was so much younger and couldn't leave him. And I had to play and play for him until we got the gramophone, he could work that himself, right up until his last stroke this spring. Have you never had anything the matter with you while you were out travelling the world?

No. I got sunstroke once.

Did it hurt?

Oh no. I was just a little light-headed for a while.

Just imagine, I've never had anything wrong with me, said the lady. It's such a blessing to be in perfect good health, I'm as healthy as I was when I was a girl.

She took good care of Abel and tried to give him her husband's hunting rifle that he used to shoot auks with. No thanks. Why not? she asked. He didn't tell her that he'd never be able to sell it on, just that he already had a gun.

She called for him now and then when something heavy had to be moved or lifted inside the house. She had a car but no-one to drive it now, Fredriksen had driven it himself until he got sick, but ever since then it hadn't been used. Abel checked it over, cleaned it, oiled and greased it and gave it a polish and drove the lady to town in it. It all meant that the business with the chestnut trees proceeded slowly, he had to be constantly ready to turn his hand to all sorts of other things for her.

She suggested to him that he sleep over at the mansion, she said: It's a long way for you in the mornings and evenings.

It's alright, he answered. Sometimes I get a lift in a lorry.

I could give you a lift into town, she said.

No, no, I'll walk.

But why, when we have the car? She didn't wait for an answer but went off to get ready.

They drove into town. The shops were closed or about to close.

The lady, smiling: Well, I can't drive myself back home again. So what shall we do?

If the lady pleases, I can drive her.

Yes, thank you.

They turned round in the market place and drove back out to the mansion.

Well you really ought to stay the night now, she said, it's so late.

He wasn't interested: No thanks, I'll walk, it's nothing.

The maids have prepared a room for you.

Again Abel thanked her and said: I need to bring people out with me tomorrow to move those trees.

Oh, those silly trees – but if you really won't—

Next morning he had a couple of men with him. He had made a platform that moved along on rollers, all the men had to do was to keep the trees clear of the ground so as not to break the branches. The car dragged the whole arrangement along.

By late afternoon the two chestnut trees had been moved to the new site and the earth replaced. They were told to see Clemens about their pay. Abel was summoned to the first floor by the lady to see the lovely view, the white lighthouse, the steamers far out at sea, and the homeward bound motor-boat with its load of milk churns.

So you're finished now? said the lady.

Yes.

Actually what I would like – there is a great deal more that needs to be done here. I have no chauffeur, he wouldn't have a chauffeur, he didn't want me driving with anyone else but him, because I was so much younger—

Silence.

I've been thinking of taking a long trip in the motor car. You could drive.

I'm leaving, said Abel.

At once? You could drive us first. Give it some thought.

Yes.

Really, will you? I just need to ring Clemens, then I'll be ready—

XXX

HE HAD MONEY AND COMFORT AGAIN, BUT STILL NO HOME. IT lasted a couple of weeks and then he was broke again.

He thought of the waffle-lady, but this time she saw him coming and wouldn't be fooled into giving away any free samples. She was actually doing pretty well, she was a good waffle-lady and did business at the railway station as well as the steamboat quay.

He broke into the shacks a couple of time and came across good stuff, from iron-piping to walking clothes, but he couldn't get rid of it. He should have been in Kentucky!

There was no point in going to the milkboat and Severin and Leonart, there was no restaurant on board. What's this about? they would say and not understand the Captain. He tried the waffle-lady again – again no luck. Of course he had a few other options, and one day in broad daylight he began painting freckles on his face, a lot of them, whole clusters of them, and made such a good job of it you

311

might've thought he'd taken freckle-painting classes. He wasn't think-ing of a bank or an office, but a particular food-store that had caught his eye. He made his preparations carefully, put on the ulster that he never normally wore outdoors, and off he went. It wasn't much later than eleven but the night was good and dark.

After he'd been boring by the window-pane for a while a dog inside began to bark. Abel wasn't about to stop for a dog and he carried on with his boring. A light went on inside the food-store.

When the light shone into his eyes there was only one thing to do: he knocked on the door. A man opened up and said what the hell? Abel wanted to get inside in case he was able to get something from the counter, but the man didn't let him in. What the hell?

Well, Abel had come to fetch the clock.

What clock?

The clock that was there. He'd received a message about it.

Some mistake. Get out of here.

The living-room clock, it needs looking at.

Get out of here immediately!

Now listen and stop being so unreasonable, said Abel. Of course it's very late, but that was the arrangement. I can't manage any other time, and I told them. I work for the master during the day and repair clocks in the evening to earn a few extra shillings.

The man wasn't being unreasonable, but he had no clock to repair and he hadn't asked for any watchmaker.

No go, no bloody go! Lawrence would have laughed at such a feeble effort, he would have ended up baring his chest and saying: See how skinny I am? And it would have worked for him. Without even the bother of the freckles.

Of course he hadn't exhausted every possibility. He could, for example, have sold the priceless socks the gun was wrapped in. For that matter, he could have sold the gun itself, if there'd been a decent scrap dealer in town. He missed having Lawrence around, missed Kentucky, Green Ridge, the river.

He could always sit down on the fish-dock and have a chat with the postman or whoever, but it never satisfied him. Self-denial wasn't his style and he said yes to a dram when it was offered him, but it didn't go down too well on an empty stomach. Same with tobacco, he couldn't take too much of it, and when they noticed that he tamped the tobacco down hard so as to have enough for two pipes they got tired of him and stopped handing it round. He took out his own box but then closed the lid again immediately because it was empty. Ah, but it had a rolled-up yellow note in it, that little yellow advertisement he'd found down on the vacant lots that looked like a ten-kroner note. You've got ten kroner, they said, you can buy your own tobacco.

It was March, times were hard. He had probably never been worse off, chronic undernourishment made his face diffuse, made him diffuse in the crowd. But still there were possibilities, there was always the barber out by the market garden.

On his way to the barber's he was overtaken by the chemist who came swishing by him, Olga out driving with her father who was, once again, a bigshot. When Abel arrived at the market garden father and daughter stood there talking by the car. Abel greeted them and walked past. Strange person, that Olga, she didn't return his greeting. The father very polite, but Olga seemed not to know him.

Hadn't they had two evenings together? Why forget them? First one evening, then another one, two evenings – forgotten! A photograph was all he had left of her. He should probably not have given in, it couldn't be undone now, but he should have been an angel from heaven and not given in. Now she was pregnant, she stood there beside the car and she was pregnant. It wasn't some kind of accident, she was testing out an idea: she didn't know if it would help her, but she was giving it a try. There was no trouble about it afterwards, she was either protecting Abel or denying him, one of the two, but she didn't identify him anyway, didn't identify anyone. But from a certain day and a certain hour onwards Volmer or was it Folmer the dentist was never invited out to the country place in Gulliksen's car again. And William Gulliksen took it all like a man and a gentleman, he really did: when people began hinting and congratulating him he responded with a grimacing pride: Yes well, that's life! What else could he say? Should he make himself ridiculous?

Everything as it should be, Abel obliterated.

He goes into the barber's, and what a reunion that is! But now Abel

313

was in a hurry, maybe father and daughter were still standing by the car, he wanted to go out again, clean-shaven this time, and say hello again.

Can you make me look good real quick? he said. I'm afraid I've got no money.

Ah, money! said the barber. As if I'd forgotten that Palm Sunday on your boat, all the hospitality you showed me and my family, that fine cabin and the rest of it – it was such a wonderful time for us, we often talk about it. So I'll shave you for free as long as I live, Captain.

Give my hair a bit of a comb too. Many thanks. Goodbye.

When he got outside the car was gone.

He couldn't now go back into the barber's and ask for a bite to eat. Okay, so he screwed up again, but it didn't hit him all that hard, it was a sort of bonus. For the sake of form he smiled.

April and May – everything better again. There was no food in the fields yet, but the cold had gone and the warm sun was back and that was half the food he needed.

Strange that he should have such a queer thought, but one day on the rubbish pile by the vacant lots he found a bone from a sheep's leg that he though he might have some use for. He took it home with him and broke it open, not to eat it but to use the marrow to grease the door lock– in case she should come! She had been before, and once or twice she had said to him: I'm the one you should have had. We should have had each other.

She didn't come.

Lili came. Defied her husband and everything and came. She brought waffles with her, from her mother, and out of the goodness of her heart treated Abel. Lili stayed a long time, it was a warm evening, she removed her coat with the grey fur trim, took off more clothes, then more clothes, the evening was warm—

Lili was unusually tender, but before she left she made it clear that 'those two little ones, you know?' ought to be getting a bicycle soon.

Yes, said Abel.

Early next morning a boy arrived with a dozen photographs from Smith the photographer.

Put them down there, said Abel.

314

Here's the bill.

I'll call in and pay.

Dammit, now it seemed as though just anybody at all could track him down. Complete strangers walking straight into the room, as though they were the ones he had greased the lock for. Strangers never came to his shack in Kentucky—

Then Clemens came, Clemens, visiting him in the shack! Actually he seemed more uncomfortable about it than Abel himself and made excuses: I've come – I'm a little confused, but I've come to settle a large debt, Hr. Brodersen. I've been trying to find you for Fru Fredriksen from the manor house. But I have also brought – he touches his pocket, his wallet – brought a thousand kroner that I owe you, that Olga got me to—

There was no hurry for that, said Abel.

Oh but, it's disgraceful, I should've done it a long long time ago. But please, here's the money now, please accept my apologies for everything.

There's no need to – I assure you—

Good. That's very kind of you. Actually it was two thousand, but I understand you already have the other thousand?

Yes.

It's disgraceful. But now to my other business: Fru Fredriksen has telephoned me many times, but I have not been able to locate you. She would very much like you to come out to the mansion, she has mentioned something to you about a driving holiday—

Yes but I'm going away, said Abel.

Yes but what about before you leave? This car holiday seems to mean so much to the lady, in her grief. So if you could go out to the mansion and talk things over—

I'll think about it.

Thank you. The lady will be delighted. Can I say hello to Lolla from you?

Please do.

She's a mother now.

Congratulate her.

A boy. Quite an event.

*

315

He saw Olga again, on his way to the police station. He greeted her and walked on, she seemed not to know him.

Yes, the police would like a few words with him – please, sit down! You once knew an Irishman by the name of Lawrence? And, you were with him in Kentucky? Well, he died in gaol. Now his family in Ireland want to clear his name, they have letters from him claiming that he's innocent. The authorities in Kentucky have asked us to have a word with you about this and to give us a statement if you know anything. That's all, just a statement that might comfort the family in Ireland. It appears that Lawrence also left a letter for you, and that this letter was found after you left.

Yes, I left it behind, said Abel.

The letter to you supports the letters to the family, apparently.

I wouldn't know, I didn't read it.

Ah, so you didn't get it before you left? But now about this statement. It'll mean quite a bit of work for both you and us, so we might as well make a start on it.

Abel: I'm going there now.

You're going there? To Kentucky? Now?

Just about to leave.

Well, that couldn't be better. There's a bit of luck. Then we can just tell them you're on your way and that you'll be giving your statement in person?

Yes.

Well well, so you're going. You've probably got things to see to there? Bit of property or something like that? Well that's fine, we won't waste any more time on that. Thank you for your cooperation. When are you leaving?

Tonight.

Well well! Have a good trip!

In the shack he left behind him a pair of thick woollen socks and some underwear. The paraffin oven was still there, and the bed, but the few other things went with him. A child's bicycle had been sent up to Lili's place near the sawmill, and he had called in at Smith the photographer's to pay his bill.

316